The family is gathering around the bedside of Ellen MacNamara but she is too angry to die. All her life she has been a fighter – for Franklin Roosevelt, for the trade union movement, for select family members she happens to respect – and damn the rest, including her daughters. Injustice done in a far-distant Irish childhood rankles yet; the grief for a son still festers. But Ellen has known how to love and how to exact a promise – and after sixty-five years of marriage, husband Vincent had better turn up to keep it. In her delirium she waits and she growls – through the bedside visits of the next generations.

It is plain to see who has inherited Ellen's *fire* amongst the intriguing procession of MacNamaras Mary Gordon holds in her gaze. For Gordon is a supreme observer of human behaviour – of private morals and public attitudes as they are dissected in that nerve-wracking laboratory – the family reunion. Past and present ebb and flow elegantly in her skilful narrative. Rivalries and alliances, misdemeanours and triumphs unfold with a compelling logic. The result is a saga of resounding eloquence, striking lucidity and humanity.

THE OTHER SIDE

THE OTHER SIDE

MARY GORDON

BLOOMSBURY

First published in Great Britain 1990

Copyright © 1989 by Mary Gordon

This paperback edition published 1991

The moral right of the author has been asserted

Bloomsbury Publishing Ltd, 2 Soho Square, London W1V 5DE

A CIP catalogue record for this book
is available from the British Library

ISBN 0 7475 0714 7

Printed in Great Britain by Richard Clay plc, Suffolk

FOR RICHARD GILMAN

ACKNOWLEDGMENTS

I received help in my research from many sources. Kerby A. Miller's *Emigrants and Exiles* and Hasia Diner's *Erin's Daughters in America* provided invaluable background information. I had great fun consulting *Irish Emigrant Ballads and Songs*, edited by Robert L. Wright. I wish to thank Angela Carter of Keshkerrigan bookstore and Brenda Parnes of the Tammamint Library. Joshua B. Freeman was extraordinarily generous in sharing his extensive knowledge of the Transport Workers' Union; both his conversation and his excellent study *In Transit: The Transport Workers' Union in New York City, 1933–1966* provided rich treasures. To Dr. Edward Bowe, as always, my thanks and admiration for his sensitivity to women; in this case, I am indebted for his advice on my characters' gynecological problems.

THE FAMILY OF ELLEN AND VINCENT MACNAMARA

THEIR CHILDREN:

Magdalene
Theresa
John

THEIR GRANDCHILDREN:

Camille,
Magdalene's daughter

Marilyn
Sheilah } *Theresa's children*
John

Daniel,
John's son

THEIR GREAT-GRANDCHILDREN:

Jeremiah
Vincent } *Marilyn's children*
Ramon

Diarmid,
Sheilah's son

Darci } *Dan's daughters*
Staci

I

1

When this happened, Vincent MacNamara thought it was the end of everything. As things turned out, it was not.

He was a tall old man of eighty-eight, and strong, but he was lying on the floor of his dark living room. He knew he had broken his leg. A thick medal of pain formed on the left side of his thigh, fanned out to thinner ribs, and flashed up and down his leg from thigh to calf. It interested him, as if it were happening to someone else. His leg was light and foolish underneath him and he couldn't move. But it was important that he move. He could see Ellen, his wife, wandering on the half-lit street, the outlines of her body visible to him through her white nightgown.

He didn't know how far she'd walk. He could imagine her walking until the land stopped, and then into the water. He couldn't stop her.

If he cried out, it would be shame for him in the world. Shame in the neighborhood. If he didn't cry out, then she could wander off and be killed.

She'd begun having strokes six years before. She'd no control left over herself, it had been months since she'd had any. It had been months since she had stood up by herself. And then she did this.

It was because she wouldn't take her pills.

He'd put her in front of the television. John, their grandson, had hooked up the remote control for her. He was in televisions now. They said he'd found himself. Vincent had put the TV on so she could see the Mass. He knew that she cared nothing for the Mass. But Theresa, their daughter, had told him she might be taking something in. Theresa stood in church now, with her arms spread out, talking directly to the Holy Ghost. She told her father he could talk directly to the Holy

3

Ghost if he believed he could, but Vincent knew he couldn't.

Theresa wanted her mother in a home.

'Swear,' Ellen had said, lying next to him when they were each no more than thirty. Her eyes were wild; he could tell in the dark. What had made her think of it? What had put the thought in her, and the wildness, so that her nails bit into his palm, as if she knew the small pain would make him remember?

'Swear you'll let me die in my own bed. Not among strangers.'

He swore. Her nails pressing made dents in his palms, a dull, shallow pain.

He'd sworn. He'd thought he could keep it from happening.

It happened because she wouldn't take her medicine. He gave it to her, but she kept it in her mouth. Three pills, red and gray, red and yellow, dark pink. He'd gone into the kitchen to get a dish of ice cream for her. He thought he'd make her spit the pills into his hand, then he'd bury them in the ice cream and she'd swallow her pills without knowing.

When he came back into the living room, he saw she'd switched the picture from the Mass to a cartoon show. A zebra family was dancing on the screen. A zebra mother hung a pair of striped pajamas on the line. Ellen was staring at the screen and her mouth was open. Had she opened her mouth to laugh? In opening her mouth, she'd let the pills roll together on her lap. He saw the three of them, wet, stuck together at the center of her lap. He bent to fish them from the valley of her lap so he could hide them in the ice cream.

And then, for the first time in months, she stood up. She put one arm in front of her breasts and raised the other against him, knocking him heavily to the floor. She walked out of the house. He could see her wandering up and down the street in darkness.

2

Vincent and Ellen MacNamara have been married sixty-six years. For sixty-three years, they have lived in one house, 128 Linden Street, Queens Village, ten miles from the center of Manhattan. He is younger than she; she was twenty-four when they were married; he was nearly twenty-three. Already at that time, they had lived other lives, mostly on another continent. Europe, from which they set themselves adrift.

They crossed the ocean to the place, America, that had been called at home 'the other side.' Now Ellen is dying. She is over ninety; no one is surprised but she. She has, of course, expected death, but now that it is near it is a shock, an intrusion, an affront. No one knows how long she'll live. She is furious in her long dying. She is powerful in her last sickness, in her dying, in the ending of what is still her life.

The thin, translucent skin stretches across her forehead, beautiful, as if the soul were winning visibly over the flesh. You would expect the brain packed down beneath this tight-drawn skin, beneath this skull that has become a feature, this skull of a saint in triumph, you would expect the brain beneath this bone and skin to be serene. But it is not.

Constant words fill the air around her bed. They are terrible words for an old woman taken up in the long business of her dying. Curses. Maledictions. Dreadful wishes. Also simple filth. What kind of life would have brought up these words? She lived a hard life, but not the kind to know these words.

Within the nearly visible skull, the brain, disintegrating fast, reaches back past houses, curtains, out to ships and over oceans, down to the sea's bottom, back, down, to the bog's soaked floor, to mud, then to the oozing beds of ancient ill will, prehistoric rage, vengeance, punishment in blood. And all the time, the bars of her hospital bed shake with her rage. She is tied down, has been drugged, but whatever she has been given fails to stupefy. She will not stop telling what she has seen. It is dirty; there is nothing; we should suffer, all of us, for it is all that we deserve.

3

Outside the room, scattered around the house Ellen has lived in since 1922, is her family. They are here because they are waiting to celebrate Vincent's return. It is the summer of 1985, August 14, vigil, for those who note such things, of the Assumption. Vincent would note this; Ellen, furious if he'd brought it up, would not. Since the eighteenth of October of the year before, Vincent has been away from the house. For two months he was in the hospital; it wasn't his leg that he broke that night, it was (much worse) his hip. After he'd been in the hospital two months, Cam, his granddaughter, who is a lawyer, arranged that he should go to an experimental nursing home. Today he's coming home.

That night, October 18, 1984, lying on the floor of his dark living room, in pain, he thought he wouldn't be able to keep the promise he'd made to his wife nearly sixty years before. That he would let her die in her own bed. But they had kept it for him. Cam had stood up to her aunt Theresa, did the things, interviewed nurses, hired people to be there around the clock so Ellen could stay home, so she could be waiting for him. Waiting till today, when he would come home to her.

Only he doesn't want to go home.

4

Nearly all the surviving members of the MacNamara family are in the house now, waiting for Vincent to come home. Almost all of them live within forty-five minutes of Queens Village, where all of them spent their childhoods: an oddity in mobile, shifting America.

One of Vincent and Ellen's children is dead; John, their only son, killed in the War. His son, Daniel, born after his death, stands outside his grandmother's bedroom, waiting to see if she's asleep.

Dan's daughters, Darci and Staci, Vincent and Ellen's great-grandchildren, are expected by the middle of the afternoon.

Vincent and Ellen's older daughter, Magdalene, is in her room, two blocks away, a room she has left only rarely in the last fifteen years. Her daughter, Camille, is upstairs, working on a legal brief.

The only one of Vincent and Ellen's children in the house is Theresa, their second-born, a medical secretary who speaks to the Holy Ghost. Her husband, Ray Dooley, is here, and her son, John, and daughters, Sheilah and Marilyn. Marilyn is the only one of the family to have moved far away. She is a registered nurse, taking her vacation here so she can supervise her grandfather's settling in. When he is settled in, tomorrow, or the next day, she'll go back to Los Angeles, to the clinic where she is director, serving a largely Chicano population, to her three children and a house without a husband now. It's another thing she's here for: she must tell her parents her third marriage has failed.

She checks the IV that leads into Ellen's arm. She sees her family arrange themselves in various positions in Vincent and Ellen's small, tree-darkened house. The net of kinship spreads around them, spreads and draws. There is a place for everyone, she thinks, but not all places are equal and not everyone is happy with his place.

Theresa and Ray Dooley are sitting in the living room watching one of their favorite TV shows, *The People's Court*. As a family, the MacNamaras have an interest in the law. Dan and Camille are lawyers, specializing in divorce; Ray Dooley is a retired cop.

Idly hypnotized, Dan sits down beside his aunt and uncle on the couch. Despite himself, he is interested in the case: a woman has been given a bad permanent – a quarter of her hair fell out and the rest will take six months to return to normal. She wants restitution from the man who owns the beauty shop. She wants enough money for wigs, hats, and scarves, six months' worth of them, and two hundred dollars for emotional duress. She wins.

Ray turns to Dan. 'As a lawyer yourself, Dan, what would you think of the verdict of the judge?'

'I'd say it's fair, Ray. I'd say I'd do the same thing in his shoes.'

But Dan isn't thinking of the judge's verdict, he is thinking of his grandfather, of what will happen in the house when Vincent walks into it, of who each of them will be then.

He thinks what he has often thought: My grandfather is an honorable man. He tries to understand what he means by the word *honor*. He's always imagined Vincent's life as a line, stretching back, emanating from Vincent's body, back to a time Dan can't imagine, through this house, curving through his descendants to him, Dan, and through him to his children, Darci and Staci, living with their mother in Seattle. But for the summer they are with him in Quogue, near the Long Island Sound, in the house he shares with Sharon Breen, whom he has lived with for twelve years, but never married.

He thinks of the differences between him and his grandfather. His life isn't a single line that stretches back to history and forward through the generations, through one house, through a life lived beside one woman, through children going out and coming back to do him honor.

His children live a continent away. One of them will never let him know her. To allow herself to be known would be to forgive, and she will not forgive her father for leaving her mother, for leaving her.

Dan walks into the room where Ellen is lying asleep. Her hair is done in two thin braids, imprisoned now beneath the sharp blades of her shoulders. He releases the braids and places them carefully one on each side of her shoulders, on the blue nylon case of her pillow, specially designed, its package said, for 'long-term patient care.' He rolls one of the braids between his thumb and second finger and he thinks: At least I was able to do that.

'Don't cut her hair.'

He'd said that to the practical nurse, Mrs. Davenport, and to his aunt Theresa. They were about to cut Ellen's hair. It was a nuisance long, they said, another thing to care for.

He used on them a voice he'd learned, a voice he'd used in court, to make someone afraid of something. He almost never used it in private life, the voice that suggested that if it were defied there would be consequences. He looked at Mary Davenport, who kept opening and closing the scissors as if by cutting Ellen's hair she could be through with something, and for good. He looked at Theresa, whose interest was in punishment. Theresa drummed her shell-pink fingernails on the white plastic armrest of Ellen's hospital bed. Mary Davenport put down her scissors. He had won.

He never told them what her hair had been to him, let down, washed outdoors once a year, on the first warm day of spring.

Once a year he would come home from school and she would be there in the fenced-in yard, her presence public but only for him, shocking, sitting in the open air, her hair undone, let down, loose on her shoulders. Her hair was gray; she must have been in her fifties. She combed it with a gray comb; its wide teeth raked her scalp that he could see a hint of: pink. Even then her hair was thin.

She was jubilant, her wet hair down, and young, an outlaw. She didn't say anything but he knew what she meant: Celebrate with me. Feel the sun. Underneath the earth things stir. You and I know this. We mark it now.

She waited on those days till he came home, till the others were away. He was completely happy then. Music rose up, fantastic music, like the music of angelic singing showgirls, forming themselves in movies into the shape of a violin, a piano. Curves of music, rising, curving up.

She never said anything about what she was doing.

He would come near her, kissing her. He'd smell her clean wet hair. 'You're home, then,' she would say.

'Yes, Gran.'

'Your school all right today?'

'Yes.'

She'd close her eyes, the both of them would close their eyes to hear the music, to feel properly the warmth that drew the wetness from her hair. In half an hour, saying nothing, she'd comb her hair, braid it, pin it up once again into the irreproachable pile at the top of her respectable, now law-abiding head.

'Don't cut her hair,' he said, and they had listened.

He'd been able to do that.

5

At Maryhurst, an experimental Catholic residence on the East End of Long Island, people keep coming into Vincent's room to say goodbye. Mothers and children knock at the door; usually, the children are allowed to knock; Vincent keeps getting up from his green Leatherette chair. He knows everybody's name. 'Well, then,' he says, opening his door to each of them. 'Isn't this a fine surprise.' Some of the mothers and children bring him presents – candy or drawings; there isn't much at Maryhurst that can be bought, and only the old people have money. The old people are there because they're old, the mothers and the children are there to be hidden, or rescued, to add life. At Maryhurst, welfare mothers and their children are mixed in with the old who can't care for themselves entirely, but don't need much help in getting through a day in which their food, their warmth, their safety is insured.

It's not easy to get into Maryhurst, particularly for the old. Vincent got in right away because Cam is a close friend of Otile Ryan; they work together on the board of a shelter for battered women. Otile Ryan, a Sister of the True Cross (formerly Sister Benedicta), runs Maryhurst. It was her idea.

Maryhurst, originally called Bower House, was built in 1887. It was the house of the O'Connell family. The O'Connells, Cam had learned, were one of those Irish families who'd come over early enough to make a fortune and manifest it by building a great house. A family trip to England had made Gerald O'Connell fix on Victorian architecture, and he built for his family, in the fashionable seaside town of East Hull, on Long Island, a mansion built of pale yellow stone with green roofs; he put gingerbread trim around the porches and windows and walls, and it was said he made heart-shaped flower beds of pinks, lilies of the valley, moss roses, peonies, and poppies in the fashion of the day. In 1934, Gerald's granddaughter, Gertrude Rose, unable to keep up with taxes, gave the house to the Order of the True Cross, who had educated her in their school for Catholic Young Ladies on Fifth Avenue.

Gerald O'Connell's mansion became the Order's Motherhouse. But by the time Otile Ryan had become Superior in 1981, the order had dwindled to fifty members, whose median age was sixty-two. Financial advisers urged her to sell the property, buy something cheaper, easier to heat and to maintain for the housing of the older sisters and send the younger ones, who could be self-supporting (they were equipped with MSWs and Ed.D.'s), out to the world, meeting like other sisters in informal consortiums, spiritual communities that involved no real estate and were

10

free from the horrors of failing boilers and French doors whose hinges could no longer be properly replaced.

But Otile Ryan, who preferred to be called O.T. (her middle name was Therese), was interested in social experiment. She decided to turn Maryhurst into a place for the aged and for battered wives seeking shelter with their children.

She'd got a quarter-million-dollar grant from a foundation to re-do Maryhurst more functionally. Each large bedroom was broken into three. The parquet floors were covered with linoleum. The money that she got from selling the antique furniture she spent to have a swimming pool and sauna installed in what was once the billiard room. She'd done it all like a sansculotte dismantling a château. When she understood that Cam disapproved, Otile turned on her. 'What was I supposed to do, spend a hundred grand so some fat interior decorator could tell me how to preserve the door frames? Or pay one of the mothers three bucks an hour to get on her knees to clean the marble fireplaces with a feather dipped in oil, like I did when I was a novice? Forget it. Look around you, Camille. People are happy here. They're living their lives without worrying all day about where they live. That's something. They're a hell of a lot happier than the people who lived here when this place was a shrine to its own woodwork. I say thank God for Formica. I'd be glad to offer my morning prayers for the inventor of Formica. If I only knew his name. I'd have him canonized if I thought he was a Catholic. But I'm sure he's not one of ours.'

Vincent has enjoyed Maryhurst. He's liked playing with the children. Although the mothers make him nervous: he can't imagine what life holds in store for them, or he can imagine, and it makes him afraid. One of the mothers, Alvira Scott, asked him to teach her how to read. He tried, but couldn't do it. After he spent time with her, he himself found it difficult to read. He wanted her to read with all his heart, but she couldn't seem to learn. He told her to tell Sister Otile or Sister Roberta, they could help her, but she said she was ashamed and didn't like people to know and if he couldn't do it no one could. He felt that because of meeting him she was worse off. Her son is nine years old; her husband tried to kill her. Vincent knew she didn't believe him when he said she was a wonderful mother with a lot of excellent qualities and it didn't matter if she couldn't read. Before he leaves, he'll tell her she must let someone know, one of the nuns, or someone. He'll

11

say it's his fault, his eyes are bad, sometimes he can't concentrate, he's too old, he wasn't the one to come to, there is someone who can help her out. He has no idea if she'll listen.

One of the children made a poster for him. It said 'We love you, come back soon.' But he knows he'll never come back. He won't make another trip from his house to a place that means something to him. He'll go places to do business – the bank, the doctor's. But Cam will have to take him, and stay with him while he does whatever it is he went there to do.

He knows that he will die. Soon, relatively soon, he'll leave his life. He will travel from the world to somewhere. He has a sense of what it will be like. He'll be watching his body. What is not his body, but still himself, will be spinning through a tunnel or a corridor. The wind will rush around him; the part of him that is watching his body will be hurled through darkness hearing the sound of rushing wind. At the end of the tunnel, the corridor, there will be silver light. He doesn't know if there will be anything to see in that light, or if it will be wholly quiet, or if he'll be alone. In the quiet, will he hear the voice of God? And then will he be joining others? Or will he stay alone?

Now he's not alone. He's got used to people. He fears the quietness of the house on Linden Street after this noisy life. He wonders how he'll eat his meals. By himself? At the kitchen table? In the dining room? He won't take his meals with Mary Davenport. He knows she stole from them, but when he'd asked her if she'd seen the silver gravy ladle, the pie fork, she'd told him she was sure there'd never been anything like them in the house. Then she said: 'I hope you're not accusing me. Because if you are I'm out of here.'

He doesn't know why Ellen likes her. She's the kind of person Ellen would have hated if she'd been herself: big-faced and loud, making herself important. Religious, yes, but Protestant. It was different, they believed in different things. The Ellen he knew would have hated her. It makes him feel that he's outlived his wife; she's still there, in the house, but she's a person he doesn't know.

He has to go back to her. She frightened him, crying out like she did, and the bad language. He kept wanting to tell people she hadn't been like that. He thinks sometimes if he could just talk to her, just the two of them. If he could ask her: Is it death that makes her talk like that, is it seeing death? He doesn't know what her eyes see anymore. In sixty-six years it's the longest time he's been away from her. He doesn't want to go back.

He doesn't want to go back to the family, the furniture, the old wood that needs care, the roof that is a worry to him, the dark carpets, and the pictures on the big piano. To his single bed down the hall from where she sleeps (she'd sent him there in the fifties, when she'd come back from the hospital after her gallbladder was taken out). He wants to ask her what it was that she's seen, to tell her not to worry, he'll be there with her on the journey. But no, that isn't what he wants. He wants to stay here with the sociable people who like a good conversation, with the mothers and the children who dart on the surface of the common life, with the nuns who believe in the future, on the grounds he has no responsibility to care for, watching while the gardener, a Spanish fellow, rides the lawn mower around the grass.

In the family they were always saying, I love, I hate, do this for me, you never did this, you forgot, I'll never forget it, I am happy, I am so unhappy, why are you like you are. He'll walk into the house and everything he knows about the lot of them will make him feel old and tired and out of hope. They believe in the future at Maryhurst; that's why he likes it. He doesn't know what his family believes.

6

In Vincent and Ellen's house, Camille isn't downstairs with the rest of the family. By simple majority, those she can't bear outnumber those she loves. She's upstairs, in the room she often slept in as a child, sitting up in the small, single bed, reading a blue-backed brief, working on someone's divorce.

She sits on the single bed, her legs stretched straight out, like a child afraid of being caught in illicit reading. She's frowning when she reads; she's always frowned when reading. As a child she did it so as not to appear to be enjoying herself too much. She was amazed from the moment that the letters of the alphabet unlocked themselves into a tray of meaning she could sample and re-combine, certain that others who read – who pretended to be reading – weren't experiencing what she did. Either it wasn't the same thing, or they were cleverly making their faces blank so that no one could guess the value of what was happening behind their eyes. At a young age, she suspected that anything you possessed of value was in danger of being taken away. Dissimulation seemed a duty. She began then to frown when she was reading so that no one would suspect her joy.

In three generations of MacNamaras, only Cam and Dan read easily, with no sense of constraint. Cam's mother, Magdalene, didn't read, nor did Theresa. Daniel had no memory of his real parents. Vincent and Ellen read hungrily, desperately, stealing time from something, needing to know something: the nature of the world. Only Cam and Dan read for pleasure. Reading was a smooth ribbon of road stretching before them. They could follow it at their leisure, or race down it, dizzily and rushed. Their grandparents always allowed them to read; they were never told, as other children in the neighborhood were, other children they knew in school, that they should be doing some-thing else.

When they were reading they didn't want to be doing anything else. They knew this was unlike other children. It was the secret mark that first bound them; it had to be kept secret – from other children, from most adults – particularly in summer, when they were expected to want to do something else: climb trees, run, play ball, look in puddles for the signs of life. Their grandmother was happy to work in the kitchen or in the garden, while they sat on the screened-in side porch, on the blue glider with its rough upholstery and consumed their secret feasts of words. They could feel the mercy in the trees whose branches hung around the house. The breeze low to the ground cooled their toes. They read. *Little Women*, *Little Men*, *Jane Eyre*, Trixie Belden, Nancy Drew, Dickens, George Eliot, a series of nurse heroines, Willa Cather, *Ivanhoe*, *Captain Horatio Hornblower*, The Hardy Boys, Dr. Tom Dooley in Laos, in Cambodia, Thomas Merton, Sinclair Lewis, *Goodbye, Mr. Chips*, *We the Tikopia*, Latin American or Canadian stigmatists. All these passed through their hands, and they could revel in the lush growth that is the territory of the untaught, unsupervised, unguided reader. At twelve Dan read *Moby Dick* and didn't understand it. Not until college did Cam know that *Two Years Before the Mast* was not a great book.

Today Cam is reading the testimony of Lorraine Barnabas. Lorraine Barnabas is filing for divorce; she claims that for twenty years her husband has regularly beaten her. Cam no longer asks women like Lorraine Barnabas why they stayed with their husbands for twenty years. She knows. They were afraid, they had no money, they thought they would be destroyed in the world alone. She understands this, sitting on the bed now, reading the deposition. When she's tired or has lost too many cases, when one of the welfare mothers she trusted loses custody of her children once again because she's gone back once again on drugs, when she has just spent time with her own mother, Cam has no patience with women like Lorraine Barnabas. Sometimes she imagines victimized women rising around her head like polluted water. She remembers once turning to a friend of hers at a meeting, one of the endless meetings she attends, on one of the endless boards she is a member of, and saying: 'Victims. Jesus Christ, I'm sick of victims, I wish I'd never invented them.' But today she isn't tired, and she hasn't spoken to her mother yet. So she is patient with Lorraine Barnabas. She says: At fifty it can't be easy to start in the world. Better late than never. She knows that Dan never has mixed thoughts like this about his clients. She knows that if Lorraine Barnabas had told Dan, weeping, that her husband had beaten her for twenty years, and said it with those startled eyes that still can't understand it, he would pity her with no impatience: his pity would be pure. Perhaps she would misunderstand this; she would want him to take her to bed. Which is why Cam thinks it's better that she should handle the case.

Cam and Dan are partners in the firm of MacNamara and MacNamara. They specialize in divorce. Their offices are in Kew Gardens, ten minutes from Cam's house in Queens Village, and an hour and a half from Dan's in Quogue.

Neither of them had planned to work in any of the circumstances in which they now find themselves. They'd planned to do adventurous things, politically active things with their law degrees: Dan planned to work among rural blacks down South. But in 1965, during Cam's last year in law school, her mother developed cancer of the breast. Within two months, Cam married Bob Ulichni in a trance and in the same trance gave up her plans to work for Legal

Aid: her focus was directed towards her mother's death. Jack Morrisey came forward and offered her a job working for him.

The MacNamaras had known Jack for twenty years. He'd run the Democratic Club; he'd adored first Ellen, and then Cam. He'd given Cam five thousand dollars for law school, no strings attached. And he had meant it, about the strings; he'd have watched Cam take a job in Manhattan Legal Aid without a hint of reproach or demand for re-payment, but when the situation arose, he could, reproachlessly, have the return of his gift; it would have been unnatural for him not to take the opportunity. He was one of those bachelors – chaste, political, idealistic – with more money than they need and an incoherent sense that they would like to do some good. The scope of his political imaginings was local; if he were a Jew, he might have been a Communist, but he was Irish; his personal chastity extended to the public view; the immodest vision of an international solution caused him to recoil, as if he were observing an endless series of random couplings.

Jack had lived, since his mother's death, on the top floor of a house owned by the sister of a former pastor of the parish. No one had ever seen his rooms. Many people spent time imagining them. The reality was a room of iron bedsteads, bookcases made of white-painted shelves, the books arranged by alphabet or subject, a mirror by the door for a last professional man's look, a crucifix, a clothes rack, a white chenille spread. He arrived at the office every day after the seven o'clock Mass, and he left each night at seven. He took his meals at the Night Cap Bar; each evening he ate the heavy, indiscriminate dark stews Herb Kennedy, his friend and fellow Democrat, served up. There were three women in his life, his secretary, Mary Dolan, who had worked for him since 1936, Ellen, and Cam. Ellen was for him the beloved past, the primitive life he glamorized and savagely cut out. Mary Dolan was the present, the law and order which made the world the barely livable place it was, and made his office the only home he treasured. And Cam was the future. Nothing of the vain, inflating, self-important, trivializing tendencies he saw as female did he see in her. If he was hurt when she married Bob Ulichni, hurt that she stooped to marriage at all, he didn't admit it to himself. Had she had children, demonstrating to his eyes that she beyond doubt was physical, things might have changed. But her infertility left her intact. Therefore, of undiminished value for him.

Jack Morrisey, along with Edith Blake, Cam's Latin teacher, had advised Ellen on Cam and Dan's education. Ellen had seen Magdalene trying to pervert her daughter's nature by attempting to teach deference and pretty ways. Ellen wouldn't have it. She said to Cam: Speak up in class, tell them what you know and that you know it. She told Cam always to defend a great man (she meant Roosevelt) when his name or memory was under attack. Cam had watched her grandmother leave a card party when one of her partners called Eleanor Roosevelt a pinko. Ellen stood up in the middle of a hand, threw down her cards, and walked away. Ellen saw that Dan didn't have Cam's courage for direct attacks; she saw her husband in her grandson, and encouraged him as she'd encouraged Vincent. Both the children ran to her with their report cards; they flowered beneath the glow of her unqualified and hungry praise.

They obeyed, though it frightened them, when she yanked them from the parish school. 'I'll never trust a nun,' she said. To her they were covered up, removed. She liked combat and engagement. You exposed yourself to the world of force; you didn't hide behind the weakness of your nature, or your privilege. The nuns' emphasis on deportment, submissiveness, their conviction that, especially for girls, the appropriate response to a challenging question was silence made Ellen fear for what she understood to be Cam's gifts. She wanted her granddaughter to live in the world; she was afraid the nuns would stop her. That Ellen secluded herself almost entirely in her house, invited no one in, went out only to electioneer – all this she never saw as withdrawal from the world. If you had told her that her kitchen was her cloister, she'd have raised her hand against you. She saw herself as living in the thick of things, because she read the newspaper with passion and discussed with Vincent from her heart the fate of the nations of the world. She thought she wasn't like other women. Although she rarely left the house, she believed herself not bounded by it. She didn't want Cam to live her real life in a house.

Ellen and Jack decided, without consulting Magdalene or Vincent, whom religion touched, that Dan would go to the Jesuits and Cam to public school. Dan won a scholarship; he took the bus and subway, traveling an hour each way into Brooklyn, where he got an education, Jack Morrisey said, as good as the sons of Presidents of Banks. Cam shocked the parish by her progress; she graduated second in her class, salutatorian, beat out only by Robert Glickman.

Jack Morrisey watched over them. He watched Dan and Cam and watched Ellen watching. In Dan, he saw too much of himself, the native fearfulness, the shy politeness he had worked to cut out of his nature and his presentation to the world. His regard for Dan was mixed with unease. But there was no dark spot on the lens of his admiration for Cam. A man unused to strong desire, he kept secret the fervor of his wish that Cam would one day be his partner, in his office, her name on the door right next to his. He kept secret, too, his fear that Edith Blake would win her from him to study classics, though he kept no secret of his ironic man-of-the-world distaste for Edith's old-maidish ways. But in the end he won Cam to the law, to Ellen's ideal of the active, useful life, and in the end both of them, Dan and Cam, came home to his office above Whelan's drugstore with its bad light and its stained, respectable venetian blinds.

They made their journey to the outside world; they met and mixed with people born far from them, people different from themselves. Then they came home to live.

In her law-school class of 1966, Cam was one of thirteen women in a class of over eight hundred. She didn't like her oddity, but it did not induce paralysis. Merely accommodation. She missed the naturalness of other women around her. But she was able rather easily to adopt the role of pal. She enjoyed her inclusion in the fraternal exclusivity that argued, sat in bars. She could almost forget the question underlying their acceptance of her: 'Why are you here?,' meaning 'What's wrong with you?' She saw her colleagues marry, purposefully, women they couldn't talk to, but it didn't bother her. She didn't want to marry any of them; she didn't even desire them. Her desires, the rare times she felt them, were reserved for distant, monkish figures she knew better than to approach. Her friendship with her classmate Anne Redmond was a free zone, in which she could be herself, without the unspoken tolerant exception generously made in her case. But she didn't realize that at the time, and since she wouldn't have dreamed of sharing her personal life with anyone outside her family, she didn't feel that she was missing anything. She shared with her friends a professional plan pointed towards service to the poor. Everything they argued and studied was geared towards this belief of theirs, that they would go into the crowded cities, to the countryside, where injustices bloomed like tough-rooted growth.

Two years after Cam, Dan went to law school out of fear, kindness, accommodation, and through comfort with the posture of defense. He would tell you, even now, he still believes it, that he went to law school to please Valerie, his wife. It's true that Valerie's father, Jim O'Keefe, had made a fortune in the building trades and was clear when he talked to his prospective son-in-law, the twenty-year-old Dan, that money was important, that he hadn't sent his girl back East to Manhattanville to marry a poor man. Dan was in love with Valerie O'Keefe, astonished, shocked, and frightened that she returned his love. She had the certainty he'd known and prized in Cam and in his grandmother, but she was small and dark, while their bodies seemed light and massive to him. She felt a commitment to domestic life, where they despised it, and Dan wanted a home. The lashings out of anger in his cousin and his grandmother, the tempers that flared up like dangerous, consuming flames, the terrible hard words, the brooding visible as smoke – there was none of all that in Valerie. Coolly she knit him sweaters while her classmates panicked in the week before their exams. She made candy for him on a hot plate in her room; and she returned his starved, shamed embraces with a steady ardor but no seeming need. Each day he knew her he believed he had to earn her by grueling, honorable labor in no way natural to him. He never felt that he deserved her. She in her turn felt, though she would never tell him and he never knew, inadequate before the love that flowed from him to her: so easily, like milk, like rain that soughed down to dry sand and was absorbed in silence. She feared the dry silence of her heart; she saw how people came to Dan and stood in the circle cast by his presence, the comfort of his large, loosely muscled body, maternal almost, and were quietened and reassured, fed, and restored to life. In her spare way she almost worshipped him. She felt she never measured up.

She would have done anything to make him happy, and she knew nothing she could do ever would. He, in his turn, revered her because he believed she didn't need him and the need of the world pressed on him all the time, he felt it like a spot on his lung, congenital, exhausting, never healed. He had always had to say of his beloved grandparents: They are weak, age weakens them, at

19

any moment those whom I most love can die. He never thought that Valerie would die.

He never told her, while they were engaged, seeing each other one weekend a month, that what he wanted was to study anthropology. He wanted to listen to the stories of people whose language was private, limited, whose language made for them a pocket or a cave away from the great world. But how could he do that and marry Valerie? She never questioned him when he said he wanted to go to law school. She made charts for him to help him study for the LSATs and read, with him, in the parlor while other students surreptitiously necked, the catalogues from law schools, noting conditions of financial aid. She said: Promise me we won't live anywhere near either of our families. The Irish genius for the local made her feel choked, balked, and trapped. Dan promised.

They married at twenty-one, moved into married students' housing at Cornell. In their last year of life in Ithaca, they conceived Darci, the perfect child, whose name offended everyone in both their families. 'I never heard of a Saint Darci,' Jim O'Keefe said. Ellen thought it sounded like an English lord; Vincent counseled her to say nothing: Perhaps it's someone in Valerie's family, he doubtfully remarked. Val's mother asked why they couldn't pick a name that would make people happy, Theresa said it was best to pick a name that told people where you stood, even Cam thought, but didn't say, for it was her business publicly to be on Dan's side in everything, that she hated women's names ending in 'i.'

The pregnancy and the first months of Darci's life were the best time in Dan and Valerie's marriage. In the converted barracks that was married students' housing at Cornell, they shared meals with other couples like themselves, protested the War, visited prisoners whom they advised about their cases, brought each other's children to be cared for by an Indian woman whose husband had got his Ph.D. in math. Clitoral orgasm took the barracks by storm; the women formed a consciousness-raising group, the men grew sullen or abashed. Val finished her library degree and got a job in the medical library, Dan took care of his infant daughter and felt for the first time that he took part in the life that other human beings always had been leading but from which he'd been cut off.

At the same time, in his classes, among his colleagues, anywhere outside his apartment, he felt a stranger, an imposter. He felt that no one knew him; if they did know him and the history of his family, they'd be appalled. He listened to complaints of friends about parents who wouldn't lend out summer houses, who wouldn't pass on a ten-year-old used car, who didn't understand their sons' refusal to go into corporate law, who wouldn't join their children for the March on Washington in Resurrection City. He listened to all this in awe and disbelief. Twice a semester he would go back home and speak to Ellen, who was avidly supporting Hubert Humphrey, hold her hand, and tell her all about his life in Ithaca, his friends. He'd listen to her worrying about the future of the Democratic party. 'You've got to have an organization in this world, they're all against you, there's enough outsiders without making outsiders of yourself.' He didn't argue with her or Jack Morrisey when they said the protesters would destroy the party. He was home when Robert Kennedy was shot and sat beside his grandparents in front of the television, all of them hypnotized, obsessed, watching as if they were waiting for someone, Walter Cronkite perhaps, to appear and tell them it was all a great mistake, a joke, a national experiment: Here is the living Bobby Kennedy and he'll be talking to you now.

He saw Cam working happily beside Jack Morrisey, saw Cam grow confident, successful at the bench, sat talking to her in her office, in the chair beside her desk, then went home to Ithaca feeling that he'd been living falsely, among strangers. After graduation, he told Valerie he couldn't keep his promise, what he wanted was to go back and work with Jack and Cam.

Val felt he'd betrayed her; it was the first rupture in their married life. But Dan was right; it was good for him to work near the town where he was born.

He's been happy, working beside Cam, but working differently from her; they split the practice, their strengths and weaknesses make a coherent whole.

She sees the people she defends as part of a long parade, leading to something. She likes to stand back from them; she likes them best after they leave her. She likes the bustle of the courthouse, the dark restaurants where she meets other lawyers over heavy slabs of meat during the lunch recess; she likes the serious municipal look of the courthouse building; she likes the mix of criminals and judges, lawyers, guards, and clerks. She even likes sitting in the unheated hall waiting, chatting, reassuring, giving to her opponents not the slightest hint of anything but good cheer and unruffled competence. She loves the word *competence*, like a classical object set apart from others in the light, without flaw. She likes standing beside her clients, making them feel that they aren't alone, that they needn't be frightened, she can stand between them and brute force, cruelty, injustice. She likes winning. She likes walking past husbands who have threatened her and her client with physical harm, not deigning to meet their brutish eyes. She likes walking with her men clients past the cruel wife and saying: See, the world is different, it will be different now, your children are not your property, the world is changing, and I am leading the change.

She hates losing. After nineteen years she still can't stand it. The only thing she likes is the rough forgetfulness, meeting the others in the dark bar afterwards, and going on, all of them going on, knowing there will be others – more victims, more cases. She dislikes many of her colleagues. But she likes the game of it, pitting herself and leading the march away from the dead world. At night she still wakes up saying: I should have said this; I should have made that point. I should have closed in this way, I should have called him to the stand.

If it is bad for her, for Daniel it's ten times worse. She sees it in his eyes, when the woman loses all her money, or the man his bid for joint custody, she sees his eyes darken with self-blame. She sees that recently he has got better. It has not occurred to her till just that moment, sitting on her childhood bed. It occurs to her now for the first time: Dan suffers less over losing than he once did. She wonders why. She wonders if it would be right to ask him.

For Dan, each case is like a postulate in science or a work of art. It exists by itself in the world. She reckons he spends three times longer talking to the clients than she does. He gives them his phone number at home. They call him at all hours. He interrupts his dinner and his peaceful sleep to comfort them. He still does this after seventeen years. He comes in early and stays late to confer with them. Many of his clients fall in love with him. And why not: for them a man, listening to them, with his blue eyes that absorb their grief, is like a gift. 'Don't worry, things will be all right,' he says, and they believe him. To her clients she says: 'Don't worry, we'll win.' She would never think of promising that things will be all right.

Their clients give them different sorts of gifts. Both of them have cakes baked for them. Cam's clients bake cakes that are large, heavy, oversweet, or cookies made with honey, spongy breads, their hard crusts shiny with brushed egg. The cakes Dan's clients bake are miracles of invention and new industry: Julia Child's three-chocolate bombe, the Pinwheel Fruit Tart from *The Silver Palate Cookbook*. In his closet, Dan has seven framed needlepoint renderings of scales of justice. Cam has, in a secret bureau drawer, a papier-mâché object, three inches high, brought back by one of her clients from her home in Guadalajara. It is the figure of a woman, robed in white, with a cavity in the center of her chest. A doctor stands behind her holding her bleeding heart with tongs. At the base is written: *'Por un amor.'*

'But, Silvia,' she'd said to her client, ten years younger than she, the mother of six, a nurse's aide, whom she'd been successful in helping to keep her children after her divorce although she was living with a new man. 'Silvia,' she said, 'I have a husband.'

Silvia laughed, suddenly maternal, superior. 'I had a husband, too. Now I have a different man. You and me,' she said. 'I know what you need. I look in your eyes and I see my old eyes. So I bring this back to give you luck.' A month later, Cam met Ira Silverman.

She'd agreed to serve, at a greatly reduced rate, as counsel for the co-op board of the building where Bob's brother and his wife lived. She told her sister-in-law, Eileen, she wasn't a real-estate lawyer, they could probably do better. 'We can't do better,' Eileen said. 'We're broke. Besides, you're good at keeping people from screwing other people. You'll be terrific.'

At one of the board meetings, a woman was talking about having taken her children to a circus and how much she'd hated it. Especially the clowns.

'Everyone hates clowns,' Cam said. 'They make you feel guilty. They're not funny, they look miserable, they're trying too hard, and you're bored to death, but you feel you have to laugh. Just because they're miserable and they're trying so hard. Circuses in general, only a real sicko would like them. They put you in an untenable moral position. You're so bored, you keep hoping that someone will break his neck just so you have something interesting to look at. Who can live with themselves after thoughts like that?'

23

The people around the table looked at her as if she'd just gone mad. Only one of them laughed, a short pudgy man with reddish hair. It happened to Cam often: she would go on talking, thinking everyone knew she was joking, and then see that she had puzzled or appalled the crowd. But this man understood. She could see, as if they were on a dance floor, that he wanted to join her, partner her, follow her lead. 'Jesus, you're right,' he said. 'It reminds me of when I was a kid, a teenager, we used to go to burlesque houses in New Jersey. Union City. The comics would go out first, but of course no one wanted to see them, everyone wanted to see the girls. Someone in the balcony threw a penny at the comedian. The guy walked to the front of the stage. "What is wrong with you?" he said to the audience. "Don't you understand, we're out here, we're doing our best, like anybody else, this is our job, like any of you have jobs, and you do a thing like that. Throw a penny from the balcony. It could have put my eye out. Suppose it put my eye out? What would happen to me? But you never think of us like that. We're nothing to you."'

'Talk about moral pressure,' Ira Silverman said. It was the first time she'd met him. Three months later they were lovers. But Cam is married to Bob Ulichni, and living with him and her mother, two blocks away from her grandparents, in the house she's lived in since she was three years old. She doesn't want to think of Ira now. She makes her mind go back to Lorraine Barnabas.

It won't go back. She wonders if she could allow herself to call Silvia Ramirez. She wants Silvia to read her palm, tea leaves, the movements of the clouds, entrails of chickens still warm from the slaughter. She wants Silvia to tell her the future.

But she won't do that. How can it be, she says to Ira, that at our age, with what we've gone through, who we are, we should be here together like this? She looks at herself in the mirror, sees herself as she believes she is seen in the world, and knows herself not to be romantic. She has white smooth skin (a good skin, she's been told; she believes that is the last-ditch compliment, the bone cast to the plain woman). She has large clear gray eyes set far apart, light lashes that can't be helped by mascara. She knows she doesn't dress well. Everybody tells her. Her law-school friends just itch, they say, just itch to get their hands on her. And sometimes she has let them, with infinitely bad results. Come with us, they say, come shopping. Shopping. To them the word suggests the vista open to the sky, the sheen of illumined buildings: points of truth in the December evenings of great cities. To Camille the word, simply the word – SHOPPING – is a February twilight in the company of a wet, dying dog. It is the test foreordained to be failed, the trial presided over by a judge paid off for years to be against you. Try this, her friends say, handing her a blouse, a skirt, a pair of trousers. This color is good for you, you need more color, brighter color, these lines will help you. How lucky you are to be so tall.

And Cam will grip the hangers, carry to the curtained cubicle the garments of her doom. Once on her body, the clothes turn against her; so promising on hangers, they bunch and hang perversely. They pucker; they cling where they should not cling. She holds her body against them. Like clever animals, the garments of her doom sense her terror and turn on her, calling up the judgment of her friends (Well, if you stand like that), the salespeople (She might as well save her money), and herself (No use, no use).

She doesn't know how to dress. She wears dark-colored pantsuits and dark-colored low-heeled shoes with chains, small horseshoes, or dull buckles at the instep or perhaps thick stitching at the toes, indicating to the world, she hopes, that she has no illusions on the subject of her looks.

She doesn't understand how she could have had the good fortune to fall in love with a man who loves her. It had never been a likely thing to happen at any point in history; now in the history of men and women, she knows it is a statistical freak. Women her age were supposed to have greater chance of being hijacked by a terrorist than falling happily in love. She'd said to Ira once that men and women together now were walking through an unlit warehouse. 'We keep bumping into furniture, things we have no more use for, names we hardly know and never say. Armoires. Credenzas.' ('Whatever happened to them,' he interrupted her. 'I remember everyone had a credenza once. That's the trouble with the world.' . . . She wouldn't let him go on. She wanted to finish what she had to say.) 'We keep walking in the dark, bumping into these things with sharp corners, falling onto overstuffed things that could swallow us up. And then we see these angry faces in the picture frames, staring out at us in the dark. Mattresses on the floor with stains from God knows what.'

25

'Stick with me,' he said. 'I'll get you through the warehouse. I've got a flashlight. I've got keys.'

She tries to bring her mind back to Lorraine Barnabas. She wonders if she should, after all, ask Dan to handle the case. Sometimes she thinks it's just good luck, the way she and Dan divide the practice. He believes in *pro bono* work, but the real, desperate lives of the people whom he works for take too much out of him. She has no patience with privileged victims.

Sometimes she worries that she's invented this neat split, that she has made Dan her victim. Would he like to be leading the march away from the dead world? Does she leave him the boring cases, the paying cases, so that she can trail glory, so that she can keep intact the image of herself she had in law school?

She doesn't ask Dan any of these things. She never has.

7

Ellen is asleep. She will no longer have a life outside this bed. The nurses, there are two of them now, one for day and one for night, Mary Davenport and Beulah Rice, pride themselves that on account of them she has no bedsores. Twice a day, they sit her up in the chair in the corner of the room. They strap her in while they change the sheets, shake out the bedding. Mary Davenport suggested an investment be made in a sheepskin pad for Ellen to lie on; it was wonderful, she said, what bedsores it kept back; but at the same time they really know how to charge. Think about it, she said to Cam. There's nothing to think about, Mrs. Davenport, Cam said coldly: If it's needed, order it. The sheepskin pad cost two hundred dollars; Cam always suspected that Mary Davenport took a cut.

The room that was once an ordinary bedroom is now a sick-room. Over the course of Ellen's lifetime in it – she'd been young when she and Vincent had come to the house – she'd filled the room with her identity. To the children, it was a little frightening, dark, overfull of furniture, smelling of liniment. There were no pictures on the walls. Newspapers were piled on several chairs; at night, Ellen would lay her day clothes on the backs of these chairs; her shapeless undergarments would graze the piles of yellowing paper. Once a year, perhaps, Vincent would grow impatient: 'Are you really going to read all of these, Ellen? Would you go through them, some of them might be ready to be thrown out?' She'd be furious at him; 'They're there for a purpose, Vincent. If they weren't there for a purpose, they wouldn't be there.' And at night, she'd read them, wearing the glasses that made her eyes look liquefied, in the light dimmed by the pink lampshade, she'd read the months-old newspapers, folding each page as it was done, putting some on the desktop underneath the scissors she used for clipping articles. Some nights she'd let Dan and Camille clip with her; she kept clippings in a wooden box and hid it underneath the bed. 'You like to have a sense of things,' she said.

But she has lost the thread. She inhabits a place that has no place inside the larger world. She can no longer make connections. She does not know the relation of one thing to another thing. The past crowds in on her, tormenting. She knows the past to be the past, but the present doesn't set itself down in shapes that she can name and recognize. She looks around the room for anything familiar. But most of her things have been taken out. Now there are only functional objects: overlarge jars containing gauze, cotton, Vaseline, clear solutions, brown bottles of medicine, plastic cups with water, dilute juice, tape, spoons, a blood-pressure cuff, a suction machine, a bellows, rubber tubes.

She is asleep among the objects that are nothing to her. Slowly, she opens her eyes; she is too tired, though, to try to understand her new place in the world, the place of all the other people, whether she is alive. She lets her eyes fall shut again. She cannot make the effort to distinguish anything about her life.

Dan sees his grandmother is asleep. He walks into the kitchen for a glass of water.

It is a meaningless room without Ellen's governance. Her objects, untouched by her, seem ghostly, artificial. The smell of her spices has disappeared: marjoram, he thinks it must have been, nutmeg and cloves, bay leaves in soups, vanilla, sage. Fondly, he looks at the table where he did his homework on the oilcloth.

There's no more oilcloth in the world and no linoleum. He remembers helping his grandfather lay the first linoleum: speckles against
a background of light gray. They never chose a new pattern; they
replaced it. Two years ago, Vincent agreed to let two friends of
John's lay a set of speckled vinyl tiles.

The shelving paper in the cupboards looks unfresh. It's the kind
of thing, he supposes, that someone like Mary Davenport can't be
expected to keep up with. He wishes he'd noticed it himself before
this. And then he realizes that, in all the time Vincent's been gone,
he hasn't once gone into the kitchen. He wonders if anyone in the
family has.

He sees his cousin Sheilah coming in from the back porch. When
she notices him, her face, which had looked as if someone had
recently offended her, or as if she's ready if they plan to, comes to
life.

'Hi, Danny,' she says. Of all the people she's known, she rightly
believes that few have genuinely liked her. But she believes Dan
does. She hopes he notices how she's arranged the cold cuts,
carefully, beautifully, she thinks, fanning out from the cherry
tomato in the center like a star.

Sheilah is a social worker. Her field is called 'Quality Insurance.'
Regulatory agencies – the State Department of Mental Hygiene,
for example – require some guarantee that the services, medical
and legal in particular, that are being provided for their clients are
up to standards. Sheilah's office handles this. In other words, she
is in charge of checking up. It's the perfect job for her. The
watchful, excluded child, the second of three undesired children,
dutifully produced, she grew expert at pinpointing failure. When
she discovers fraudulence, carelessness, incompetence, neglect, or
an attempt to cover up, she doesn't move quickly or even seem
to be responding. Then she issues reports that are triumphs of
meticulous devastation. She believes that she does this because she
is the champion of the poor: a legacy of the years when she was
Sister Raymond Theresa, a Sister of Charity, from 1965 to 1970.
She left the convent scandalously to marry Father Steve Gallagher,
her fellow picketer and witness to draft-card burnings, participant
in vigils, marches, folk-song fests against the Vietnam War. In fact
what makes her good at her job is her talent for finding fault.

As a social caseworker, helping the poor to a better life, she was
a disaster. Unlike Cam and Cam's sister-in-law, Eileen Ulichni,

28

also a social worker, she was angry at her clients for their continued stubbornness in the face of her good advice. 'The trouble with Sheilah and her clients,' Eileen once said to Cam, 'is that she's pissed off because they're not like her. Thank God, most of them have too much sense for that.' Whereas both Cam and Eileen were content with rare and temporary progress, Sheilah had felt betrayed when her clients seemed to be taking her advice to heart, and then, leaving her office, acted exactly as she'd urged them not to, exactly as they'd always acted all of their disorderly lives. She moved into administration, saying she was 'burnt out.' But in fact she'd never caught fire; as a caseworker she had failed; running the Office of Quality Insurance, she is, in the circles where she moves, a universally acclaimed success.

In her childhood, she was a failure, the one who woke unbeautifully with crusted eyelids, who fell over her open shoelaces in the middle of a game of tag and stopped the game. In a circle where wit was prized she had no sense of humor; she never got jokes, especially the ones she was the butt of, the ones from her mother's mouth. Always cringing, she would cave in almost entirely at her mother's sharpness. But in adult life, since leaving the convent, she's placed herself in the center of circles of earnestness, of serious, sincere people who believe in something, who use their spare time to act on what they believe in for a better world. She is the head of her parish council; she is working on her master's degree in family history (for which she has tried to interview her grandfather, with results that frustrate and anger her), she travels regularly to Manhattan for meetings of a society dedicated to the preservation of Irish culture; with her son, Diarmid, and her husband she takes weekly classes in the Irish language and in Irish dance. In these circles of earnestness, she is respected and looked up to. But in her family she is seen by the kindly as pathetic, by the less kind as a joke. She is never seen as a success.

Even Dan, with his merciful eye, looks at Sheilah and sees failure. He sees the plate of cheese and cold cuts she has arranged to fan out like a star from the cherry tomato at the center and does not think, as she had hoped, how original, how pleasing. He notes with pity that this simple infantile arrangement took his cousin an hour and a half to effect. He would love to run up to Cam and laugh about it, laugh that it took Sheilah an hour and a half, think of her trying to slice Muenster cheese with an electric knife, so they can become children again, cover their faces with their pillows to stop the intoxicating bubbles of illegal laughter.

Sheilah sees in Dan's eyes, which can hide nothing, that in looking at the plate of cold cuts for a second he wanted to laugh. She'd been proud of the arrangement. She had hoped that Dan would come in first and see it, see what she had done, and compliment her on her work. But now she sees the shadow that passed over his gaze. She understands that everything she has done is ridiculous, always will be, nothing will change it, when she thinks that it has changed *she* is the fool and they are laughing at her. Nothing will change.

Then angrily she blames him for making her feel this way. She thinks: Why has he made me feel this. I have arranged these things attractively on a plate. None of them would do it. None of them cares about these things. They'd have put it any old way, horrible, disgusting how they would have put it. I see what they never see. I do what they would never think of doing. I am happily married, and they are not. My husband and I stand on the edge of the new world. We have courage. We left our orders for each other. We are at the center of a movement which allows the Irish to reclaim our heritage. *We* study the language, *our* child learns the traditional dances. Not theirs. He competes each year in the city-wide Feis. One day he will win ribbons for me, medals. I know a history they never even knew they lost. How dare they make me feel a failure. They are the failures. She wants to say: You are a failure, Dan, not me; your ex-wife half a continent away, your one child unmanageable, the other who will never love you. Never. And the woman you won't marry. It is you who fail.

But Daniel doesn't run upstairs. He could only laugh with Cam about it if Cam, too, felt sorry for Sheilah. But she doesn't; she's impatient with Sheilah, she wants to dismiss her like a pesky fly buzzing on the screen door of the family life. And he won't disturb Cam. She's working; they are partners. *Partners*, the lovely word. His cousin. *Partners*. He won't go up to Cam to laugh because he pities Sheilah, and fears Cam's scorn, which falls on Sheilah, and turns her vicious. He hates the sight of all of it: Sheilah's failure, Cam's scorn, Sheilah's viciousness, Cam's shamed withdrawal, then her guilt. Cam knows that she has never been able even to like Sheilah and that Sheilah has always needed love. She has known this for forty years. Knowing it has helped nothing.

'How's Diarmid?' Daniel asks. Diarmid is Sheilah's eight-year-old son.

The question, as always, frightens her. She can't answer truthfully. She's afraid if she makes her pride in her son public it will be taken from her. She will be punished, mocked. For her boy is a miracle to her. She has been, since she has known that people looked at her, aware of that great minus in the glances that have fallen on her. The inevitable minus of the unloved child. No one, not even her husband, ever looked at her as she looks at her son, with joy and gratitude. From birth she was a disappointment to her mother, who had hoped in having children to gain the respect her own mother had withheld from her, on account of her sex.

When Sheilah now looks at the old pictures of herself, among her family, she'd like to cry for the child standing apart who inserts herself into the family grouping next to Daniel, and desperately holds his hand. Dan, when he was allowed to choose his own place in the pictures, always chose to be with Cam. In the pictures, he holds Cam's hand, not merely kindly, as he does with Sheilah, but with joy. Cam in the pictures, bold even as a child, makes Sheilah rage. Cam the thief, the pirate. *If you had not been, I might have been you.*

So her love for her son frightens her. Suppose it can be stolen, lost? She has to hide it, no one must know of this gift she gives her child. She and her son are weak. She won't allow anyone to steal from her or from her son. So she says to her cousin Dan, who asked about him, 'Well, you know, he drives me crazy.'

Dan ruffles her hair. 'He's a nice boy,' he says.

Now, secretly, she preens. This is the sun that she can, for a moment, bask in, Dan's praise of her boy. For he could never say anything like that to Cam. Cam has no children, Sheilah thinks, as always with clear joy. And never will.

A childless woman, Sheilah thinks, and barren. To think in secret of her cousin and to use the word, the terrible, the cruel word, *barren*, lights a joyful flame in Sheilah's heart. She could almost be kind to Cam, or could at least not be hateful to her. She thinks that maybe when Cam comes downstairs later she won't be hateful to her. She wonders once again why Cam's marriage is childless. No one has ever told her; she has never asked.

8

Ellen MacNamara made a happy marriage. But it was not enough. She came into it from a life already scalded by shame, stiffened by disappointment, judgment, fear. So her happy marriage could not make her a happy woman. Her husband's happy marriage almost made him a happy man.

Until that thing happened, ten months ago, he was almost a happy man.

Cam thinks of Vincent sitting now, not in the house where people fan out from the center of his dying wife, but twenty miles away. He is sitting in a room that looks out to a sloping garden. It is summer now; the roses bloom, the zinnias, nasturtiums, marigolds, planted by him and the other residents, flourish in the black soil of Eastern Long Island, famous for potatoes. Three months before, Vincent had said to Cam, 'Bring my garden tools, my work pants, my old shoes.' He made this request on May third, more than three months ago, and Cam went into her grandfather's workroom in the basement to get these things. She was happy to do it for him, remembering how happy he had been there, in this room that really was not a room, a slice of cellar, where no light entered, where the naked bulb hung from the ceiling, where the air presented an unvarying cold damp, where seasons came and went, leaving no mark. He worked there, he made things, and he was happy, singing tunelessly, or whistling without song. He thought his thoughts.

And what thoughts were they? In that room, seeing his constructions, his inventions, Cam had always thought: My grandfather was a genius. He was a genius at design. He had a gift for abstract thought. She could say this only to Daniel, and to her lover, Ira Silverman, for to anyone else it could become a joke. This man, leaving behind him abstract shapes in tin. Left over from his models. His work was wonderful for a child to watch. He worked as a machinist when she knew him; his days in the Transit Authority shop were over before her birth. His job was to make models of scaffolding. Seven inches high. He had no interest in the scaffolding itself. Or in the skyscrapers it made possible. She'd asked him if he'd ever visited the finished buildings. 'No,' he said, 'I never thought to.'

As children she and Dan had walked behind him, asking him things he was pleased to answer fully and at length. They played among his abstract leavings. No tempests there, no dangers; that was safety to them, it would always be their memory of safety, sitting with their grandfather, courtly even to children, patient in the cellar.

He was a gentleman, Camille would say. A word she honored, despite who she was politically. All my desire for a life that had a shape grew here, Cam thought, looking for her grandfather's garden tools. And for a life that had a vivid pattern: this I learned from him in the garden. Dahlias, marigolds, flowers of line and pattern. There was nothing shifting in his flowers. Dark-colored sweet peas. Flowers that stood out in the world.

Walking by his workbench that day three months before, she put her hand on the vise and the grindstone. On the racks she looked at screwdrivers, wrenches (crescent, monkey, ratchet, pipe), tools with their proper names and places, and their exact functions, their specialized tasks. The hammers, some clawed, some with a ball head. In her memory, not the traditionally comforting smell of wood: the smell, instead, of burning tin, industrial and unpoetical.

She passed the metalwork bench and walked to the woodworking section, which he used less often: plane and lathe, the puritanical nails in their jars. On the other side of the cellar he kept pitchforks and rakes, bags of manure, spades, paper bags of bulbs, now sprouting from neglect (he'd had his accident in autumn), grass seed in boxes.

He was interested in life, so was Ellen, always interested, thought Cam, bending and choosing only light tools for him, the tools of simpler labor. He was old now, he was eighty-eight, but it was wonderful that he was working in the garden. She picked up his gardening gloves, put them on her own hands. She stroked the gloves as she had stroked his hands to comfort him the night that Ellen had knocked him down and she had come to see him in the hospital. The neighbors had called Theresa. They had been unable to get Cam. The night that it all happened she was with her lover.

Panic rises up. *My fault, my fault.* The sex was still wet between her legs when she came to the hospital. She wanted to kneel down before her grandfather, ask his forgiveness. Had she been wrong to go along with him when he said he could care for Ellen after she'd had the last stroke? 'I can care for her, Cam,' he had said, 'at least at night, after all these years. She is my wife, I just don't want a stranger in the house. Just not at night. Please, Cam. You can see to it.'

She had seen to it, and had been wrong. 'Judgment calls,' her friends who spent their lives in meetings, on committees, called them. The kind of words she hated and made fun of that these people who did such good works always would use: 'ballpark figure,' 'bottom line.' And yet these were the people who could make money trickle through the world so that her grandfather could be in that nice place, Maryhurst. You had to thank people who said 'Let's interface' for things like that. 'It was a judgment call,' her friends said, thinking that was comfort. 'You called it wrong. We all do.'

Called it wrong. As if it were a ballgame or a square dance. But what had happened that night was like the gunshot that sets off an avalanche.

Vincent had lain on the floor, calling out to anyone for help. He couldn't move himself into the hall, where the telephone sat on a stand that he had painted black. It was autumn and the windows all were shut. No one could hear him calling out. He could see Ellen walking in her nightgown. He was afraid drivers wouldn't see her in time; he had to do something before somebody in a car ran her down before his eyes.

On a table near him, low, within his reach, were the historical figurines they had collected. Roosevelt, the Kennedys, an inscribed ashtray from the Democratic Club, a brown-and-green statue of the Bicentennial eagle. He picked one up: a statuette of Robert Kennedy. He threw it through the window. He picked up six more figurines and broke six windows in the front of his own house. A man whose life had been devoted to respect and care for property, he did this shocking and disgraceful thing. He knew he had to. It had worked. Somebody called the rescue squad. The ambulance arrived with its flashing lights and its good citizens: trained neighbors, paramedics, lifting her grandfather onto an air cushion not larger than himself. 'It's a shame there's so much furniture,' one of them had said, Vincent had told her later. Even then he was able to notice things.

When she finally came to the hospital, he didn't look at her. When she came to the room, his eyes were fixed on the ceiling; the attentive eyes, the courtly glance, grew fixed. He was trying not to think, he who had always passionately thought about the world before him. She could see him looking at the ceiling, willing himself into an abstract noun, two nouns: age, death.

9

He didn't stay that way.

For two weeks he lay on his bed in Mary Immaculate Hospital, trying to make himself let go of his life. Then he grew courtly again, shaved, and asked about the nurses' families. But he did not inquire about his wife. Something was sloughed off, some burden shifted, then laid down. First in terror. Then relief.

Now, in the room he is about to leave, he fears returning to her anger. All her anger had become corrupted like her body in old age. As a young woman, she'd been beautiful in her anger, he remembered, looking at the sloping garden, far from her. He thought of her anger at the Irish countryside, the harsh soil and scrub growth, the gorse she hated. She'd no memory of tilled field, of the elm or the potato, tender when in leaf. Anger had been Ellen's chief food. And she feared sympathy like a disease. Do not give it, do not take. Action was what she loved. Is there nothing I can be doing for you, she would say, when he would say he loved her and she couldn't answer back.

She'd never believed in happiness. The mention of it put her in a fury. *Happy*. The word could make her bang down pot or scissors, shovel, garbage can, whatever hard thing she was holding. Her hands were never empty. Even when she sat in company she held something in her hand: a glass, an empty ashtray she'd turn over, a coin, a scissors, or a handkerchief, a knife. But she liked to laugh. Jokes made her happy. Jokes, songs, toasts, speeches, arguments, political and passionate. Her angry politics, words that sprouted up like buildings overnight. Words hard and blunt: stone axes. He thinks of her walking out of the butcher shop she'd patronized for twenty years because Joe McNulty said some bad thing about Roosevelt, then six years dead. She chose to live with meat of lower quality and more expense, chose to put her heavy black foot down on the gas pedal of her 1940 Chevrolet and loudly drive past Joe McNulty's store each week to a strange butcher, an Italian. Vincent was proud of that. He was not proud, though, of all the parties she had left and made him leave, the First Communions, graduations, barbecues, if somebody said something anti-union or Republican. He'd been shamed by that.

He won't think of her now. He'll look at the sloping garden. He'll think of dahlias, asters. He'll think of herbs the sisters want, whose use he cannot understand. He will go back to Ellen. But he won't think about it now.

10

Sitting on her childhood bed, Cam thinks about her grandfather. She plans her visit to her mother, bringing her mother here (she's pretty sure this won't happen, but she has to plan for it anyway). She thinks of her grandfather in his pleasant room, of Ellen in the room below, cursing again and refusing her death. She asks herself: How have I got here, how have I come from all those people?

When she thinks like this her thoughts turn to her mother. Magdalene's face swims up in her mind, bobbing like a discolored ball pushed under water and then rising up. She thinks first: 'I don't love my mother.' Then she says: 'It's not her fault.'

It would never occur to Magdalene that Cam, her daughter, doesn't love her. She would always say that daughters love their mothers. She assumes she loves her mother, Ellen. She doesn't question, doesn't wonder over what she takes to be a natural order. 'My mother is a great woman,' she says, 'my mother is a saint.' Only when Magdalene is drunk she says: 'My mother never loved me.' In this state, even now, when her mother is dying, when her mother could never come to the phone or even understand its ring, she calls her mother on the telephone; she wants to wake her up. She says to Mary Davenport, to Marilyn, to Theresa, to whoever is on the phone, 'My mother didn't love me.'

As a child, Cam would try to stop her. 'Don't, Mom, it's late. Don't call Gran, Mama. Don't, you'll wake her. You'll make her upset.' Her mother would push past her. 'Goddamn it, she deserves it. She deserves once in her goddamn life to be upset. The cold bitch. She never loved anyone but John. Me and Theresa, she never cared about either of us. I'm going to call Theresa. She's the only one who understands. Not you, you're a cold bitch just like she is.' Cam is seven, eight, nine years old. 'A cold bitch, just like her.'

'Don't call Aunt Theresa, Mom. Please don't.' She has to protect her mother against Theresa. Theresa the collector, holding, hoarding, storing up damning information, instances of offense. She herself never offended. 'It's not that it bothers *me*, Camille. It's you and her I think about. I'm upset for you, what you have to go through. Just remember, sweetheart, if it gets too bad, you just walk out and come right here. There's always a place for you here.'

Never. I will never leave her.

Cam, seven, eight, nine years old, becomes a craftsman building up a carapace to protect her own life and her mother's. Always afterwards when she thinks of hate, the things that people do out of hate, the crimes that she defends her worst clients for committing, she understands. She remembers what was in her heart towards her aunt Theresa. *You are a liar and a murderer. I am a child, but I would kill you if I could.*

She'd meet her aunt's eye; it took all her courage but she'd do it. 'It's fine here with us,' she'd say to Theresa. 'In the morning she's always fine. She goes to work. She makes my breakfast.'

Then she would see the closed face of her aunt stiffen, knowing she had been lied to. She would see the eyes sharpen, the teeth working behind the lips trying to smile. Theresa was caught up in her hatred. Her hatred had no brilliance; it was functional, and she loved it in its function: to do hurt.

Theresa saw Cam in her carapace. She thought that the child had made herself impervious. But underneath Cam bled, whimpered for her mother, for the fragrant, coiffed woman who walked out of the house in the morning, perfect for the ones who paid her to cut their hair, to do their nails. To this mother she cried: 'Why do you leave me to this hate and shame and force me to build up this hard enclosure to protect our lives? I am a child. Your child. Why don't you protect me? I will always protect you from your mother, your sister. Anybody in the world. I will protect you always. Therefore, you must not ask me for love.'

In the mornings, after her mother's nighttime telephoning, Cam would walk the two blocks to her grandmother's. She was seven, eight, nine years old. She would walk silently into the kitchen. She would slip into a chair; she'd watch her grandmother's clever hands, deft but bluntly molded: their padded fingertips, their pinkish palms. She would watch her crimp pastry, fill it with fruit, shut the oven door angrily, hard, bang down her pots, chop violently, stir deliberately, slip silently to Cam a nip of pastry, a tender carrot, or a spoon of soup. Her grandmother would say nothing of Magdalene's shame. And Cam would see her grandmother, seriously busy, listening to the radio as she ironed, *Our Gal Sunday*, *The Romance of Helen Trent*, or cursing at the news, calling out to her husband, 'Dad, it's lunch now.' And Cam would see, from behind her carapace, her grandmother's similar edifice, and feel safe then to break out of the enclosure she had built up to protect her mother's and her life. So that by the time her grandfather came to the kitchen, washed his hands at the sink, Cam's cramped limbs had relaxed. And she was able once again to speak to him, her darling grandfather, speak her first unchoked words of the day. She had been set free by her absorbed, purposeful grandmother. And Ellen had been in turn set free by her own skill, and her consuming tasks.

In adulthood, Cam has retained her carapace. Some who have flung themselves against it have sprung back in shocked anger. But nobody hates Magdalene. Magdalene has always had her champions, who burrow in the soft flesh of her nature and find love. They find there a bright, wounded creature, an example of originality in her heroism. 'Think of her,' her champions say, 'let down by her husband, then him killed in that way that only was a shame to her, the no-good, and the kid just six. And what did she do then? Lay on her back and die? Not her,' they say. 'She went back to her hairdressing. She never went to school for it, learned it herself watching John Impanata, working as a cashier, then a manicurist, working herself up till she became a hairdresser herself. Then getting back to it while the husband was away. Then buying into the shop, then taking it over when John got sick. Today she'd go on welfare,' say Magdalene's champions. 'But no, not her. Not with her spirit. No. With everything she did for that kid, college, law school, big success, the kid treats her mother like dirt. Does for her but acts like she's too good for her. But not too good to live in the mother's house. Of course I guess they have to, with Magdalene always on the edge like she is. So sick.'

Her champions see Magdalene the invalid, gallant in her prison-bed. They visit Magdalene, they tell her all their sorrows, and they come away refreshed.

In 1965, the year that Cam got married, Magdalene developed cancer of the breast. Your mother won't live, the doctors said to Cam, a law student at Columbia. What shall we tell her? Cam thought: There is no one to ask. Her grandparents were too old, and Magdalene was their child. It would be too terrible to ask someone for help with the death of their child. She longed to talk to Dan. But Dan had a wife, a baby. She thought it was his first real life, she didn't want to mar it. Finally she couldn't stay away. She went up to Cornell, sat at his table in the married students' dorm, and said, 'Magdalene's going to die, the doctors say. What should I tell her?'

She wished she hadn't come to Dan, for the grief passed so visibly over his features. And she couldn't bear to see him grieve, she couldn't bear to watch his face when it was like this, so porous to unhappiness. As a child, she'd do anything to take that look away, run to exhaustion, dance, tell jokes, make up stories, offer money, steal food, ransack anything. Seeing his face, she wanted to say, 'It was wrong, what I said. I got it wrong. She's not going to die. I have to go now.'

'How long does she have?' he asked.

'Six months.'

'Don't tell her.'

From the shadows, the quick certainty rose up that made him good at the law. But, hearing him say it, she thought he was wrong.

'I have to tell her. There might be something she wants to do. Or say to someone.' (She did not mean herself.)

'Magdalene? Your mother? What sense does she have of the past? What's her memory: the dresses that she wore, the dances, the nights out before she met your father? Do you think she'll tell you she's sorry for what she's done? Never. She thinks she did everything for you anyone could do. She kept on working, she thinks that is everything.'

'Maybe she's right. Maybe she did all she could do.'

Always when her mother is criticized, even by Dan, the glittering enclosure shoots up. *Don't hurt my mother. Praise her. Understand.*

'So you're going to tell her?' Dan asked.

'I don't know.'

'Remember, Magdalene never minds being lied to.'

But she should have the truth.

So Cam came in one evening to her mother's room, not too late, and told her what the doctor said. And Magdalene rose up to the second great act of her life: the calm acceptance of the news of her death. She reassured the nurses who prepared her for surgery. She was every doctor's favorite patient. In the hospital she had her hair washed and set twice a week, put on her makeup every day, and changed her bed jacket the first thing every morning. She made black jokes about her missing breasts and urged her fellow patients to get up, try to walk, not to malinger. She had a parade of visitors like an ambassador: her customers, pulling at their hair in mock horror: When will you be back?

She came back home from the hospital. She redid her bedroom all in purple, with the advice of a decorator, one whose hair she dyed and cut. She bought herself a bed fit for a dying queen, a purple velvet spread, lavender sheets. She had built into her bathroom a black marble tub and shower, she filled brandy snifters with small soaps in the shape of shells or flowers. She built a special closet for her shoes. She took, then, to her bed, waiting for her suitor, death.

Who did not come, as false to her as her betraying husband. It is twenty years later; she is cured, but still is waiting. She never goes outside her house; hardly outside the two rooms she invented for herself, for her role of dying queen. Every five years she buys a larger television. Last year she installed a microwave. In one lavender cabinet she keeps her foodstuffs: Cup-a-Soup and

Noodle-roni. Waverly Wafers. Swiss Knight cheese. Every week she gives her daughter a list of foods to buy, a list of liquor for herself and guests, handing the piece of paper to her, holding it at arm's length, holding it with her fingertips, as if they were distasteful to her, all these bodily needs. Twice a week Kevin, her old partner, comes to do her hair. He runs the shop now, and has hired four more cutters, but he and Magdalene are partners. Kevin and his companion, Dennis, and their friends pop in and out, gossip, bring her the *National Enquirer*, the *Star*, *People* magazine, sometimes *Harper's Bazaar* or *Vogue*. They advise her on her health and dressing up.

She lives now in the joy and peace of one in love with her vocation. She has found her calling; all her talents are put to use: indolence, a limited but well-formed vanity, a desire that people should come to her. Once they have come, an infinite desire to hear their stories, no unwillingness to hear the stories repeated many times.

She is of real help to her visitors: Kevin and Dennis, and her old customers, retired couples whose children have moved south or west, or died, or grown into disappointments to their parents. Cancer victims who can see she is alive. She gives the cancer victims holy pictures with a printed prayer on the back to Saint Peregrina, patron saint of cancer. To her gay friends, terrified of AIDS, she gives out holy pictures of Saint Anthony. For some time, she had trouble coming up with a saint appropriate to this special cause. She settled on Saint Anthony, as she told her friends, because he is the patron saint of *finding*, and she prays to him to find a cure for AIDS.

Magdalene is in a strange position with her gay friends. She is devout, although she hasn't been inside a church since her illness (she says the crowds make her faint, she'd just pass out and God doesn't want that). And she doesn't *believe* in sex. She never believed in it in relation to herself. Sex, she thinks, is something that men need and women put up with. Her picture of sex is this: a man, his nature crystallized in his tumescence, looms above a woman, who, eyes closed, pretends to be a corpse. She allows this to go on because she wants a child and wants a house and wants things paid for and not to worry or have to go out to work. Because of these ideas it is difficult for Magdalene to include in this picture a man with a man. She can't talk to her old customer

41

friends about it; she knows they understand even less than she. Nor can she ask the priest who comes once a month to give her communion. Priests are consecrated temples. They do not want sex.

And she doesn't want to ask the men themselves, for fear of hurting their feelings. So she comes up with theories she keeps to herself. She is proud of these theories; she believes she is the first to think of them. She says to herself: *They're like this because their mothers didn't love them. It could be in the blood. The genes.* She makes her mind go blank from creating a picture of what this sex might actually be. What she knows is that from these men, these friends of hers, she gets praise for herself as a woman, the praise she always wanted from her daughter, still living beside her in her house, still withholding the smallest word of praise.

Cam lives in her mother's house because both she and her mother believe that Magdalene is too sick to live alone, but it is as though they live in different towns. Their sections of the house are separate and distinct. Cam has her bedroom, and the living room and dining room, her study, and the kitchen. And Cam's husband, Bob Ulichni, has his zone: male, scientific, and apart. He has his bedroom and his study and the finished basement, where he has installed what is called a kitchenette. In this way he need never see his wife, her mother, or her mother's guests. And yet he doesn't leave. None of them leaves.

Bob and Cam's marriage is a failure. Looking at the painful life of Bob Ulichni in his kitchenette, the flourishing life of Cam in the world, in the happy bed of her lover, anyone might point and say: 'See what you have done to your poor husband.'

They never should have married. Bob should have married, at nineteen, a nursing student, supporting her on his scholarship money. He should live in a long, one-story house: the basement, in any house he lived in, would be his. There, as here, he could have his ham radio, where he could talk, as he does now, to Europeans, to Southeast Asians, and in his study, there, as here, he could install his homemade telescope. With which, in that one-story house which he will never now inhabit, he could show the constellations to his many children, each of whom, in his or her suburban school, would be outstanding in science class. Still he would be nearly mute, but it would be better. He would have a place to live.

42

Their marriage is a story of the middle-1960s, and of Catholics in Ivy League (or nearly) colleges and universities, where they feel they do not belong. Cam went to Bryn Mawr in 1959. Miss Blake, Cam's high-school Latin teacher, had studied at Bryn Mawr. Bookish, tenderhearted, pigeon-breasted, plain, a competent but uninspired student at Bryn Mawr, she watched the student body of the high school turn from light-haired Protestants, with the occasional infusion of a German farmer's child, to a postwar salad of Brooklyn refugees. She grievously misunderstood these children, thinking, for example, the Italians would be interested in Latin since it was the language of their ancestors, and the Irish, in their devotion to the Church, would be in love with Latin as she was, having heard it from birth. The students were polite, it was the age when students were polite, the students of working-class parents who worshipped teachers as the incarnation of the intellectual life they despised and feared. But after ten years of teaching, Edith Blake knew that her students thought her odd and finicky, and so, when she met Camille MacNamara in 1955, in her freshman class of Latin I, and saw returning her gaze the clear, level eye of sheer intelligence, she poured half a century's love into this brilliant child of such a vulgar mother, grandchild of the charming, heroic grandparents, poetic-looking and political, though they were Democrats and Edith Blake's people had always been Republican.

Edith Blake convinced Cam's grandparents (she phoned them, wisely stepping over Magdalene) that Cam should apply for a scholarship to Bryn Mawr so she could study classics and teach Latin at a university, as Miss Blake never could have done.

So Cam went to Bryn Mawr, enabling Daniel, two years later, easily to go to Haverford. And they were caught, Cam, Dan, and Bob Ulichni, on the moving staircase of American upward striving.

There they were in college; Bob Ulichni, Camille MacNamara, working-class Catholics at Haverford and Bryn Mawr, with their endless part-time jobs in restaurants in town or in the library, and then, after a Saturday night studying late or washing dishes, up for Sunday-morning Mass. They lived the anxious, crabbed life of the scholarship student, but darkened, hardened by the Newman Center and the chaplain, warning and reminding, 'The others are not like you. But they would like to take away your treasure: this jewel, this faith, this your salvation. Date each other, Catholic men and women. Do not set your roots to twine among the Protestants, the Jews. Come to our dances, our discussion groups on contraception and divorce. Sign up here for the bus, the Catholic bus, to register black voters down in Mississippi. But remember your kind. Look around you at the students in your classes. They are not your kind.'

Thinking themselves liberal, the priests allowed guitars at Mass and even had days of recollection with Methodists and Presbyterians. But they still said, 'Marry each other, Catholics.' They spoke about mixed marriages (like mixed drinks, mixed nuts, mixed economies). They said, 'Look, we're not saying it's impossible the other way, we're only saying that our way is easier.'

They made it easy for Bob Ulichni to love Cam MacNamara, to worship her white skin, her coloring: the perfect Irish rose. To worship her wit, her squarish, competent fingers. To go, because of her, to register voters in Alabama (where she didn't speak to him, didn't notice him), to oboe concerts that he had no interest in where she sat with her girlfriends, her legs heavy in blue knee socks, and forgot his name.

He studied chemistry and was at the top of his class and was able to go to Columbia Engineering because Cam chose Columbia Law, though in three years in Pennsylvania they had barely spoken. In New York, reminding her who he was the first time he bumped into her (she had forgotten, she apologized, his name) that they had known each other from the Newman Center, and the concerts, and the Mississippi bus. He kept asking her out to experimental plays, thinking she was interested and that he ought to be. In fact, neither of them was. In the taxi, he'd hold her hand as stiffly as a paralytic, and then, after dinner, he would kiss her with closed lips. And she would say, 'Thanks, Bob. We'll see each other sometime soon.' He knew that when she closed the door of the graduate dorm she never thought of him. But at the end of the year, he'd phone and say that he was driving to Long Island, could he take her things home, would she like a ride?

Who knows what would have happened if in 1965 Magdalene MacNamara hadn't developed cancer of the breast, and Cam had not had to think about and plan her mother's death? In the summer of 1965, just before she was to begin her third year of law school, Cam was told by all the doctors that her mother was about to die.

Dan was in Cornell, framed by Married Life. She was alone. There was no one to whom she could explain the complications of her mother's nature and their joint history. She didn't want to expose her mother and reveal the oddness of their life. And to whom would she reveal it? To her law-school pals, who sat around after classes in dark bars, talking about old cases, their professors, telling jokes, or talking politics, but never mentioning their families? They had no families: they were living in the world. The mention of a family past in the dark, conversational air, among the spilt beer and the peanuts and the ice cubes melting horribly in the full ashtrays – the mention of family life would shock. It would introduce the notion that, at one time, these people around the table had not been adult. It would be as if someone had set up a crib beside the bar and then crawled into it.

Cam knew that to tell the truth about her mother would be a betrayal, for to tell the truth she would have had to say: 'My mother is a failure.' Worse: 'My mother is a failure in these ways.'

And now her mother was dying.

So, when Bob Ulichni called to ask her did she want to see the in-the-round production of *Citizen Tom Paine*, she said no, she was spending her time in the hospital seeing her mother. He said, 'Let me stay there with you. I'll bring sandwiches.' She let him wait in the green lobby with the picture of the Sacred Heart, and Sister Dismas, founder of the order of nursing nuns who staffed the hospital. She let him hold her hand during her mother's operation, had every meal with him in the three weeks of her mother's hospital stay, let him visit with her mother, let her mother flirt with him, and listened, and was pleased, when her mother told her, 'Hold on to that one. A good man is hard to find.'

She married him before school started in September, through fatigue and gratitude and fear that she was twenty-four and no man before this had seemed to love her.

Nothing good came of it. Not one good thing. At the start there was the blank self-blame of genuinely moral natures, the tender guilty gestures never met in kind and never simultaneous, the outings of the childless young: the restaurants, the movies, theatre evenings, nights with other couples, always failures, always friends of Cam's (he seemed to have no friends) and Bob Ulichni sitting silent, trying to project a quiet geniality when what he felt was black despair. Cam had her rings of pals: the men she worked with, the women friends from college, the few like her, lawyers and women both. They took part in the proud, uneasy mating of the middle-sixties, marriage not quite passé, but almost, no one yet unfaithful or yet dreaming of it. And at night, less and less frequently, Bob Ulichni would approach his wife, and she, brought up above all to be dutiful, lay back, her eyes fixed on the ceiling, in excruciating pain. She thought, *It will get better, this is my fault, just relax.* She felt the muscled nature of her heart, its chambers distinct and hardened; she saw the straining worried face of the man she had never loved but married out of gratitude and fatigue and thought: *This is my fault and I deserve it.*

Now Bob Ulichni is almost destroyed. This is the fault of a disease. Not a disease of his. Nothing in Bob Ulichni's body has been touched. No silent organism tunnels through, or eats, or weakens, lodges, tears apart. He is the victim of a disease that never touched him: it touched Cam's womb. Her womb was victimized by endometriosis.

Endometriosis: a disease affecting tissue of the endometrium, outside the uterus, of unknown etiology. Called by the men who do the calling, and think this kind of thing would benefit from a good joke, 'career women's disease,' because it is supposed to go away, or at least the symptoms dissipate, if the uterus has once contained a child. But the joke is that the disease encourages sterility, is cured by that which it prevents. Its symptoms are, to the clinician, dysmenorrhea and dyspareunia. To the sufferer: severe cramping large parts of the month and painful intercourse.

Severe cramping. Painful intercourse. The descriptions make it sound as if the two effects were the same in a life: a monthly tightening of the abdomen and the impossibility of making love. But if Cam MacNamara had suffered only menstrual cramps, the life of Bob Ulichni would not have been destroyed.

She saw the face of a man who she now knew had loved her many years and had desired her. She saw his simple nature close, close in. She kept trying; most of the time she was in pain.

'Let's see the doctor,' Cam said after several months. Abashed, Bob agreed, although it meant he had to present to Larry Riordan, who had been Cam's doctor since her childhood, the evidence of failure: the failed husband and his victim wife.

'You're not the first, you think you're the first?' said Larry Riordan. He sent Cam to sit in the waiting room and talked to

Bob Ulichni, man to man. 'Look, these Jewish bastards, these Protestant guys, or guys with no religion, they've got a leg up on us. You know what I mean? Who'd you have in high school, Christian Brothers?'

'Jesuits.'

'Jebbies, Christians, same difference,' the doctor said. 'The trouble is, we grow up thinking we're what they tell us, temples of the Holy Ghost. So we're afraid to touch a girl, won't put a hand on a girl's tit till we've brought her to the altar. Am I right?'

Bob nodded.

'And with girls it's worse. So give it time. They don't want to do it at first, so they say it hurts. They really believe it. But don't let her get away with it forever. You're a man, you've got needs. You don't want to knock the whole works out of commission.'

'You don't think there could be anything wrong with her? Physically, I mean. She has a bad time at her time of the month.'

'Listen, what's wrong with her is what her grandmother and her mother told her men did to you on your wedding night. They probably made it sound so awful it scared the poor kid to death.'

'But she said she's always had trouble at her time of the month.'

'What she needs is a baby, that'll take care of it. Try putting a pillow under her behind.'

They put a pillow under Cam's behind. But this did not relieve the pressure. The pressure built, until even contact suggested pressure, and all contact ceased.

The fall of 1969 was the last time Bob Ulichni had sexual contact with a woman. What he saw was this. He had admired Camille MacNamara and his admiration caused her pain. He had been all his life a studious, reclusive, secretly romantic boy, with a gift for chemistry and engineering. He could say: The elements behave this way, and this and this. He had been kind and deferential to his mother; in the welter of her seven children, giving no trouble, he was ignored. He had dreamed of a tall fair woman he could honor. And his honor would mean marriage. So he married Cam. And all this, his experiment in the world outside the elements of the periodic chart, ended in nothing but failure and pain.

Three years later, in 1972, Cam, doubled over with cramps, was forced by her sister-in-law, Eileen, to see a gynecologist. She was given a laparoscopy, and was told there was a name for what she suffered: endometriosis, extensive in her case, involving the uterus and both ovaries. She was given various drugs. Nothing worked. She was asked if she wanted children and was told that in any case the possibilities were slim. The doctor recommended a hysterectomy. A tragedy in a young woman, thirty-one. But really, he said, the best course. She didn't think she had a choice. She had no marriage, but she wouldn't leave Bob. It wasn't his fault. He shouldn't have to go to Ulichni family Thanksgivings, Christmases without a wife. She agreed to give up her womb. 'And then,' the doctor told her, 'you and your husband can resume a normal life.'

A normal life. By which, of course, the doctor had meant sex. So it can be said that Bob Ulichni has not resumed a normal life.

Cam, over the years, allowed herself halfheartedly to be pulled into brief extensions of her friendships with male colleagues: a night here or there in a conference hotel room, a weekend at the beach. None of it came to anything, and she had begun to tell herself that it wasn't in her nature, as it wasn't in her mother's, to love and be beloved. But at forty-one, she met Ira and her life was changed.

Nothing could change the course of Bob Ulichni's life. He had a nature built for one and only one journey out of himself, out of the world of elements. But on this journey, he was smashed up; he was shipwrecked. Too distant, too impoverished of experience, too abashed and shamed, he couldn't try again. Bob makes himself frozen dinners in his kitchenette, then disappears to his basement ham radio to converse with people in other hemispheres. 'And how's the weather in Bangkok?' '*Spasibo.*' '*Au revoir*'.

But Cam's life has changed. 'I've never known anyone like you,' she's said to Ira hundreds of times, like any lover. And it was true. He wooed her with stories. In her family, the storytellers had been women: her grandmother, her aunt Theresa, herself. The stories were always linked to judgment; they were correctives, proofs, signs that someone in the world had thought too much of himself, the storyteller would show how. This amused Cam in her grandmother, but she dreaded it in her aunt Theresa, and she feared that she herself shared the qualities of her aunt's styptic heart. She understood the pleasures of judgment, the taste for condemnation like a taste for salt. A racial trait, she guessed, of preserving, self-preserving Irish women. She'd seen them thrive on judgment, finding in it nutrition, healing, the reward for hours of exhaustion and for years of self-control. Refusing alcohol (they saw its devastations all around them), they filled themselves on judgment, and then gave it out, as calmly and with as much confidence as if they nursed the people whom they judged. She'd felt the effects of judgments, cold as an iron railing in the winter, to be feared, you thought you'd never be free of the mark of them – those words and looks, as if you'd put your hand on the cold rail in winter and torn it away, leaving behind some leaves of your flesh. She'd both felt the effects of judgment and known the lust for it, the utter pleasure of it, the buildup of excitement, as in sex, but unlike sex, the high, sustainable plateau. As if you stood up on a high point: (butte, mesa, bluff) open to the winds, and saw the view beneath it of the sea, ice cold and dazzling. The stories told by the women in her family were always in the service of this: this judgment, without whose proximity they could not, any of them, think of pleasure.

But Ira's stories weren't tied to judgment. They were surprised, bemused descriptions of the world. Once, after she'd bought a new nightgown, he told her a story of his childhood.

Before or after they made love, he cooked for her; she didn't like to be naked when she cooked and she didn't want to be clothed. He wore a robe, but she had nothing suitable. So she bought a thin pink cotton nightgown. It allowed her breasts and sex to be visible, but why not, she thought, why not with him? The neck was high and square. A lace border grazed her collarbone.

She walked into the kitchen wearing her new nightgown. He was cooking. She'd just bathed; the ends of her hair were damp; the lilac scent of her expensive soap was on her skin. It was hot in the apartment. They hadn't yet made love, but she knew how it would be that night: slow, expressive, punctuated by pauses filled with reverie, returns to languid, half-absent caresses, leading, almost surprisingly, to an active end. Sex that night would be in favor of the female, she thought, walking towards him; that night, she predicted, women all around New York would sleep in peace.

'How nice you look,' he said. He put his spoon down. He forgot his cooking; he walked her to the bed; he asked her to keep her nightgown on when they made love.

Kissing the lace border of the nightgown, he followed it, half-inch by half-inch, with his lips.

'That nightgown brings back pleasant memories to me,' he said afterwards. 'We'd go away each summer to the country. To the mountains. There were these houses, farmhouses called *kuchelaines*, big houses, with several families. There were these long days when you did nothing. Rainy days when you played games with other children. Or fooled around on a piano. Or one year someone played the banjo. Another year some aunt had a guitar. It was just women and children, mothers, grandmothers, aunts; the fathers came on weekends, some of them, or on vacation for two weeks. In the evening, all the children would take baths, and then we'd go outside for the last moments of light. The dark would come, the mothers would turn the lights on, you could see them sitting in the kitchen, at the table, playing cards. They were happy to leave us alone. Everyone's hair was damp from their baths. Like yours,' he said, kissing the ends of her hair. 'The girls wore cotton nightgowns with lace trimming. Like yours,' he said, kissing the lace border once again. 'The cloth of those nightgowns was fresh and beautiful. It had a beautiful fresh smell. And the grass smelt wonderful. It wasn't sex, but all your senses were alive and at the same time calm. Well fed.'

She'd liked the story for itself, but also because it allowed her to feel the bracing deprivation of race difference. It's one of the things they enjoy about each other – their riffs, Ira calls them – long descriptions or analyses beginning with large generalizations: 'The Irish,' they say. 'The Jews.' Once Cam said to him: 'God, it must be a burden being part of a superior culture. It's kind of a relief coming from a bunch of third-raters or self-destructors. Flops.'

'What do you mean, flops?'

'Flops,' she said. 'Who do we have? You have Jonas Salk, Isaac Bashevis Singer, Artur Rubinstein. Who do we have? Teddy Kennedy. Phil Donahue. You know, I'm the only person in America who really understands Phil Donahue. He's just mimicking a particular kind of priest. There was always one of them, not the pastor, the assistant pastor, prematurely gray. The middle-aged women always went to him to confession. He was the moderator of the Rosary Society, the Catholic Daughters. They felt they could talk to him about birth control. At the parish picnic he

50

walked around with a mike, breaking up fights, making sure nobody drank too much. The women all said to their husbands: Why can't you be more like him? Eventually, he became a pastor and he stopped talking to the ladies. But while he lasted, they were in heaven.'

Things like that would make him grab her and kiss her on the mouth. 'All my life, I wanted an Irish girl,' he said. 'But I was afraid the Irishers would kill me if they saw me touching one of them. Finally,' he said, 'I get my reward. All those rocks your people were throwing at us on the way home from Hebrew school, they were all worth it.'

When he told her the story about his childhood vacations, she felt it was another clue she needed, another piece of the puzzle, *Why are we who we are?* When he'd finished the story, she said to him: 'Why weren't the Irish interested in pleasure? Why didn't they give it more attention? Some Jew had the idea of buying farmhouses, building bungalows. Because he understood that people without money needed things like that.'

'And he could make a good living off it,' Ira said.

'Never mind. Two cheers for capitalism. Why didn't the Irish have pleasant ideas?'

This is a false question, set up only so that she can answer it. As a gift, he will become conductor to her: tap the baton, give her the signal so she can begin the aria, the virtuoso piece.

He gives her her cue: 'Why do you think that they were like that?'

She says: 'It's no accident the Irish built the subways. And then stayed there. It was the perfect place for them, dark, underground, dangerous, hidden, but the men could get together and tell stories. Drink. And once a year there'd be a party or a picnic and the women would dress stiffly, call each other Mrs., and the men would dance. The next day the women would talk about it in their kitchens. With relief: it was all over for another year.'

He says: 'There's more than that.'

She thinks of Vincent and Ellen's faces. He knows she is thinking about them.

'I loved them so much,' she says, 'I love them.'

Refusing to judge even an absent group, nearly all of whom are dead, he asked her to remember that she loved two of them.

He isn't interested in judgment. By profession, he urges people to forget their early judgments and to compromise. He is a labor arbitrator. He doesn't judge Cam when she behaves badly; when she loses her temper, he attributes it to fatigue; when some cruel sentence comes out of her mouth, he forgets it. But unlike Dan and her grandfather, he doesn't seem diminished by her attacks and displays. Sometimes she's so grateful for his mercy that she could go down on her knees to him; she wants to tell him that because of him the world is a new place, she sees it fresh, it is a place that she can live in without fear. But sometimes she suspects and judges him for his lack of judgment. How can she trust him when he is so rarely strict? Once he came and heard her in court. He waited in the back of the court, after she'd finished her opening statement; his smile was so extravagant it made her blush. 'You were incredible,' he said. 'You were a star. I felt like the guy in the audience who gets to take the girl singer home after the show.' For a little while, his praise delighted her. But then she began to mistrust it. She imagined he thought she was eloquent because he was in love with her. She imagined that, with his nature, he would have thought anyone was good. She didn't want to relinquish her pleasure in his praise. But to be safe, she didn't give herself up to it entirely; she held on to her portion of mistrust.

She believes that his faults are connected to his lack of judgment. Sometimes she thinks he doesn't judge because he isn't paying attention to the world. The same trait, she thinks, makes him careless and forgetful of her. Once she'd agreed to pick up a chair he had bought and to bring it to his apartment. She had a Jeep with a roof rack; she could have the chair tied to the top of the car. He was supposed to be there when she came. But he forgot; he'd gone to get a hamburger. In a rage, she untied the chair from the top of the car and left it on the sidewalk, hoping it would be stolen. Each year he forgets her birthday. Compounding the fault when he apologizes, he says, 'I always forget women's birthdays. I forget my mother's birthday. I've forgotten the birthdays of both my ex-wives. It made them furious.'

She is often angry with him. She wishes it weren't the case. But she learned how to be in the world from her grandmother, who judged the world in anger, who is judging even in the midst of drawn-out death.

Dying gradually in her bed, her family around her, Ellen judges. She is judging Theresa's children. She doesn't know who these people are or what she is judging. But she is furious at the terrible noise that intrudes upon her dreams, the buzz and whine of the power drill John is using, making last-minute repairs for his grandfather's homecoming. And Sheilah, in the kitchen, using an electric knife. Sheilah and John, at home in the world nowhere, always use wrongly anything to which their hand takes hold. John should not be using the electric drill when his grandmother is having one of her rare peaceful sleeps. There is no reason for Sheilah to use an electric knife on a block of Muenster cheese; it is a useless gesture, a misuse of power: it will get her nowhere, it will open her to ridicule, create a mess. But Ellen rails unjustly with an equal fury against Marilyn, who has tended her for two weeks. She rails against her because she has just used a machine to save Ellen's life. She has put a tube into her grandmother's mouth, and then has flipped a switch and sucked out the phlegm that would have choked her.

'Leave it go,' Ellen gurgles, but no one can understand her. 'Leave it go.'

It is one of the times when she would like to die, it feels so easy, and she rages because no one will let her do this easy thing.

She is lying in the bed, her dying in the center of the house. She feels she has become her death, feels that they wait for her to be her death, the one event that they have made her. When it is easy she thinks she can accept this one event that they have made her. This bright thing from which all other things fan out. But then, preparing to accept that she *is* this, she can't. She does not want to become her death.

She doesn't know that everyone is waiting for Vincent. She thinks Vincent has left her to her death, in justice punishing her for the offenses of a lifetime. And that they have collected in the house, all of them, because they think that they know something she doesn't know: that she is dying. They are here because of her. Each of them is here on earth because she lay three times and pushed three children out of her living body to the light and neutral air. So they fan out from her body, once the source of life and now merely the source of the one event, her death.

Vincent has gone away. Did Vincent never know she loved him? He has the right to leave her to her death; in justice, that's his right. But he made that promise. Was it a mistake? Could that be it, then, all the years and all the promises? Could that be it? Mistakes?

Ellen MacNamara lies in her white net of cloud and sees only glimpses. Lucid rhomboids of the past. She sees her mother rocking in the darkness, gibbering in the dark. She sees her cruel father and his mistress, and the mistress's ankles, and her cruel back. She thinks of her father and his mistress fornicating in the room above the pub while a mile and a half away, in the countryside, in the desolate and gorse-surrounded house, built on the brown grass where nothing else could grow, her mother rocked and gibbered in the dark. In her bed now, more than seventy years later, weakened beyond action, beyond speech, beyond the power of coherent image making, Ellen renews her vow. That she will not forgive.

While upstairs Cam sits on her childhood bed, her legs stretched out in front of her, holding a blue-backed legal brief, not thinking of her grandparents, not of the law or of the case of *Barnabas* v. *Barnabas*, but thinking of her lover in a rather common way. She is amused that she is now part of the democracy of women yearning for their absent men. Sixteen-year-old girls, she thinks, their red nails bitten to the quick; brilliant undergraduates, stars in the sciences; professionals making their way across large cities dressed for success in copies of men's suits. Repeatedly betrayed hairdressers, waitresses. Single mothers sitting by the phone. Game sixty-year-olds back from the museum or a game of squash. All of us, she thinks, fed by the songs of half a century, musical comedy, Jerome Kern, Irving Berlin, the Gershwin brothers, Rodgers and Hart: 'I'll Be Seeing You,' she thinks, 'The Man That Got Away,' 'But Not for Me,' 'Where or When.'

Cam knows all this, she'd like to stop, but she is buoyed up on the dense ocean of her longing. Ira Silverman can't be with her now; she is in her grandparents' house; she is responsible. You can't be publicly adulterous, she said once to Eileen, and be the one responsible for three generations of family life.

Some people say this is a ridiculous thing, her failure to leave her empty marriage. They say she could do it anytime. But if she did, she would have to give up the idea of herself, in her own mind and in the mind of others, to whom this idea gives and sustains life. If she left Bob Ulichni she would not be the one to get her grandfather, to bring him home, here to this house, where everyone is waiting. For her to bring him home.

She's never sure if this is idealism, dutifulness, self-sacrifice, or complicated stubbornness mixed with self-love. Whatever it is, she knows her life is better than it was, even torn as she is between states of longing and happiness, at least it's much better than the life she lived before, the life of duty and achievement, comradeship, the built-up victories of her professional success, then coming home to hear her husband in the basement with his radio, to her mother, watching her sixty-five-inch television in her purple room.

It is twelve o'clock. All morning people came to her for things they needed. She got to her office at seven; knowing she'd leave at ten-thirty, she wanted to have a certain amount of work to give her secretary, Joan Reilley, who arrived at nine. At nine-fifteen, Joan, with whom she is moderately well pleased, brought her pieces of pink paper: calls she had to return. A woman, one of her clients, is nursing her child, who is two and a half years old. Her ex-husband wants to take this child to see his family for two weeks. According to the law, he has the right to his children for two weeks a year. He left the family when the two-year-old was eight months. He has never asked for the younger child before; he left her with her nursing mother. Now he wants to have the younger child as well for his legally agreed-on two weeks. He says there is no need to nurse a two-and-a-half-year-old; it's time, he says, the baby should be weaned. The mother doesn't want to wean the baby. Isn't it her right to make the choice of when her child should be weaned? If her husband takes the child for two weeks, her milk will dry up. How, she asks Cam, can she stop her husband drying up her milk?

Another woman owns half her husband's business. Should she give it up and agree to his offer of alimony, tax-deductible for him? She doesn't want to give him her share of the business; she wants to know that he requires, if nothing else, her signature. Even though the alimony will be financially more profitable to her and without it the husband will not sign the separation agreement.

The office manager from the Battered Women's Shelter has called. Cam is their unpaid counsel. If they break the lease with the company from whom they rent their copier and buy one outright, they will save a thousand dollars in two years. But can they break the lease? The company, says the office manager, are incompetent criminals. They never service the machines. But will they sue us if we break the lease?

Dan's daughter Darci has called. The message: If you don't take me shopping today, I'll have to throw myself out of the window from boredom.

Her mother has phoned. The message: I'm low on Cup-a-Soup. Get the tomato, not the vegetable like you did last time. I hate those little peas.

For all of these she has responses.

To the mother who asks: Can he make my milk dry up, she says regretfully: 'You won't win this one. Your child is healthy and happy, he's two and a half years old. It's time to wean him. In a court, you'll be forced to do it anyway. Decide yourself.' She doesn't say: Don't be unfair, it's the father's right to have his children as the contract says. It's not her job to speak about this kind of justice. She says: 'Probably this won't work.'

To the vengeful wife she says: 'You might win this in court. But financially, it's ridiculous. Why take a loss?' She doesn't say: Do not be eaten up by thoughts of revenge.

To the secretary of the shelter she says: 'Cancel the contract. Let them try to sue.'

She tells Darci on the phone: 'We can't go shopping today. Great-Granddaddy's coming home.' She comforts her when she sees her sinking into the bog of seventeen-year-old shame.

She does not return her mother's call.

And on the piece of paper she has put on the bottom, the message: 'Mr. Silverman called. Please return his call.'

This is what the piece of paper records. But she sees: 'I love you, you are wonderful, you are mine.' And now, lying on her childhood bed, all she wants is to be with him, to kiss his shirt, his face just underneath his sideburns, his temples and his knees, to be kissed, to talk, to be held, to look, be looked at. His mouth on her breast. Her sex. To be entered. To be with him now. She rolls onto her back, right there in her grandparents' house, right on her childhood bed, she puts her hand behind her head and dreams. The August heat brings heaviness. She dreams of herself, the tan blinds drawn in her office, where they most often make love. They can only go to his apartment when the Ulichnis are away. She dreams of herself and Ira on the fold-out couch, the red light of the telephone signaling that there are messages she doesn't answer, there in the place where clients weep, shaking their fists at the betrayal of what they had thought was love. Her grieving clients reach to the glass table for the tactful Kleenex, they rock back and forth in anguish, rage. They cry: 'He never loved me.' 'She never really meant a word she said.'

11

From a phone booth on the corner of 57th Street and Seventh Avenue, Darci phones her father to say she's on her way. Standing next to her is her best friend, Rebecca, whom she's known for seven weeks.

'Daddy, I'm getting on the train now, right this minute. So forty-five minutes, give it fifty maybe, I'll be at the house.'

'OK,' Dan says.

'Daddy, I did this incredibly stupid thing this morning. I'm so embarrassed. I called Cam in the office and I left a message that I wanted to go shopping. I completely forgot that Great-Grandaddy was coming home today. I don't know why I did that. I've been thinking about it for weeks, I know how important it is to everyone. I don't know what the matter is with me.'

'You really didn't forget, Darci. It just slipped your mind.'

'You know I don't believe in euphemisms. Euphemisms are for those wonderful people that brought us Vietnam and vaginal sprays, I'm not one of them.'

'It's true, darling. No one thinks Vietnam is your fault.'

'Thanks, Pop.'

'Darci, you are a splendid human being with the moral fiber of many saints. Just get on the train. I'll take you out to Howard Johnson's if you get here soon.'

'I probably won't eat anything. A Diet Coke.'

'Whatever you like. You can watch me. Just get on the train. I can't wait to see you.'

Darci knows that he means what he says. She knows she always makes her father happy.

'I adore my father,' she says to Rebecca. 'Any woman would be so lucky to have him. It just pisses me off that he's with that idiot. I mean, he could have anybody, anybody. He feels tied to her by guilt.'

'Let's promise never to do anything in our lives because of guilt. Let's make an absolute promise. Not one thing.'

'Not one thing,' says Darci.

They fall into each other's arms.

'What if he makes you go back in September? What if your mother won't let you stay?'

'Cam will let me stay in her house. She wouldn't throw me out. They don't want me to end up on the Minnesota Strip.'

'What would you do about school?'

'Oh, do an Equivalency,' Darci says, as if the thought didn't appall her.

'What about college? You're not going to flush college down the toilet?'

'They're going to let me, Rebecca. I'll go to the high school Cam went to. I know my father thinks it's a good thing. I'll make Cam talk to my mother. Even my mother's afraid of Cam.'

'God, you're so lucky in your family. What do I have, Bernie and Miriam, twin shrinks? My uncle Al, my aunt Lorraine. Who'd be interested in them? Your aunt Cam is really great.'

'I know, I think she's great-looking too, except she dresses like shit. She's got these really great boobs. You'd never know it. God, if I had *them*.'

'So I'll see you tomorrow,' Rebecca says.

'Yeah. I'll call you tonight. After we get home. This could be extremely strange. But I'll be able to use it. Like Mona says in class. You can use everything.'

Darci gets on the train. She thinks how lucky she is, to be an actress, to have an unusual family, to be in New York, to have her father, to be the kind of person who can use all her experience. Her teacher Mona Labourdette had quoted them some words of Henry James. 'Be one of those on whom nothing is wasted,' she advised her seventeen-year-old students. Darci is determined to do that. She will use everything in her life, her pain when her parents separated, her estrangement in the house where she lives with her mother and her sister and stepfather. She wishes she had known her great-grandparents. She can't remember what her great-grandmother's voice was like; she wishes she could, she could use it; she'd love to play Pegeen. She wishes her great-grandfather didn't make her feel so far away, as if she were always listening to him from another room. She wishes her great-grandmother didn't scare her, lying in her bed with those eyes that look so frightened, or so horrified. She doesn't know how they look. She doesn't understand them. Today she'll make herself go in and look at her great-grandmother. Lately, she's been too afraid.

This summer, she knows, has been the best time in her life. She's taking courses at the Actors Studio. It gives her an excuse not to live with her father and Sharon in Quogue – it's too far, they all agree, for her to go into the city every day. She's living with Cam and Magdalene. She takes the bus and then the subway into the city by herself, a child and yet a worker among workers. She has lunch with kids who get their education at the Dalton School, Brearley, among the children of ambassadors and movie stars and meter maids. She makes a passionate friendship with Rebecca. They walk through the magic summer of young girls who believe the world will one day know that they are great. In class, they read the parts of Clytemnestra, Peter Pan.

In June, when she arrived from Seattle, she put a cot in Cam's study; Cam took off the walls her Spy prints and her Dürer violets and allowed Darci to put up Rothko posters and a poster advertising Judith Anderson playing Medea. Darci was too horrified by Bob to speak to him; there were hints about Cam she didn't want unveiled – like everyone else, she found it easier to forget that Cam had a husband. Secretly she liked her great-aunt Magdalene, but saw that Cam both did and didn't want her to – in her confusion, she tried to pretend her attention was only kindness, but Magdalene's sense of drama was too kindred to her own for Darci to feel mere pity. She saw the way Magdalene used Cam; she saw her beloved Cam grow into a hard stranger in her mother's presence. She saw, too, with the vision of the gifted young, that the adult world was a series of armed camps that demanded loyalties that she was glad to give because they must be absolute. The excuse for her living with Cam was that it was closer to the city, but everyone knew that she didn't want to live with Sharon, and everyone knew that was for the best, and so said nothing.

Only Staci dropped the odd remark about how pleasant it was with the swimming pool, the hammock, and her father barbecuing every night. Just for the three of them. So pleasant.

But she didn't care. Not living with her father meant she could talk him into meeting her in New York. The City. It was hers.

She'd been seven when she'd moved to Seattle with her mother and sister, and her memories of New York City shone: the treasures of a child for whom childhood is an imprisonment, a temporary, senseless stop on a road she can sense will open up if she can only get going. For Darci, the games of childhood were a torment and the company of other children an enforced, unnatural situation. Early on, she dreamed of sleeping in hotels, riding in taxis. While other children her age wished for ponies, she wanted an apartment with a view.

And New York – she called it, even in Seattle, The City – was her father's. Her father, in whose company she could feel joy. It wasn't that she didn't love her mother. She felt bolstered up and braced by her mother's quick, definite, and dry view of the world, and by her sure movements through it. She was proud of her mother's looks, of the costumes she made for both her children on Halloween, of the envied and enviable birthday parties she created. She loved the cool sheets her mother arranged for her sickness, and her deft hands, her way of measuring out medicines that could inspire faith. But she felt beside her mother and her sister overfleshed and overheated. She made her way through the world crying, 'I love, I hate. How happy I am; no one in the world has ever been so miserable.' Valerie looked on her kindly, was amused, impressed by her daughter's passions, by her paintings and compositions and uneven, undisciplined bouts of piano practice, which the clever teachers loved her for and which the mediocre feared. But Darci knew her mother saw the world she lived in from a distance. She knew her world was, for her mother, overgrown. Her mother watched her from the high place where she lived: a cleansed place, an empty place where nothing hid or bred in secret or disappeared.

But with her father, with his jokes and his apologies, like her jokes and apologies, his miscalculations, his perfect plans, his going into court, the fool he lived with (she had been told why), Darci saw the life that was her blood life. When she stood beside her mother she felt her white flesh insulted Valerie; she felt her physical existence like a living rude remark. Her body lived beside her sister's only to be reproached. But she could walk in happiness beside her father or Camille. This was for her the emblem of her happiness: to walk between her father and Cam on Fifth Avenue, MacDougal Street, Central Park West.

She is riding on the subway. She looks around her. Everyone on the car is interesting; she thinks they are all living interesting lives. She thinks about her great-grandmother. Today, she won't be frightened. She can learn something from this. She will be someone on whom nothing is wasted. Someday, she knows, she will be great.

12

Cam sees that Dan is standing at the door. He says: 'Let's go for a walk.'

She puts her papers in her briefcase and she smiles at him, taking her glasses off, happy at the prospect: they'll walk on the streets they walked as children with the same flat gray pavements, unambitious trees, the green leaves that show their undersides in a light wind.

Dan looks around the room, Cam's room in childhood, though she'd never lived in the house, as he had. The house hadn't been, as it had been for him, the only childhood home. It had been his address. In the front covers of his books, his notebooks, it had said: 128 Linden Street. The numbers and the words described his life. For Cam it was the refuge, the occasional escape. They kept this room for her; they kept it for his sake, too, knowing how happy he was with her.

She was two years older than he; she had never not been there. He'd always come to her as the younger boy. He'd come for comfort and she'd understood. He had been orphaned by two violences: the War itself and the theft of his grandmother, who had stolen him from the simple weakness of his mother, had kept him for herself.

'Five minutes,' she says. 'Three.' He decides to look in on his grandmother.

Ellen is sleeping. The skin is stretched so tight against the skull that Dan is afraid that it won't hold. In sleep she seems not angry. He wonders about these last images. What memory or current sight swims up behind those eyes that, when open, seem dull moons of accusation, discontent, regret? What is the function of that sight?

He walks past his cousin Marilyn. Calm, angelically calm. She has the nature of their grandfather. He sees: She is my grandfather now. Marilyn moves away, out of the room, so Dan can be alone with Ellen.

Is there anything to say? He takes the hand, a claw now, of the woman whose soft flesh was bolster, shelter, refuge, and reward. She stole him from his mother with the righteous grasping of the victim of a great disaster. Most likely she was right to steal him from his mother. He saw his mother for the first time when he was thirty-five. All Ellen's predictions had come true. At fifty-three she was a ruin. And, soon after, dead.

But she was his mother. And he couldn't know if she was born to be a ruin or if Ellen made her into one.

By which he meant he wanted to ask his mother: *Did I? I didn't mean to abandon you. I was a child.* And now, a continent away from his two children and their mother, he wants to say: *I didn't mean this separation. I never meant to be apart.*

Now he takes Ellen's hand, which is claw, paper, bone. He thinks: After all this time I have not found the right name for you. What can I call you? What should I have called you? Grandmother. Too long, too indirect. No word comes, so he thinks of pictures: her apron over her flattened breasts, the thin ring sunk into the flesh of her fourth finger, the fingers themselves. The smell of her, he was unable to forget that she was physical, unlike the mothers of his friends. Those mothers of the fifties were corseted even for housework; they wore scarves around their pincurls and their housedresses were not like Ellen's; on theirs you smelt detergent and felt the fabric stiffened by starch. His grandmother wore dresses limp from washing, sweaters even in the summer, cardigans with silver buttons, thick stockings the shade of milky coffee, in the forties worn-out pairs of old black shoes and in the fifties sneakers, navy-blue. Her hand, still covered with wet earth, arranged tight bunches of flowers in a glass. Vivid flowers, and unfashionable, shocking combinations: night-blue, purple, and then orange, yellow, red. Cosmos, marigold, cinque-foil, pansy, flowers with simple facelike centers, sweet peas, lilies of the valley so abundant they were nearly wild.

When Dan thinks of how he came to live with his grandparents, he wants to shut off his mind. He knows that Ellen took her grief, her loss, her hatred, greed, and sharpened it against the weak and unarmed nature of a girl. Dan's father, John MacNamara, his mother's favorite, only beloved child, married Doris Butler a week before he went into the Air Force. She was four months pregnant with his child. Ellen never would forgive her.

Once Vincent had told Dan the story of Dan's father's death. He'd said: 'I never thought a son of mine would die.' But Vincent had never said anything to Dan about how his mother had been made to go away and he had been brought up by Ellen and Vincent. Over the years, Dan had constructed pictures he could comprehend. He placed his mother at the center.

Doris Butler, a weak girl, with a weak spirit and a kind, undiscriminating heart. It was her bad fortune to mature just as young men her age were going off to war. For Doris, the world was fluid; edges disappeared; in her vision pastel discs merged and recombined. Her effortless good nature fed itself on images flickering from films. She thought the world was made of brave men terribly in need of comfort. She would comfort them. They told her she was pretty; they were only boys: why shouldn't she believe them? Her physical ignorance was as complete as if she had grown up, not twenty miles from Manhattan, but in some tribe where it was believed that a baby was implanted in its mother's womb by mist, rain, or a visit from the moon.

It didn't matter how she met John MacNamara. Anyplace at the beginning of the war. The Roadside Rest, where you could drink beer and dance. John MacNamara told her she was pretty. She *was* pretty. Small, pale: Look at you, I could put my hands around your waist; see, two of your hands don't make one of mine; watch, I can hold you like a flower.

Or it might only have been that Doris Butler and John Mac-Namara drank too much one summer evening, had each other in the back seat of a car. Brute hunger met brute hunger; it was simple; it resulted in a child.

Or they might have talked about their families, their jobs, their friends from high school, the War. And John might have thought: I could see her in a kitchen, smiling easily, as my mother did not smile. And one day I would like to have a child and leave my parents' house. To come home to her singing, to her lightness, unlike my mother's heaviness, her serious quiet reading. But first I will go to war, and I will see her every night before I go. Tenderly, almost brother and sister, lying down outside somewhere, night after night, one summer. And one night, almost not frightened, she tells him: I think I'm going to have a baby. John is almost not unhappy. Until he thinks of his mother, of her face.

The face of Ellen MacNamara in 1942. Her life shaped by two men: her son and Franklin Roosevelt. Passionately driving around town, campaigning for local Democrats, handing out leaflets, arguing, creating rifts, her black shoe heavy on the gas pedal, her mouth tight with threats. 'Good, vote Republican. You hardly have a pot to piss in as it is, and they'll take that.' Three causes – Roosevelt, the unions, and the War – took up the love she should have given to her daughters, whom she saw as torpid, truculent, and weak. Proudly she went with John to sign up for the draft. It did not seem possible that he would die. She saw him safely under the protection of Franklin Roosevelt. She didn't think about her son with women, but she supposed that someday he would marry. She didn't like young women; she didn't like women much at all. She thought they lacked the edge that made a cut through the world's murk, the murky atmosphere she hated. One kind of young women she liked, the indefatigable girls at Democratic headquarters. Up till dawn and ready for the next job, girls with short, overmuscled legs and jokes that made the thought of sex ridiculous.

Dan had imagined the night his father had to tell his parents. Perhaps John found them sitting at the table after dinner. He knew this was the night he had to tell them, he'd been with a girl, now she was going to have a child. Theresa had done the dishes and had gone upstairs. His parents were reading the newspaper. Ellen sat, leaning into the paper as if the wind were at her back, hungry for details of the War. His father leaned against his chair, courtly in his posture towards the baseball score. Was this the worst moment to tell them, or as good as any other? Who could know? John at nineteen, who had never done a thing not pleasing to his parents, who had been head altar boy and Eagle Scout and high scorer at basketball though he was not exceptionally tall, this same John had to say: I've been with a girl. Now she is going to have a child.

Perhaps Ellen stood and, turning her back to son and husband, left the room.

Or perhaps John had spoken to his father first. Left it to his father to break the news. Male first to male. No, John would not have done that. To keep something from his mother would be to deny her place in the family, the first place. With his mother out of the room he might have said to his father: Watch out for Doris if I don't come back, then gone out once again to be with Doris, to tell her he'd broken the news, to say: 'I've told them. They're fine. Everything's fine. Everything's all right.'

But it wasn't all right. It was never all right. Never once did Ellen MacNamara come near Doris Butler with anything but cruelty; she would not approach her, except to hurt. Injury to this girl was Ellen's only pleasure in her company. 'It's your fault; he was never like that,' she said, not in words, but over and over in her acts to Doris. And when John died she blamed Doris, thinking: If he'd gone into battle pure he'd have been saved.

John married Doris, and moved Doris into Ellen's house the week before he went away. Dan imagined Doris living there throughout her pregnancy. Ellen silent except to injure, Theresa contemptuous, horrified by the proof of female physical life that Doris gave. Perhaps John had told her that Theresa would warm up, that before long she'd be coming upstairs, bringing her cigarettes, her ashtray, would sit down on Doris's bed and chat all night. But Dan knew she never did. He knew Theresa came in late at night from dates and shut her bedroom door. He knew how they all were. Only Magdalene was nice to her, but she was married, had her husband and her baby girl. She made packages of baby clothes, gave advice, but she was busy: in the day she had her job at the hairdresser's and at night her family to tend. Vincent bestowed on Doris a constant, furtive kindness, worried always that Ellen would see, would hear him saying to her, 'Drink your milk up, now, you want the baby to have nice strong bones.'

Why did she stay? Her family was just across the town. Why didn't she go home? Because she knew that she had pushed herself out of the estate of girlhood. How could she go back pregnant to the sisters' bedroom in the family house, four beds in the room, her youngest sister six years old? It was a house full of eight children; she, the oldest, was eighteen. Where could she put her baby there? As each brother and sister was born, the two-year-old would move out of the parents' bedroom and be placed in a crib in the middle of the sisters' room, near Doris's bed. Dan could see that room. The crib in the middle surrounded by the sisters' beds, their white chenille spreads pulled tight each morning. How could Doris bring her own baby there? And who would pay its expenses? The MacNamaras had more money than the Butlers. Dan had never met his mother's family. Sometimes he walked past what used to be their house. They'd moved to Iowa soon after he was born.

In the MacNamaras' house Doris kept the light on in her room. John's room: the baseball pennants still up on the wall, the wallpaper pretending to be knotty pine. With the light on, she thought that she would try to read; she thought that John would like that. But she never did. She'd never read before. How could she? In her sisters' room, with fights and chatter, and giggling and then the command: *Silence!* shouted by her father up the stairs, then the silence that fell on the room, sudden and absolute and violent: the crack of a whip. When she began to feel the baby move, Doris treasured it as company.

And then the news came – John was dead – and his cruel mother became terrifying. She who was cold and perfect flew apart; her wildness made the house a danger, and made Doris fear for her child moving in her. How could she be safe when the mother at the center of the house first raged and then collected all she had left of herself beneath an iron sheet of hate? No one thought to comfort Doris; she had known John so short a time they felt she didn't need much comfort. And her family? It was as if, in leaving the house, she had dived down below the surface of the water on which they, as a family, sailed. The waters covered over; she was gone.

She moved in the house of mourning as a foreigner. They spoke, when they remembered to speak to her, more kindly now, except Ellen, who never spoke to her at all. When labor began, Vincent took her to the hospital, sat with her in the evenings after work; her sisters came, her mother and her father. But she felt that no one wanted to be near her. The nurses kept the baby from her. Mostly she would sleep.

So she was clumsy when she took the baby home, and frightened, although she'd cared for all those brothers and sisters. She was grateful when Ellen took him over, comforted him when she could not. Little by little, she became convinced that she could do nothing for her baby that was right. She felt he stiffened in her arms and relaxed only in his grandmother's. Ellen suggested that Doris might like to go back to work. The feigned kindness in her offer frightened Doris, like the witch's offer of sweets to Hansel and his sister, Gretel: to eat was to be poisoned, to refuse was instant death. She went back to work in the 5 & 10, and was happy there, happier than she was in the MacNamara house. She tried to feed her baby, change his diaper, but under Ellen's eye she failed at everything, and Ellen's eye was never off her. The child gagged on the food she spooned him, or screamed so Ellen thought she'd stuck him with a pin. 'Don't touch him, you upset him,' Ellen would say, taking the baby from her, turning her strong back. And how could Doris not believe her? Her son became a stranger to her; she feared to approach him, for the sound of his refusal of her each time pierced her heart.

She did well at the 5 & 10 selling makeup: lipstick, rouge, compacts of powder, bobby pins, hairnets, nail polish (thirty shades whose names she knew) and the clear bottles of remover, emery boards, orange sticks, nail buffers, files. Her boss began to praise her. Harvey Kelley was his name. He had a wife, two children. But he wasn't happy, he told Doris, he dreamed dreams. He drove her to the beach and they walked there in the evenings. One night they made love. They were both very lonely. When the time to go away together came, they felt that they were leaving no one.

Dan couldn't imagine how they lived, what they felt, how long they stayed together. Or if Doris thought of her son, Daniel, company for her when in the womb, after his birth a stranger. Doris ran away, with no word, no forwarding address, leaving Ellen her child. Ellen allowed the child to bring her to life; she made for him a living heart and housed him there. For him alone she dug up roots and boulders, created a moist living place, and said to him: You can live here. And made a place for another child, a girl, his cousin Cam, his sister, she could see they both were orphaned, saw them huddling together, warming each other with their breath.

So Dan became a boy brought up by grandparents. His ex-wife threw it up to him when she felt he'd failed her: 'You don't know how to love. How could you love, the way you were brought up?'

He thinks that's wrong; it's not that he can't love, it's that he can love only in the way of orphan children, brought up apart from ordinary life. He'd been spared the anger of young, overtired parents but burdened with the fears of two whose bodies were beginning to let down. As a small child he felt archaic. The ordinary objects of his life marked him as different. The other children brought to school bologna sandwiches in lunchboxes with blazoned pictures of Roy Rogers, The Lone Ranger, Mickey Mouse. But he carried, in a workman's black, serious lunchbox, leftovers his grandmother had put aside or re-invented for his taste: meat pasties, ham salad made from Sunday's meat, a chicken wing, a thermos full of pea soup or beef stew. Each lunchtime was a mortification to him, though he knew his food tasted better than the other children's. He hated the smell of their flat sandwiches, even as he craved them. But he would never tell his grandmother; she was old, he loved her, why open her up to his shame.

Upstairs in the grammar school, two grades ahead, Cam, carrying the same lunchboxes, but, combative, adversarial, and quick, made the other children think her lunches were a prize and made them buy the homemade cakes and tarts her grandmother had baked. For Cam her grandmother's foreign life was an adventure, but for Dan it was the shame he loved and must protect. So, when the fracas came about the chickens, he hid in the living room, abashed, while Cam stood on the sidewalk with their grandmother and stared the policeman down.

'Who do you think you're talking to now, Jerry Flynn,' Ellen had said to the policeman. 'I had to chase you and my John off the neighbor's apple tree, you'd both have been in jail. Which would have been the end of you at the policemen's ball, and all your dreams of glory.'

Dan stood on the screened-in porch, ashamed to hear his grandmother talk that way to a policeman. Even Cam hung back at first, he saw, but then she took hold of herself and stood beside her grandmother.

'Mrs. M., look here, the neighbors here filed a complaint. It's just my job.'

'What neighbors?'

'I'm not at liberty to say.'

'Don't bother. It's the two over there. It's not refined for them, chickens in the neighborhood. Too bad for them. I was here with chickens when they were in a dirty tenement sucking at their mothers' tits. So let them come to me if they have a complaint. I'll tell 'em.'

Ellen's chickens. In the twenties, when she first moved to Queens, there were only two houses on the street: the Mac-Namaras' and the Bakers', who were Germans and who had five girls. Mrs. Baker was sick and for long periods could not care for her children. Ellen would take them in, not asking Vincent; she would bring mattresses up from the basement; one child slept on the living-room couch. In the night sometimes the knock: Mr. Baker calling for Ellen's help: 'My Mrs. is bad.' Always they called each other Mr., Mrs., through the years of nursing, burying, the marriages and christenings, the food passed back and forth. They didn't visit each other in their houses; they talked on the sidewalk and the porch. Then other houses sprang up, gradually, magically, the street grew full and Ellen built a chicken fence, a wire pen so she could keep her birds. At first she'd had a rooster, but by the forties, she'd given that up, thinking it would be her one concession to the neighborhood, and vowing she would make no more.

Of course the two policemen, half her age, one in the class in grammar and high school of her late son, the hero of the War, could not stand up to her. And the disapprobation of her neighbors wouldn't have stopped her; she'd have enjoyed it; combat thinned her blood, like warmer weather; it made her feel the joy of movement and its force. But she did kill the chickens; it was Dan who wanted it. He couldn't stand the shame of it. She would not have him unhappy. She saw he was but he would not say why.

He heard Ellen ask, 'Camille, what is it with him?'

Camille was nine. He knew that she knew his double shame; he was ashamed of how his grandmother stood out in the world, that she was not like others, but he loved her and was shamed by his own shame. He longed to be like other people, and he hated the chickens, for their part in keeping him from this. He knew Cam had seen him that winter afternoon doing the one cruel thing he'd ever done: she'd seen him throwing snowballs at the chickens. And another time she'd seen his face grow horrified when Ellen had them catch the old hen, no longer worth her feed, and hand it over to be beheaded, dropped then on the floor, flapping until its heart had lost sufficient blood. Ellen had thrown the hen's head to Tramp the dog, and never seen Dan's horror. But Cam saw.

They both knew Ellen wanted the chickens to stay in the yard. Dan knew that Cam loved her grandmother's defiance, loved that they had stood together on the sidewalk and made two policemen walk away. But she saw that he suffered, and she would always act to keep back suffering from this boy, more than brother, orphaned even more than she and even more bereft.

She said to her grandmother: 'He got upset about the chickens. When the two policemen came.'

'For God's sake, what's the matter with him.'

Cam looked at her grandmother. She said nothing.

Ellen understood. So one day when the children were at school, Ellen MacNamara killed the chickens, demolished the chicken house she'd built twenty-five years before, took down and cleared away the wire that made up the pen. And when Dan and Cam came home and saw it, she said nothing, and allowed no comment on this corner of the yard now naked, derelict, bereft. She served the children custard, warm and liquidy in soup bowls she called basins. In the houses of their friends, they'd eaten from small cold glass stemmed dishes of chocolate pudding with black skin on the top and over that a rosette of whipped cream. Eating the custard at his grandmother's table, Dan had to think: Am I happy? Am I glad the chickens are gone? Have I failed her, failed what she thought I was? He could see his cousin Cam entirely absorbed in her enjoyment of the custard; a dart of simple love shot from his heart towards her and he wondered: Why am I like this? And then his grandmother began to sing. No words he knew, or even understood. They helped her with the dishes. The warm suds, the music with no words he knew blanketed his heart. He could be happy.

Alone now with his grandmother, holding her papery hand, he thinks about the chickens, of his mother, of the custard and the music and the dishpan and the suds. He sees her eyes; he sees that they see nothing. The eyes try to find him in the room, give up, and close.

'She's sleeping now,' says his cousin Marilyn. 'You go now for your walk. Go on,' she says, 'go on with Cam.'

II

1

This is the way she told the story out in company. Her best story: she made everybody laugh. She told them this when they asked her why she came to America, could she not have stayed at home?

She always began in the same way. 'Bit by bit the news spread through the town.'

She'd look around to make sure everyone was listening well. She didn't want to waste her effort. She refused to. Lying now, refusing to become the one event, her death, she sees herself talking.

'The news spread through the town. 'Twas not a big town, you know, Tulla, but a market town. So Thursday, market day, everyone was gathered in the square, or I should say the men were gathered, God alone knew where the women were.

'"The bees are in the church now," they were all saying, as if it was good news, some relative from America, or that the roses were full out, or you could get a good price for your bullock.

'"Bees, then," they were saying, and that was the end of it.

'Of course we lived in the town, my father was a publican, right in the main street we lived, so of a Thursday morning, market day, I'd pull the curtains of the parlor windows and see a bullock's face pressed up against the glass. And what the street was like after they left, the pack of them, the people and the cattle both. I'm on your side, I'll keep it from you. So I'm hearing there's bees in the church, but never in my wildest dreams could I have thought of what it was. On Sunday, we went up to the church, of course, my dad and myself walking. Everyone was there, just in the usual way. Then you walked in and, Holy God, 'twas nothing but a swarm, sounding like thunder. And not a blessed person saying one word on the subject and the priest up there on the altar, normal. Though he had the sense to cut the sermon short.

'You couldn't hear a word of any part of it, Mass or the sermon, for the swarming. And after Mass, like always, each went about his business, not a word was said. I thought 'twas safe back home to ask my father couldn't anyone do anything about the bees and was cuffed right then and there for my damned insolence. Three weeks this went on, once a week the woman who cleaned out the church went in to sweep away the corpses. The fourth Sunday the place was spotless. There'd been these lines of honey, and then clots of it dripping down the wall, they'd stuck there, but the woman, God knows I don't remember her name, who cleaned up the church had got rid of that somehow. The priest stood in the pulpit and thanked God that through this tribulation no one had been stung, especially the children, and he offered three Hail Marys of Thanksgiving to the Blessed Mother, Patroness of Ireland, who sheltered all within her motherly embrace.

''Twas then I packed my bags,' she always ended the story. 'And I booked my passage.'

'How old were you, Ellen?' people would ask her.

'Sixteen, but I knew 'twas not the place for me. And right I was.'

'And you don't want to go back?'

'What would I go for? Pigs and dirt and begging relatives. No thanks, none of that "I'll Take You Home Again Kathleen" cod for me, thank you. That's my husband's department. Say the word *bog* only and he's drowning in the water of his tears.'

2

In reality, the sound of swarming bees has been, throughout her life, the sound of all her terror. She was sixteen, that much was the truth, but she wasn't living in the town, not living in her father's house, but in the country with her mother. Her mother, who sat in the darkness gibbering. Supplicating in the Irish tongue: 'God take me from this life.'

The year is 1911. A quarter-mile from the main road, and

never visited, is a stone house. The others in the countryside are whitewashed and their roofs are thatched. Their look is welcoming; inside these houses could be cheerful life. A woman bending at the fire, and at least the possibility: a steaming kettle, laundry whitening on the hedge. But this house belonging to Tom Costelloe, Ellen's father, is a place where there can be no hope. It is the house where Ellen lives. Its stones are dark; in the whole house there are only two windows. The roof is slate; in a storm the slates loosen and fall off. When Ellen tells her father this, he sends a man to fix it, one of his men, the one perhaps who drives her in the dog cart to the Presentation Sisters every morning and in the afternoons is waiting, when she walks out of the door, to drive her home. She will not board there with the sisters, though her father many times has said that he will pay. She won't board; she won't leave her mother.

It could be the man who drives her who comes to fix the broken roof, or it could be another. Her father has many men in his employ. For he has many occupations. He is a publican, a grocer, a seller of animal feed. He has been clever with his money; he has prospered.

Her mother has not prospered, and will never prosper. They are in the house because her father saw this and put his wife away, from his sight, and from the sight of all his customers. The trouble, Ellen sees, has its source in her mother's womb. From that womb she alone escaped alive. Three ghost brothers and sisters perished in the womb: born dead, their green skeletons all in the graveyard. And the other five, too young for bone: the bloody messes and her mother lying on the floor. 'Go call your father, tell him come, tell him it's too late. It's all over.' She would leave her mother lying in the blood that was the brother or the sister, bloodying the bedsheets with the family blood. And she would hear her mother weeping to her husband, 'I'm no good, Tom. Once again I've failed you.' And Ellen would see the father leaving, sickened by the woman's mess of it, not coming back till morning, or for days, saying the business took him, it was unavoidable.

3

Tom Costelloe had trusted his daughter with money from the time that she was young. It was nearly half her life, then, being with her father. He was proud of her, he wanted her beside him. They were living behind the pub. All day long it was dark, and noisy in the evening, and the smell of beer was everywhere. You would have thought they'd be unhappy there. They weren't. He was free much of the day. It was just the three of them, and they went walking in the countryside, long walks, sometimes to his parents' farm; the land belonged to the elder brother now and to the brother's family: his dour wife, Kathleen, and their four boys, who frightened Ellen, meaning to – they hated her for living in the town. Her father'd saved his wages working for the Shaughnessys across the road; his elder brother, too, had helped him buy the pub and start himself, a part of it was his. It did not make the brothers love each other. Tom Costelloe resented Jack, his brother, for his place as firstborn, his smaller talents. Jack in turn thought his young brother fast and never to be trusted, though he saw that these same qualities made him prosper, and he loved prosperity, kept his brother near him to be near its touch.

The pub had a back door that opened onto the Protestant graveyard. They had a morsel of a garden where her mother set the washtub in fine weather; she would sing then as she washed and when they finished, she and Ellen would take a piece of bread and butter in a napkin and walk among the dead Protestants till they got to the hill above the graveyard with the best view of the valley. She would sit beside her mother. Sometimes they sat silent, sometimes they talked like sisters, sometimes her mother would unplait Ellen's hair and hold it in her hands then plait it up again, just for the pleasure of it. Sometimes the father joined them. They would look down at the valley below, spread around them like a lap. He'd put his daughter on his back and run down the hill with her, and the mother, laughing, would beg them to slow down, she'd never catch up to them, they were merciless, the two of them, they were two villains, they must take pity on a poor old woman's tired bones. He'd slow down for her. When she caught up, she'd wink at Ellen and say, 'Race you, then.' Ellen would jostle on her father's back. She knew he let her mother win. He'd put his daughter down and say: "Tis a terrible thing to be married to a woman that cute she'd deceive her husband.' He would kiss the hair his wife was pinning up and for a moment Ellen hated her, the beautiful mother, who had only to pin her hair atop her head to steal the father, turn him into her husband merely, and the two of them turn away, away from Ellen, in their pleasure in each other, and their pride. They were better-looking than the parents of the other children. When they stood up for the Gospel during Mass she was proud to stand beside them. She imagined herself envied for her parents and it was the secret jewel she hoarded in her mind: the stranger's envious stare.

Her father bought up the grocer's shop next: then they were happiest. She sat beside him on a high stool. She was seven years old, she was eight: she gave change back to customers. Occasionally she'd get something for her father, when he said, 'Would you run for that, now, Ellen, like a good girl. Get the brown soap in the back for Mrs. Lavery.' She loved the ledger books her father kept, the black ink of his writing, the thin red line of the columns separating numbers.

That was the time of the first stillborn baby. The mother in the room above the shop, a nice room with curtains you could open to look out. Ellen had been sent to fetch her aunt Kathleen, expecting she'd come home to find a brother or a sister. But nothing, no word. Silence. Her father grim-lipped, coming for her in a week. Her mother white-faced. Slower-moving. Only when they were alone, her mother took Ellen to her, to the arc her body made. 'The poor babe was born dead. There's nothing for it.'

It began then. She'd catch her mother out in weeping, in the vague looks, in the silence and the slower tread. And people told her, 'You must be kind to her, poor thing.'

As if she ever had not been kind. As if the mother, beautiful in movement or stillness, ever had called up from her heart anything but yearning, pride, the pull to be as near her as she could. The first day she'd gone out to school was death, just down the road, but really exile. All day in school she longed to be running up the road, dusty from chalk, back to the heaven of the room she lived in with her mother, to hear the sure click of her thimble, the wooden spoon against the pot side, the rustle of her mother's dress as she lifted up her arm to the high shelf for salt, for flour.

When had she not been kind? When had she not seen her mother as the treasure she would die for? Die for in an hour, gallant, soldierly. She would feel privileged to lay down her life.

Her mother took to resting in the afternoons. She was nearly always pregnant, or getting over the loss of a child. But she was never whole with child. The children broke her, or they broke her heart. He went on doing it, the thing he did to her that made it happen. Every few months something terrible.

He hired Anna Foley then to help the mother with the housework. She was younger than the mother, eighteen, ten years older than Ellen was herself, but she seemed much older than all of them and she worshipped in the mother the traces of preserved youth she had never seen in the overworked women she'd been brought up among.

So they created between them, Ellen and Anna, a shelter for the mother. Anna, unhoused, the middle girl of a dreamless family, called up a romance from some hidden part of her and pressed it down: a lozenge of devotion that expressed itself in furious domestic passion. To the linens lately bought through the father's prosperity, the crockery kept from the first days of marriage, the white curtains, the long table where they took their meals, she paid the homage she would once have paid to the person of the mother, whom she counted herself blessed to serve. The mother's voice, her thin hands, her kindness, the lost look of her, all seemed to Anna Foley emblems of the fineness of the world that made life sensible. Why live if it was only what her family thought to live for? Better to be done with it and dead in the gray river and at peace, if there was nothing but the endless labor she was born to with no object but itself.

She saw Ellen as far above her, to be aided, praised, and feared. Ten years younger, Ellen seemed to Anna to have taken in a manly understanding of the world. At twelve, she worked beside her father, ran the grocery on market days while he sold feed, wrote figures down in books so beautifully it would do the heart of anybody good to see them. In silence Ellen and Anna had come to understand and had agreed. The mother was their charge. Ellen could give the welfare of her mother's body up to Anna. She'd seen too much for a young girl. The mother felt that, felt she had done harm. 'Four times she came upon me, Anna, in the midst of losing one of them. It was a thing she never should have seen.'

He was a brute to keep her going through it, Anna thought. She couldn't offer the father understanding, or justice. His attentions to his wife could have in Anna's eyes nothing of the love that he professed. She could not imagine that the mother begged for it, begged for him to come to her, so they could try again, so she could prove that she was not a failure, she could do it, be beside him once again, stand up beside him with a healthy child. Anna could not believe that her devotion to the mother had been shared once by himself. She had the simple, deadened views on sex of any girl brought up on a half-ruined farm, with animals that were a misery and too many younger children to feed. She saw that the father had brought her to the house so that he might feel easy in withdrawing his attentions, his responsibility from the mother. She saw that and was glad, for she believed that her attentions were more suited to the mother than her husband's, bruised now and wounded as she was.

She had her work cut out for her. It was important work. She understood it perfectly and did it well. She saw herself the solid prop that held up the abode of two superior creatures. The mother losing her strength, the daughter just beginning to get hers. Anna Foley took a pride in Ellen's looks and her quick answers, in her black eyes that stood no nonsense and her hair that one day every man would want to touch, in her success with the Presentation Sisters, her fast retorts to her cruel cousins in the country, too slow-witted now to hurt her, the way she walked up the high street, swinging a slate, a book she'd borrowed from the sisters. (Unlettered herself, Anna would beg Ellen to read aloud whatever it was she had in her hand. While Anna baked bread or peeled potatoes, Ellen read to her: Sir Walter Scott, a catalogue of feeds. It was the same to Anna, the act itself was of importance.)

Ellen's love for Anna Foley was the pure love of a child who has been rescued. She need no longer preside over her mother's ruin, started by the failure of the mother's womb, completed by her husband's treacherous withdrawal. She was slipping from them daily, the mother, they could see it, growing slighter in existence, but physically heavier. Less capable of movement now, less willing

81

for it, she fattened in her idleness. Her color darkened and her hair grew lusterless and flat. More and more she sat beside the window now. 'What's that, dear?' she would say when one of them asked her something. Less and less captured her interest; less and less, they saw, she understood.

The father moved them to the country. He took over the feed business; he became the money man in town. On market days he kept Ellen home from school, braving the ire of the Presentation Sisters. It was his gift to her, his daughter, facing down the nuns to show them his regard for her, her value. 'She'll work the grocery for me on Thursdays, Sister. There's not a man in the village with her intelligence, you'd be right to be proud of it yourselves. I'm grateful, Sisters, you can rest assured, and there's ways I can show you my gratitude. But she's my only heir, and never too early to learn the way of things, and who would I be trusting if not her?' Thirteen years old then, at her full growth, she stood beside her father, not his daughter now, but his partner, business people facing down the poor, unworldly nuns.

This was the time that held the seeds for everything to come. His faith in her, his teaching her the ways of money, giving her the care of it, his moving them away into the country. It was his pride in fine material that made the house miserable. He demanded that it be a stone house, a grand house, he believed, but everything around it darkened, and he picked a high spot without trees for its good view of the valley, its glimpse of the river, like the glimpse of a concealed knife on a thief. But nothing grew there. Desolate brown grasses, tough and springy, dry at all times of the year. The land ate moisture up; the house devoured light. Why could he not have put in more windows? Because he built the house to keep his wife from sight. He had no thought of her seeing.

The seeds of everything were planted then. He kept the house in town. He'd stay there, he said, when the business was heavy, not ride the five miles out to the countryside. He was that tired some nights, he said.

But Ellen and Anna knew, and the mother knew that he could not bear to set eyes upon his wife. She'd darkened, coarsened; her flesh was treachery to him, and accusation: he had done this thing.

He said he let the rooms in the house on the high street to commercial travelers. Later they found he'd hired a girl from Gort to run the pub for him; he moved her into the house in town, her and her sister, for respectability. The Monahan girls, Rose, the sister, and the name of the offender: Marin. A name that brazen, Anna said, what could you expect from her but brazen actions. Although at first he was not open with her, Anna saw the woman made him be. As proof of love.

He would not let his daughter and the woman speak. He kept them far apart. The woman was glad to go along. On market days, if they met on the street, Ellen crossed over to the other side, pretending she saw nothing. The hate filled Ellen then, and from that time grew up in her a love for vengeance that would mark her life, a cruelty that gave her strength, a knife she always held close to her body. Ready at any time.

In that time, too, there came together the dense sediment that later hardened into hate. She knew that she must hate her father. Looking at him, she knew that she took after him. Like looked at like. She saw the man whose shirts she'd loved, whose boots she had admired, whose posture, upright and commercial, she'd chosen as the model for her own. She understood she could never move as her mother had once moved, silently, the sources of the movement in themselves mysterious. Unfixed. She liked her father's purposefulness, not the hidden actions of her mother's world.

But it was her job to hate her father. To punish him for leaving them alone in the stone house with only two windows, for allowing Marin Monahan in the house that had once been her mother's. To soil it with her filth. He'd made the mother darken, coarsen, till she looked out at the brown grasses from the moment of her waking until dark, her only pleasure food, eaten fearfully and greedily, like an animal. Her mother, once beautiful, now ruined, was her father's work.

She felt bound to punish him. To hate the pleasure she had had in him. Hate the easy pride, the joy in his company, his words. She would distrust from now on pride and pleasure. She would bind herself to this. She would know that what looked like charm could easily be murderous intent.

She began to plan how she would cheat her father. The idea came when Delia Mullins and her family left for America with much less money than what Ellen had imagined was enough.

Delia was the one friend she had made. The one child who had had the faith, the courage, the desire to stick with her through the father's scandal and never say a word. Ellen admired Delia for this, but for nothing else. Compliant, biddable, good-natured (it was said with literal truth) to a fault, she was a pretty, fattish girl with round arms and light hair who seemed to want only a place at Ellen's feet. It took years for Ellen to unbend to Delia, years of Delia's presents, secret notes, false errands, false favors asked. Gradually, Ellen grew accustomed to Delia's attentions. She would not have admitted this. But Ellen depended upon Delia, like an abstemious person who tries liquor, at first to go along, and then acquires a thirst she wrongly believes she can at any time give up.

From the age of ten, Delia had come to Ellen to sort out her muddles. First with the nuns or with her spending money, later, in America, with the power company, the bank, the income tax, the dangerous insulting bill collector, the landlord, the parish priest. For seventy-five years Ellen spoke to Delia, whose existence she required so that she might recognize her own, in a tone of exasperated, hard-pressed impatience. Not a word in all this time of gratitude or love.

And yet she did feel grateful, for Delia had been the only one to see the mother in her ruined state. And had said nothing, knowing that her silence was the coin that bought her treasured place. In the whole of Ellen's youth, Delia was the only child to sit at the long table beside her and Anna Foley, to smile at the mother and meet only the dead eyes. Delia's father was a farmer prosperous enough to send her to the Presentation Sisters. Her mother was gregarious and easygoing, happy in her kitchen, but struck dumb with terror of the outside world. There were two sisters who had gone to Dublin. But the imaginative center of the family, the knot of color around which it spread, like a peacock's tail, was the life of the oldest sister, Moira, in America. She'd trained as a baby nurse there. She'd married a doctor. She lived in Montclair, New Jersey, and whenever the family was ready, she had always said, she and her husband would bring them over. Money was no object, she told her family. She missed them every minute of her life. But money was an object to Delia's father, Jack Mullins: an object palpable and looming and immense. He would not go to America a beggar. He would save up money till the time was right. They would not sail in desperation, like the people he'd seen go over when he was young, running from grim lives and from poverty, as if it were the plague. The Mullinses' planning and their saving up impressed Ellen from her thirteenth year.

Each month her own father drew back from them more and more, drew himself towards the woman. Or was drawn. In weak moments, when conscience struck him or a sense of the lost past, he turned to Ellen for forgiveness and was given stone. He admired this hardness in his daughter; he wished for punishment. He respected her for this as he respected her as a keeper of his accounts. He bragged to everyone that his daughter had a great head for business, better than any man in the district, she was born to it, like him. His idea that she was honorable and precise enabled Ellen to steal, over the course of four years, enough for him to pay her passage to America.

The year Ellen and Delia were fifteen was the year the Mullinses left. Ellen had taken Delia into her confidence, as she had taken Anna Foley. The secret was that in the bureau drawers where Anna kept her underclothing Ellen had hidden a pile of money she had stolen, the pounds a term she overcharged her father for tuition, and the daily coins she pilfered from his till. They sat around the kitchen table, Delia, Anna, Ellen, while the mother hummed across the room, a weight of ruin, and heard nothing. Anna told Ellen she was right to go, right to leave the father to his shame, and the mother to Anna's care. On Delia's shaky sense of things they depended for the facts, the details of costs, the papers. Ennobled by the importance of the one serious task she'd ever in her life been given, Delia made no mistakes and rose to the occasion like a boy who is useless at home but grows invaluable to his sergeant at war.

Delia said she was sure her sister could be taken in on the business. Anyone would sympathize. She didn't name the thing that needed sympathy: she knew that she must not. But anyone would understand, she said. Particularly any woman. She said this though she had no memory of her sister, who'd gone to America when Delia was six. But from her sister's letters she was sure she was a sympathetic person. She was sure Moira would help.

The mother darkened and the father's actions grew more brazen every day. Yet as he defied the town, the parish priest, his brother, and his family, he grew more to fear his daughter. Most likely, had she asked him, fixing him with the gray look, unforgiving, obdurate, he'd have given her passage money then and there. He'd have railed first, said the business was for her, he couldn't do without her, but he'd know he lacked the necessary weapon of a good name. He'd have given in. But she never asked him. She took pleasure in her deceit: it was a way of punishing him and only punishment could bring her peace.

She stole and saved money. She obeyed the Presentation Sisters, learned the things they had to teach her, deportment and fine sewing, though she thought them rot. Her mind was fixed on commerce, revenge, and escape. What the sisters could teach her were contemptible, weak-minded female tricks she needed only for camouflage. With Delia gone, she was alone, proud in her refusal of the other girls' society yet shocked sometimes at her own common loneliness. She turned even more inwards; she tried to curb her pleasure in her father's business. She would leave it soon. Her purpose was to leave it. At nightfall, she would sit beside her mother. Bringing her chair nearer, she would sit and watch the window filling up with darkness. She would hold the hand that had been lively, clever, magic in its ministrations, dead now, fat, the flesh growing over the wedding ring so that the gold was barely visible.

The news from Delia, good at first, became dispiriting. There was no love between her and her sister. The sister treated Delia as a maidservant, ordered her about, and left the children to her care exclusively. She gave her not a cent for her work, and introduced her to no living soul. Delia was lonely in America. She was a prisoner in her sister's big house. She lived only for the day when Ellen joined her. They would get a room together, go to dances, join clubs, meet young men. She hadn't spoken to her sister about Ellen's plans, and she had to say she wasn't hopeful. But she'd think of something. Something would turn up.

Ellen wrote Delia terrible letters, blaming her for everything. It was her fault Ellen ever had the first idea of leaving. Because of her and her daft schemes, Ellen had become a thief. She now had a drawerful of useless money, stolen off her father's back. Because she'd thought that she was leaving, she'd made no new friends at the school and could not now look to the sisters for a character. If she'd never had the idea of leaving, she'd have long ago resigned herself to settling in the town and put her energy into making the best of a bad lot. But Delia'd put ideas in her head and for the rest of her life she'd be tormented.

Delia took the blame. Alone and miserable, she was cut off from her parents, who in turn couldn't reckon where their loyalties should be: with the older daughter, in whose house they lived, whose food they ate, or with the younger, whom the older persecuted. Her friendship with Ellen Costelloe and her responsibility for Ellen's happiness had been the only source of meaning in Delia's life. Now she'd failed Ellen, so she was nothing but a failure. In her dark room at the back of the house, the room that looked out on the somber, joyless garden, insulted by her sister, ignored by her brother-in-law, disobeyed by her nieces and nephews, who, she knew, thought her a fool, her failure made her desperate. It was desperation, then, or perhaps loneliness or the high sense of purpose that grew higher with lost time, that gave her the courage to make friends with Jimmy Flaherty, who drove the baker's wagon, to offer him morning tea in secret in the kitchen, to meet secretly with him in the garden when everyone in the large house slept, meeting with him all that long summer so that in September, she had to present him with the news: somehow they'd made a baby.

Neither of them was displeased. The shame she carried made real what had been their desire: to fly in the face of family expectations. They ran off. They married and moved to New York. She brought the baby to visit her mother, her sister wouldn't see them. It didn't matter. She was married now; her husband was a citizen. He had a job with the Sanitation, could vouch for Ellen anytime. He'd be pleased to, Delia wrote with pride to Ellen. She told her friend what her husband had said: 'She'd only to name the day; they'd meet her at the boat with bells on.'

A stronger character than Delia might have written back to Ellen, refusing blame. She might have written, 'Don't say such things to me. You're young and you're intelligent, go off to Galway City or to Dublin, do a teachers' training course, a secretarial, come over by yourself, others have done it.' A strong character wouldn't have married, out of loneliness, out of necessity, literally the first young man she spoke to in America. But

Delia was not a strong character. As a child, she'd looked at Ellen and saw what she herself lacked. Had she known the terror Ellen lived in, a terror similar to her own, she would have suffered a dreadful loss. In seeing Ellen as she really was, she would no longer recognize herself; she would become a different person, would have to have a different life. But she never saw Ellen's terror, and so her nature stayed intact.

Ellen would wake in the night and see the moonlight fallen on the bare floor like a wafer, like a slice of mirror, an oval of white gold. She'd look at it for portent, but it gave her back only her own fear. What she'd despised in her life grew, in apprehension of its loss, now dear to her. She'd never traveled to a city. What would happen to her in New York? To her father, she would be as dead, and he would be as silent as the dead to her. The mother would be silent too, only just alive, in the dark stupor she'd grown into. And suppose, Ellen would think, her eyes wide open as if they were propped on stalks, suppose I don't succeed and make the money that I need for my mother? She saw herself locked in a bedlam of a factory room with hundreds of other girls, and dragging herself home through streets that swarmed with thieves. She could be hurt or robbed or cheated. And she saw her mother, sitting by the window, asking for her, calling her by name. She'd never leave, she couldn't. She'd been deceived. It was Delia who deceived her, then had forgotten her, then married, and had left the sister's grand house, where there would have been room for both of them to live.

And in her father's store, she'd tie her apron on, feel the cool coins between her fingers and the satisfying thump as they would drop down in the till. And she would think: Why leave? Her father's silence, and his fear, she'd lose that prize as well. Then she would hear the words of Marin Monahan. 'Tommy-love,' she'd say. And Ellen would think: I will leave this. I will take the mother; you, Marin Monahan, will die without your own kind, a barren woman on your bed alone.

Everyone in town had turned against Thomas Costelloe, his own family and Marin's too. Behind his back people called him adulterer, and usurer, and thief, though he stole nothing: all his money he had earned from his intelligence and his hard work. She'd not let anybody say a word against her father. If they tried, if anybody tried – the townspeople, her ax-faced aunt, one of the nuns at school – she'd turn to them the proud face that was his face. They would be silenced. She wanted the job of his punishment for herself; she'd not let others share in it. She hadn't a friend in the town now, only Anna Foley, who'd asked on Ellen's sixteenth birthday, 'When is it that you think you'll make the trip?'

Would she have left if the bees in the church hadn't so terrified her? Their noise was the clamor of her fear, the drone of her entrapment. Their stain, their leavings were the family sin. That day in church, the first day of their swarming, she'd broken into a sweat; each movement terrified her. But what appalled her most was her sense of being alone in her terror. No one in the pews around her seemed to fear the horror she could see about to strike them all. They moved their lips; they knelt, and sat, and rose again; they understood or did not understand the Latin. They didn't break and run; they didn't search for cover. Kind- and stupid-faced as the sheep on the hill outside, or unperturbed as stone, they formed a ring she couldn't break or break into. Outside the church, the priest who called her 'Ellen dear' and never felt the duty to bring the mother the sacrament joked with the young mothers and wondered at the weather.

In those nights she woke in terror at the sound of swarming in her dreams. But she didn't leave for that. Her anger drove her out, anger at the gratitude of all the congregation when the bees were gone. They had done nothing to prevent the horror, but it had been prevented. Her idea of justice had been mocked; they thanked God for the mockery. She couldn't wait to leave them.

She wrote to Delia saying she would come and Delia wrote back with information about her passage. She sent lists of prices and departures. The father never came to the stone house now. It was easy to deceive him. Anna Foley paid her brother from her own wages to bring back the trunk that Ellen bought at Gort, and then to drive Ellen to Cork in the dog cart.

Coolly, Ellen did all the things that needed to be done. She wrote to Delia; she arranged her passage and her papers. She was nearly seventeen but looked much older. Yet the day before she was to leave, when she saw her father's back in the town for what she knew would be the last time, the pain she felt was like a spike through the center of her chest. It was a child's pain, allowing no hope of future relief. She longed for the father's back, his boots, the harsh tweed of his jacket. She would not forgive him; he was a danger to her. Yet she knew these things of his were all she treasured; she longed to give herself up, to be carried on that back like a child, the weight of her life no longer her own, but a man's. Her father's.

'No use in staying any longer,' Anna Foley said, sensing the impatience of her brother's horses. The mother looked out on the deadened grasses, did not look at her daughter. And the child's heart in Ellen's breast cried out, 'Mother, tell me I can't leave you.' But the dead eyes would not turn towards her, nor the hand return the pressure she applied.

She left by moonlight and the countryside she hated was saturated with beauty. The invisible meadows loomed in her mind. Her feet ached for the touch of the white road. She closed her eyes; she made herself desire nothing of what she passed.

The light came up as they approached Cork City. By the time they were in Queenstown, it was morning. Anna's brother left her, silent, as he had been since she'd known him, on her own with her trunk at the office of the steamship line. Too frightened to talk to a city person, he took tail and left her by herself to sort out her business. And she was glad to see him go; his country boy's sense of inferiority was right: he was a lesser mortal. It was her first time in a city, but she felt that she was born to it. She liked the bustle of the quayside, the forms she must fill out, and herself in the tumult, her own fixity within the moving crowd.

On the ship, she kept entirely to herself. She watched the other girls, who flirted and ate oranges, showing their large white teeth as they popped sections of the fruit into their mouths just to torment the men. She watched them run upstairs and downstairs, share their biscuits and their mother's baking, speculate about the rich passengers, and look up longingly at the first-class deck. She would have none of it. She stood out on the second-class deck, letting the cold wind hurt her. And thought of her mother, sitting, noticing nothing, and the father's high, proud back that she would never see again. She'd be interrupted in her thoughts by the foolish buzzing around her, the ridiculous girls talking, their words in the air around her when she stood out on the deck or when she tried to sleep. That buzzing that she hated. Nothing she could distinguish. But a danger to herself, that thing she was by herself, apart from other people, that thing that people had to keep their distance from. Throughout her life she's had to fight against that buzzing, keep herself from it, tell the truth about it: it's a danger, it makes you lose the things about yourself you know: who you are, what the truth of the world is. It makes you forget what's important. Insistent, confusing, trivial: never going beyond itself, doubling back upon itself, thickening and crying out. *Listen to me. Me.*

That clear call from the outside world, the horn note sounded through bright air, the music that rang out, pointed, singular, it could so easily be lost in the buzzing, the swarm. You could so easily forget who you were, that large acts were possible, that the world could change, you could change, could get away. All her life it's been around her; she's had to fight it using all her strength. The hateful buzzing of the bees in Knock James Church that no one told the truth about or knew enough to fear. Lying in her bed, a ninety-year-old woman, her hair on her shoulders in the thin braids her granddaughter has plaited, she mutters against the girls aboard the ship. She clenches her hands that are claws now and she curses them all. The fools in her life that have crowded her, have buzzed around her. They're round her again, buzzing voices, words said by whoever they are straightening her bedclothes, putting tubes into her mouth, her sex, taking her blood, making her eat when she can't bear to eat, when she would like to be simple, empty, easily taken up into death, but they won't let her, they won't let her alone, they never have, she's had to fight them. All her life.

She's vanquished them sometimes, she's been free of them, felt herself grow straight, become a bare branch against a brilliant sky, a spire pointing upwards, a lance, the dark horizontal stroke beneath a column of correctly added figures. She sees with satisfaction that her hands and arms are bone; the sharpness of her body is a source of pleasure to her. She will raise her bone hand to anybody who comes near her. She can't move her body but she still can raise her arms. She will keep herself untouched. The touch of anything on her skin now is agony. They know it and keep on touching her. 'Don't touch me,' she keeps saying. They don't listen.

She would like to die. But she refuses to become only her death.

★

91

At night on the ship she heard them crying for their mothers. She hated them for that. Grown girls, she said between her teeth, crying like babies. They'll never make it in America. She created for each of them a separate dire end: for each of them a fate: drunk, slattern, streetwalker. She thought that in a few months, she'd pass them on the street and not give them the pennies that they begged for. Not a cent to any of them. Not a one of them. Not a single one.

She is horrified by her physical weakness. She hasn't liked her body. Times with Vincent, though, she did. Now she regrets what she let him do to her. She allowed him to unseal her; it is his fault now that life spills out of her, spills over into death. She wishes herself intact. She curses Vincent for the thing he did. Why did she let him? She wants a stone now for a body, smooth, a weapon, closed. Now her body keeps nothing back. The buzzing now is able to enter through her openness, travel through her blood into her skull, confusing everything, eating away the healthy living matter of her brain. She can't distinguish and she cannot recognize.

Out of her mouth come filthy warnings. Words she doesn't know she heard but understands. It must be stopped; she must tell all of them. She says the filthy things about the bodies of all men. Their filthy hands and mouths and hidden parts they show as if it were their glory. They do it to you and you lie in pools of blood. Your life goes out of you because of them.

She wants to warn someone, a woman, she does not know who. But no one understands her. She says the wrong things. She remembers now. The faces around her cannot understand her words. When she says, 'Bring me my glasses,' they bring her a toothbrush, water, a handkerchief, a pill. When she throws it at them, knowing they're trying to trick her, they say, 'You asked for this. You asked for water.' She tries to find the word for glasses. She shines the light of her mind into the store of words and looks in the place where she sees the image of her glasses. There is no word there to go with the picture. Darkness. What was the storehouse of her words, stocked, overflowing, is a dusty emptiness. There are no words that name the things she sees. She shines the light of her mind backwards and forwards on the shelves of objects that she means to name. The light searches. Backwards and forwards. There is nothing. She used to think someone had done this to her as a punishment. But now she understands. There are no thieves or punishers. Nothing has been stolen or kept back. Everything is simply, for no reason, gone.

She is remembering the boat now. She remembers landing, but she can't remember what she saw: the buzz around her took her up, so she saw nothing, barely heard her name, knew only that she'd been let through. Her father hadn't sent the word ahead about her. No one in America had learned she was a thief.

Delia was there to meet the boat. With Jimmy Flaherty, her husband, born a fool like Delia, but good-natured like her too. That's it, she remembers now. She wanted to forgive them for their natures. For not looking at the truth. For Delia making her say all these years: 'Look at this, Delia, look at it now.' From childhood she'd had to push the truth under her friend's nose. And even then Delia wouldn't see.

She calls out Delia's name. She hears Delia's name in the room. She's done it, it's the right name, fitting the face she sees in her mind. The buzzing stops; the fog lifts. She remembers objects of the past and has the names of them. She remembers the kind of things she liked to look at. Things seen best from far away, or set apart from other things surrounding them. She sees posters slapped up against a wall: MEETING TONIGHT − FUN FAIR − VACCINATIONS FOR DISTEMPER. She sees brass numbers on a black door. A steel bridge. A steep-roofed house. She tries to make her mind stay with these things. If she can do it, she can break out of this dead light. The light she always hated is the envelope containing her whole life now; it is all she sees. As a girl, she'd hated the tall conifers outside the house her father had built to hide her mother. Their heavy needles hid the lines on the branches; their thick growth devoured light. She'd run, as a girl, to get away from those trees, out to the place on the road that opened up, where beech took over, larch, and the hawthorn began. Now there is no breaking out. The distorted light that won't allow her to distinguish one thing from another, that won't let her say: This thing, and that, and then the other − is the only light available to her. And yet she fears the loss of it. She's not ready to relinquish herself to what she knows will follow. Darkness. Silence. The end of everything that is.

If she could see a face around her she could put a name to! But there is no familiar face. The objects merge and lose distinction. The fog covers over. The buzzing begins again. She'll never find it now, that thing she wanted. She slips back; she feels tears coming; she has lost the thing she had a glimpse of. All she can see is Delia's face.

She always had to keep telling Delia everything. She didn't understand a blessed thing. But sometimes Ellen was grateful to her. Delia had seen the mother and been silent. In the town, in the stone house of the mother's shame, and after in America. So there was that. But Delia *did* too much, Ellen couldn't stand that, she could never stand it. Delia cried too easily; she laughed too loud. You could never get her to sit still and just look at a thing or listen long enough to get it right. The nuns were after her for it every minute. Delia'd be twisting in her seat, fiddling with her hair, examining her nails, her skirt, her handkerchief. She'd be wiping her eyes after a fit of laughing, with a fit of weeping on its heels. She'd be up getting you something: a cup of tea, a biscuit, a cardigan. She'd open a window for you. Did you feel a draft? She'd shut the door. No stillness. Vincent was the one for that. He could be still and listen to a thing and get it right. Bring up an angle of a thing you hadn't thought of. But never Delia.

She wants to rise up so she can correct Delia. Then she remembers: Delia is dead. She wants to rise up against her old friend's death. And then she understands: she can't rise. They've strapped her in. That's it, she remembers now. They've tied her up. A prisoner. A head of cattle. She won't let them make her an animal. She'll strike at them now. They can't keep her down. She feels that, even dead, Delia needs her. Needs her to hold on to the image of her face so she won't be swallowed up in darkness. She's impatient now with Delia's calling out to her, needing her to pull her back, to keep a hold on her.

She always needed something, Delia. Always needed help, always mucked up her life, always needed pulling out. Always Delia came to Ellen. At the Presentation convent: 'Cripes, I've lost my Latin, I can't find my Rosary, I've spent my mission money, El, I'm in the soup.' Delia that everybody liked. The yellow curls, pinchable cheeks, bottom asking for a man to slap it, round white arms. Too free, too thankful. The nice children she could not keep fed. Tears then. 'I'll have to give the youngest up. I'll have to send him to the orphanage. I haven't any choice.'

'I'll take him for a while. You'll not be sending him to any nuns.'

A nice boy, Delia's Tommy. Grateful like his mother. Nicer than her own. Her own had hated it that she'd brought in a child to live with them who wasn't of their blood. They'd grudged him every spoonful, every drop of medicine, every stitch of clothes, every kind word from her or Vincent. That was the girls. Did John? No, he couldn't have. John had been kind.

Her girls were never nice. Vain, primping, thinking only of themselves. And supplicating. Do this for me. Give me that. Their greedy voices. Their refusal to take part in life. No, that was Magdalene. Theresa didn't ask for things. Theresa refused. I'll take nothing from you, she'd said, turning from the breast at six months, drinking from a cup to spite her mother. Vincent saw none of it. 'They're good girls. Be a little softer with them.' One a coward and the other heartless. Lacking the important thing, both of them, lacking what was needed. What would count. Life. They weren't interested in life.

It wasn't just that they were girls. Cam wasn't like them. Cam was like Bella, her real friend. Where is Bella? She calls out to her. Why is it Delia's face she sees when it's Bella she wants? The both of them are dead; why is it Delia's face that comes? Bella is somewhere in the fog. Among the other dead. She's furious at Delia for taking the place she wants to give to Bella. It's Delia's fault, just as it had been Delia's fault that Ellen's first job had been in service. Delia with her greenhorn's fear, her hiding out among her kind, her terror of the first thing not out of the same bog she came from. 'My Jimmy has a cousin has a friend, says there's a place. All ready for you, El, you'd never have a moment's worry.' Of course, she took the place, grateful as she was to Delia, and wet behind the ears, not knowing one thing about America, relying on Delia and Jimmy for advice. As good advice as she would have got from their Brendan, who was two when she arrived, or Margaret, who was just six months.

She'd never get over the disgrace of it. Even the words themselves shameful: 'in service.' And why should she serve? Cleaning the shit of people she was better than. 'But, El, you've such a lovely job,' Delia would say. 'Mrs. Fitzpatrick's lady's maid. I'd give my eye teeth for it. Any girl would, Ellen. All the lovely stuff, the clothes, the hairbrushes. Tell me about those hairbrushes again.'

'I'll not talk about the nonsense one more time to you. They could clothe and feed a family for a year, those hairbrushes.' She gave Delia the look she put on when she wanted Delia to know she had been stupid. She did it when she felt the rage coming on her, rage that she could do nothing about the circumstances of the world that held and choked her and kept back her life.

She had not had the strength to make her father do the right thing, leave that woman, come back to the stone house, cure her mother with his living there. Make her mother beautiful, make her sing. Make up for the blood. Make up for the body that would not hold. The failing body, all the parts of it that must be hidden, covered up.

That was her job for Claire Fitzpatrick: hiding, covering, so that the woman could appear before the world, walk down the dark staircase, a woman in civilization, covered up and holding in. She hated the lie of it. Service. She was in service to the clothing and the body of a fool.

She was good at it.

'The hairbrushes, Mrs. Fitzpatrick.'

Claire Marie Jameson Fitzpatrick. Wife of James. Mother of James, William, John. All of them gone to their graves old men. None taken from their mother untimely.

Claire Fitzpatrick. She was a machine with moving parts: legs, organs, pumps, bolsters, entryways. Producing substances. Some of which were useful, most of which were waste. Her whole life was about her body: to preserve, to ornament her body, more important, to conceal the nature of it from men's sight.

'Tell me about the hairbrushes, El,' Delia had pleaded.

She'd have liked to throw them through the glass, that was it about the hairbrushes. She dreamed of a clean break, silver, glass, the window frame gaping shamefully like a ruined mouth, the ragged hole unstable, dangerous, glimmering in the clear morning sun. And the brushes themselves, lying on the sidewalk. Would anybody pick them up? Step on them? Sell them for money or trade them in?

Who are you to call me by my name?

Ellen. She was Ellen to any of them. They were not her betters. No. Not one of them was.

The hairbrushes with their patterns of leaves – acanthus, laurel – pressed or cut into the metal, was it? And what for? Nobody thought of the weight of them. In all her life Claire Fitzpatrick, and the women like her, had not done their own hair. So what would it matter to them, the weight of the brushes? The arms lifted above the thick hair were servant's arms.

Each morning as she dressed her own hair, Ellen thought how glad she was to have it, not Claire Fitzpatrick's. Her hair was a pleasure to her. Smooth. She'd pull it so it lay straight against her skull. She loved the fineness of it, loved taking it, forming it into a roll, pinning it low against her neck. She could imagine the pleasure it must be to look at, that thick knot of hair against the white skin of her neck.

She'd loved her hair.

And Vincent had loved it. Lovely moments they were, he would take the pins out of her hair, sometimes he'd kiss each of them as he took them out, then lay them down, always in perfect rows. His ardor didn't let him lose that part of his nature. He respected tools. Hairpins, he tried to tell her once, were tools. She doubled over laughing. She'd tease him for it, his laying the pins in rows, call him 'the engineer.' But it was lovely, when the last pin would be taken out and then there was a moment of real stillness when the hair would hold of itself its own shape, and then it would fall, wonderful, onto her shoulders. He'd take her hair in his hands, kiss the smooth hair he loved and kiss the places of her body. She allowed him everything. He understood, he learned of her. His hands, his mouth learned. He knew.

Claire Fitzpatrick's hair was dreadful. Coarse and no color, not a hint of sheen, no smoothness, to arrange it was to battle with it. And Ellen had clever fingers, she could do things with the rough, unpromising material, quicker than the others. Claire Fitzpatrick praised her, for she knew the value of a thing. She'd been brought up to it. Her father, Owen Jameson, had made the money they lived off in his business, furs it was, she'd never known exactly. The hidden sources of the Irish money. James Fitzpatrick's father's money, too, came from a source that no one spoke of. James himself was a great lawyer, he'd a way with money, so even the Protestants took his advice, although it stuck in their throats.

Claire and James Fitzpatrick. Both of them brought up thinking themselves royalty. The Jesuits, the Madames of the Sacred Heart, the dancing classes for the children of the wealthy Irish so that they might mate. They'd known each other from their cradles, Claire and James Fitzpatrick told Ellen a million times, as if it were a smart remark. It made her sick. 'I see you're a good girl, Ellen, and a clever one,' Claire Fitzpatrick would say, smiling at Ellen in the mirror while Ellen looked down at the ugly hair, would not meet Mrs. Fitzpatrick's gaze. 'Mind that the one does not get in the way of the other.' And she'd quote her a poem about the Virgin Mary that was supposed to be clever because the BVM was never mentioned:

And was she clever in her words
Her answers quick and smart?
We know not: we know of the secret love
For her son in her heart.

'I understand from the others you have a quick tongue in your head, and find yourself ready with an answer. But remember, Ellen, a girl in your position can lose everything by forgetting who she is.'

'Yes, madame,' she would say, refusing in her resoluteness to meet the eye that searched, demanded that she meet it in the glass. I know who I am. And where I've come from. She longed for the relief of the abuse that could come from her own mouth. My father, a gentleman. My education, the Presentation Sisters. And my mother. She would see the mother in these moments, young and running, singing, lifting the towel on the bread dough as she checked its rising. But then it would come to her, the real truth of her mother, silent or gibbering, an animal, no woman now, bearded, with lifeless eyes. Ellen had feared that any slip, any faint hint of her past would reveal the truth of her mother to Claire Fitzpatrick's eye. So she remained above reproach and when Mrs Fitzpatrick questioned her about her past she made up what she knew the woman wished to hear: the small farm, the countless brothers, cheerful sisters, stoical hardworking father, and her sainted mother, who slaved for the family but was never too busy for a laugh.

'You must think of me as your mother now,' Claire Fitzpatrick would say from time to time, in love with herself for her good heart.

'Yes, madame,' Ellen would reply. The perfect servant with her eyes kept down because of her emotions: gratitude and missing home. And in her heart: 'I'd slap the face of you for that suggestion if there was a way on earth I could. I'd tear out your ugly hair. I'd leave you here, bald and disfigured from the blows of my fist on your face. You'd be unable even to find your underclothes, so little do you know the workings of your own life. Never dare to speak of yourself and my mother in one breath. You are unworthy to kiss the hem of her garments. The strap of her sandals you are unworthy to loose.'

Ellen is lying strapped to her bed, over seventy years later, and refusing to become the one event, her death. Refusing to forget. No one remembers but herself and if she lets go of the memory, it will be lost forever. The memory of the young mother singing, her bare arms covered in soapsuds to the elbows, singing as she scrubs her husband's shirts. The clever fingers making shapes out of the dough: birds, animals, a pointed flower. If I forget, she will become nothing, will disappear, will be homeless in the universe, wandering, her arms outstretched, rootless if I lose the picture of her.

Do not speak to me, Claire Fitzpatrick. Do not say that you would be my mother. Did you lie in blood, the children of your life lost to you not once, but again and again? Your husband's money, your father's keeps you from your body. That is its purpose, so the men can tell themselves: The bodies of women which we covet we will never know the truth of; because of our wealth you must let us believe that what we feared has ceased to be. Cover, muffle, pare, remove, keep down the evidence, the secret smells.

That was her job, they paid her for it, used her talents for it and her wits and her dexterity, her nimbleness and memory, her understanding of the place of things. And of her own place.

At first she'd been taken by the size and richness of the house, and felt grateful to be there, grateful for the woods and porcelains, the dinner gong with its somber, reproachful tone.

Her early pleasure fed her subsequent rage. She knew they

counted on that pleasure. The homeless girl, the unhoused voyager, taking her solace from the house, taking the measure of her worth against its objects. They'd counted on it, and in her case it had served them for a time. Until her understanding choked her and stopped her breath. People like Delia and Jimmy Flaherty were their meat. Their excitement when Matt Corrigan, chauffeur to the Fitzpatricks and a pal of Jimmy's, suggested that Ellen present herself to the Fitzpatricks' housekeeper, for they were looking for a ladies' maid. An Irish girl they wanted, no French or English for them, no, they were that loyal, but a girl with breeding, like Ellen herself, who made a good appearance, spoke well, and had her wits about her. 'I'd just put in a word for you,' said Matt Corrigan, thinking she'd be impressed. She was; he had been right to count on it. On him more than the others her anger fell. In her bed, old, dying, she curses Matt Corrigan. Then curses them all, their sense of gratitude and having been well situated. WE ARE OF THE HOUSE. WE ARE THE HOUSE. *We count for something, as the house does; we weigh, as it does.* The greenhorn cod that kept them slaves. She'd been taken in at first, because she had been frightened. Even now, her hands claws and her mind a fog in which she has misplaced her present life, she won't forgive herself that weakness. A slave's weakness. She was not a slave.

You must possess yourself.

She'd known that early. There must be a place, shored up, defended, reconstructed daily, where that thing that kept itself that was yourself, could stay intact. Fragile, pointed, dark, sharpened. Precise. You kept it from the sight of others. You could not soften, open. You kept yourself held in. Then you belonged to yourself. 'She kept herself to herself,' people had said about Ellen all her life. Resentful, not knowing it was her triumph. Weakness made you open up. Weakness and fear. You had to stop it happening.

She thinks now, making her claw hands fists, what she has always thought, that it was living next to Delia, in the house with Delia, that gave her her first weakness. Delia with her tears, her fatness, her too-quick confidences, dreams, obedience, remorse. Her delight that Matt Corrigan thought so well of Ellen, her friend. The honor beamed back to her, to Delia. Matt had worked first with Jimmy Flaherty. He came by on the evenings he was free, when the Fitzpatricks didn't want him, in his uniform (Livery, she corrected him, an ugly name, but call it by its right one), he'd sit with his beer and tell them about the Fitzpatricks at the opera, what the cook had told him, what was eaten: champagne, canvasback duck. Mr Fitzpatrick was the finest gentleman in all New York, he put the Yankees all to shame, they knew it. The finest houses in New York he'd driven to. Later she knew that he was wrong, they weren't the finest houses in New York, the finest houses in New York would not receive the Irish. How could he live among them and not know?

Matt had complimented her on how she poured the tea, her lovely diction, her white hands, her talent with a needle and the way she'd write a letter for any of them, and read the papers from the government, and know the right way to reply. She'd taken comfort in his praise. She curses him now for this comfort. All her life she'd hated Matthew Corrigan, and he never knew why.

Life in the city, in the flat with the Flahertys, had tormented her, the lack of solitude, life lived among strangers. Unlike the Flahertys, she could never go back home. A criminal in her own town, she had escaped by night, with stolen money. If she put a foot in the town, her father would have her arrested. They could dream about going back, sing about it. How she hated them for every song, and every tender word that was denied her. 'My mother died last spring/ When Ireland's fields were green/ Snowdrops and primroses beside her bed.' Her throat closed up when she heard them, with their Irish mother songs.

Would you like to know about my darlin' mother? Gibbering, a beast now in the darkened house my father built to hide her in, not a green field but desolation, dead grass and the colorless sharp choking weeds that cannot and will not be cleared. My darlin' father that would jail me if he saw his darlin's face. So sing on. Choke yourselves with lies about what you never had, and weep now for not having.

She felt her shame amidst the other greenhorns and held it up against their sorrow. Families that wept to see them go and letters of lament. *Come home and let me see your face before I die.* She was the criminal among them. Only Delia knew. Ellen would die grateful to her for that. For all her foolish tongue, she'd always kept Ellen's secrets. But among the weeping sons and daughters who'd been sent off with tears, with grieving, Ellen felt herself flayed. It made her credulous and grateful, grateful for the presence of Matthew Corrigan, who'd no more mind than the horses he tended. Grateful to be told by first the housekeeper, then Mrs. Fitzpatrick herself, that she would do. She seemed a girl of promise, but she must work hard.

The work was never hard. It was the nature of the life that killed her. All the lies that stopped her breath.

The room they gave her could so easily have been a pleasant room. Its darkness was no burden to her, nor its size. She brought in small objects for pleasure: a postcard she liked, showing the harbor, and one handpainted one, a scene of Brooklyn Bridge; a tin she'd asked the cook for, Famous Cake Box; a picture of a blonde child and a large black dog. It was the cast-off, the rag-endedness that was the room's cruelty to her, and the sense that what was deficient could so easily be fixed. Nails for her clothes instead of hooks. The comforters stained, marked with the waters of who knew what life or what disaster. The mantel and the floor inadequately varnished, ready to splinter, to cause pain. At least the door closed: she thanked God for that. But it didn't lock. In time, when she thought she had her mistress's favor, she asked: 'Could a lock not be put on my door? It would mean something to me.' Claire Fitzpatrick didn't hesitate, didn't give it a moment's thought. 'Our servants' rooms are never locked.' Reminding Ellen of what she hated most, making her hate herself and all of them because she had forgotten or assumed it could be otherwise. She was a servant, what they wanted was that she would not be herself to herself, but lay herself out to them for their own use.

The worst of it was living among the others. Coarse, ignorant, filthy girls, thinking themselves so great and fortunate. Matt Corrigan the king among them; the undermaids, fighting for the joy of polishing his boots. The cook a drunk, the housekeeper a pious ninny, always pressing on Ellen holy pictures and novenas, urging her to thank God for her good situation, offering her suggestions about underwear as she offered her mints so strong you'd kill your stomach with them. And all of them – the trades-man, the butcher's boy – thinking they had the right to call her by her first name. The impudence, the theft of it. She'd stopped them talking to her by her coldness, her coldness was her joy.

Delia had begged to visit, wanting to see the inside of the Fitzpatrick house. 'Maybe you'd slip me up to the mistress's room itself, one day when she's out, El. I could take a look.' But Ellen never would. Her job meant something. She was paid to keep things concealed. The thought of Delia in the mistress's room shocked her. It was Ellen's place to keep back the intruder, the violating eye or foot, the hand that touched and spoiled. She knew her part in the conspiracy: it was her understanding of the nature of the human eye, that thing that leered and gaped and sought to steal the good of everything, that loved defilement and the ruin of a thing, her understanding of all that made her good at her work. She hated the fine lace, the covered buttons, the exact folds, the silk ribbons, veils, false flowers, the embroideries, the small stitches: she knew the blood of slaves went into them. And yet they were her province. She was honorable; she valued, above all, her honor. Why would she let Delia into places that were not hers? Why would she let her into the library, the dining room, let her finger the silver or the coffee set that stood out on the sideboard, the chintz draperies with their pattern of choked carnations, holly-hocks, chrysanthemums? Why would she invite her friend? She hated all those objects but they were not hers, and she respected separations. She would not let the trespassers trespass.

So, when the day came that she couldn't stick it, it wasn't the disliking of the job itself that pushed her over, it was the sudden awareness that the Fitzpatricks, in paying her, thought they had bought her life.

'Ellen dear, stay in today, I must ask you this favor. I would never insist, you know that, but my sister . . . from Chicago . . . very suddenly. . . . We were, of course, surprised . . . and all must pull our weight. . . . Three weeks she'll be here, and her girls. She's always been that way, thoughtless, perhaps, but charming. Very charming. Well, I must ask you this favor. . . . Your day off, I know . . . but stay today, and help me. . . . Nothing I can name right now, just to have you around . . . a million little things.'

She'd had no plans that day. It would have been an easy thing to give it up. But, seventy years later, she can feel what she had felt then. She raises the claw hand that will not obey her. Memory enlivens it, makes it quick-witted; life flows through her arm. The memory of her refusal gives her back her biddable, compliant limbs. 'I will not stay in,' she hears herself say aloud.

'Surely it can't mean that much,' Claire Fitzpatrick had said.

It means my life. It means I draw my breath outside your presence and your will. It means that there is justice and you too abide by it. Shining justice with its buckler and its shield. I want no part of mercy, womanish and yielding. I will live by justice. My day free from you you may not have. My life apart from you you may not have. My life.

She did nothing on her days off. Walked. Bought thread, elastic. Rice powder she admired. Paper for her bureau drawers. Ink. Buttons. Throat lozenges. Not stamps. She was not one of those who needed to send money to the other side. To whom would she send money? The mother sitting in the dark? The father who would have her put in prison if he could? To Anna Foley, she had sent her address. Just that. She had money for luxuries. She did not covet clothes. But hats, ornaments for her hair. Yes, those she liked.

It was the walking on her free day that she loved. The wide high avenues, their carriages and trees. She knew those avenues were not meant for her kind, except as far as they were meant to be the servants that kept the fine houses running smoothly. Invisibly her kind held up the houses, were the stones of their foundations, their beams and props. But she did not begrudge the streets as she begrudged the rooms in the Fitzpatrick house. No, not at all. These avenues that were meant for the pleasure of the rich could do you good in spite of themselves. They gave hope; your lungs filled with the rich air of them, your tired bones could let themselves enliven and grow light.

She'd walk downtown, among the busy men so full of import and real destinations, and the girls, younger than her they looked, bank clerks and secretaries, stiff with responsibility and pride. Among them she'd take a cup of tea in a shop, as they looked at her and knew her as not their own. As they moved to rush back to their offices, she would languidly expand: Another cake, please, she would say to the cool waitress; tired, she could tell, of ladies and their small appetites. She would walk farther downtown and see what she'd been spared: the filthy tenements, the street-lived life, the bumptious children, the displayed life she hated, envied, feared. Gratefully, then, she'd walk uptown, her packages secure in her bag, her feet that she was proud of sore in their well-made boots. Content, she'd close the door behind her, watch the shadows thickening on the wood floor, comforting, reminding her that she had hours left, hours when she must answer to no one.

She would soak her feet.

She'd not give that up to please anyone. But what would have happened that day had she not, in her anger, run into Laura Fogarty? Laura Fogarty, whom she had met a year before, when they were each sent by their mistresses to do a two-month course with the genteel Miss Berringers in their rooms at the Gotham, a residence hotel on Madison and 89th. The rooms were weighted down with the sisters' plush draperies, the tiny marble bowl up which climbed alabaster doves, the replica of the Leaning Tower of Pisa (which she remembered from one of the nuns' books at school), the cracked carved wood of the large chairs. Five ladies' maids came there for a two-month course. The connivance of it. Now she makes a fist and brings it down, unsatisfying, on the white plastic arm of the bed. Where did that bed come from? It wasn't the bed she'd shared with Vincent. She'd never had a bed like it. She never would. Nor Vincent. Flimsy stuff they hated. Would not have it in the house. 'Two months,' she remembered the Miss Berringers saying, 'two months to learn the art of perfect care of Madame's clothes.'

Two months to listen to those old sticks, with their surprisingly youthful teeth that they showed when, lifting their lips like horses to get sugar, they smiled. Two months on brushing, folding, packing, invisibly mending. Buttonholes, handkerchiefs, preventatives against the moth, or remedies against the mud that stubbornly adhered to Madame's hem.

'D'ye call yours Madame, then?' Laura Fogarty had said.

'I do,' Ellen had whispered, resisting conversation.

'I wouldn't be caught dead.'

After that, Ellen disliked her.

But what if she hadn't run into Laura that day, the day she had refused Mrs. Fitzpatrick, the day rage bulked up against her line of sight, as solid as a building?

'I'm out of service and I thank God for it. You're a fool if you don't get out. A slave. Your life's never your own, and what's the use of living it that way?'

Ellen's pleasure in the free time they'd granted her became hateful from that instant. Why should she be grateful for the free breath, the moments free of another's power to order her seconds, minutes. Surely this was every human's right: each day to have some time alone. It was a dreadful thing, a terrible unnatural thing, she saw it now, to have your ear poised to answer a bell that tinkled – so genteel Claire Fitzpatrick thought, almost silent, she imagined. The slight, unobtrusive sound of wealth. You answered to a bell. Dogs did that, came not to their names but to the signal. The abasement of the name repeated constantly was as bad. 'Ellen, I'm tired to death, get my book, will you?' A dozen feet away from Claire Fitzpatrick the book sat. But she would ring for Ellen to run up three flights of stairs rather than rouse herself to walk a dozen footsteps. 'Ellen dear, help me with my sewing for the charity. I'm perishing of boredom. And while you do it, tell me something of your life.'

She made up lies. You will not have my life.

A slave's trick, lying. A slave's gratitude.

Laura Fogarty said: 'The lady runs my place is looking for a girl. You're a good needlewoman, I remember. Throw your chains off. Come with me.'

She followed Laura up a side street within sight of Union Square. The business signs were few, and her heart quickened to see the famous name on the brass nameplate. Madame de Maintenant. Claire Fitzpatrick yearned one day to have a dress made by Madame de Maintenant, but knew it was beyond her. Ellen and Laura passed the row of carriages, walked down a stairway to the basement, proud, were let in by a woman prouder than them both who nodded merely when Laura said: 'She's a good needlewoman. She needs a place.'

Ellen tries to sit up, but she can't; she's strapped.

She can't remember the look of that old place. She sees shadows, gaps, then objects disconnected from each other and their names. She sees scissors on a long white table. The ornate black legs of some machine. She sees sleeves, a set of sleeves it was her job to put into a dress someone has made.

She sees her own hands working with the sleeves. Her hands are real, they are palpable in the grasp of her eye. The room holds promise. She can recognize her hands. And a voice, severe, noting a fact. Answered by her own voice, noting another fact. Two girls, working together. Helpful to each other? No. Contingent to each other. I will get you something you have dropped. Praise? No. But later, the fierce, shy friendship of two girls, made up of adoration, mutual humility, a sense of honor, and momentarily the lifting of the curse that is their life: poverty, hard labor, the female sex.

Now through her mind pass all the bodies she has been. The girl child running behind the easy body of her mother, the mother's body like a ship, then older limbs, light, long, and painful in their joints, and the new arrivals: breasts, hair, blood, monthly pain. Grown used to that at last, the self lost, and herself a mother, who does not see herself a ship at ease in movement, but is disquieted by her unbalance and the shock, splash, danger-cry of giving birth. My body not my own but empty once again. The heavy softening: Where are the girl's light limbs? How have my breasts become this shape? Did you, child, do this to me? Take all that? The veins, the feet, hardening like trees and growing roots. And now she once again has taken on a lightness. She has become a leaf now, insubstantial to herself, in the light body of near death.

She is remembering the bodies she has been. And yet she understands: at any moment to herself she always has been the one body. The lost body forever lost. But not the voices. No. Not lost. Bella. She hears Bella's voice, as she has always. Bella. My friend. She calls out. Tries to remember: How did we first speak to one another.

First in shame. Shame that they passed each day the other girl, the courageous girl, shamed that they said nothing, shamed by the girl's brave eye.

Ellen had been at Madame de Maintenant's two months. She felt she'd bettered herself; she was delighted to be free of service, left alone, left to the silence of the workroom where she served. After work she could leave behind the person she was to them in that room, the wage earner, could take herself up once again, at no one's beck and call. For a few hours each night she had quiet, she had what she desired of silence, emptiness, where the ideas could sift down, the sights turn over and over, stones, dry stones: The thoughts I have.

Delia was living in West New York with Jimmy and three children now. At first, saving herself expense and helping Delia, Ellen had agreed to live with them, but she couldn't stick it. The noise of the children, Delia's hurt if Ellen wasn't speaking to her every minute of the day, her hurt if Ellen closed the door, her timid knocking: 'I've got a cup of tea here for you. Would you just take a look at this paper from the government. . . . It worries

107

me, this envelope. Does it look important? Can it be Immigration? We've done nothing wrong.'

Every brown or yellow envelope she thought was Immigration. That made Ellen furious. 'It's nothing, Delia. City water. Why would you think it was Immigration? You're a citizen, for God's sake, have been since you married Jim. Fortunately, they weren't giving out intelligence tests then or they'd have sent you on your horse forever as a fool.'

Delia cried when Ellen left them. One day she saw a sign in the window, rather near to Delia's, 'Room for Rent.' Her wages were quite good, and unlike other girls she had no family needing her money. She climbed the back stairs of Mrs. Devlin's boarding house and was shown the dark room with a view of a garden, and, if you leaned out and the night was clear, a glimpse, like a strip of mirror, of the river. 'That's fine,' she told the landlady, hardening her heart to what she knew would be Delia's pain. Delia was pregnant once again: she put it that way. She said: 'You need the room.'

'Oh, El, I can't believe it,' Delia wept, watching her friend pack, as if she were crossing the ocean, not a few streets. Jimmy Flaherty, jovial and addlepated as his wife, had helped Ellen with her things. So it was hers, the place she could close the door of, every night now if she wished. She knew Mrs. Devlin charged her too much. The other boarders in the house were rough and loud; she had nothing to do with them. The window of her room was cracked; the water in her basin froze over in winter. But it didn't matter. She could put her own things around her. She could keep herself to herself.

Her work at Madame de Maintenant's did not displease her. She was valued, praised by the stout forelady, whom she despised for meanness. Mrs. Bellamy thought herself a lady, above them, but Ellen knew her for what she was: gossipy, ignorant, a creature fattened and made solid on her greed and pride in being above others. Ellen was praised and was not interfered with. Each day they were given lunch, a privilege, the forelady told them, each day, nearly tearful over the mistress's generosity. 'Look at the sandwiches, the tea carried to you. Where else would you be getting this? Ladies: remember Madame every evening in your prayers and in the morning as you kneel beside your bed, let her name be first upon your lips, before your family even, for she gives you everything, and none of you know what she suffers.'

When she disappeared, racked with emotion, into the glass office that was an island in the center of the room, from which she could see them at every moment, see each thing they did, the girls would keep their eyes down on their lunches. No one would meet another's eye. But it was over lunch that she and Bella spoke, she and Ellen, who didn't know each other's names. They sat together; Ellen was pleased by the dark girl's angry look. She liked somebody looking as angry as she knew she was herself. Each day at lunch the dark girl's hunched back hid the book she read as she ate, not looking at her food, not looking up. But one day, reading, not looking, she knocked Ellen's full cup of tea onto the floor. Mercifully, nothing was soiled. They were on their knees together, swiftly cleaning up the evidence, for it would cause a reprimand and any moment the forelady could roll towards them, seeing the spilled tea as proof of everything she always knew: they were uncouth, ungrateful girls; they did not deserve a bit of Madame's kindness, and they never would.

Kneeling, acting with swift, efficient motions, they kept the damage from the enemy's all-seeing eye. And their eyes met. Ellen, kneeling, said to the other kneeling girl, 'Every morning on your knees let Madame's name be first upon your lips, before, even, your family.' They could lose wages if the laughter that they recognized in each other's eyes spilled out. They allowed their mouths slightly to twitch. Meaning: I single you out.

After that, she got the courage from Bella Robbins to do what she wanted: bring a book to work. She knew the world, the times were terrible. The year was 1913. Danger from Europe threatened the innocent Yankee air. She wanted to understand how these things came about. She wanted to read history. Not just the newspapers, which she devoured, but history. She found two books on the dustbin in the alley between Mrs. Devlin's house and the Farley house to the right: she plucked them, frightened of the defilement of books cast out, of the books themselves. Two books, one brown-covered, one blue. The brown: *A Shorter History of Ireland*. The blue: *The Course of Positive Philosophy*, by Auguste Comte. 'Would you be reading these?' she asked Mrs. Devlin. 'Would it be any trouble if I took them?' Mrs. Devlin shrugged, incredulous that a book could be of value.

At night in her room, feeling that she stole grace, she read the books that she'd found on the dustbin. She was unused to ideas: the reading was difficult. It was labor. Her mind strained, moving a heavy object. She cursed her mind. It was impermeable with stupidity. She cursed her training at the Presentation convent. Catechism and the simplest pious poetry, needlework (that she was grateful for: it earned her living), cookery, the painting of china or of fans. Ideas they feared, and in the house she lived in with her mother in the dark, in shame and hiding, there was not one book. Not even the Bible, which in Ireland was thought dangerous, to be read only with the guidance of a priest. Although the ideas she tried to take in overmastered her, she was in love with them, and even when she beat her temples with her fists – it was impossible, she was too dull – just after that, she would feel calm and honored by the grandeur of the enterprise she was allowed to have a part in.

So, while the other girls ate quietly and decorously, talking of their families, their beaux, dress patterns, Ellen Costelloe and Bella Robbins sat in silence. They ate and read. For months, in silence, saying nothing of what they saw behind their eyes, because the printed words were vulnerable: who knew what would become of them if they were turned to speech.

Ellen saw that Bella's book was not in English. German, she thought. She saw the writer's name, Schopenhauer, and the name abashed her. She was happy simply to know someone who could read a book by someone with a name like that. At the end of the day they walked out the door together, and wished each other good night. Respecting one another's silence, knowing the treasure of the other's anger, pride.

And then there was the day when they passed the accusing girl. Sitting on Madame's doorstep, saying to each girl who went in: 'If you go in and do her work and take her money, you put in your pocket money soaked in blood. She owed my sister wages. She still does. For the honor of working for Madame Maintenant,' the accuser went on, 'who could not pay her [the so-careless customers, they did not pay; and what could Madame do? they'd heard the forelady say], my sister went for months without her proper wages. Madame said she'd pay her in the spring. For now, would she take half? She would. Her shoes wore out; she didn't buy new ones. My sister died of her old shoes.'

Small, wild-eyed, mad, the girl cried out and the policeman was ashamed to move her. 'Do not believe her, the disgrace of her,' said Mrs. Bellamy.

Madame herself appeared, the first time any of the girls had seen her, a full figure and a beautifully coiffed head. She stood before them. Her carriage stupefied them all. She said, 'It is my deepest joy to know my girls are working happily and well.'

And then she disappeared above the stairs.

After she left, the girls, discommoded as if by a royal visit, blushed and giggled. Cookies were sent down with tea. The girl on the steps was made to disappear.

Three days after the girl was taken from the steps, Bella Robbins turned to Ellen Costelloe and said: 'I'm worried sick about a war.'

And her words were a knife slicing the thick air of the room of women sewing. Women stitching fine, beautiful stitches, women ignorant as dirt, skilled women, making things for other women who need do nothing for themselves, the unreal dreamwork of the dresses of the period. Bella's sentence let in life, breath, pulse, the whole world of ideas. It set the tone for the whole of their friendship. They did not, like other women, say to each other sentences beginning with the words 'I love, I hate, I fear.' Ellen told Bella nothing of her mother, not until it was too late. And Ellen never knew her friend had been for years the lover of a married man until he died (they were in their fifties) and Bella tried to kill herself. Bella's sister accused Ellen, 'You must have known.' Bella did not forgive her sister for telling Ellen. She said to Ellen, 'Don't believe her, what she told you. About why I did this. I don't know why I did it. There's no reason. I don't know why I did.'

Ellen allowed Bella, her cut wrists crossed on her bosom like a corpse's, to see the face it had pleased them both to turn a thousand times towards the world. The face of their shared superiority, of their contempt: two girls above it all.

'Who'd listen to that dope?' said Ellen. 'If she ever had an idea in her head it would have to leave the neighborhood. Driven away by its own loneliness.'

They said nothing more about the subject.

Ellen never disbelieved the sister. She feared the depths of her old friend.

Throughout their lives they gave each other names and information as other girls give each other pastilles, or open up their lockets, show their photographs. Bella would tell her about Spengler, Comte, German philosophers whose words could turn the world.

They would say, 'I believe in the religion of mankind.'

All Bella's family were atheists. Bella's father, a tailor, and her mother, and all eleven of their children believed, they said, in the divinity of man. 'Why do they invent pie in the sky except to keep your eyes off what's in front of you,' Bella's father had said. From Bella she first heard the sentence, 'Religion is the opiate of the masses.' She heard the bees in Knock James Church; that sentence could break up the swarm: it could dissolve the buzzing. 'Religion is the opiate of the masses.' Bella's family said sentences like that. Large sentences they were not afraid of. 'To drink tea is not to hew wood.' 'To cross a field is not to live a life.' Sometimes Ellen didn't know what they meant, but she was thrilled to hear the courage in them. The courage to make a sentence that could cover the whole world. No one else she knew would do it. From Bella's family she heard the words that made her see lives she had never known of. Hooves raised above the faces of women and their babies, dark modest girls torn apart by mustached brutes who said they had a right to, and a right to burn the towns. She heard in these stories the quiet of ruin, the silent aftermath, the departure of the men on horses, the respite till the next disaster struck.

The Robbinses trusted her. They said she didn't seem like other Christians. She was pleased at that. She'd never thought of herself as a Christian. A Catholic, yes, but 'Christian' was a word for Protestants. To them, she knew, it was the same.

Bella and Ellen preferred not sharing their time together with Bella's omnivorous, hard-breathing family; the warmth, drive, of all that life pressed on their leisure and they couldn't talk. Their talks were dark, night-blooming, violent bouquets. They were defiant: they were females who felt free to speak to each other about anything on earth. Except they would not talk about themselves. They did not speak of men or love. As if a flag had been flung out between them: None of that for us. No time. Hunger to know the world consumed them. They felt their deprivation and all their lost time. Bella wrote to Ellen from a cousin's in the mountains of upstate New York:

What matters most is time is passing. Time is passing and everything is missed. We are not living. I have been thinking: girls must get a living wage and then a shorter workday and many more girls must begin to think. It isn't that they don't want to think; they are all too tired to think. Thinking makes you interested in life. To be interested in life makes you a thousand times better as a person.

In the fog that is her current life Ellen sees perfectly the face of her friend Bella. She thinks of Bella in her dark dresses, with the white collars and sometimes the little bows that did her chin, her face, no good. It made a mockery of all that seriousness, of that understanding. She thinks of her friend's mouth, lovely, the fine, neat teeth, bluish in some lights, like skim milk, but strong: you'd think that they would last her. And the dark under her eyes so she never looked young or well. But the eyes themselves, the wonderful dark eyes. There were no eyes like that at home, so brown they had a touch of red in them, nothing like the brown eyes of animals, which were the only brown eyes in her childhood. You'd look at Bella's eyes and know there was nothing she couldn't understand. And she wouldn't be likely to think well of a thing. She'd fix her eyes on you, at first you would feel frightened. Some people never got over this, some people never relaxed around her. Delia. Vincent, too; she didn't like to say it but it was the truth. Vincent was always a bit frightened around Bella. Her hair, smooth and lusterless, collected into rolls around her ears.

Ellen pitied Bella's hair, the only thing to pity in this girl she worshipped as a creature far above her, yet who, miraculously, listened to her, was interested in her. They listened to each other. And she made Bella laugh. 'The world's a brighter place for you than me,' Bella had said to Ellen once. Wounding her to the quick.

She wanted to say to Bella: *Do you, my friend, not know me? This laughter, these words of mine, my way of putting things that makes you laugh, and that I mean to make you laugh, do you imagine that I do this out of joy? For pleasure? That I don't see as darkly as you see?*

I have seen more than you know. The children, born unborn, blood, mess, on the floor, the stain that was the hope of family life. My mother moaning: 'How can I have done this. Why do I do this?' My beautiful mother (her thin fingers transparent almost when she held them to the light to show off, to admire her ring), my mother turning, before my eyes, into a man, an animal, in darkness, in the total darkness of her mind, gibbering words no one can understand, her feet in black men's boots, like trees rooted, taking root. And in the pub where the money was made to send me to the Presentation Sisters, I have heard things, in the first days when my father would take me, thinking I didn't understand. I have understood what men think: they wish nothing but misfortune to their neighbors. Every good thing for another is a blow to them. They crave a stupor, a calamity. Anything to break the rhythm of the life they strap themselves to like a wheel that turns and never stops.

I have seen more. The woman taking my mother's place beside my father. In his bed. Her broad back I see, her thief's mouth, her fingers thick with the life she lives and doesn't even cry to keep a secret. I know what they do. I stiffen all my life against them. I become a weapon. I become an eye, a glass, a fire burning up their pleasure. You think the world is a bright place for me? I have always known. Men are brutal animals, the yellow teeth, the red eyes, and the damp, destructive breath. I see always in the darkness, in the silence. I keep it all in my mind, which, though not as good as yours, lets go of nothing.

She never said anything like this to her friend. They talked endlessly of life at the workshop of Madame de Maintenant. It was crucial that they demonstrate to one another in minute detail their knowledge of the workings of the place and their precise awareness of the injustices, tyrannies, falsehoods, insults, chicaneries, and downright thefts which they witnessed every day. Most important, they had to make clear to each other their contempt for the other girls, who believed themselves honored to be working in so fashionable an establishment and with so prized a clientele. So when the forelady, weeping in Madame's name, asked would they not wait for their wages till the slack season was over and the so-forgetful clients paid their bills, the girls fluttered their honored agreement like sweet birds.

Bella and Ellen said they wouldn't wait. 'Fire us if you like,' they said to the forelady. 'You'll never get two as good as we are for the sleeves.' The forelady's face turned red; the other girls feared she would die of heart attack, of shock. None of them would join Ellen and Bella, who were not fired, but were no longer given tea.

They reassured each other every day they weren't dupes, like other girls. Yet they didn't leave the workshop. They dreamed of escaping, but they knew that what they could escape to would be worse.

They stripped their dreams of the domestic with a devotion that was female in its thoroughness, as if they stripped a house for a spring cleaning. Their dreams came from their discussions at the Women's Trade Union League, a club for working girls: international governments, living wages, decent work. Being female, they could not dream dreams without rooms. The rooms they saw were not rooms with warm, inviting beds, or round familiar tables, around which the beloved few gathered to be fed. The rooms of their dreams were large and public. Underheated meeting rooms, lecture halls, the daunting rooms of the new Public Library, where they were told (but did not believe it, and feared to see for themselves) they had a right to be. They saw themselves at the heads of audiences, crowds of women like themselves listening to them, acting on their words. Or *they* would listen and then act. The men in their dreams stood at lecterns, or beside them, not too near, pointing out to them important passages from crucial books.

Streets were in their dreams. They walked the streets where trees flourished before them; they walked across a bridge. The lights fell on the river in drops, wafers, coins. They leaned over the bridge, rested for a moment, talking, then went on. They walked along a boardwalk; they could smell the ocean, it excited their talking, and encouraged their belief. They did not, in their dreams, talk to the young men in straw boaters; these were not dreams with places in them for young men. They were different from the other girls they saw. But they would change the other girls.

Outside the dream the girls around them did not change. And their notions of their new heroic selves were smashed not by the falling action of some fist, some whip, but by the silent power of the forelady and of Madame herself. At the Trade Union League, the organizers said: 'It's places like your shop that most need organization. The injustices in the name of gentility. Girls starving thinking it's an honor. Wages almost as low as sweatshops. But a nice room, a fire, tea.' Ellen and Bella thought but did not speak of the young girl who sat on the stone steps demanding her sister's wages, the girl whose eye they did not meet. They took with them the union cards, with the blank spaces for names and addresses. They tried to talk to some of the more friendly girls. But they were met with silent, fearful glances, or the genial upturned face of the non-listener. They decided they would put a card down at each place. Lying on her bed, Ellen remembers, though there is no act she can perform now, therefore no reason to fear action, strapped in her bed whose plastic armrests are the color of a poisoned shell (*This was never mine*), even now she remembers her fear. She remembers lying in her bed at Mrs. Devlin's, the street sights through her window: the stiff, city trees, bunched, conical in the darkness. She was rigid in her fear. She remembers digging her nails into her palms for courage. She remembers saying to herself, fear making her organs light, acute, and lively: Tomorrow we will do it.

And they did. On the dark wooden tables among the mix of threads, scraps, scissors, tissue papers, they placed down cards that said: I _____ wish to become a member of the Women's Trade Union League. They did not meet one another's eye. Then, suddenly, one of the girls, one of the ones who most disliked them, rose, pretending she must show some work to the forelady. But they knew where she was going. The forelady, looking at no one, disappeared up the stairs. And, a few minutes afterwards, she came back. She opened the glass doors of her office. Everyone in the large room was waiting, pretending all the time they weren't.

But nothing happened. Nothing ever happened. Ellen and Bella gave out union cards. But no one responded, not one of the girls.

In their discussions of this, which they had endlessly that winter, walking at night up and down streets where the air challenged their failure with its expectant breath, in the tea rooms where they allowed themselves their weekly luxury, they puzzled out their failure. At the meeting of the Women's Trade Union League, no one could understand why they failed. But no one blamed them.

Bella blamed the Church, the state, the family: those things of which she refused to declare herself a part. Ellen pretended baffled anger. But she knew, although she never said, that she and Bella

116

were not successful for the simple reason that they were not well liked.

In their friendship there was room only for themselves. They were exclusive and excluding; their friendship had a force no marriage could approach; they spoke of the world only as something they would put their mark on. They'd excluded Bella's family, and Delia, who cried every Sunday when Ellen refused to go to church, saying that her religion was the religion of humanity, her divinity the divine human soul. Delia would cross herself, pushing her children from the doorway so they wouldn't hear. 'God forgive you, Ellen,' she would say. 'God bring you back to the True Faith. It's being friendly with that Jewish girl that did it.'

Ellen would turn on Delia: 'You belong back in the bog. This is America. We're all equals here. If you say a word against my friend, I'll never come to your house again.'

That threat was too terrible for Delia. 'You're right, Ellen,' she said. 'It's America. We're all alike.'

But they were not all alike and there were times when she knew that she was more like Delia than like Bella. The home fear, the home silence: 'Mind you, I've said nothing,' you'd hear them say at home. They wanted things kept in the dark. In some ways they were right. But then your tongue stuck to your mouth and wouldn't give out information, you spoke to placate, fob off; cause forgetfulness. To entertain. Bella could speak up at the Women's Trade Union Lectures. Ellen could not. She thought that if she said the first word everyone would know her ignorance. She would be banished, her huge lacks would be seen. They would have no choice but to turn her away. She thought that if she kept silence she might be safe.

Delia would come to Ellen's room, touch the covers of the books as if they were dangerous or sacred objects, look at her old friend whom she had known from childhood, and from home, look at her with that wide gaze that understanding never touched, and say: 'I can't get over it, El, coming where we come from, reading books like that.'

She raged that Delia should speak out the thing she feared: that it was all ridiculous, you were who you were born, and you were born nothing. She heard the home voices, buzzing at her: 'You particularly, Ellen Costelloe, we in the church, among the swarm, know who you are. We know your father and your mother. We know you from your birth. You are no different from us. You are no better.' One of the favorite sayings in the town was this: 'Two things never change: the mist, and the nature of man.'

When she'd heard them at home, in the churchyard, in the market, saying things like that, she'd wanted to stand beside her father, saying to them: *He and I are together, the same. Whatever he is it's better than you ever thought of being.*

Her father didn't have thick, dead eyes like the rest of them, reflecting the belief that nothing could be done in the world, it was useless to begin to raise your hand. Their heavy feet trudged like those of the cattle they fattened and led to death, trudged from one day to the next, the day of their death no different from any other, the last, only, in a series of identical dead days. Her parents hadn't been like that and so the parish was relieved by their disasters, reveled in them as if their touching pleasure, liveliness, had brought as a matter of course illness, sin, madness, the betrayal of a daughter, and her leaving in the dead of night. When these thoughts came to Ellen, in her bed in America, she wanted to get up, go back, stand with her father, stand against the town. She'd force the other woman out, then stand beside her father, help him with the business, they would prosper, they would stand apart from the thick crowd of the townspeople, whose envy would rise up, steady and predictable as coins in the till, rising up like the incense at Benediction in Knock James Church. They'd have their place, she and her father, at the head of things, the other woman gone, their pride well earned, and justified. Not to be cast down.

But how could there be pride in the mother, gibbering in her chair, in the darkness? She could not be brought out to the light of day. The noise of her words that weren't words was low and repetitive and damning, like the swarm noise. It was the worst curse in the world: *Forget your efforts. Nothing will prevail.*

The parish had been right about the bees. It had endured their swarming and had not been harmed. Action was danger, and the lie that there was nothing there needing their action had been their safety. Who had cleared the walls of all those clots, and spreading stains? The honey that spilled down and that she knew could ruin the walls? It hadn't. Who had prevented ruin? Secretly, at night? The priest? Old women? Young, married ones leaving their babes at home at the priest's whispered request? They had prevailed.

Nothing had happened. She had wished them the harm of their lie and it hadn't harmed them. Only she had been harmed. The sound of the bees swarming came into her dreams, telling her everything was useless. There was nothing to be done.

It had prevented her, the sound of swarming and the lie that had not brought its rightful punishment, from speaking up about the books she read in the Trade Union League reading circle. It had caused her to fear the others, caused her to crawl, shamed as a child who vows to run away from home and turns back at the first sign of a stranger, back to Delia and Jimmy's house for the old food, the soda bread, potato with butter and a drop of milk, the stirabout, the meat cooked black, the dense, muffling comfort of the sweets: rice pudding, trifle, custards, sago. Delia dishing out plate after plate. She came to them after the meetings where her silence was her shame and talked to Delia and Jimmy about the books. She abashed them into silence as they fed her the meals she craved and gave her the false homage that she craved like the soft foods: 'El, you're a marvel. What you know. Imagine, Jim, from my own town. My best friend knowing that.'

Did she go to Vincent for these things as well? No. Yes. Yes and no.

He said, like her, that you could do something in the world. The world could change. But she had never known if he believed it, or said it to keep her love.

The memory of Vincent's body comes back to her on her bed, known as she has no other thing: face, chair, ring, article of clothing. Better known than her own body, for she has looked freely at the whole of his as she has not looked at her own.

Warned against her own flesh, she never caressed it as the loved object that Vincent's had been. They would never tell you not to touch the man's body, assuming that no girl would want to. But she had wanted to. From the beginning she had. It comes back to her now, his body, but gradually and not at once. The shoulders first, high spurs of bone, the lively tendons of the neck, the chest with its enchanting whorls of hair, flat, smooth, that she has followed with her lips, for she was never shy with him once she had given herself over. Her belonging came to her like language. This body, the words, the phrases she had known. Following the path of hair down to the narrow waist, the hips, the sex she did not fear, the satisfaction of its rising up with yearning for her, and the strong, protective legs, the feet, boyish, white, surprising for a man who worked as he did. The hands come to her next, then the arms. Hands that had traced and found her, smoothed and calmed and then aroused. Afterwards holding her face, kissing it as he held it in his hands, kissing her eyes, her nose, making her laugh with boyish kisses on her neck. Saying: 'Imagine, you, my wife.'

Wife. A simpler word than *husband.* Older, preferable. More intact. She was glad of being Vincent's wife. Whatever else she might feel, she had never been wrong to be with him. How dark he'd been when she had met him. Like an Arab prince, like an Italian, she had thought. She'd loved the darkness of his hair against the white skin, surprising a man's skin could be so white. The hiddenness of it, his whiteness, so that she'd wanted to protect it. And as he grew older age spots appeared on the white expanse of his back. How? She could never see them coming. Only knew that they were there. His hands, small for a workman, were covered by sparse, dark hairs.

Vincent.

She calls out to him now. He doesn't answer. He has left, as she has always feared he would. No, that's not right. She thought he never would. She had believed him. She had made him promise. He would never break a promise.

Vincent.

No answer.

Where is Vincent? Why doesn't he hear her calling out for him? Is he pretending not to hear, to punish her? Because she knocked him down? She knocked him down because she thought he was making advances towards her. He was reaching towards her skirt. She wouldn't let him. She wouldn't let him come to her in the state she was in. She knew what she was: a wreck, a horror. She must hide herself from him. She owed him, out of respect for what they once had been, that much.

They had been beautiful, young. High-colored. They had talked, though not as well as she could talk with Bella. Vincent hadn't the quickness of Bella's mind, hadn't read as much. But talk with them had come from and gone back to the body. Garlands their words were, that twined around them, joining them, limb to interlocking limb. It was more truthful, what they said, because of that other knowing. And excitement, at the first, when she had talked at Delia and Jim's table, about the reading circle. She watched how his eyes were fixed on her – riveted, he'd later said – when she talked about the effects of the War and the sacred rights of every worker. As he looked at her she knew her power. She'd smoothed her hair around her ears to draw attention to it. She'd let her eye fall boldly on his, though he'd not met it. She'd got up, gone to the shelf for more sugar, though she hadn't the need of it, so he could see her figure and her walk. And for the first time in her life she felt that stretching outward, stretching up, and felt him moving towards her steadily, inevitably, like a flame. How many times they had sat at Delia's table, him saying nothing, or saying, 'It's just great, the thoughts you have. It's a great education for me just to hear you speak.'

And then, after some months of sitting, listening, he'd invited her for a walk, and told her he was a great union man himself. It was the way of the future, unions, he said, it was a tide that couldn't be turned back.

He's gone, to punish her. She knows she deserves it. Over all the years, she'd done things to deserve his punishment. Not telling him about her mother. Lying, saying her parents both were dead.

He'd turned from her when she told him finally.

'Why didn't you say anything? Why did you lie all these years?'

She said nothing. She deserved this from him; to raise her voice in her own defense would be to block justice. And to expose her mother and her own life, spent keeping her mother in the dark.

'I always wondered why you married me,' he said, refusing to look at her. 'I knew I wasn't up to you. Now I know you did it for this trick.'

She told him she was afraid to go back home. Afraid of what the father would do to her. He didn't believe her.

'Afraid? You've never been afraid of anything. You wanted to play me for a fool.'

Afraid of nothing? You, too, my husband never knew me. Almost always I have been afraid. You think because I stand up to employers, have a sharp tongue for poor souls who haven't got the wit to cut me back, because of this, you think I have no fear. I have always been afraid. No. Not always. No. Not before, when she was happy, well, when we would run, sing, make things in the kitchen, when my father would come home, embrace us both, and call us 'my two beauties,' dancing with her, twirling me, my cheek against his jacket, I was not afraid then. No. Why would I be?

But afterwards, my mother, shamed and shameful, lying in her failures, in the mess, the family blood I had to find, my mother growing darker and the father turning from us (you are turning from me: you will not be back), always after that I have been afraid.

She'd wanted to kneel before him, not in supplication, but to take his face in her hands so he would have to look at her. But she didn't. She turned her face to the wall; she closed her eyes; she accepted her punishment: that he would never understand.

Now, lying on her bed, sixty years later, she remembers his face. She understands: he has been waiting all these years, pretending to forgive, to punish her for what she did. It's why he isn't with her now; she understands it all; he is away from her to punish her. She is alone, more alone than her mother ever was.

She calls out. Strangers she has never seen approach. 'Mother,' someone calls her, but this stiff face can not have been a child of hers.

When the letter came from Anna Foley she'd felt her life unraveling. Everything that she had: her house, her husband, children, safety in this new world, disintegrated. Alone in the house with her two babies, she sat at her table and wept. She ignored their cries until she couldn't any longer; absently she fed them, not seeing them for her tears. She put them in their rooms to sleep, not caring if it was time yet. She got into her own bed, shameful, in the middle of the afternoon, she'd never in her life done such a thing, and hid in the darkness of the blankets. Over and over again she read the letter that Anna had sent; not that Anna had written it herself: she couldn't read or write. She'd had a nephew do it. Someone whose face Ellen didn't know had written to her, 'You must come and get her now. I have a sickness, and it will get worse. I cannot do for her like before. I've said nothing to your father. I'll give you the chance. As promised. But act soon.' Before she'd left, on the night the moon made the road white and the flat fields shone before her, Ellen had made Anna Foley promise: 'If anything goes wrong with you, don't go to my father. Get in touch with me. I'll provide for her. She's my charge. He'll not have her to himself.'

122

They shared a horror that he would have any charge of her. Him and that woman. They could imagine what the two of them might do. Leave her to grow into an animal, in her own filth. Ellen and Anna knew what she required: bathing, feeding, like a baby. But she had none of a baby's loveliness. She had her heaviness instead. Still, they honored what she had been. The other two would not.

It had been in the back of her mind; it was what she saved her money for, when other girls were sending it back home or spending it on dresses. She was saving it, not knowing what could be done with the mother, but thinking she would buy a house for her, where they could live beside each other, and the mother could be sheltered, kept from view.

After two years in the apartment in the Bronx, Vincent began to mention to her dreams of a small house, out in the country, raising her own food (would Ellen feel up to it? He'd teach her; it would not be hard). His wages were good, he was a machinist now, they could afford it. He saw greenness, animals, the warm eggs under the hens, the gardens he would dig for her, one for vegetables, one for flowers. While he saw that, she saw a place to hide the mother, and in Vincent a man who would help her keep the mother from sight, who would take the mother in. She saw not the children's health, not all the money saved on homegrown food, but a place with an upstairs. A room with something for the mother to look out on where she could live her life in peace. Where she could die kept from the tearing hands of the deserting father, from the hard eyes of the woman in his bed.

But now the time had arrived, and she knew she couldn't do it. Lying in the dark, pulling the covers over her for protection, she saw her father's face. The harsh eyes, the prosecuting mouth. She saw him gathering the strong boys, the muscled men in his employ. And around them, all the people in the parish, calling her thief, ringing around her, swarming in their accusations, lifting up stones to strike her. But her father won't let them. He waits for the police, who take her from the square, where all the town have assembled around her. Her father turns his back. He allows her to be taken away; he tells them to show no mercy. But she doesn't care; it's his eyes she fears, more than the policemen, more than the accusation of the parish, the eyes that turn from her, the back that stiffens itself against her, the arm that links up with the arm

123

of that woman who shares his bed, their backs turned to her, disappearing down the road.

She lay in her bed, weeping, shamed in front of Vincent. He should never see her in this shameful state. She had to tell him that she couldn't do it, and he had to help her. She said she'd never ask him for a thing again, not even a word between them. Only he had to do this thing.

She wanted to cry out to him. She wanted to open her arms, beg him for comfort, throw herself against the hardness of his body, pull him by the hair, say to him: *You have to understand me. This is why I couldn't tell you. What if you said no before we married? Then I could never have you, and I need you, you are the one thing in my life I cannot be without. You never understand you are the stronger of us. You can live without me. Without you I have no life. In all my life, only you have not been a stranger.*

But she said nothing. She lay in her bed, covered herself, and wept. Her life was lost to her. All the years, plans, self-denial and renunciations, acts of courage. And now that it was the time she couldn't go. The sight of her father's eyes, his back turning against her, his sending her to prison while he went off with the other woman – none of this would she be able to bear.

Vincent refused to sleep beside her. He didn't speak to her for several days. He took the children away to stay with Delia. He came back into the house. He turned the light on in the bedroom. 'I was thinking about things,' he said. 'Suppose I could arrange it, then, to go there for you. Do it square. Talk to your father. Tell him we could pay him back the money you took from him. Say she'd be better off here. He'd have to see it.'

She nodded, she barely had the strength for assent. His goodness overwhelmed her. She was overwhelmed with love. She couldn't meet his eye. His goodness was like a natural thing, like rain, or clement weather, growth in the earth, shade when the sun was merciless. *Vincent, can you love me as much as this? So much? Really as much as this?*

'Thank you,' she said. 'It would be good if you could do all that.' She never said another word to him before he went. She packed his bags.

She did the necessary things. Bought the tickets from savings she had hidden from him for this purpose. The papers: the mother was old, she was infirm, but they would be responsible, they both were citizens, her husband had a steady-paying job. 'A machinist. Very good,' the man said. Protestant. 'A very steady job.' 'Yes,' she said, her large heart beating, spreading like a stain, 'there'll be no problem sir.' 'No, not with your husband and you vouching; and she'd not be taking away, like so many of them now, some citizen's good job.' Laughed, she had to laugh now with him. 'No, sir, I'll see to her all myself. We've a nice house in Queens. Sir, another time I'll bring you some of our good eggs.' The greenhorn palaver they expected and gave things over for. She took the papers from him, left in terror: he could change his mind.

He never told her what he saw in the town she had left as a thief. He only came home, bringing her mother with him. She understood that, on the boat with her mother, he must have seen to her needs. She wasn't filthy on arrival. Did he do everything, or did he pay someone, a stranger, a woman he'd never seen? Would her mother have let him wash her on the boat, or would she have kept her modesty? She was ashamed that he might have had to do these things. But after all that, all that he'd done, how could she have done what that stiff-faced one, her daughter, said she did? She wouldn't knock him down. She'd die for him. She'd always been ready to do that.

A shadow, spade-shaped, the width of a hand, falls on her brain and she remembers that it isn't true, that after that she'd never hurt him.

After the son's death, she turned from him, again.

Because he kept her from her grief.

And, she remembers now, she pushed him down, because he reached for her skirt, and she knew what he wanted, she couldn't let him, she had to keep her body from him, in honor of what they had been.

She didn't mean to push him down.

Only away.

She weeps now, for the things she never meant to do.

Vincent, you must know the things I never meant.

She thrashes in the ugly bed, as if she can wash it all into a blankness if she moves her head wildly enough. Why will the blankness not come now?

The blankness will not come. The sight comes back now, when she doesn't want it. Where are you, lovely mother, your

complexion pink, your hands transparent, and your clever feet?
*I cannot forgive you. Because you must have let my husband see your
shame.*

Her mother lived with them in the house. Her eyes were dead.

Vincent said: 'I think she's happy here. She's happy for this
change.'

Almost, sometimes, the mother looked as though she could be
happy. Ellen let her hold the baby; the mother almost let her dead
eyes come alive.

John was born while the mother lived among them. Was that
why she loved him best? Did the presence of the mother bless his
birth?

She felt the other two were born to be against her, by their
births to thwart, balk, halt her progress, press her down. The first
one, Magdalene, named foolishly, she thought, for Vincent's
mother, who had died in childbirth shortly after he left home. He
blamed himself, she knew that, for he'd helped her as the others
in the family did not. 'You were in Cork, Vincent,' she said, 'for
years before that; she'd grown unused to your help by the time
she started this baby.'

'No, I could have helped.'

So she allowed the daughter a foolish name, and it began a life
of foolishness. She never could respect the child. All of her a
softness. No resistance to the world. She felt she must resist against
the softness of the child or else be swallowed up in it. Already she
felt, in marriage, in motherhood, that which she most valued in
herself beginning to be lost. She had no time to read or think. She
grew ashamed when Bella visited, ashamed when she had to admit
she'd not read the last books Bella had left her, ashamed when she
saw Bella slip the new books back into her bag, trying to be tactful,
trying to keep Ellen from feeling shame.

But she felt shame that her mind was being softened and pressed
down in service to two babies. The second one knew her anger,
and pulled herself back, stiffened herself, and made her body a
refusal to be supplicant, like her sister. The second child understood
what the first had not. She turned away.

Ellen was jealous of Vincent, popular and successful in his job.
Jealousy and pride. The two strands: *Why him and not me?*

But with the mother in the upstairs room, she felt herself

becalmed: a small boat moored in shallow water. She gave herself up to it. It pleased her to have given birth to a male child. She felt that she did not have to resist this one. She allowed the days to wash over her. She didn't try to read. She lost track even of the newspaper, until Vincent chided her. 'You must keep up,' he told her, 'it's a great world out there, a great day for the workingman. You have to keep up.' At night he wanted to talk about it: the new world he saw growing outside the house. Once, in front of Bella, he said, 'It's time men knew there are some women have twice the brains of them. It's certainly the case in this house.' He said that to honor her, in front of Bella. She was spooning out tapioca. She banged down the spoon in rage. Furiously, she shook a spoon of tapioca under her husband's nose. 'That's the brains of me, and not an inch above it.' His praise mocked her, she felt, before her friend. Bella and Vincent looked away, pretending to see nothing.

Did Vincent like talking to Bella? Or was he too afraid? He never did relax with her, but he admired her. 'She's a person you can learn from,' he'd said. And she listened to him talk about the union, about the Democratic party. Sometimes when they talked, Ellen would feel her eyes grow heavy, would realize that she had fallen asleep a moment, because she was so tired from the children, from the mother, she couldn't follow their ideas.

Sixty years later, the events of what has been her life stretch out before her like a river covered over by a mist. The mist clears in patches; the water becomes visible, and then from the leaden band of water rise up mountains: events in her life. Then the mist falls once again, and nothing is distinguished. She is lost. She can hear sounds through the mist, like conversations in fog. The voices fade and even her fear fades: she gives over to the undifferentiated blur, it's better that way. It will lift, or it will not. The mountains, the islands, will show themselves or will submerge forever. She is quiet and no longer angry. It is summer evening and the sun, late in descending, vanishes. The birds are silent. In the heavy darkness nothing more will come to pass.

But where is Vincent? The moments when she is free of fear have gone. He has left her among strangers.

All her life, she knew she would live out this moment. It always came to her, this fear, pushing up through fog: she knew it would become her life. The night she made him promise, she was lying awake, feeling her sleepless, lively skull, she saw herself alone like this, in fog, and among strangers. The sound of swarming came to her, a young woman, alone with her new husband in a bed in the first light of the morning of a sleepless night. She couldn't stand the mocking voices she couldn't shut out. She heard the swarm, the voices once again, but now in fog, she called out to him, knowing he was happy in his sleep. She said his name to wake him. She wanted him to give up his happiness. She dug her nails into his palms.

'Swear you'll let me die in my own bed. Not among strangers.'

He has tricked her. She brings her lips together and forms the curses she heard from the drunken men in her father's pub, from the sailors or the seasick men on the boat coming over, from ancestors, dead a hundred years before her birth. The curses and the filth rise up. She opens her mouth to release them.

The stiff face comes towards her. 'Calm down, Mother.' The stiff face says prayers.

Now she will curse the prayers, brought to this place from hatred.

'Banish this evil spirit,' the stiff face says.

'Get her away from me. Send her back home to hell.'

'All right, Theresa. I'll take over now.'

Bella. 'Religion is the opiate of the masses.' Bella will send the lying stiff face from her, back to her home in hell.

'Gran. It's all right, Gran. I'm with you. I won't leave.'

A man's voice. She remembers now. It's Daniel. She can tell him. She can ask where Vincent is. He will tell her the truth.

'Where's your granddad gone to?'

'He's been sick. He's coming home today. That's why everyone's here, for a celebration, Granddad's coming home.'

His hand is warm and full of health. She remembers this hand, and the other one, the girl's hand. These were the children who made her want to go on with her life. She can't remember why. Only that they were interesting to her. She could watch their minds absorb the world. Knowing. Watching them take in the world made her willing again to be alive.

Those children, Dan and Cam. She had told them they must go into the world. She had allowed them to do it, she had made it easy for them. And they had done it, and come back to her, with the world in their hands, laying it before her, so it could be hers as it was theirs.

So she could, again, wish to live her life.

Vincent. Forgive me. I was proud of you.

'The union,' she shouts out.

'The union, Gran?'

She tries to sit up. Her vision clears. She can see Daniel's face, knows that she can say something that he will understand.

'Brave,' she says.

Now the mist comes up, exposing one patch of the river, one island becomes visible. The decade of the 1920s, once a blur to her, her young motherhood vague, a watery existence she can never settle on. But she remembers the excitement of the years when Vincent, risking everything, worked to build a union, when they could have killed him for it. He told her that, 'I could be killed for it, they could kill me, they'd be glad to do it if they could,' and she was proud of him, 'but let them try.'

'The hell with them, then, Vincent. No sense living if you can't stand up and say who you are.'

She couldn't remember what the issues were or why the bosses fought them. But she could bring back the feelings, the excitement, code words Vincent would tell her, jokes played on the company spies, 'beakies' they were called. Tuesday substituted in the code for Monday. 'We know they're listening in,' Vincent would say, 'so we say on the phone, "We'll have a meeting on the Tuesday. By the way," we'd say then, "I'd a letter from the family at home, they're extending the cowhouse on the west side of the farm to accommodate twenty-three new head of cattle"; that means, you see, El, this is great now, that we're meeting at the place we all know about on Twenty-third Street, on the Monday night.' Excited as a boy and boyish in his ardor, he would come to her at night, home from a late meeting, now older, heavier in his body, and his rough cheek, cold from the outside, would arouse her. In the mornings he would talk at the breakfast table to the children about starving workers, and the hope of the trade unions, about Sacco and Vanzetti, the tragedy of it, Al Smith, he's Irish, children, but he might yet be the President, about how the Pope himself would sooner or later endorse labor unions, he knew it on good authority, they needn't fear what the priests said. She'd get angry then: 'What do you care a damn for the priest's word, there's not a one of them who's not a liar or a thief. Or a pansy on the top of it.'

She'd never go into a church. Vincent would take the children. The parish priests would try talking to her, series of them coming to the house over the years. *Now, Mrs. MacNamara, don't you think.* Some pretending they had just stopped by. One, threatening her with hellfire, in her kitchen, told her of her melting bones to come, her crackling flesh, eternal separation from the ones she loved. 'What kind of God is it that you worship, a God who would do that?' she said to him. 'The same God you say separates babies from their mothers if they die before a splash of water hits their heads.' The face of Bella clear before her eyes. *I believe in the religion of mankind.*

'You're nothing but a Red,' the priest said, with his heavy accent. 'No better than the satanic Communists of Russia.'

She thought of Bella's family.

'I'll be asking you to leave, then, Father. I didn't cross the ocean so I could be insulted in my own home.'

Arguing with Vincent against religion. 'You're a union man. They've threatened every Irishman who has a union card with eternal damnation. They've held the labor unions back for fifty years.'

Turning the radio up so he would have to hear the voice of Father Coughlin. 'This is the mouthpiece of the church you want your children brought up bending the knee to. Filth. Poison. And you want their veins opened up to that.'

I will not close my mind or bend the knee.

The children, though, were pious. Seeing of course their father, who was kinder than she, who never shouted, did not turn away, had not the tongue that mocked. They thought, perhaps, his kindness was from God, that perhaps God would keep them from her anger.

Even John: 'I'm going to be an altar boy. You wouldn't stop me, Mom.'

'No.'

'You'll help me with my Latin.'

'I'll help you learn anything.'

'But you won't come see me serve the Mass?'

'I'll not set foot inside a church.'

He didn't say 'Even for me?' As Magdalene would have. Theresa would not, she'd have made her mother feel she was missing something, and was glad she was able to keep her mother from a thing of value. Her prayer a thorn to pierce her mother's flesh.

Her John.

Her boy. His body growing up, a tree beside her. Honor, shelter, and a place of pride. Her son. Intact, he seemed to her. And safe. The only one of them not frightened by her mother. Although Ellen understood why she could appear frightening. A woman with hair growing on her face. A beard. Like a goat.

A man.

'Does Grandma have a beard? Why, Mom? Is Grandma a man?'

'*Your grandma loves you. You must love her back.*'

John sitting on the floor as she cooked. Knowing her need of his company but saying nothing.

The girls refused to look at their grandmother. Magdalene: Don't make me, Mama. Theresa: I will not.

Then Vincent getting sick. How scared the children were, and her anger at the children for the fear they wore so he could see it on their faces. 'You're no good to your father with those faces.'

But she was angry at Vincent when they brought him to her sick, near death. The doctor said a heart attack. 'At his age, Mrs. MacNamara, barely forty, he will have to find another job, an easier one, and the union work is too much for him.' Shop steward he was, and meeting every night. 'Tell him the decision is his, the doctor said. Stop it or die.'

She was angry at her husband's white, sick face. She wanted to scream at him: 'How could you do this to me?'

He knew that her voice lied when she was so sympathetic, that she made her body lie. He cried when they told him he had to quit the subways. He turned his face to the wall so she could not see the tears on his face. 'A change will be good, I guess. Everyone needs a change.'

The strike happened while he was in the hospital. It hurt her to see the others come and tell about it. She was dying to know, but she wouldn't listen. If he'd missed it she would miss it too. She saw him drift away when they talked about it, the pain of it sickening him once again. She was angry with them for going on with it, angry at them for having had the strike without him.

She wanted to scream at them that they were selfish, disloyal, they should have waited for him, all the thousands of them, she didn't care; it was unjust that it should happen while he lay in hospital. She wished ill to the union. She was furious when they offered her a job in one of the change booths after he'd used up all his sick pay. 'We were thinking, since you've this great interest in the union, you could become a member. Sort of take his place.'

'Thank you, I've found another situation,' she said, clenching her fists so as not to strike out at them. As if she'd be a part of something he couldn't be! As if she'd jump in and watch him on the shore, separate, ill, ashamed of the failure of his body, as if he'd failed her as a man.

Bella got her a job in Ratner's millinery. Once again with silly girls she had no patience with. But her fingers were dull now; she didn't like the work, the heavy materials: wool, felt, pushing the needle through: no fineness to it, skill was nothing. Bella talked her into joining the union. She couldn't refuse, but she'd not go to any meetings, though the talk of them excited her, and she pressed Bella for every detail of what was said. But she'd not do that to Vincent. He never knew she had a union card. She was happy to quit the job after a year; it made her feel old, out of the swim of the young girls.

She quit when Vincent took the job with Patent Scaffolding. She didn't understand his work. Making up models of scaffolds for buildings. Engineers would give him plans. He'd make up models, like a child's toys, she thought, she didn't respect the work as she did when she believed he made the subways run. And working for a company that didn't have a union.

'How could there be a union, El, there's only five of us in the whole operation.'

He knew she'd lost her pride in him.

With this new work, he wasn't a man Bella could understand her pride in being married to. Though Bella was kind, said he'd done the right thing, Ellen knew that Vincent's step down from union work meant he had lost his footing in Bella's life. It was never the same between them.

And then, when John died, Bella, too, told her not to grieve. She closed her heart to her then. *You have not understood that I have lost my life.*

132

Why was he taken from her? Of them all the most beautiful, the bravest?

And before his dying why were those last hours with him spent fighting about a whore? The girl he'd got with child. 'The foolishness, the filth,' she'd said. 'Why were you with a girl like that?'

Like her own father, foolishness with a woman.

When she thinks about the ways of men, she tries to get out of the bed, but she is strapped, she tries to tear herself free. I will not submit to the ways of men. She remembers why she struck Vincent. The ways of men do damage in the world.

And her own son. Like that as well. Like her father. With that foolish girl. Who sat, smoking her cigarette, painting her nails, crying into her bunched-up tissues. Her perfume so cheap it made the house stink of sex. And nothing in her mind but what's between a man's legs and her own and how to make the most of the whole foolish business.

Unable to keep herself pure for memory of the dead man she claimed she loved.

Like most women, her word meant nothing.

I was right to take the child from her. He meant nothing to her, I knew it all along. That is why I did it. Her grief, her memory were nothing to my own.

She recalls her towering grief. The telegram. 'Your son, an honor to his country.'

Her mind, she could see her mind, a door blown off a house in a wild storm. I have lost my mind.

She felt herself become an animal. From pain she threw herself against one wall and then another, pulled the pins out of her hair and then her hair out of her head, scratched at her flesh, happy to draw blood.

I will not live my life.

I will no longer be in my life.

The grief that towered, cut off sight.

My son is no longer in the world. I will not, either, live. My lungs will stop, I will not allow them to draw breath. My heart, I will allow my bones to crush it. For the best.

I hate this life.

The buzzing noise inside her head. Mocking. Like the electric noise at the power station Vincent took her to. The lights that flashed in darkness.

To stop the buzzing she banged her fists against her head, her head against the floor, on the hard table. Vincent tried to stop her.

'Stop, Ellen, stop, you'll kill yourself, you'll hate yourself for throwing yourself around like this.'

'I want to.'

'I won't let you. You have other children to think about.'

She spat in his face then. 'Let me go.'

'I won't. I'll hold you. I will never let you go.'

She scratched at him. He held her tighter; he was stronger than she. 'I won't let go of you so you damage yourself. Stop it, Ellen, you have to stop this in yourself.'

She looked at him with hate. He didn't understand her. The wild nature of her grief.

Because of this grief that towered, because they said she must stay alive, she had to take the child. Daniel. She knew his mother never really loved him. She never even loved his father. She was incapable of love.

And now, lying in bed, holding the boy's hand, Daniel, whom she took from his mother, she hears the buzzing come again. *You had no right. You stole the child from his mother.*

She cries out, 'I had the right. Her grief was nothing next to mine. She was nothing. Bad from the start. Look what became of her. I kept him from all that.'

The buzzing says: *You made her be that way.*

NO, *she always was. And Daniel never minded. Listen, he'll tell you. He always told me when I asked him. But I never asked him. But he would have said.*

He was glad to be mine. He was glad not to be hers.

I know it: he was happy.

'Dan,' she calls out.

He comes to her. He holds her hand. She confronts the buzzing. *I'll ask him now.*

'I'm with you, Gran,' he says, holding her hand, a claw, with his live, healthy hand.

He puts the bars of the bed down. He lays his head against her chest as if he wants to listen to her heart.

'Rest now, Gran.'

She pats his head. She can sleep now, she understands that he has always needed to be hers. Even now he needs her comfort.

Everything is over. But he is here with her.

Vincent will not be back.

But she can sleep.

And she is falling into sleep, and dreaming now, of all the things for which she cannot be forgiven.

III

1

'It's only a matter of time,' Theresa says. 'I think we should start packing things up gradually, the things they never use. They won't notice and we can keep on top of it, not have some huge mess all at once.'

'We're not going to do that, Theresa,' Cam says. 'It's their house. He's coming back today. He'll be here living in it.'

'It's ridiculous, him rattling around this house like that.'

Marilyn and Dan listen to them, standing in the doorway of Ellen's room. They watch everyone fall into place: Cam and Theresa fixed at the center, the antagonists; Sheilah in back of her mother urging injury; Ray and his son, John, outside the circle, knowing no act of theirs can have weight. Marilyn hangs behind Dan a little, waiting for him to walk between the two antagonists, to fool them, to distract them, sing, tell a joke, make a remark on the weather, anything to make them stop.

'I thought we were going for a walk,' Dan says to Cam.

Cam walks out of the house ahead of him and bangs the screen door. He can see the line of it, starting with Ellen, hating herself, refusing to love her daughters, stealing him from his mother, taking Cam from Magdalene; he sees John and Sheilah in their mother's blackened house. And he and Marilyn, always a little desperate: We'll fix it, wait a minute, we'll do something; it will be all right.

He knows he has to make something move in Cam, Cam's anger is like a foreign power that can colonize their lives. When she's angry (she is never angry at him), the look of the world changes for him, as if a war had happened. The peaceful streets where you could live a modest, public life have been demolished; where there were cafés, churches, simple houses there is rubble: you sit on the bombed-out site searching in the wreck for the familiar things.

139

'Look around at all this,' he says, pointing to the new houses. 'Look how it's changed.'

He knows that, even angry, she can be interested in the world.

'I mind,' he says. 'You wouldn't think I'd mind, considering we weren't happy here. You'd think I'd like it all wiped out.'

He knows she has begun to listen, but he hasn't got her yet. The engine of her anger still runs, he can hear it; it slows down but doesn't stop. She knows he's trying to distract her; she can feel his effort.

'I guess that's the oldest story in the book, right, talking about the neighborhood going downhill? They probably said it in the Stone Age – "Look at those assholes, iron' – and in the Middle Ages, "Who wants those goddamn spices from the East?"'

She pities him. She sees him floundering, desperately trying to be interesting, to make her laugh so that she'll give it up, this anger that she treasures, that she doesn't want to give up, that she enjoys hoarding, fingering. Its sharpness creates borders she can understand: a skeleton, a frame. Pleasant to feel that bone, that wood, like lying down and feeling the jutting pelvis, like touching rafters, beams, before the ornamental camouflage is once and for all in place. She can know who she is in the world if she is somebody's antagonist; to be Theresa's enemy, therefore *not Theresa* in the world, satisfies her, gives her certainty and hope. But Dan is drowning in his efforts to make her stop; what gives her certainty and hope brings him anxiety and displacement. She won't do that to him. She'll give it up for him, this anger, desirable to her, valuable as medicine or wealth.

'Do you remember that magazine with house plans in it?' she says.

He remembers it; it was a magazine Vincent brought home for them, made up of photographs of houses with blueprints of the houses beneath. He thinks of them poring over it as children, looking for something. What? The book itself enchanted them. They loved the shiny pages, heavier than those of ordinary magazines, the photographs of new-built houses among trees that in themselves looked modern, unencumbered trees, trees without sad histories, trees that would give the right amount of shade, but wouldn't, for a moment, cut off from the wonderful and lucky family who lived among them even an inch of light. The man outside the house, the father, wore a plaid shirt, smoked a pipe;

the mother wore a Fair Isle sweater. He forgets the children, their faces, what they wore. The children, boy and girl, were not important: it was those young parents. Those young parents who had nothing at all to do with Europe. He and Cam got the magazine in 1949. He remembers: she was eight and he was six. Europe seemed to him still covered over by a cloud of danger and shame, the War, the ruined streets, children hidden for years in basements. Europe was Ireland, which Ellen called a bog, a backwater, a filthy hole. She mocked the rich first-generation greenhorns who took their families back home. To see what? she would say. The cattle shitting in the streets, right up to your door, the children with their teeth rotted out of their heads, the beautiful thatched cottages swept only once a year, the tinkers carrying their filthy babies in their filthy blankets? Oh, this beautiful thing, Ellen would say, through furious cruel teeth, we loved it so, that's why we couldn't wait to leave. And when his grandfather would send into the air a nice memory, rising like a balloon to give them pleasure, when he would say: The greenness of the grass, the goodness of the milk, the lovely bread, the songs, the smell of the peat fire, she would raise the hammer of her scorn. She would begin to talk in a false brogue. 'Yes, Dad,' she'd say, ''tis little enough ye knew of it. You left at fifteen and lucky for you. 'Twas a lovely life you had. Breaking your back on the farm that went all to your brother, then apprenticed out at twelve. 'Twas what ye wanted for yer children, wasn't it. The lovely bread, the lovely singsongs by the peat fire. Everybody slaving till they died or wore out. 'Twas wonderful. If only I could have it back, my carefree youth.' And she would flap and dance and invent a song. 'My carefree youth/ The cowshit and the toothless mother/ And the starving tinkers out to steal me blind/ Back, back to the auld sod of my dreams.'

Dan would see his grandfather pretend to laugh, or genuinely laugh, for Ellen could do that, she could make her husband laugh, and when her wit was cruel and meant to draw fresh blood he would go quiet. She could see that she had hurt him, and she would regret, but not apologize.

So that was Europe: the War, the Ireland he could not make a clear picture of. Was it the green country of his grandfather, or the hard, filthy place that she spoke of? He'd traveled to France and Italy, to Spain with Sharon, long before he went to Ireland. He'd gone only two years ago, with Cam and with the girls.

Cam and Darci loved it. But for him, the country was a sign: they could never be happy, any of them, coming from people like the Irish. Unhappiness was bred into the bone, a message in the blood, a code of weakness. The sickle-cell anemia of the Irish: they had to thwart joy in their lives. You saw it everywhere in Irish history; they wouldn't allow themselves to prosper. They didn't believe in prosperity. Perhaps, he thought, they were right not to.

He saw it everywhere he went in Ireland, the proof of the Irish temperament, the doomed service of the ideal, the blatant disregard of present pleasure. He could see it in their politics, their architecture, in the layout of their living rooms, their towns. He compared the way the Irish lived with what he'd seen in France and Italy. In Ireland, there were no glimpses of shocking, reassuring brightness: a plate with overlarge, loud-colored flowers, a milk jug in the shape of a bird's head, a rectangular pillow in a dark, primary shade, a fountain, just for nothing, in the center of a town, the trees extravagantly leaved, the chestnut, and the willow. It was fine for Cam and Darci to bend over laughing at the decor of their Bed and Breakfasts, but for him it was a dreadful talisman. It seemed that in every dining room of every B & B in Ireland, even in those that took in only three or four paying guests, there was an inexplicable presence: a tableau of animals that appeared from a distance to be the work of a skilled taxidermist, but upon a closer look (and Cam and Darci planned their mornings around the opportunities to get a closer look) turned out to be plastic animals frozen in deadly attitudes, about to swoop or perch or use their talons, beneath a sheet of Plexiglas.

He understood the Irish. They were a colonized nation and had taken from their colonizers all their symbols of prosperity and of success. The English gave them their model, and like the colonized everywhere, they learned their lesson only halfway: they learned the wrong half. They copied from the English the jarring printed carpets and the half-glass doors that closed as if they kept out someone dangerous or insane. And, fearful of their reputation as slatterns (fatal to the tourist industry), they put dust-resistant covers on their furniture, and on their mattresses quickly drying nylon sheets. They seemed, Dan thought, to have been taken up by an obsession with concealment, or protection, by impermeable plastic. On the graves were arrangements of plastic flowers, in what looked like plastic cake dishes, the kind churchgoing women would use to transport their layer cakes to the bake sale or the parish tea. He watched the furious, the desperate, the anxiety-filled cleaning of the Irish women who had taken paying guests. He saw that there was nothing natural about their cleaning, nothing learned in childhood, practiced over the years. The cruel, expensive vacuum cleaners (*Just doing a bit of Hoovering, so*) set the rhythm of the day for these genuinely nice women and their families. A few hours of frantic activities: the breakfasts, the cleaning up. Then the long day of waiting, like unsure lovers, for the rented car, with its Americans, its Germans, for someone to come out and say, 'How much?' The tourists didn't say, as they should have, 'How much for the family beds?' For Dan had seen how they had done it – the Americans, the Germans, the English, by their holidaying – turned the children from their beds. He'd awakened in the night and found the children sleeping in their sleeping bags on the sitting-room floor in front of fireplaces that sometimes held peat, but more often facsimiles of peat in neon-colored plastic. How nice they were, how friendly, these children and their mothers. The fathers you never saw: they drove away quite early in the mornings, or they were outside with the cows all day; they came back for a silent dinner; they went back out then to the pub. Sometimes if you were at the same pub as one of these men in the evenings he would smile, embarrassed, for he knew and you knew: his wife was making money off your need for shelter and a bed.

The towns displayed their own kind of blindness, not mistaken and mislearned, like the distressing ugliness of the private houses, but a willed, blunt disregard for beauty, a blank, punitive, ungenerous self-presentation, a reproach to ornament, to prideful style. The towns were built for commerce, and stripped down for it. They had been market towns once, cattle had been brought from the surrounding areas into the large central square. He saw the trees brutally pollarded, the unwelcoming pebble-dash faces of the houses, the thin sills painted dull blue or prison-green. Some curse of money-changing, money-making, had come down upon these towns. They stood for commerce, but with none of its excitement: no goods flashing, bright stuff disappearing, then appearing once again. No, what Dan could see was that this was the idea of 'the town' thought up by people whose genius was rural. Real life was in the countryside. And the country was miraculous.

So they had both been right, his grandmother, his grandfather.

Ellen, brought up in town, had seen the bleak, commercial greed; his grandfather had seen the land's beauty. Dan had wanted to see what they both had seen. So they had driven south to Cork and found Vincent's village, Dromnia, lush and gentle, a female landscape full of hidden brooks and noble trees. And they had gone north, to the west of Clare, and had found Tulla, Ellen's town. A steep-streeted town with mute, gray sooty houses all connected, as if they'd all been poured from the same batch of concrete, all at once. They'd found her father's pub.

Darci and Cam, who loved pub life (Darci was, to her great joy, served her first drink in Tulla, a shandy, beer and lemonade), were adopted lovingly by Ellen's town. 'Can you imagine, this one is the granddaughter of Ellen Costelloe.' No one remembered Ellen; they couldn't have; no one they met was old enough; they pretended that they did. It was a kind pretense; Dan didn't mind. But in the stones of the streets, in the blank cement faces of the houses, Dan felt the child Ellen's misery, imagined her a little girl living above the pub noise, the men's sickness, the dark small rooms. For he could feel it when he walked into the rooms she knew. He saw the countryside around the town, brief fertile patches, taken over soon by brown grass and the gorse the farmers cursed. Everyone but tourists cursed it. He understood. He couldn't sing and joke like Cam and Darci; he was happy to take Staci home to the room, to read while she made perfect sketches of the hillsides and the furniture and wrote brief, numerous, and uninforming letters to her friends back home.

He felt they were his people, the Irish, and he pitied and admired them. He enjoyed them, but he felt that, like him, they had no idea how to live.

He takes Cam's arm as they walk down their childhood street. They look across the street; their eyes fall on the same sight; they are thinking the same thing. Some children, young teenagers they must be, thirteen at most, are getting on the bus for Jamaica. Cam and Dan know from the way they're dressed (uneasily) and standing (tentatively, as if they are afraid someone will come along and tell them they have no right to be there) that these children will take the subway at Jamaica and get off in midtown Manhattan. The City. They travel only from borough to borough but it is as if they travel to another continent. They are leaving home.

Dan says: 'Remember when you took me into the museum. It was so exciting. I felt like you were taking me in a covered wagon.

Cam isn't listening. They are about to pass by 163 Linwood Avenue, where Cam lives with her mother and Bob. Cam's eye is on Magdalene's window, facing out onto the street. Dan sees Cam's mouth go tense. He knows she won't suggest that they go in. It occurs to him that in all his life he hasn't been in that house more than twenty times. *That* house. It was a place that you got out of, quickly, into the fresh air, to the city, or to Vincent and Ellen's, or away somewhere in your car. Cam never wanted him in that house; he never particularly wanted to be there. There was something dangerous about it: infected, forbidden. Magdalene ruled there, making Cam behave her worst.

Cam sees that the drapes of her mother's room are drawn. It makes her furious; she'd like to bang open the doors of the house, run up the stairs, open the curtains, and say, 'Mother, it's the middle of the day. How about letting the sunshine in.'

She knows it's a bad sign, the drawn curtains. She wonders how much time she has before she'll have to go into the house and find out, once and for all, whether Magdalene will do it. Whether she'll walk out of her room, onto the street, back to her parents' house. To be there for her father.

Cam expects the worst. She doesn't want to think about it now. She takes Dan's arm and steers him forcefully around the corner, as if he were a stranger, as if he didn't know where they were.

2

Behind the drawn curtains in Magdalene's room, the telephone is ringing.

Magdalene answers it as she always does, expectantly, flirtatiously. 'Hilooo,' she says, drawing out the last syllable. It is Kevin Browning, her partner in Maison Magdalene.

'Oh, darling, I'm so glad you called,' she says. 'I've been trying to get dressed and I just don't think I can make it. I have these terrible spots in front of my eyes.'

'Sweet, you've got to go. What will you wear? Let's plan what you'll wear.'

She can't listen to what usually enthralls her: this description of the contents of her closet, which he analyzes and embellishes with his devoted eye. 'The teal shirt with the green stretch slacks?' he says. 'The purple pants with the white blouson top?'

She isn't listening. He has betrayed her. He has left her. The world is made up of sides. He hasn't taken her side. He has taken *their* side. Cam's. She pities herself.

In the first months after her operation, twenty years earlier, Magdalene was entirely without self-pity. Then she began to resent everyone who had allowed her to be brave. She saw the way they swallowed her stories as evidence of their brutality. They believed she was all right because they didn't care if she was not. She retreated to her bedroom. She had expended her reserve. The energy that she had used for the eighteen years of her widowhood to cut a figure of public bravery was used up.

She'd had no notion of herself apart from the responses that she could engender. Her parents' early disappointment in her left her hungry, as if she'd been permanently underfed. Her nourishment came from the eyes of strangers, it had to. The only other choice left her was to take the grudged minimum, whatever the parents had left.

But she had only to walk onto the street to know that her parents were wrong. She could tell that her physical presence was a gift to everyone that she passed by. It was her looks, but not only that, it was the conviction that came over her after the first glance fell on her that she existed with a wholeness that was perfect and almost abstract. The wholeness of a geometric shape. She existed in the minds of those who looked at her with the solidity of a mathematical idea. She felt herself grow more durable every moment she walked in the world. Soon she could feel herself impermeable. Nothing chipped or marred the surface of the self they made for her, those who looked. She didn't have to give them anything. It was perfect; it was what she liked.

Even in middle age she could command the look that made her, to herself, substantial. It was given to her by her clients, by the men who took her to expensive restaurants and told her she ate like a bird, she needed someone to take care of her; they gladly would if she would only say the word. She never felt her grip on men slacken. Before that could happen, the men became unnecessary. Kevin came into her life, providing everything that she had wanted in a man. He was her handsome escort. From him came the praise that fed and made her whole. She could trust the praise; it was discriminating, like a woman's, but he said it as a man.

In June of 1963, at the height of bouffant, beehive, those exhausting, challenging architectural days in the world of beauty parlors, Kevin Browning walked into Maison Magdalene with his diploma from the Robert Valli School of Beauty. He was hoping to be able to find a job in his hometown. His first choice was Maison Magdalene, because he had known Cam in school. Awed, like everyone else, by her public achievements, he would never have talked to her, but her connection with Maison Magdalene gave it the suggestion of solidity he craved.

Kevin was one of those inexplicable flowerings that grow up in a household marked by nothing but drabness and a numbed attention to the plain details of daily life. His father was a postman and his mother raised five children with the withdrawn, unoriginal stoicism of a financially pressed woman whose dreams are of 'sets' of furniture – a bedroom 'set,' a living-room 'set' – that she will never have. Early on, from a source he could never place, came to Kevin the dream of a glamorous mother. Her nails would be polished a shade called Tudor Rose. Smooth nails, untouched, unused to dishwater, not cracked and striated like his mother's. The dream mother would walk, high-heeled, through light rooms smelling wonderfully of perfume. She would take him on vacations, to the movies. She would take him out to lunch. Inside her heart would be a suffering maiden she would hide with jokes that everybody loved. She would see how he stood out among his family. For, although his dream mother was not his mother, he peopled his dream family with siblings from the life. 'A rose among thorns,' she would call him. She would tell him, 'We are just alike.' When Kevin walked through the door of Maison Magdalene, he experienced a searing moment when the dreamer sees, shockingly embodied, the figure of his dream. Magdalene smiled, turned, shook a can of hairspray, joked as she sprayed the tower of hair she'd crafted for a customer, then swiveled the customer in her chair so she could see the effect of the back of her now perfect coiffure.

He said, 'I'm Kevin Browning, I'm a hairdresser, and I'm looking for a job.'

She answered, 'Dream on, Macduff.'

He wasn't daunted. 'Well, at least you could talk to me. You could give me a cup of coffee, for God's sakes,' he said.

Of course she hired him. They soon found in one another natures generous but enclosed, imaginative yet easily discouraged by the world of fact which they both hated and revered; ambitious, concerned with fashion, interested in money, pious, sentimental, attentive, but often surprised by the effects of their own acts.

Kevin's presence changed the tone of Maison Magdalene in ways that were alarming or invigorating, depending upon who spoke. It was said at the same time 'He's ruined everything,' and 'He's a real breath of fresh air.' He and Magdalene spent all their time together, endlessly turning the pages of magazines, not idly, speculatively, but as professionals who needed to find the precise objects that could make their vision real. What they had in mind was a blending of the most desirable of Magdalene's old clients with the new young faces Kevin could bring in. There was a middle range of women who came to the shop three or four times a year, seen to by Betty or by Myrna, whom Magdalene and Kevin thought of as so much underbrush, more profitably cleared away. In a while, their attitude towards Betty and Myrna's clients extended to Betty and Myrna themselves. Sensing rightly the danger to their positions, Betty and Myrna took exactly the wrong approach. Their relations with Magdalene had been impersonal and formal. Resolutely, Magdalene had discouraged their confidences. If she saw them approach her with a need to unburden themselves, she became jokey, hyper-urban: an Irish tough. She lifted up one shoulder; she looked in the mirrors that were everywhere to check her lipstick. She shot at the sufferer, from halfway out of the room, some bracing platitude. And then she was gone: her high heels tapping, beating out the truth: *How futile is self-pity. How relentless is the world.* When Betty and Myrna tried to speak to Magdalene about their worries, they never got her ear. She was always off somewhere, to lunch with Kevin, or to church, a decorator or a salesman was soon coming and she must look over the samples which she hadn't had a God's blessed minute even to think about.

'You know how my brain is, like a rag picker's bag, my mother used to say.' Then she was flipping through brochures; she was writing numbers out on scraps of paper. She was not available to them. They were out of her world, and soon they quit working for her.

With the advice of decorators, salesmen who could supply, at the crack of a whip, a dreamy array of new products, Maison Magdalene transformed itself between May 30 and August 15, 1964 (Feast of the Assumption, chosen by Magdalene for luck), into Maggi's. Young women in short skirts began appearing so that Kevin would cut their hair into geometric shapes. At the same time, Magdalene kept her older customers, and got some new ones: doctors' wives, the wives of one judge and a local politician, women in their forties frightened that perhaps they had lost their lives. Kevin learned the new boyish haircuts thought up in London and Liverpool. Magdalene continued to arrange the hair of her old customers in homage to the widowed Mrs. Kennedy. Maggi's was the home of two friendly but unrelated tribes, who watched each other with amusement and regard, occasionally communicating by means of their few words of shared language. At night, when the tribespeople returned to their separate tents to sleep, the two priests, Kevin, Magdalene, met and came together. Cam was in law school; Kevin lived at home and saw each meal he took there as the death of all he loved, so every night he and Magdalene ate out, or bought food for the one meal they would prepare and eat, not at the kitchen table, but on lacquered Chinese trays Kevin had bought for just this purpose, trays they would place on their laps as they sat in front of the TV.

When she came home for weekends, Cam felt she'd walked into a strange house, presided over now by strangers.

She saw how the house she'd grown up in had changed. Kevin and her mother spent their weekends in Suffolk County buying antiques. Magdalene had bought all the furniture in the house in 1952, when she shocked everyone by moving out of the apartment she had lived in as a bride, then an envied mother of a single child, then a widow pitied first, then feared. She was tired, she said, of throwing rent money down the sink. She was tired of the smell of meat that came up from the butcher shop, though for fourteen years she hadn't said a word about it, and hadn't seemed to notice that there was a smell. She bought one of her customers' houses

when the customer's husband died. She furnished the house per-
functorily, as if it interested her as an investment rather than a
dwelling. But with Kevin, she became acquisitive. Large, dark
pieces of mahogany, plush couches took over the spaces occupied
by insubstantial, tired Danish modern she had bought on the
installment plan from Montgomery Ward. Gilt mirrors sprouted
everywhere like spores, Cam thought, and heavy damask curtains
kept out every possibility of light. Only Cam's room remained
untouched, its maple single bed with plaid spread and matching
curtains a kind of shrine, to an unknowing, under-ripe virginity.
It was a mixed homage they paid the room, ignoring it. It was the
only light room in the house. Leaving it so, they must have seen
how it would comment on and mark the others. When she took
Dan around the house, Cam said her room looked like the
madame's daughter's. They both laughed but Dan understood
Cam's sense of defilement, of the desecration of the dwelling that
had been her address if not her real home.

Dan and Cam were right in understanding that the decorating
scheme had everything to do with sex, but the connection wasn't
simple. What they couldn't know was that Magdalene and Kevin
worshipped the accoutrements that were supposed to lead to sex,
but found the act itself abhorrent. High on their list of valued
attributes was elegance; they were, in addition, both possessed of
an extreme bodily consciousness. The act of sex required that they
give up both; they both preferred, therefore, to avoid it. And for
Kevin to think seriously about the act of sex would require that
he acknowledge that the lovely perfumed women who peopled
his other dreams were not the bodies that he wanted near his own.
It was the body of a man that he desired when desire did intrude.
The idea of that in himself disgusted him. He could only endure
himself if he pushed from his mind those pictures that grew of
themselves (he tried to stop them) in such lush and frightening
profusion, like, he thought when he made his Act of Contrition,
a jungle growth.

So together Magdalene and Kevin created a place which was
meant to do homage to sex by replacing the act of sex with its
effects and its surroundings. And in the center of it all they kept
Cam's room, their thoughts, their stories about Cam herself.
When Cam came home, Kevin was prepared to worship. But she
wouldn't let him. He was ready for a cool and unmoved goddess.

150

He wasn't prepared for the clear, freezing glance that fell on his every act and killed his spirit.

Cam knew that what she did to Kevin was terrible; she knew it and she didn't stop. She couldn't find in anything he had done a single act for which to blame him. But he had done the one thing she could not forgive. He had become to her mother the child she had always wanted.

Cam heard their confiding, easy conversations. Her mother saying: 'What's up, love? You under the weather?'

And Kevin saying, 'I'm depressed.'

In twenty years she and her mother had not had an exchange like that. Hypnotized, Cam listened in.

'"Depressed,"' said Magdalene. 'That's a word your generation made up. In my day, we had the blues.'

'So, whatever you called it, what did you do when you had the blues?'

'I'll tell you what I've always done, because, let's face it, my life has not been one long picnic. I got the idea from my eighth-grade teacher. Sister Mathilde. The woman was a genius. I think she had a Ph.D. from Europe. But she was humble about it. She told me one day when we were alone, just the two of us, I was helping her with the altar, she said, "What's up, Magdalene?" I said, "Sister, I've got the blues." She said, "You know what I do when I've got the blues. I take a piece of paper, a piece of ordinary paper. I fold it in half. On one side of the page I write down all the things I have to be grateful for. On the other side I write my problems. Then I take the piece of paper. I rip it in half, and I throw both halves in the garbage."'

Cam knew that she could never, hearing this story, have presented Magdalene with the kind of rapt, grateful look that took over Kevin's face. For years, in exasperation, she had listened to her mother's non sequiturs, astonishing misinformation, conclusions drawn from premises impossible to trace. A night or two before, when Kevin had told her about a dream he'd had, Magdalene had said, 'My generation didn't have dreams. We were too busy.' And Kevin seemed to believe her. Cam stood in the kitchen, at once furious at their complicitous stupidity and jealous that someone else could make her mother feel so happy, so intelligent, so prized.

When Magdalene got sick, Cam didn't notice Kevin. He stayed in the background, visiting, but only when the family wasn't there.

151

At that time, Magdalene turned to her daughter in panic; feeling herself near death, she felt only someone of her blood could keep her from it, or accompany her to it when the moment came. As Magdalene withdrew for her demise, Kevin stayed around, keeping the business going, reporting to Magdalene, making money for her, giving her more than her share. In the early years of Cam's marriage, as it gradually became evident that Magdalene wouldn't die, Kevin took up again his role as Magdalene's companion, but only when Cam and Bob were out of the house, which they were often, in the days when they went out together, meeting up with other couples to avoid being by themselves. By the time Cam looked up from the bombed-out site of her marriage, she found she wasn't without help in her problems with her mother. By the time she understood, Kevin had been helping her for years. He had matured; he was no longer the moonish boy whose skewed erotic source was Magdalene. He lived with a companion; he had become part of a circle in which he could be himself. Cam and Kevin developed a relationship of co-conspirators.

Magdalene doesn't know that Cam and Kevin speak to each other every day. They talk about their own lives, but mainly they have grieved or anxious conversations, sometimes carefully sardonic: the talk of connoisseurs. Their subject is Magdalene. They've never allowed Magdalene to know that over the years they have become a bulwark to each other. It is a necessary fiction for Magdalene that Cam and Kevin are antagonists; it's the tension without which her life would lack shape.

Magdalene hopes Kevin will tell her she doesn't have to go to Vincent and Ellen's house. She takes one earring off as she talks to him on the phone.

'Cam doesn't know what I go through,' she says. 'She thinks everything's as easy for me as it is for her.'

'I know, darling. Just try. One step at a time. You never told me what you'll wear.'

'I can't make up my mind. What did you say, the purple? I was thinking that too, only the shoes kill my feet.'

3

Harriet Duffy knocks on Vincent's door. Without his answering, she opens the door a bit, and sticks her little bird's head in the room.

'Yoo-hoo,' she says. 'I hope you weren't thinking of shoving off without saying goodbye.'

He wishes he were wearing a hat, so he could tip it. That would be an acknowledgment she would like. He realizes that men no longer tip their hats. In the old days, you'd tip your hat when you passed a church. He wonders when all that stopped. It was something to do with John Kennedy; after him, men stopped wearing hats.

'A little going-away present for you, then,' she says. 'I couldn't resist.'

She hands him a package wrapped in rainbow-colored tissue paper. Stuck to the top is a yellow bow. He opens the box. It's a tie, red plaid, wider than the ties he wears.

'I made it myself,' she says. 'It's my new hobby, making ties. My daughters bring me their old clothes, their old dresses, and I just make ties out of the scraps. Sometimes they've got big stains on them or holes from I don't know what. But I don't let anything go to waste. We were brought up like that, you and me, Vincent, weren't we? Waste not, want not. People today never heard that one. I'm just grateful they let me have my machine here.'

'My wife was an excellent needlewoman,' he says. He wants Ellen's presence in the room. Harriet Duffy makes him uncomfortable. There's something funny about the way she treats him. Wanting to give him her desserts. Asking if he wants to watch a game on the television in her room. He knows she isn't interested in baseball. Knocking on the door for him, so he can walk her down to dinner. He feels it's wrong. He feels it's wrong to Ellen. Ellen can't help herself. If she was her old self, she'd never allow Harriet Duffy to get this familiar. Whenever women seemed to want to get too friendly, Vincent only had to introduce them to Ellen. Seeing her, they knew they didn't have a chance.

This Harriet is taking advantage of Ellen's position. Ellen's position: lying in a bed, her eyes looking up at the ceiling, or at nothing. Ellen might not even recognize him anymore. He feels that Harriet is hovering around Ellen's bed, waiting for something, like those witches that waited around deathbeds at home, and then, when the moment came that they'd been waiting for, the death itself, they'd set up their wail. Except you knew they weren't sorry. Harriet wants something from him as a man. He'll have no part of it.

'I'm much obliged to you,' he says.

She walks over to him. She opens her arms. He can tell she wants him to kiss her. He holds his arm out stiffly to her, keeping her back. He shakes her hand.

When she goes out the door, his eyes fix on her disappointed back. He is sorry to hurt her, but he can't help it. You have to be who you are.

4

Dan and Cam turn towards the two local stores: Johansen's Deli, Friedman's Candy Store. 'Do you remember, that magazine had floor plans,' he says.

'That was the best part,' Cam says.

Dan tries to understand who the magazine was meant for. Contractors, builders, someone his grandfather came across at work? What genius made him know children would like something like that? Or did he simply bring it home? He and Cam studied the floor plans, they talked about the architecture of each house. They never talked about the photographs. He knew that she, too, had her treacherous, her shameful dreams.

It's thirty-six years later, a summer afternoon. The light is changing. The trees that are rich with leaves now were saplings when the houses they walk in front of were built. Slapped up, their grandfather had said: the only contempt he ever showed, a workman's for bad work. Each summer when they were children walking down this street a house, two houses would grow up. The vacant lots they treasured disappeared; the exposed roots, the colorless, downtrodden grass, the severe wild chrysanthemums, the rose hips and choke cherries, the cracked bricks, the shards of broken glass, the inexplicable and random objects they found frightening – a single shoe, a handbag – all these were dug under. And the new houses slapped up. There was a moment when the mourning for the lot was over and they couldn't decide which they preferred: the flat space where they could invent landscape, or the bare, challenging, inviting bones of the new house and all the objects that the workmen left at night. Useful by day: barrels of nails, work aprons, cement mixers, wheelbarrows, files, yardsticks, rolls of tape. By day the things were taken up. The barechested men pushed the heavy wheelbarrows full of wet cement, frightened the children with their hammer blows, the noise of their electric saws, but stopped, some of them, for a minute to be friendly till a mother saw and made the children leave. 'Don't play by the new houses,' every mother shouted every morning as the children banged the screen doors running out. Even Vincent was adamant. 'Don't go near those houses. Keep away.' But the children obeyed no one, and no one was hurt.

Dan looks at Cam, walking beside him on the streets they've walked on all their lives. All the romance children might have put into trips, holidays at the seaside, vacations to the mountains went into these walks he took with Cam. For they never went anywhere else. Not once in all their childhood had they gone anywhere. And was it a mistake? He thought of the failed vacations he had taken with his children. He thought that really what children loved was routine. Change as an idea delighted them, and the voyage itself might give them pleasure, but a strange place was a danger: they were always wanting to be home.

Better, perhaps, these walks, these trips to vacant lots or half-built houses, than the trips he took his children on. To Disney World, when they were nine and ten. There was an unexpected cold spell in Florida that Christmas week. The girls had brought with them only summer clothes. They shivered; then, ineptly, he had to buy them an overpriced, unsatisfying wardrobe of warmer clothing in a shop in the hotel. All the time that he was buying the girls their pants and sweaters, he was worried that Val would be angry, accuse him of trying to win them by one more indulgence that she would not or could not match. 'You have them for a month, buy them everything; then they expect it from me and throw it in my face. Be real, Dan, just for once,' she'd said to him the last summer. How could he be more real? They wanted; he could give; he gave. Was a father's real role denial? Was that what she meant? He had had no father; he would never know. Perhaps he was not a real father.

They'd stood on the interminable lines of Disney World. He told Cam later what it was like. Disney World, he said, is the Lourdes of divorced fathers. He stood behind men he had nothing in common with, men he would never have spoken to, except they now shared an estate: they were waiting on lines with impatient, cranky children. Men with sunburned necks, white creases where they bent their heads. Beefy half-boys wearing satin jackets with the names of high-school teams, recently left, embroidered on the back. Blacks in leisure suits or sweating, as he did, in too-warm jackets: proof and uniform of uneasy tenancy in the middle class. These men who in any other setting would have fallen within minutes into insult or tense silence made sympathetic comments to each other on the weather, the scandalous price of the drinks. They pointed out to one another the locations of the bathrooms. Failures in the company of failures, they became kinder. Almost womanly, they shared domestic troubles; they gave advice.

For the first day of the vacation, the children were amused. But he had rented the hotel rooms not for one day, but for a week. The children fell into a pattern of bored fighting. Fights like brushfires that started from nowhere, were quenched, and started up in the same place, for no reason, again. It was Darci who dissolved in tears. What she wanted, Dan could see, was her father to herself. And Staci wanted no part of either of them. She drew back into the armor of her discontent, disliking everything, but silently, or saying why didn't they just stay in the hotel room and watch television, everything was so expensive. 'Such a rip-off,' she kept saying, 'Dad, you're being so ripped off.' Then Darci would say, 'Jesus, Staci, you have got to be the world's most boring human being.' Staci would walk out of the room, as if responding to such comments was beneath her. Dan agreed with Darci; he felt they should keep trying to enjoy this place where others of their kind so famously had enjoyed themselves. But they didn't enjoy it. Everyone was happy to go home.

★

Dan and Cam walk on a street that's changed entirely within their lifetime. They link arms. Male, female, but children together. They can walk, their arms together; they're no danger to each other; in this difference of sex there's nothing of fear, desire, contempt. They share blood. Memory. A childhood. They were brought up by people who were old when they were young, whose death they had to fear each morning, whose love had too much in it of anxiety. They were fatherless children of mothers who were absent or useless in their love. They have only to look at each other and all this is understood.

They head back to the house. Once inside, they walk into their grandmother's room. For this moment, she sleeps, her mouth open, miraculously not grotesque, her hair in two thin plaits under her shoulders. Dan stands on one side of the bed and Cam stands in the doorway. Ellen wakes. Her eyes focus on nothing. Are they terrified or angry? Who can tell? She cries out: the sacrilegious cry of someone who has lost her place among her kind.

Cam hears this sound and feels terror first, then anger. She can't do anything for her grandmother. She doesn't know what her grandmother sees. She's horrified by the avidity for life those eyes express; as if simply to be *not dead* was what she craved with a hunger that was unseemly in its plainness. What could inspire the look behind those eyes, that terror, that anger, that unmediated request for deliverance? But deliverance from what? Cam feels that if she could simply name the thing her grandmother sees, could describe in solid language what goes on behind her grandmother's eyes, those eyes that aren't dead but are perhaps not quite human, she could help her. Not knowing how to name the thing, she's helpless. Her helplessness makes her angry. She hates that, being of no help.

John, Theresa's son, comes and stands beside her in the doorway. He's been in the garage, doing the repairs he'd promised to do months ago. On the last day, working too hastily, Cam sees, he's bungled. She worries what this will do to Vincent on his first day home.

'I'll sit with her a while,' John says.

Cam nods. She never knows what to say to John. His life is ruined. He is a wreck, Cam thinks, thirty-seven, sitting in a wrecked life. She wonders who is to blame. She'd like to think it was Theresa, but her work has made her chary of the automatic blame placed on mothers by everyone from Ann Landers to the Family Court judge. John was one of those boys living on the margin all their lives. Should you look to coded genetic messages: did something in John's body program him for marginal living? Should you look to the neighborhood, the schools, and say: If not this friend, if only this teacher? Or should you look to history and say: Drugs, Vietnam, the dropout generation, they despaired, or they were lazy, they lost heart. In the end, what did it matter, Cam thinks, looking at John. She sees that somehow sitting beside Ellen – she's quiet now – John is happy. She wants to thank him for all the time he's spent with Ellen this year. But she doesn't thank him; she could never talk to him, and it's dangerous, with someone like John, to interrupt some moment not devoted to making his life worse. She won't say anything to him now; he seems happy.

John holds his grandmother's hand. He is thinking that perhaps he'll study to become a nurse. He checks his grandmother's pulse, as if for practice. He looks up at the IV tube sending glucose to her arm as if he could discern its proper function or its failures, be the one to rightly raise alarm. His sister is a nurse. He likes his sister. He has always liked his grandmother. She left him alone. So he is almost happy and he thinks he's had a good idea: he'll study and become a nurse. He thinks he'll work in a veterans' hospital. Or else a nursing home. He sits, holding his grandmother's hand, a claw. In his mind, he performs perfectly at two interviews: one at a veterans' hospital, one at a nursing home. He tells the interviewer that he's had so many offers, he'll have to sleep on it, be sure he's making the right choice.

He wants to tell his grandmother he knows what he'll do now. He will study, he'll become a nurse. He thinks that this would please her. It will please his sister Marilyn, whom he likes. He could have a job like her. Sitting beside his grandmother, he has already done it, gone to school, trained in the hospital. It looms before him, solid as a house, all this accomplishment. Accepting it as fact, he now refines, in great detail, all the particulars.

Outside the door, John's father, Ray Dooley, is thinking: My son, my ruined son. He doesn't know how to begin to understand him. How can he understand this son, how can he understand himself, how can he recognize himself as a father? He's so different from his own father that they should call themselves by other names. How can he understand this son? The refusals, the sleeping until three o'clock on filthy sheets, the joblessness accepted like a natural fate or a deformity, the anger if someone suggests that he should do something, anything, the freedom this son feels to say dreadful things to his parents, profane or wounding. To the parents in whose house, at thirty-seven, he still lives, and shows no sign of leaving, or wanting to leave. And watching all of it, as he has always done throughout his family's life, Ray Dooley stands back, puzzled and uncomprehending, certain that his wife knows something he doesn't know, she must know something about this son, something that he does not. Ray stood at the side for all the family life, clumsy, balked, and silent, frightened by his wife's clenched-teeth anger, by her punishing cold gestures to the children, whom he could see wither in her presence, whom he did not see prosper beside her. They should do that, he thought, mother and children, prosper and be pleased. But she was the woman, she must know about the children, he knew nothing, his world was the world outside, the precinct, money, the silent life of men.

She was the one that spent all day with them. He came in only after they were fed, dressed, ready for sleep. How could he know them? On the weekends he held another job at a box factory as a security guard. And then, when the kids were grown, Theresa went to work, as Larry Riordan's secretary. For a while she made almost as much as Ray. Now that he was retired, she made more. She runs the place, Larry Riordan had said, before he, too, retired. Now she works for a group practice, knows computers, everything. The things he doesn't know.

He saw how the cold knot of her contempt and her indifference froze the family life. He saw it but did nothing, could not raise his hand to cover or to shelter the three children, his and yet not his, whom he had loved in silence, in confusion, in despair. He'd loved them paralyzingly from birth, and couldn't say it; he'd watched them grow into their unhappiness like some dark coat passed down, one to another. And the youngest, John, had never given it up. The girls seemed all right now. But John was drowning in his life. Ray saw it, and said nothing. He watched and he grieved.

John is not unhappy now. He is thinking of comradely jokes about bedpans and midnight shifts. The young girls, fellow student nurses, are wonderfully impressed with his other experiences before finding this work. They are shyly grateful, honored when he asks them out. His grandmother interrupts his dream by opening her wild eyes that see nothing. She screams and bares her gums. He doesn't see this as he formerly did, in horror, in terror. Now he sees her with a professional's eye. Professionally, he moves her blanket half an inch. He smooths her pillow. She settles down, as if he did the things she wanted. And he takes it as a sign.

He thinks that after a while, he'll quit the job in the nursing home (he's decided that he'll choose the job in the nursing home rather than the V.A. hospital: he likes working with old people), he'll move somewhere warmer. To the Sunbelt, out West, maybe, not down South: he hated that, it makes him think of being married and he doesn't want to think of that. Arizona, he thinks, New Mexico, or maybe Colorado, maybe he'll learn to ski. He wishes he hadn't thought about the time that he was married. First it was a good time, then it turned bad.

Everything started making him sick. The way she looked – he can't call her his wife, even to himself. And then the way she kept apologizing all the time. It wasn't his fault that things ended that way with the job. He was installing and repairing air conditioners. It was all right, he'd liked it at first, but he got sick of it. He was ready to walk out. But not like that.

The day it happened, he was fixing a central air system in one of those fucked-up houses like *Gone With the Wind*, with the pillars. It was a big job, but he was on top of it. Then the bitch came over and said would he turn down the music, it's disturbing her. Like she owns music, like she owns him, his life's not his own, she bought it when she paid the installation charges. He just turned the music up louder. She asked him again – I said the music is disturbing me, I have to have it off. He just kept working on the system like he was deaf. The next thing he knew his boss, that guy Lannie that he always got along with, was on top of him. I guess you didn't hear the lady. Well, listen up. Turn the goddamn music off. So he laid him out on the broadloom and just took off in his car, he doesn't remember where. He didn't take a thing from the apartment, never ever went back, just kept driving. Till he landed up here.

He knows it's ridiculous, his idea of being a nurse, he'll never do it, he's never made anything work, he's ruined everything in his life. His grandmother begins thrashing, but he doesn't try to quiet her. She cries out; he gets up to look for Marilyn. He sees his mother. At the sight of her he knows that he will never be a nurse, or anything. He hates himself for all the details of his happy dream. And then he hates his mother.

'Where are you going?' she asks.

'Out,' he says.

'That's a good answer,' she says. 'You finished up that work in the garage?'

He pushes past her, out of the house, banging the screen door to offend her.

She refuses to show she is offended. Instead, she holds her body so its posture can be read as a reproach.

Theresa knew from childhood how to hold her body so it would be a reproach. She took her father's admiration in like moisture, without the slightest gratitude or sense of having been marked by it. Her movements, swift, deliberate, yet drawn out, he looked on with delight. He loved her singing voice, her size-five shoe. Ellen looked into her child's heart and found it empty, and this left her terrified and punitive, eager, in her fear, to inflict upon her daughter any quick, surprising hurt. As if she always wanted some ambush of her daughter so that she could find her, in the glance of her surprise, comprehensible and alive.

Theresa's coldness has been helpful to her in her life. It helps her, daily, in her job. She is a medical secretary. She is the one who hands the patients a form clipped to a clipboard; if they ask her for a pen or pencil she provides it. Many of the patients feel their spirits shrivel as they are passed the pencil or the pen. But should the patient know that he is dying, or discover herself unhappily pregnant, Theresa will behave as if she didn't know or hadn't noticed, as if she weren't the kind of person who could take the trouble to read a patient's chart. This can be helpful, if the patient's need is for privacy, rather than fellow feeling. It often is.

In her fifties, she became taken up by the charismatic movement of the Catholic Church. She is one of those people who stand in churches where there are still highly colored leftover statues of the Virgin, still plaques that represent the fourteen stations of the cross. She is one of those people who lift up their arms and cry out, lay their hands upon the sick and dying, expecting to be healed or that they themselves will heal. These people, mostly in late middle age, brought up on a ritual impersonal and formal as a face of stone, then told to leave all that, feel moved to stand and cry out 'Praise the Lord' as if they had just been given the good news of their salvation from a wild-eyed preacher holding in his hands his oversized and rusty hat. They stand together in these churches built with bingo money or with dollars that parishioners thrust in the basket, dollars sealed in numbered envelopes recorded by the pastor for his records and the IRS. They stand together in these churches, crying 'Praise the Lord,' 'Amen,' 'I hear it, brother.' If they are teenagers they sing and play the tambourine.

At the age of sixty-four, Theresa Dooley's days are shaped by morning Mass (in which she stands at the Consecration with her arms outstretched), lunchtime prayer meetings (attended by local housewives or people employed in local businesses who give up their lunch hours to hold hands together in a circle and to pray for guidance, healing, world peace, the end to pre-marital sex, abortion, homosexuality, divorce). Two evenings a week, after she has dried the dishes from the modest, pre-frozen meal she slipped into the microwave for herself and Ray, and John (if he decided to come down), she gets into her car and travels to the house of one of her group members for Bible study. She remembers that until the Council she, a Catholic, had been told it was a sin to read scripture by yourself without the guidance of a priest. They laugh, Theresa's group members, to think that they might need the guidance of a priest.

Her group believes in healing. Every day they pray for Ellen, whom they call only 'Theresa's mother.' Hearing this, Theresa feels a flame of inward joy that her name in the group has blotted out her mother's name. And as she sits beside her mother, she turns her mind to God and readies herself to lay her hands upon her mother so that she may heal.

But she does not lay on hands. She looks at her mother, sees her mother's eyes, which wildly focus upon nothing, hears her mother mutter words of unimaginable filth, hears her cry out with no sense that someone might be listening, like an animal who lives for herself only. Hearing all this, seeing this, she is satisfied. She says in her mind: This is the will of the Lord. She does not touch her mother. Deliberately, she folds her hands.

5

Dan goes to the telephone, more public on the hallway table than he would like. It occurs to him that his grandparents never felt the need for privacy on the telephone. Nothing important was communicated by them over the telephone; they always answered uncomfortably, anxious to get off.

He is phoning Sharon Breen, whom he lives with. She works as a paralegal for a law firm in Riverhead. Even answering the phone 'MacIntosh, Canino and DeFries,' even with her professional upbeat timbre, he can hear the underlying weariness. He hears her voice and thinks: 'I've failed to make her happy.' They haven't married after all this time.

'How's it going?' she says.

'Nobody's killed anyone yet. Not bad for the house of Atreus.'

She laughs. Once, when she was taking a course on Greek tragedy at the community college where she got her associate degree, she read *The Oresteia*. She said she'd enjoyed reading it because it was a relief to find a family that was worse off than hers.

He wants her to come today, he'd like her to be there with him; it's an important moment, he thinks, his grandfather's coming home, and he'd like her to be there beside him. But he knows she won't come. She'll never come to Vincent and Ellen's house. She's too ashamed. Shame, he thinks, that unmodern emotion, stains Sharon's life like a dye. It weakens her, it slows down the growth of muscle, bone. She's still ashamed of what happened twelve years ago, in June 1973.

In January 1973 Cam hired Sharon Breen as a secretary, causing scandal in local legal circles by announcing that secretaries were exploited and underpaid and giving Sharon a salary a third higher than the highest-paid secretary in town.

Sharon had graduated from the nuns' school that Ellen had refused to allow Cam to attend. She was the child of an electrician and his Irish-born wife, one of eight children. Her good grades in high school didn't mean that she'd go on to college; she went, instead, to Wood Secretarial School on a scholarship and married, at nineteen, the boy she'd one year earlier danced with at the Senior

Prom. She was attentive, quiet, naturally sweet; she'd been told she was pretty, but she had no idea what that meant.

She liked herself in the mirror – her light-brown hair, her wide blue eyes, her skin with its high color – but it seemed to her to count for nothing in the world. A melancholy hung around her, but she told herself her life was good, and there was nothing to explain why she seemed to herself unhappier than other people. She moved into an apartment six blocks from her parents and was happy to be hired in an office near her home; it meant that she need not commute and so would have more time for household occupations. She enjoyed her new apartment, enjoyed decorating it; she was fond of her husband and assumed most wives discovered they had married boys. She worshipped Dan and Camille Mac-Namara; she loved her job. She would do anything for either of them.

Cam was delighted with the arrangement. Sharon was a satisfying slap in the face to Mary Dolan, Jack's secretary for thirty-seven years, who had known Cam all her life and insisted upon calling her, even in private, Mrs Ulichni, although it was Camille *Mac-Namara* on the letterhead and on the door. Each morning when Cam walked into the office, the sight of Mary Dolan, always there before her, made Cam feel petulant, resentful, in the mood to pick a fight. Sharon seemed to have all Mary Dolan's virtues and none of her lacerating faults. Her efficiency was rich and maternal where Mary Dolan's was deprivational and dry. Sharon blushed easily and seemed overcome when praised; at the same time, she soon felt free not to ask permission or advice on every detail. Cam began inviting her to lunch and then to family functions. To Cam this was proof of the success of democracy and justice in the workplace. No need to treat your employees like lepers or like slaves; there was a place for everyone and everyone could be happy in his place.

But then Cam noticed that Sharon and Dan had fallen in love. She saw that Mary Dolan knew it, and watched her eyes sharpen in joyous recording of Cam's error, and in expectation that Sharon would neglect her work. She never did; it was Dan whose work suffered.

There was no way that Cam could talk to Dan. He'd moved away into a state where he'd become unrecognizable, carried out of reach. He floated in some atmosphere of sexual intoxication, absorbed, oblivious, addicted: closed. She saw him float away from her and from his work. And from the family. She saw that he was happy and that made it worse. She felt as if he'd been picked up by the nape of the neck, seized in the beak of some predatory bird: swirled through an atmosphere of confusion and disregard.

Dan was amazed at what had happened to him. He thought he was the most fortunate man in the world, and the most cursed. His adolescence had been free entirely of coupling: the school life of the Jesuit academy, where females were kept out with rigor, with contempt, made it unlikely that he would come into normal contact with girls. Overlarge and awkward, he believed himself so undesirable that he pitied in the abstract any girl he might attract. Pitying them, in advance he spared them, spared himself. Morosely he attended dances sponsored by the CYO; he stood in corners with his buddies, smoked, desired silently, went home. He joked with Cam's friends but they were older. They thought he was wonderful and wished there were somebody their age like him that they could talk to. He understood.

He met Valerie O'Keefe in freshman year at Haverford; she was the roommate of his roommate's girl. Valerie felt what every woman did about Dan: that he liked her, that he wasn't asking questions to make a fool of her, or as filler until the moment when he could make a dive for one of her breasts. She knew that she could happily, freely read with him the poetry of García Lorca, the essays of Thoreau; they held hands on the buses to Mississippi. They kissed in dark places or behind trees; once they kissed lying down together at the shore of the lake where her family owned a cottage. Val was surprised by Dan's desire, her surprise made him ashamed. In marriage they could give each other pleasure, but Dan felt always the force of his wife holding something back, something he couldn't name, place, or describe, but guessed was there for other women, other men.

But in the arms of Sharon Breen, whose desire for him seemed to him the same as his for her, Dan felt himself allowed into one more part of life. Another door he'd feared closed to him because of the flawed history that marked him an outsider, was now open. He felt blessed, anointed, miraculously reprieved. Astonished, he saw himself the lover of a beautiful receptive woman, who wept after orgasm, begged him to hold her, make love to her once again,

165

whose body he understood, whom he believed when she said: 'No one has made me feel like this.' His pride made him feel what he'd never felt with a woman. Fully adult. He thought he made her happy. He was right, she loved him, and, to his surprise, bloomed underneath his fattish body, its chest covered with red hair that she called gold. He wanted to give her back the pleasure he had had, to make her feel that she could open up and flower, then collect, grow still in her success, and rest. He felt he could.

He waited to see what would happen. It couldn't go on, the daily lovemaking at six o'clock, when the office had finally emptied, saying they couldn't leave, how could they leave each other, but then leaving, going on to the rest of their lives. Dan felt he'd tainted each part of his life that had, only a month ago, been nourishing. He would leave Sharon and go to his grandparents', sit in the dark crowded living room, watch the news, curse Nixon with his grandmother. He stopped by his grandparents' each day after leaving Sharon, wanting, really, to put his head on his grandmother's lap, smell the overwashed smell of her apron, hold the hands he'd as a child played games with: this finger, and this and this.

At work Cam's pretending not to see grew up like a wall between them. At home he hid from the flaring heat of his children's lives and Val's efficient managing. He saw himself a boy running from locked door to locked door. They had been right, he thought, those people who had warned against pleasure. He had followed pleasure, and it had brought him here, desperate, and once again without a home.

Both he and Sharon knew that something would happen to change things. It was almost as if the incompleteness of the situation was fatiguing; later he wondered if Sharon had done what she had done out of boredom, as someone might dive into a lake during a thunderstorm because she couldn't endure one more second waiting for the weather to break up.

She told her husband about Dan, one night when they had been comradely, unsexual: the childhood friends that they always were to each other in some way. It seemed then that she could simply tell him, and everything could go on as it had. Only there would be no need for the burden of her deceit. He would understand that Dan gave her something she had always dreamed of but had never thought could be hers, something that had nothing to do with

166

him: they were husband and wife; in a year or so, she would stop things with Dan and have a baby. She imagined that Jerry Breen would be momentarily saddened, then permanently ennobled: she would love him more than ever, things would be better than anyone had dreamed.

But the moment she had got the words out, she saw what she had done. Jerry let out a hissing breath, as if his body tried to make sense of a blow. He pulled the car to the side of the road and turned the engine off. He didn't move. She told him they had to go on, go home now, she would stop with Dan if it meant this much to him, she had been horribly mistaken, could she take it back? But he wouldn't move. She was afraid that she had killed him, so she sat in the dark with him silently, comforted that at least she could hear his breath.

He refused to sleep in the bed beside her. In the morning, he didn't go to his job at Friendly Frost Appliances; he went to his mother. Rita Breen was Irish-born. She made corsets in the back room of her house and sold them to portly, old-fashioned women who kept up in their persons an out-of-date physical pride. She'd taken the stiffness of the product she manufactured and built her nature on it. Unbending, she kept her husband and her sons in terrified and grateful places, fixed far below the one she settled on herself. She was ashamed to see her son forced to weep, and she felt he had been violated in some tribal, public way. It seemed to her that the reparation for this should also be tribal and public. She drove him first to the parish priest, who approved the course of her action. She took him next to Sharon's parents, who accepted what was told them in grim silence, and assured the Breens their daughter would not be sheltered in her old home once again. Then she took him to Valerie's house in Stony Brook; she told her son the other injured party had the right to know; it would be unfair to Valerie, Rita Breen said, that one part of the puzzle, hers, should remain incomplete.

She left him at Val's house; she didn't get out of the car. She drove to a luncheonette and had a tuna sandwich and a cigarette. In half an hour, she came back to get him, honking the horn, refusing to come in. Jerry got in his mother's car; his talk with Val seemed to have bucked him up.

'She said that everything would be all right,' he told his mother. 'She said it would be seen to somehow, that we shouldn't worry.'

But Rita Breen was still unsatisfied. She drove her son to the office, where Jack Morrisey, and Cam and Dan and Sharon were at work. She came up the stairs with Jerry; she said she didn't think he was a match for them, three lawyers, and himself not even with a college education, and too forgiving in his nature: he'd be scalped.

At the sight of Sharon, sitting at the front desk, Jerry broke down in tears again. 'I suppose you know why we're here,' Rita Breen said, and of course Sharon did. She showed them into the conference room and shut the door. Her cheeks burned and she didn't know whom to go to. Obviously, they had come to see Dan. But she felt Cam should be there. She felt that only Cam could stand up to Rita Breen.

But how could she get Cam from her office to the conference room? They'd never taken Cam into their confidence; it would be terrible to tell her now. She knocked on Dan's door. He greeted her with a look that was so full of pleasure that for a moment she forgot why she was there. But then he saw that she was troubled, and she only had to say: 'Jerry and his mother are in the conference room. I guess we have to speak to them.'

He held her for a moment and said, 'It's all right, it's going to be all right,' but neither of them believed it. On the way to the conference room, they ran into Cam, who'd buzzed Sharon and was prepared to be annoyed that she wasn't responding. She saw Dan's and Sharon's faces, which shared, perhaps because they both were so fair, a kind of transparency: when there was trouble, it showed; nothing in their features was designed to hide distress. The three of them went into Cam's office. They explained the situation.

'All right,' she said. 'All right.' She started walking. 'They can't do anything to us. They have no right to be here. Don't worry. This is the twentieth century. And I have a lot of friends among the criminal classes. We can always have her shot.'

She led the way into the conference room. She began speaking as she walked in the door, closing it aggressively, aware that Mary Dolan had a good idea of what was going on and hoping to make her afraid to speculate further.

'Mrs. Breen,' she said. 'I believe you think you have something to say.'

For a moment, Rita Breen lost her bearings. Cam sat across

from her, and stared hard at her hands, having noticed that Rita Breen bit her nails and hoping to make her feel found out and therefore at a disadvantage. It worked, until Jerry began to cry.

'Don't think you can push us around,' Rita Breen said, turning her eyes to Dan and Sharon: she hadn't yet the courage to look straight at Cam.

Jerry's infantilism and Rita's protectiveness made Cam impatient. 'What exactly do you want to happen now?' she said.

They were silent. It was as if they hadn't thought of it: all that had occurred to them, to Rita Breen particularly, was to make a scene. No subsequent, resulting action had crossed any of their minds.

Cam pressed her point. 'Well, there are several alternatives. Would you like financial recompense, Jerry? Is that what you have in mind? Recompense for loss of rights of consortium, it's called, there are precedents. Or you could sue for, I believe it's called alienation of affections. Or perhaps you'd like a divorce on the grounds of adultery. Of course that would involve private detectives, you need to have direct proof. Any of that appeal to you, Jerry?' she said.

'Nobody's talking about money,' Rita Breen said.

'No, Mrs. Breen?' said Cam, standing. 'What are we talking about?'

Rita Breen seemed to remember. She stood up, across the table from Cam.

'I just think people should know what's been done,' she said. 'I just don't think people should get away scot-free.'

Cam saw that Rita Breen was getting brave. 'If we don't make much of a fuss, everything will die down and things can go on as they did before,' Cam said.

'You're saying you want them to get away scot-free.'

'Well, Mrs. Breen, I've asked you. What's your solution?' Cam could see inspiration spread over Rita Breen's face. She pulled at the waistband of her cotton skirt. Cam thought she saw her tugging at her corset.

'I said, I just think everyone should know. I'm taking Jerry over now to see your grandparents.'

This was more than Dan could bear.

'You won't do that, you can't,' he said.

Rita Breen wore a look of triumph. 'I'm going to right now. Try and stop me.'

She walked out the door, quickly, before she could be stopped. Like a comic parade, Dan, Cam, and Sharon followed her and Jerry. They said nothing as they passed Jack Morrisey and Mary Dolan, who looked as if they knew everything. On the sidewalk, Cam grabbed Rita Breen roughly by the arm.

'If you go near my grandparents' house I'll —'

'You'll what?' said Rita Breen with a sour smile. 'Sue?' She walked down the sidewalk, swinging her hard, rectangular pocketbook, letting it bump against her leg.

Cam's car was parked behind the office; she, Dan, and Sharon piled into it like policemen chasing robbers. They were determined to get to Vincent and Ellen's first.

'You stay in the car,' Cam said. 'I'll tell them.'

Vincent was not at home. As plainly as she could, Cam explained the situation to Ellen.

'Foolishness from beginning to end,' Ellen said. Then she remembered it was Dan who'd been attacked. 'If that cute bitch with her hen's-ass mouth comes over here thinking she's about to shock me, or I'm about to stroke her poor boy's brow, she's stupider than even I think she is. Going to the parish priest. I'm sure she made him feel right as rain. She'll be sorry she set her foot in this part of town when I'm through with her.'

Ellen walked to the front porch wiping her hands on her apron. She was standing on the porch when Rita Breen walked up the path.

'I know what you're here for, Rita Breen, and you can take yourself off my property or I'll have the police on you for harassment.'

'I didn't want to upset you, Mrs. MacNamara. I just thought you should know the goings-on in your own family.'

'If I want the news I'll listen to the radio. Now, get out of here, and fast, or you'll spend the night in jail.'

Dan and Sharon watched this from the back seat of Cam's car where they sat holding hands. It made neither of them happier, Ellen's performance; it didn't make them feel vindicated, or protected, or redeemed; their gratitude and pride in her made their shame unbearable. Sharon saw that Ellen kept her back straight until the Breens were out of sight. Then she saw that Ellen leaned on Cam a moment to walk into the house. She thought then that she should leave Dan forever, since what they had done had made Ellen turn a corner; they had made her old.

But Sharon and Dan didn't separate. It would have been possible, after Ellen's victory, that everything could have gone back nearly as it was before. Sharon would have had to find another job, but she and Dan could have stopped seeing each other; she could have gone back to Jerry; no one outside their families knew anything about it, except Jack Morrisey and Mary Dolan and Father Lynch, who would use their information for silent punishment, but keep it silent all the same. But Val wouldn't take Dan back. Or, rather, she insisted upon giving him away. She wasn't outraged by his infidelity, she'd been unfaithful first, and realized how little it could mean. It was that in seeing Dan choose Sharon, who was beautiful and sensual and lush, she understood how wrong she was for him. She realized that beside him she would never feel quite like a woman; he needed somebody who was, like him, slightly overfull. Sharon's physical being supported all the ideas Val had about men and women. She didn't blame men for it: who wouldn't prefer Sharon's voluptuous, dreamy abundance to her own tense, highly wrought spareness. She perceived, too, that Sharon was weaker than she; she convinced herself that Sharon needed Dan more than she did, and therefore she should give him up. The weakness of women had always been a sacred idea to her; her mother had been an invalid; Val had seen her own energy as a failure to come up to the female ideal. She saw how lovable it was, this idea of woman's weakness. She understood what had come of it, the cluster of ideas that grew up around the picture of the vulnerable woman, the inventions it inspired: fashions to encase, enclose the soft bones that surround the emptiness at the center, sanctuaries, stories, operettas, tragedies, things she never would want given up, the rituals of adoration, of protection that were so touching and so beautiful they must be true. She saw herself a skeleton: functional, dry. She had produced two children freakishly, the goose who laid, because it had been called for, golden eggs. She could use what she was to protect these children, who, having come from Dan as well as herself, would need protection. She would not take them away from him, but she could no longer live beside him. She made him see that she wasn't angry, but that he could no longer live beside her in the house. It was jarring,

171

their contiguity; it was a false picture. He belonged with Sharon now, it was impossible that he could go on living in the house, beside her, as if they belonged together, as if that were right. To Dan she said only, 'It's better if you move out.'

Dan had no recourse; if she had said he had to go, he felt he should. She never told him all the reasons she had for his leaving; she grew harder, colder, every day, until both of them understood that life together was impossible.

Jerry Breen had moved out of the apartment; Sharon was there alone. It was unnatural that Dan stay away from her; they came together in sadness, in shame, but they made a shelter for each other and a place where each could live.

After a month of living in the apartment that, after all, belonged to Jerry Breen, Dan made the dispiriting search of the unhoused adulterer for an abode. He spoke to bored and surly building managers in apartment complexes horribly designed to seem opulent. I have two children, he would tell them. Maybe in the summers this could be good for them: the swimming pool. They'd seen it all, the building managers, the children in the summers, on the weekends, bored and anxious and impatient to go home.

In those days, Dan walked around like a man recovering from a gunshot wound. Sometimes he and Sharon would rouse themselves from their miasma of shame and lethargy, punctuated by tentative withholding sex, and go out to a store to shop for furniture or linens for the new home they felt themselves forced to make. She could see how, beside Dan, she appeared desirable, enviable, even to other men; sometimes her pride in him filled her veins with joy like a transfusion of fresh blood. She could pretend that they were starting out together on a wonderful adventure, that Dan would be hers now, forever; this wonderful man would be hers. Almost, then, eating cheeseburgers in the shopping-mall luncheonettes, they could feel they had not been shot dead.

But then he'd see something – a tricycle in a store window, a horse that could be made to buck by the insertion of two nickels, a child the age of one of his – and he'd feel himself a danger and a poison, he would look at Sharon and think: Sooner or later, I will poison her too. He visited his children in the house that was no longer his. Darci at five had grown already into her real nature: ardent, tense, alert. She was vengeful, terrible, when he prepared to leave. He would drive away, seeing in his mind's eye her sullen and destructive tantrums behind the closed door of her room. But Staci, who was only four when he left, had a notion of him as only absence, a language the others in the family spoke easily that she had never learned, a blank door she would never open, never even approach.

It went on like this for two years, the time of the subpoenas, the divorce (his friend Joe Murphy represented him, but could not hold him back from giving away too much). It made him feel slightly less monstrous to see that his wife and children lived like the others on the street, the ones with real fathers who planted grass on the mean, unhopeful lawns and in the winter shoveled the thin sidewalks. After two years, the divorce became final; Sharon's divorce, much simpler, had come through a year before. Dan asked her to marry him, but she refused. They've been together for twelve years; he's asked her to marry him many times. Each time he asks her, she thinks of Ellen, turning her tired back on Rita Breen, and she feels that she has no right to a legitimate place in the MacNamara family.

It wasn't only Ellen, she believes, whom she'd weakened and made old. Six months after she and Dan moved in together, Jack Morrisey retired. For thirty years, he'd kept up a correspondence with a Paracletist missionary who'd spent his priesthood in the Philippines. Jack had never met him, but when the priest retired to a small parish in South Carolina, where his family had settled, Jack joined him and bought a house nearby.

Sharon knows that Jack left because the direction in which Cam moved the practice didn't please him. He lost his bearings in Cam's wave of feminist energy; he never wanted to handle divorce, wife battering, difficult custody cases; now these made up the bulk of the firm's cases. That was true, Sharon knew that, but it wasn't all the truth. The truth, she felt, was that seeing what had happened with her and Dan made Jack Morrisey want to give up.

She will not go to Vincent and Ellen's house; she sees Cam, rarely, at the house she and Dan built in Quogue; she likes serving Cam meals, but she can't be at ease with her. She carries the shame of what she did to Dan and to his family, a weakening disease. She lives her life always a bit under the weather; like a patient getting over pneumonia. Her employers encourage her to go to law school, but she refuses. She and Dan live quietly, devotedly, but she is not his wife, she won't allow herself to be. She took him from his wife, and she insists they both remember.

Approaching middle age, they understand that they will be together, now, for life. But they have never said this to each other; they feel they have no right to promise. Their house is half a mile from the Long Island Sound; they walk, each morning, by the water; they see friends from Sharon's office, they collect antiques. But they are never lighthearted; sadness hangs over them, a cloud everyone can sense, so they aren't popular with other couples. Dan will never get over the loss of his children; she can't give up her shame that it was through her this loss came about.

Every year, the girls come for August and life is different. Sharon accepts her displacement in the situation; Dan cooks for them: hamburgers, Kraft macaroni and cheese, Chef-Boy-Ar-Dee ravioli, coral-colored in the pot. Her attempts with the girls have always been hobbled by her sense of shame in their presence: naturalness is impossible, and she knows what takes its place. Darci despises her, she's glad not to be living with Sharon, but with Cam. And Staci uses her. Sharon is not deceived that the presents she buys Staci earn anything for her but contempt; still, she's afraid to stop; at least the pretense of connection is better than the freezing look in Staci's eyes when she isn't being distracted by a new acquisition. The girls stay for a month; Dan speaks a new vocabulary: their friends' names, the names of the songs they like, their favorite movie stars, their jokes. Then, cruelly, the thread is cut, and in September, she and Dan go back to being what they were: modest, melancholy, and responsible.

'I've got to go,' Sharon says. 'We're so shorthanded. Lisa and Joanne are away.'

'Where'd they go?'

'Lisa went to Paris with her mother; Joanne is in the Islands with God knows who.'

Dan realizes that it's been three years since he and Sharon have gone away on a vacation. A damp spot of guilt spreads underneath his ribs.

'Let's go to Paris in the fall,' he says. 'Or to some beach.'

'What beach? It's hurricane season in the Islands.'

'It's not hurricane season in Paris.'

'Oh, Dan, for heaven's sake,' she says. He doesn't know what she means. He knows that any movement – forward or out – makes her a little anxious. But he thinks he hears in her voice her willingness for him to lead her out. He thinks of them on a plane together. The thought arouses him. After all this time, whatever else has happened, they have not lost that pleasure.

'Come on, Irish,' he says, 'a plane is a very sexy place.'

'Dan,' she says, 'everyone can hear you in the hall.'

'Only my aunt Theresa,' he says, and they both laugh.

But it isn't Theresa who hears them, it's Sheilah. She hears Dan's words and understands what's behind them: the easy life of men and women, the playful life that starts in bed and moves into the world. Love-play. She's never been a player. She has watched, always outside it, both yearning to be *of* it and taking her pride and sense of safety from being apart. The sense of apartness has marked her life.

She was the quiet girl in glasses with pastel rims, tortoiseshell barrettes held on to past their usefulness, their rightness. She counted up the errors of the others moving out of childhood, out of the bones and flat muscles, the quick legs burnished by the heat of local games: red-rover, ring-a-levio, street games played to the point of death, faces flushed from the last sun of autumn, faces shocked by the quick curtainfall of night in late November. She watched those faces, those bodies; once they were faultless, but no more. She stood away from them, recording everything.

That's what she's always done, it's who she's always been, the one who watches and stands apart. She can never have what Dan and Sharon have. She'd stumbled into being joined to Stephen Gallagher; their coming together had the elements, not of romantic comedy, but of the most common sort of farce. When she met him, he'd been Father Gallagher, a Dominican; she'd been Sister Raymond Theresa. They met when they participated in a draft-card burning on the steps of the City Hall of Keene, New Hampshire, and became lovers while their vows were still in force.

The integrity of their political activities was called into question when they were found by the police in a motel. Just a routine check, Miss – or Sister, whatever it is. Their spiked hair, combed wet from the shower, made a joke of everything. The police had brought reporters along. The flash camera, the headlines that read 'Nun and Priest Protesters Found in Love Nest.' The day before, they had been heroes, Steve leading the psalms in his workshirt and liturgical stole. Was that why Steve married her? Because they'd had their pictures in the paper, with their hair wet from the shower, in front of the Thunderbird Motel? He wasn't interested in sex, not really, even at first. He was interested in being able to say that he, a priest, had *had* sex. Their marriage, even Diarmid's birth, never made up to him for losing the distinction of his priesthood. For having become, once again, simply himself, her husband, rather than a priest of God. It hadn't measured up.

She watches Dan; she is the child she's always been with him, yearning, envious, vengeful. Putting down the phone, he turns to her, realizing that she's overheard.

'Hi, there,' he says, self-consciously.

She sees that she's made him uneasy. One of the few people in the world who like her, one of the few people whom she likes. She's half sorry, half something else she doesn't know the name of but recognizes as familiar, partly satisfying: right.

6

Staci rounds the corner of Linden Street and Roberts Avenue and begins to slow her pace. She has just run two and a half miles from the G. Michael Hobbs pool, where she is a lifeguard. Running, she is the person she wants to be, the person she admires herself for being. Now it's all over: the fight she always wins against the heavy body, heavy in itself despite everything she does. She can't make herself entirely weightless as she would like, and yet that isn't really what she wants: she dreads insubstantialness; it would mean that she would have no force. She would like a body that is muscle and bone, dry, unneeding. Yet that isn't what she wants either, because no one would look at her like that. Without this flesh – tan now, the way she likes it, the gold hairs on her arms shining like metal – no one would look at her. She couldn't sit on the high seat of the lifeguard stand, move her leg an inch, a quarter of an inch and know that she has caused something to happen in the world, know that the boys who jackknife into the water to get a better look at her, who pull their hard white lifeguard hats over their noses to pretend they aren't looking, are doing it for her. For *her*. A movement of hers, even the slightest, is a pull: the vector of the earth tilts. She is the equator, the pole. She is in charge of gravity. When she runs, when she feels her heart like a knife pressing its blade against her and her lungs two spots, sharp and hot, she doesn't succumb to them, she delights in them. She lifts herself above them, and she is lifted up, but moving, nothing can stop her; they can be looking at her or not looking, she is moving, she is all alone, she couldn't possibly need anyone, no one could do her harm.

She slows herself down. She is about to lose it. At the first sight of her great-grandparents' house, she will begin to succumb to its lowering, decelerating, darkening force. She won't give herself up. She hardens herself, she makes herself a stone against the force of the house pressing down. When it presses down on her, she will press back. All her life she has been expert in resistance. It is her safety from harm and desire.

She sees her father sitting on the front porch steps beside her cousin Marilyn. She would never let anything happen to her like what happened to Marilyn. Like what keeps happening over and over, though she's old now, she ought to be finished with that, but it will never be over for her, and Staci doesn't know how she could stand to live like that, just waiting for a man to come and do something to her. Staci can tell by the way she sits.

Staci doesn't want to talk to them. Her father lifts his heavy shoulders. She can tell how he's dying to talk to her, dying for her to come over to him. She won't. Every time she sees him everything about him is always telling her something depressing: how much he misses her, he loves her, how sorry he is that he left, he wishes he could love her as much as Darci. Why would she want to be around that? She always wants to kick her father over, like one of those bottom-heavy clown toys that you can tip over, but they just come up again and again, asking for it, asking for it, over and over. She won't give him what he wants. 'Oh, Daddy, I adore you,' Darci is always saying to him. She'd like to kick the both of them over, running off, just on her way somewhere, one flick of the foot, the two of them. They're disgustingly fat. She doesn't know how they can let themselves get that way. Neither of them says no to themselves for one minute.

Pointing to her watch, and then grabbing hold of her wrist, she pantomimes to her father and Marilyn that she can't talk, she's trying to take her pulse. They wave and smile at her and go on talking.

'You look terrific,' her father shouts out.

That's just the kind of thing she hates, he knows that. Why doesn't he just shut up? At least her mother never does anything like that. At least she leaves her alone. That's all she wants from people, and they can't seem to get it. It's because they're always needing something; they can't believe that other people don't.

Opening the latch of the backyard fence she sees her cousin John walking with a hammer in his hand. He scares her. He never says anything to her, just looks at her with those eyes that mean he wants to do something to her, hurt her or punish her. He looks at her in that way that's already taking something from her. She won't let him do that. He looks disgusting. He's the most disgusting one of them all. He's always smoking and his teeth are brown, but it's not just that. Some of them are missing, like he got into a fight. She knows it's not impossible that he could hit her with that hammer, make the blood come out of her head, and just walk away, leave her there, not look at what he'd done, not even remember it. And her father wouldn't be able to stop him. She can see her father kneeling over her, crying. 'Staci, baby, how did this happen?' Letting that pig get away. Forgetting to do what he was supposed to do: revenge her. She's never seen hair as horrible as her cousin John's. He probably doesn't wash it, ever.

She's opened the gate now, and she won't let John know that seeing him makes her want to walk away. She's got to make him know that he could never make her do anything she didn't want to do. Anything she would do would be because she wanted it. She walks around the backyard, pretending to cool down. To return her pulse to normal. But her pulse is faster than it was when she was running.

She's afraid of him, but he'll never make her do anything she doesn't want. He sits down on the step and lights a cigarette, but she knows he's sitting there to watch her as she walks around the backyard. His eyes are half closed as he looks at her. His legs are open; he lets his hands, one holding a cigarette, dangle between his knees. Something about his looking at her makes her feel he's locked her in somewhere. She keeps walking around, not ever getting closer to him, but not wanting him to stop looking at her either. The circles she makes are getting smaller. It's making her dizzy to keep walking around like that. But she can't stop. She turns her back to him and stares at one of the hydrangea bushes. She hates those flowers. She doesn't know why anyone would want flowers like that. She lifts the front of her shirt to wipe the sweat off her face. She knows he can probably see her.

She's sick of it, she wants to take a shower. Even the shower in her great-grandparents' house is disgusting. She loves her shower at home. Her own shower in her own bathroom: white tiles, chrome, as much hot water as she wants any time, coming out of the shiny metal shower head. This one is greenish on the bottom, where the holes are that the water shoots from. She likes the water in the Hobbses' pool: bluish, sharp, like it was never near anything dirty. No one ever uses this shower; her father said that when he lived here he was the only one in the house that ever did. That's exactly the kind of thing he's always saying. So that you have to think of him in the shower, and his grandparents taking baths. That's the kind of thing he's always making you think about.

She doesn't look at John as she walks by him to get into the house. She can walk through the house the back way, through the kitchen, which is empty, and up the stairs, without having to talk to anyone. She opens the bathroom door. She can't stand that the floor is old linoleum, not tiles or a rug or anything like an ordinary bathroom. She goes over to the window to close the curtain. Then she sees that he's up on a ladder, forty feet away, right across from her, pretending to fix the gutter on the garage, pretending to nail something tight, but she knows it's not that, she knows he's there to look at her.

If he sees her closing the curtain, he'll know she did it because of him. And she won't let him have that. She walks away from the window, leaving the curtain open.

All the time she's taking off her clothes, she's telling herself that he's not making her do anything. She gets into the shower. She can smell the dust in the water; even the water doesn't seem clean. The shampoo on the side of the tub must have been there for a million years. Prell. She wonders who bought it. She smooths it on her hair, taking a long time, making him stand on that ladder.

She hopes he'll fall off. She hopes he'll fall off and break his neck. She'd love to see him on the ground with his head snapped to one side and his eyes open and his mouth open showing his disgusting teeth. She soaps herself as slowly as she can, but it starts to bore her.

She takes the towel off the rack and begins to dry herself. She makes sure she does it the way she always would, no special way for him. She bends down and shakes her hair out, then wraps a towel around her wet hair. She reaches for another towel, then walks to the window, stands there for a second and wraps the towel around herself. She stands there staring at him so he knows she knows. She tries to make him get down off the ladder, but she can't. She pulls the curtains shut.

7

Cam is on the front porch, sitting on the blue corduroy glider. Theresa walks out and sits beside her. Cam stiffens; she doesn't encourage Theresa to relax, to stay. Theresa looks down at her peach-colored nails.

'Have you talked to your mother today, Camille?'

What is between them – hate – flourishes at the sound of Theresa's first word. It unfolds, like a paper flower in water. It exfoliates, intricately, as if touched by some seasonal impulse. It unrolls and throws itself out like a bolt of cloth. It grows in its extent: familiar, useful, interesting. This hate began for Cam in childhood. Theresa attached her hate to a still-growing child. Ancestral, it would go on, and it would be passed down. There would be no end to it.

'She wasn't at all well this morning,' Cam says. 'I'm not sure if she'll make it today.'

Cam says this, knowing her enemy, therefore unable to look in her eye. She knows she's the weak one in this encounter. Her sense of her weakness makes her angry at her mother. She'd like to shout at her mother: 'Why do you always make me lie?'

8

Magdalene is in her room, wondering what she'll do. She is still focused on what she'll wear, as if, after finding the perfect outfit, she'll be fine. Her life is largely the body's, more particularly the eye's. It's not that she's observant; she has always missed the most obvious, the grossest or most clearly impressive aspect of any scene. Even her interest in clothes is limited largely to those she wears herself.

She walks into her closet, a small purple room. A sense of peace comes over her at the abundance of her clothes. She doesn't get rid of clothes once they've gone out of fashion. She pretends that this is done from thrift – things always come back, she says, and then you're glad you have them. But actually it's that she can't bear to betray her clothes. Having touched her body, they became loving relatives. How could she put them out, expose them in their old age, in their marginality, to the cruel world whose cruelty they kept her from?

She gave her clothes the tenderness she never gave a lover. Her clothes had given her something: her clothes had added to what she was. But sex only took away. She would gladly have kept herself a virgin had there been a way for her to do it and still leave the family house. Every act of sex to her was an ablation and a loss, total because it took place in private, and she could gain no recognition for what she had given up. But she had to marry to leave the house. And she had to leave the house.

Magdalene's bad luck was to have been born into a family, the one, perhaps, in fifteen hundred, where good looks wouldn't matter enough to see a daughter through. What could Ellen Mac-Namara treasure in a pretty girl? To Ellen, prettiness was a lure, a snare, at the best a distraction. And to Vincent, who was by nature genuinely intellectual and moral, and by habit practical and interested in the functions of things, his daughter's looks were merely a confusion. Her prettiness, soft, blonde, white-skinned, and prone to change, seemed insubstantial to him. He couldn't understand why she didn't look like her mother; he'd expected her to. Ellen's was the kind of beauty that he liked, suggesting action or resistance. But Magdalene wasn't like that; she was the ideal of her age: light, curly-haired, with wide perplexed or indolent blue eyes, a pliant, uncomprehending mouth. She was not her father's type. Finding her vague, scattered, easily distracted, he turned his attention to the other two children, Theresa and John, whom he found solid, who were able to follow an argument, a plan, a blueprint, the directions on a box, the line of a journey on a map. When he tried to explore his older daughter's character, he felt as if he'd stuck his hand into a pile of feathers. He couldn't fully love that which he couldn't grasp. The soft and shifting substance which he believed made up his daughter's inner nature caused him to recoil.

Magdalene knew she didn't please her father, and she was confused, for she could see she pleased all other men. Her failure with her father turned her radically outward. To live her life at home was to acknowledge that she failed. The words, the gestures that made her mother call her a fool and made her father turn away brought her in the outside world friends, laughter, the place of the chosen child. By the time she was eight years old teachers had marked her in this way: *Magdalene is sweet-natured and amusing; she will cause no trouble; her sunny disposition is an asset in the class.* On her, these words meant, no effort would be expended. She would marry early; there was not much that she need learn.

If she had had a family that made her feel prized, perhaps she wouldn't have married quite so early. Eighteen. A week after her high-school graduation. Perhaps she wouldn't have been so obviously foolish in her selection. Was it that her tastes and fantasies, bred in the movies, were bound to mislead her? They did not suggest a recondite, surprising choice. She was the prettiest girl in the class; she married the best athlete. Who could have predicted it would come to such grief?

Magdalene married Jimmy Laughlin in July of 1938. From the beginning sex was bad. The problem was one of misinformation, a sexual education so incomplete that Magdalene believed, and still believes, that her husband was fiendish when in fact he had the ordinary hungers of a young and healthy man. She was shocked by the transition from kissing to intercourse. Or it was the lack of transition that shocked her. The unrushed, silent embraces that were all she had allowed before her wedding turned into a frantic, feverish performance while she lay inert beneath a man she never knew. His face, his voice, his body were all unfamiliar. He became, she felt, possessed, and she herself entrapped beneath a stranger.

He did well enough in his job selling iceboxes so that they could afford, as so few of her friends could, not to live in their parents' home, but to be independent. Independence is better than a college degree, Jimmy would say, as if he had been tempted for even a minute by the prospect of further education. Living in three rooms above a butcher shop, they felt successful. They felt too that, in living as they did, they had moved one step closer to the America they saw in the movies and had known nowhere in their own lives.

In this spirit they decided they would wait to have children. Defying the pastor, Magdalene lied in confession (later she would see what happened as a punishment for this), they used condoms for a year and a half, then gave them up when Magdalene turned twenty-one. In two months she was pregnant, in another month she lost the child. Their sex life, which had been for him the swift release of some uncomprehended pressure and for her a bafflement, turned into the grim, purposeful friction of two people who felt they must overcome a curse. In 1941 they had Camille, named by Magdalene after her favorite movie.

Before Camille's birth, Magdalene had worked as a beautician in Mr. John's House of Beauty, a salon owned by John Impanata, who had begun his working life a barber and switched, in the twenties, to the newly profitable female clientele. Magdalene's working life had given her the time and money to build a wardrobe, learn to use makeup, find and maintain the perfect hairdo that would make her not just a natural beauty, but an invented one. With her cork-soled shoes, her Marlene Dietrich trousers, her high-maintenance pompadoured hair, she frightened and made humble the young mothers on the street. She made it appear that Camille's birth was a subtle, highly styled event in opposition to the force of nature the other mothers, still girls, were victims of.

In the pictures Jimmy Laughlin took of those days, Camille, a smiling, photogenic baby, radiates her parents' well-toned pleasure. Her mother in shorts and a midriff top lifts Cam, incandescently laughing for Daddy-Papa-look-at-Daddy in the camera. Or muscular, smiling Jimmy holds his treasure like a basketball. In these pictures it is summer, always clement weather. It is also 1941, but to look at the photographs, you would imagine that the War in Europe was a bad joke that the pessimists made up to stifle the good times of the fun-loving and clean-limbed Americans at home, who obviously knew the score.

But then it was March 1942, and Jimmy was drafted. All the noble, sentimental feelings Magdalene saw in movies actually grew up in her breast. She thought her husband looked heroic in a uniform, though even this sight didn't transform itself into desire. Photogenically, they parted at the railroad station, holding between them their adorable child. When Jimmy spoke to Magdalene sentences that began 'If I don't come back from all this,' his words lacked conviction. He believed himself immortal, and she knew it and resented it, wanting him to throw himself upon her in real, if only temporary fear.

During the eight months that Jimmy fought in Burma, Magdalene went back to work as a beautician. John Impanata sold Magdalene Mr. John's House of Beauty, which she rechristened Maison Magdalene. Having seen her behavior, knowing her nature, people predicted ruin, chaos, joked about disasters, scenes of Magdalene begging bank managers for a reprieve in a tableau of flutterheaded supplication and distress. But Magdalene made money. It turned out that she had a gift for money. She was excellent at managing her business, hired two more girls, Betty and Myrna, who did manicures as well.

When Jimmy came back, he observed Magdalene's achievement with the pride of a dog owner who has left home and returned to find his pet performing in a circus, wearing a crinoline, a sailor's outfit, a beret. He expected that Magdalene had had her fun and would quit now, stay home full-time now he was back, take care of their miracle daughter. She did not. She went on, facing her husband's anger and his scorn, leaving her daughter with her mother. Ellen felt a satisfaction in her daughter's making money, it was the one thing she could like her daughter for, and she fell in love with the girl child in whose baby eyes she saw what she had not seen in her daughter's: something of herself.

So, every morning, dressed in stockings and high heels, while the other mothers slopped in housedresses and slippers, her clothes crisp, exciting to her daughter, Magdalene got into her blue-gray Buick, pressed her high-arched, polished shoe on the accelerator, dropped her daughter at Ellen's, said no to coffee, she was busy, she was rushed, the child had dawdled. But the truth was that she didn't want to be detained for a second longer than need be in the domestic world her mother's house embodied. She loved the moment when she put her key into the lock of the shop, smelt in the dark the strong, dangerous smell of permanent-wave lotion, stood alone and turned the light on with a sense of awe. Seeing it then – the empty chairs, the sinks, the dryers, the trays of nail polish and emery boards – she thought every morning: I own this, this is mine.

Jimmy had to understand that his wife was well off. The baffled look with which she had, before he'd left, greeted everything from the male orgasm to the size of the telephone bill had smoothed itself out. He could see she wore that look now when it could be useful to her. It could help her get something from a man. But he watched her sitting over the salon's books and he saw the secure, serene face of a mystic. She seemed to have nothing to do now with domestic life, that dream he and his friends had dreamed together in the Burmese jungle. She wouldn't cook. It wasn't that she refused to. She simply indicated that they would be eating dinner at her mother's, and if he wanted a hot meal he should turn up there. He could see that he was of no interest to her, except to be beside her with the other young couples, and to be her partner in the fox-trot or at bridge. Whereas she had been abashed before him sexually, she was indifferent now. He felt she humored him. He saw that she regarded sex as the childish preoccupation of the childish gender, the male. The men whom she admired, like her father, she believed had reached maturity and given it all up.

Magdalene was right to see her husband a boy. Defeated by his wife's prosperity without him, he grew every month more into the child she thought him to be. He tried to pick up the thread of his pre-war success, the shining high-school years when he courted Magdalene, impressed and won her. It was embarrassing to see him with the teenagers. He coached the CYO team, but ruined the practices by hogging the ball and showing off. He trained his daughter to be an athlete. Flattered by her status as the chosen girl, proficient in the world of males, delightedly Cam let herself be tutored in sports that were her father's calling and his pride. She became a girlfriend to her mother; she became her father's pal. All this was established before she was six years old. Her two good-looking parents knew they had more to say to her than they did to each other. She assumed that was the way with all parents. She was close to no children but Dan, who had no parents, and she had no way to verify what she simply took to be the norm.

Then the news, the policeman at the door at 3:00 A.M. Jimmy Laughlin was dead, drunk, off the highway with a parish girl. Eighteen years old and dead too, drunk like him. Because of Jimmy, her heartbroken parents took up in the town the honorable position of the shamed bereaved. But Magdalene turned all her shame to gold. Betrayal gave her stature. She became the movie image of the gallant widow, prematurely middle-aged. Without comment, offering no one an explanation (none was needed), she gave up her husband's name and changed her own name and her daughter's, legally, to MacNamara. In fact, she'd loved her name, loved the alliteration, 'Magdalene MacNamara.' She had thought it distinguished; now she thought it would be good for trade.

Camille saw that her mother did not mourn, and closed part of her heart against her. One room she kept cleansed and sanctified for the handsome young man who had pretended, all along pretended, to have been her father, and now, dead, seemed in fact to be. She clung to Dan, who had always been the one child she'd enjoyed. She clung to her grandparents.

Thinking of all this makes Magdalene feel trapped. She feels her clothes have conspired against her. Punishingly, she pulls the string on the light bulb at the center of the closet that is the size of a room. The string sways back and forth; the little metal flower at the string's end clanks against the bulb like a lost soul. She feels she has nowhere to go. Nothing is of interest to her. She thinks angrily of her daughter. How could she be a happy woman with a daughter who's always treated her the way Cam has? She feels like she needs to calm down. She decides to pour herself a drink. It's Cam's fault that she's drinking at this hour. Thinking of her daughter's defections, beginning at Jimmy's death, makes her feel that her nerves poke through her skin and she needs something to put them back, take them away from the surface, where they are too susceptible to hurt.

She pours herself a drink. Sherry, she thinks, will be a nice drink, a light drink for this hour of the morning.

Magdalene begins to drink. Whenever Magdalene admits she drinks (which isn't often – and when it occurs it happens only when she is alone) she tells herself that she does it because her daughter always wanted to make her feel bad. She was so upset at

186

that time, after her husband died, that she couldn't sleep. If Camille had just been nice to her then, it would have made all the difference. But Camille turning against her kept her up at night. She wouldn't even let Magdalene put her to bed; she wouldn't let Magdalene unbraid and brush her hair. 'That's OK, Mom, I can do it. You're tired.' But she wasn't tired. When she lay down all kinds of things came into her head, things it wasn't any help to think about. Somebody suggested she take sleeping pills. But when she asked Larry Riordan, the doctor, he said, 'I'd hate to see you getting caught up in dope. Just have yourself a good stiff drink, that'll bring sleep on you.'

Camille did everything to turn against her. She shortened her name to Cam, she spent all the time she could with her grandparents. On Saturdays, she didn't wake Magdalene up in the morning, she dressed herself and walked to her grandparents' for breakfast. 'Why didn't you wake me, I told you I'd take you to the luncheonette for breakfast? We talked about it last night, you said you'd get French toast.'

'You looked tired, Mama. I wanted to let you sleep.'

Sometimes she could catch her daughter off her guard by making some warm, female nest, not womanly, but girlish: a lush refuge where two equals could retreat and settle. The two of them could sit on Magdalene's bed with its varieties of pillows and watch the Late Show and eat foods of great comfort and pleasure with no nutritive value at all. Modern foods Ellen would never serve. She could take her daughter out to lunch. For a while, they could go shopping. But as Cam grew older, she took on her grandmother's asceticism. 'Don't spend money on a restaurant,' she'd tell her mother. Or: 'Let's not go shopping, I don't need more clothes.' More and more, Magdalene was pushed out of the life her daughter lived by day. Vincent worked with Camille on her homework; he made her and Dan the stars in the school science projects, coached them for spelling bees, and drove them anywhere for oratorical competitions which they nearly always won. With her grandmother, Camille talked politics. Together they campaigned for Stevenson, together they cursed – the real untrammeled curses Ellen encouraged in her granddaughter – they cursed the fools who voted for a mediocre bald golfer when they could have had such an obviously great man for President.

Magdalene thought Camille despised her. Camille was always

trying to make her look bad, to punish her. For what? She'd worked hard, worked her fingers to the bone, to get the best for her daughter. She didn't know what else Camille wanted. What else could she have done? Whatever she did, it wouldn't be enough. You'd never satisfy Camille. She never understood what Magdalene had been through, what she had to go through every day of her life. Even now, forty-four years old, she doesn't have the maturity to understand her mother. Even today, she wants to put her through it. Doesn't she understand how hard it would be for Magdalene to go to her parents' house? In this weather, with this humidity and her trouble breathing? It's like she doesn't know a thing about Magdalene's health, after everything the doctors told her. She doesn't see how she can be expected to do the things Camille expects her to do. Her hands start shaking just thinking of getting dressed and going out. Suppose she fainted on the street. When she gets shaky like this, anything can happen.

Another drink will steady her. Maybe, she thinks, with another one she'll be steady enough to get herself dressed and go outside. The sherry bottle is empty. She walks over to the place where she keeps unopened liquor. The lower cabinet, violet enamel, with its white scalloped trim. Sherry is a light drink for the morning. Soothing. She pours herself another half-glass and sits down on the purple chaise longue.

It is twenty years after Magdalene's first sickness, twenty years after her operation, which was a complete success. She is in her room now, August 14, 1985, knowing they are waiting for her, her family, knowing they think she won't show up. It would please some of them if she should fail her father: Theresa, Sheilah would be pleased. Dan would sympathize with her but he would sympathize more with Cam. Her mother won't notice. Her mother doesn't notice anything anymore. She wouldn't recognize Magdalene even if she came. John wouldn't notice; Marilyn would be kind either way. Her father would understand. Nobody's like her father. She knows he'll understand. It's Cam, Cam's the one. The only one it's important to is Cam. She knows that Cam believes that if she shows up they've proved they're all right, the two of them, and if she doesn't they're shamed.

She doesn't want to go. She's full of dread. She blames her

daughter for this dread. Why does her daughter make her feel these things? Nobody else has daughters that make them feel these things, these terrible upsetting things Cam makes her feel. Someone should know about Cam, the way she really is. She wants to tell someone, about everything Cam does to her. Cam never understands. Cam's never on her side. She needs to call someone. She decides to call her father. She has the number, somewhere; though she's never called him at that home. She fishes in her drawer for her telephone book. The number is there, written in Cam's hand. The problem is that she's never confided in him. He hasn't understood because she's been afraid to tell him. But now she's not afraid. He's got to know. He's got to know the score, the way things are.

'Hello, dear,' he says to her, uncertainly. She didn't remember his voice sounding that old.

'So, you're all ready to hit the road, Pop?' she says.

'Right you are,' says Vincent.

'I'm hoping to see you later, Pop, at the house.'

'Well, that would be nice,' he says but she can tell that he doesn't believe her. She hasn't been in the house for fifteen years, but that doesn't mean anything. If she says she's going to come, he should believe she'll come.

'It's only that the heat is terrible, and the humidity. I feel so dizzy in this kind of weather.'

'Don't push yourself,' her father says. 'Remember your health.'

'No, I'm not as strong as I used to be,' she says.

'You do wonderfully well for yourself,' he says.

'It's twenty years, Pop, that I've had to live with this. A death sentence for twenty years. I never said this to you, Pop, but it's the truth. I looked into the face of death. Do you know what that's like?'

Her father doesn't say anything.

'Every day of my life I have to face the fact that I could die.'

'It's true of all of us, Magdalene,' he says.

This makes her angry. 'You never looked into the face of death,' she says. 'None of you know what it's like. Especially Camille. She has no sympathy for me. She just tries to make me look in the wrong.'

'That's not true, Magdalene. She's very good to you.'

'That's my cross, Pop. That's what you think, that's what

189

everybody thinks. My cross is nobody sees what she does to me. Always wanting to make me look in the wrong.'

'Well, I don't know about that, Magdalene. I think I'd better finish packing. You take care of yourself.'

'You too, Pop. Maybe I'll see you later.'

'Fine,' he says. She knows that he doesn't believe her.

None of them knows what it's like. 'I've looked into the face of death,' she says, aloud, to no one. The worst thing about it she doesn't say, that she looked into the face of death, and she prepared herself, submitted herself, not just to having her breasts cut off, but to the thought of death, which she awaited like a just and longed-for punishment. But then it didn't come, and the failure of the sentence she had believed in made her see death as untrustworthy. That was the worst. It could be anywhere, and could appear at any time, and she might not be ready.

Alone in her room, Magdalene imagines her daughter in Vincent and Ellen's house. She knows what Cam is thinking. She knows the words behind the thoughts. Hearing the words makes her angry. Her anger has no lightness; it weighs down her limbs. Could she walk anywhere with legs like these? Her legs are like lead. The lead rises up her legs, it fills her ribs. Her ribs are leaden straps around her lungs. How can she breathe? She sees herself on the street. There is no self there, no shape, nothing to keep her from spilling over into air, into life, into anybody's life. Outside this room she can fly off, she will, there will be no more *her*, nothing will press down on her to create a shape. The room creates the shape. Outside the room, everything will be lost. Nothing will stay, she will be terrified, alone: she knows that she will not be able to hold together. She sees a picture of herself on the street: organs flying off, limbs here, there. And falling, everything is falling, but not falling into shape.

How painful the straps around her lungs are. She can't get her breath. She stinks from terror. How can my daughter make me do this? she thinks. She wants me to feel like this. She tries to make me do what I can't. I'm sick. I am a woman who could at any time be dying. I can't leave this room.

She can't possibly be expected to go outside. How can she, when she is as she is, when she can't be looked at, when she can fall apart? The space where her breasts were throbs like a burn. She is loathsome; she is mutilated. Her body, hacked so it must

190

be hidden, is the true sign of herself. She has to hide. She is ugly; and she can fall apart. Cam must know this. She won't be angry. Or she will be angry whatever is done. So nothing can be done.

Magdalene thinks about her father and mother. Better not to see her mother as she is. Better remember her. No need to see her now. Think of her as she was.

She knows her father never made her do what she couldn't do. He never wanted that. He understands, or doesn't understand, it doesn't matter.

She decides that she'll stay here, in her room.

Nothing is that important.

No one cares enough.

IV

1

Vincent is sitting in a room that pleases him as much as any he has lived in. He is packing up his things. In his shaving kit he puts his razor, shaving brush and soap, an orange tin of foot powder, a cake of soap (Cashmere Bouquet) which he has rewrapped in its original paper. He folds the cotton rug that lies beside his bed. Sheilah his granddaughter brought it to him from Mexico, where she went once on vacation. There are pink, turquoise, and scarlet animals cavorting among branches. Their paws and haunches intertwine. He has never liked the rug, but kept it on the floor to please poor Sheilah, who'd never had the knack for pleasing. When Cam visited, her eye would fall down to the rug. Vincent could see Cam weighing the two possibilities: Perhaps he likes the rug, I mustn't spoil it for him; or he's doing this for Sheilah to be nice.

When Sheilah visited, she always said, 'It really livens up the place.' Under those words, though, he could hear what she was saying: 'I have traveled. I have given you something the others never would have thought of. Now let me be first.'

Able to hear the words below the words, how could Vincent take up the rug, which he dislikes? Even when she was gone and would not be back for a month, how could he? It hurts his eye. The room is square and plain and institutional. This is why he likes it. Sister Otile and Sister Roberta covered the decaying wooden floors with squares of tannish vinyl tile. Slabs of sheetrock they hung themselves cover the exposed laths and deranged plaster. They took a house that was the ruin of great beauty and made a place where people could be comfortable and live their lives. He honors them for this, and for their labor, whose full scope he knows. At the same time he honors the house for its loss, as you would honor a woman, formerly beautiful, who has lost her money and been forced to take a useful job.

Without the rug, the room was only what it was: a place

where people could enter and collect themselves. The room would disappear around them. What they made of their lives was theirs; the room would never help or stop them. Vincent likes this state of things, he likes its possibilities. His friends had come into this room and sat and talked and smoked their cigarettes. They had played cards, traded magazines, shared the advice and homemade things the families brought. They didn't admit that it was pleasant when their families left again, and they could come back here, to Vincent's room, or to another, where no one looked at them with the heavy eyes that said, 'I have abandoned you. Forgive me.' Vincent is grateful to have had a room where people could come and enjoy themselves. Now he is leaving. But he doesn't want to leave. They have done everything so he can go back home. He can't tell them that he wants to stay here; he can't disappoint them. He's been a man who didn't disappoint. At this age, you could only finish the life you'd led, and be the person you had been. Otile Ryan, Sister Otile, he can't help but call her, thinks it isn't so. She believes in change. They all do, all the sisters. On Sister Roberta's desk is a framed card, the message written in the slant, well-known handwriting of someone who had been a nun, but had got famous and had left the convent. 'Today is the first day of the rest of your life,' it says. For these last months, he's believed them.

He thinks of Ellen now. Sitting in her chair, up out of bed an hour, two hours a day, muttering curses, cursing offenders for their seventy-year-old crimes. Nothing is forgotten. Now her heart and brain have grown gelatinous, transparent. You can see the old slights, the offenses, come together and the punishments beside them. It is as if you could see them when you saw her eyes.

Neither of them had believed much in change. You are who you are, they'd always said. But were you? Who was Ellen now? He had to admit, she's changed. But has her change changed him? Does it mean he isn't the person he has been? Who, then, is he?

He remembers a road in Ireland: white; flat; and walking on it in hard boots. His heart was hardened against his wife. But then his hardness left him. He became Ellen. He became the girl that she had been. He'd thought that after that he would never again not know her, since she was a person he had, for a moment, been. He'd thought it was a thing you wouldn't lose. He'd lost it now.

Nothing more would change for Ellen. Or only one thing: she would die.

The biggest change for him had happened when he'd left his home in Dromnia for Cork City, thirty miles away. He lost his home. If he told the truth, that was the biggest thing that ever happened to him; bigger than losing his son in the War. Bigger than meeting Ellen? Maybe. Yes.

Even leaving for the other side, crossing the ocean to America, wasn't as hard as the day he left home to be apprentice to O'Donovan, the ironworker who'd learned from Leary at the mill in Dromnia that Vincent had a talent with his hands. He hadn't wanted to leave home. Except he knew his older brother and he knew the younger brother's place that was his own. He didn't want it to be his place for good.

Terrible, the way it was in families. He'd never understood it. Why they weren't what they were meant to be, what they could almost be so easily. Children grew up there, little children, and were never difficult. The faces of children come before him now, parades of them, Julia and Margaret, his two younger sisters whom he'd barely known, dead now, both of them. Julia in the blitz of London, where she'd worked as a trained nurse. She'd been the one who had been sensible, though it was Margaret that he'd preferred, in trouble all the time for giggling at nothing, but she was affectionate, warm in her preferences, and candid. She'd married a farmer, a boy from a nearby town he'd never met, and died a mile from home at fifty-six, of a ruptured appendix. In America she would have lived. He should have brought her. But she wouldn't have come. They liked their home; they had no wish to leave it.

Then his own two girls. Magdalene, never sure what was her place or if there was even a place for her. Her prettiness gone to her head, or maybe not: she'd been unhappy. He'd always felt he had nothing to say to her. Their conversations flooded up and then evaporated, senseless, and with nothing left behind.

He preferred Theresa. Even her looks were preferable to him. Had she ever loved him? She was religious now, the only one of them so pious. Probably to spite her mother. She said, 'I thank God every day for the gift of the faith you gave us all in spite of Mother.' He'd liked Ellen's derision of the faith, though he himself

197

had been devout, not knowing why. It had seemed right to be. He could see Theresa now, her head bent over some acquisition. She liked collecting, then discarding. Keeping straight. She'd come behind her mother, cleaning where she had just cleaned, reproachful. Ellen would turn on her: 'If you'd an idea in your head, or an interest worth a shilling in the world, you wouldn't have the time to be behind me with a dustcloth.' When Ellen sat down to read something, Theresa would destroy her peace in it. She knew how to torment her mother, it gave her pleasure to torment.

Vincent knew why. Her mother had felt nothing for her, nothing for either of the girls. The son alone was her treasure. Of course the girls were upset by it. Yes, of course. He used to think they could all stop it if they wanted. They could all say: 'Now we will love each other. And our unhappiness will end.' As he grew older, he thought he'd been wrong.

In his own home, in the town of Dromnia in County Cork, there had been hate. Even now, an eighty-eight-year-old man, he is frightened by the memory of that hate. *I am weak, a child, there is nothing I can keep back.*

His brother always meant him harm. And why? Because the mother had loved Vincent best. And because the father wouldn't listen to the older brother's thoughts about the farm. (It was the brother who was right. When the old man died it was the brother who made money. The brother died a bachelor with the richest herd for miles.)

When they were boys, the brother did him damage. Little cruelties, abandonments, exposures to the world from which he needed, as a younger child, some shielding. Older, the brother used his strength to hurt. He need not have. But why think that way? He was born as he was.

He remembers them on the road to school, his terror of his older brother's strength. His pride in it.

They'd once raised together a lamb whose mother had jumped off the rocks to her death. They'd found the mother smashed up below and the lamb wandering on the cliff above. Each morning Vincent and the brother, friends for once, came out to nurse the lamb. Secretly, knowing the father'd think it soft. Bluebell, they called her, cradling her. They'd even sing, some song of their mother's to calm down a baby. Then one day the thing was done, the father never mentioned it. It wasn't the father's idea. After all the years of thinking the thing over, Vincent was sure of it. (Did other people do this to their lives? Go over them like this, nothing changing in the details of it, the picture coming out the same, it had to, of course. Over and over he'd shuffled the things that had happened, as he shuffled cards the slow way that made Ellen so impatient when they played. As if it wasn't worth it. Still, he kept it up. He felt he owed the past that much, at least to go over it. Ellen didn't do it that way. She cut up the past, she recombined it, in false ways that shocked him. Colorful new ways, any way she liked, as if the things that happened were just furniture, you changed this or moved that. Then you were satisfied.)

He'd tried to make himself think, when the thing first happened, that the brother'd done it because he thought it was the father's wish. But what he knew, had always known, was that the brother did it for the pleasure of it, because he'd liked to hurt.

Vincent had come home late from school. He'd received special praise from Mr. Boyle, the schoolmaster, on his sums. That was what had set the brother off. He'd walked up the road, his heart singing with the praise he'd got from Mr. Boyle. (Who'd later been murdered by the Black and Tans. No one had known he'd been political. He was stalwart and taciturn until his rage flared up when a boy would not meet his eye, would not answer. It had mattered to him that the children learn. 'D'ye think in the Midlands of England there are boys full of dumb insolence like you lot?' he would say.)

Mr. Boyle had given Vincent a book of Irish poems. 'To Vincent MacNamara. For proficiency in Mathematics,' he had written on the flyleaf. And Vincent had shown his brother. And the brother had done that thing.

'It's done, then,' the brother had said, staring at Vincent to show he had nothing in his mind to be ashamed of. 'I saw no sense in waiting for you. Who knew when he'd let you out?'

He pointed to the place behind the house where he had done it. The dead animal, his throat open, red and revealing where the knife had gone in. The fresh blood oozing into the wool. He must have waited till he'd seen Vincent coming to begin it. Must have stood up on the rise and waited. Then rushed down. And taken up the knife. The lamb would have come out to him, thinking it was milk he carried. He'd have taken the lamb on his lap, as they'd

199

always done to feed him, and then taken out the knife and done the thing.

While Vincent looked down at the animal's body, he knew everything. The first thing he took in with calm; it was simple: the animal was dead. The second made him frightened: he could see the remnants of life still within the animal. What happened had just happened. The third thing he knew made fear and anger grow inside his brain, like trees that grow from the same root beside each other, harmful and competitive, yet bound. His brother had done this to harm him. It was Vincent's throat, not the poor animal's, he would have liked to cut.

He should have struck the brother. But he was a child. Tears blubbered up. Shameful and undistinguished tears, fat tears that dripped, and his nose running and his throat too fat and hot for speech. Nothing in him was to the purpose; nothing in him could punish or revenge. His weakness was the truest thing about him. It was the only thing.

And then the mother came, saying she'd heard the screaming (he must have screamed, although he had no knowledge of it), his mother walking with the baby, walking to the back of the house, where they stood, crying out: 'In the name of God, what happened?' He could only run to her, out of his formlessness. His shame made him the shape he was: legs without sinews, body without shoulders, boneless feet infantile as his sister's, still a suckling. He'd let himself be taken on his mother's lap, because he lacked the shape and force to stop it. He let the mother cradle him, knowing that for his age the place that he was in was shameful.

'What else?' the brother cried. 'Run to your mother. Go tell Mr. Boyle. Both of you can write a poem about it. Sell it to the newspaper. For myself, I'll savor every bite of the meals the animal makes, and so will all this family if they're honest. As if we could afford the cost of feeding it. Strapped as we are.'

He threw the knife down. The point of it stuck in the dirt.

'Pick that up, now,' their mother said, but Vincent could hear the fear inside her anger and he knew the brother never would pick it up.

The father had whipped the boy, but he'd not repented. And there hadn't been a soft word spoken between Vincent and his brother from that time until the last day they saw each other, the day that Vincent went off to America knowing that his brother would always be happy only at his harm.

He'd been right to go to Cork, and it was shocking to remember how quickly the pain of leaving home had passed. In some ways it had been the best time of his life. Had he been wrong to leave there? Blind ambition. He remembered Father Sullivan warning of it from the pulpit, how it was the curse of Irish life. The countryside stripped of its youth by the ambition that considered only self. He spoke of emigrants, 'the type, of course, who left their homeland for selfish, materialistic reasons, not carrying with them one single reminder of their nationality, not a shamrock, not a ribbon, as if they were casting off all allegiance to the motherland.' He told a tale about a priest friend of his who'd come back from America. He'd walked one night, fresh from the bed of a dying child, to see a woman of ill repute walking behind him. Intoxicated, flaunting herself in the most lascivious manner, without the shame, even, to conceal her intent from a priest. He turned round to warn her sharply of the jeopardy in which she was placing her immortal soul and the immortal souls of others. To his horror, he heard the name Eileen spring from his lips. It was a girl from his own town in Kerry, who had been the treasured playmate of his youth. She wept, recognizing her old friend. Thank God he'd been able to talk her into returning home, and she worked now in Killarney, a respectable and happy seamstress, able to put the horrors of America behind her in the clean and bracing air of Erin, her true home. Ask that Eileen about the streets they pave with gold, the priest had thundered, bringing down his fist hard on the pulpit wood. And she will tell you not the honeyed lies of lucre-loving wretches whose great fortunes have been made by the foolish credibility of the young who cannot wait to leave their homes.

Vincent is an old man, sitting in a room thousands of miles away from Cork. Father Sullivan is dead, must have been dead for fifty years. Still, his voice is alive in Vincent's ear. Yet he wonders: could that have been a true story, the priest friend, on the way home from the bed of a dying child, just running into his old playmate in the way it had been told? He doesn't like to think a priest would lie just for effect, but maybe it was what they called poetic license. On the other hand, stranger coincidences had happened in the world. The words of Father Sullivan still make him afraid. The loss of faith, of virtue and of health, the ruin, mental, physical, and spiritual, the coarsening of every human feeling, and the break of every human tie – that none of it had come to pass was, is nothing to Vincent now. He can hear in his skull once again the words, the hard words, the important words 'apostasy,' 'damnation,' 'treachery,' 'the bone and sinew of the Irish nation brutally cut out.' He'd sat in the church in Cork, trying the words out on himself: 'traitor,' 'apostate,' 'lucre-loving materialist.' He feared to say them to himself: what if they fit? At night, in his bed in Mrs. Tierney's house in the Barrack Stream, he tried them on as well. Suppose he was not yet any one of these things now but could become them? He might not notice it happening. He might have lost his soul, have lost it without knowing.

Fortunately, he confessed his fears to Father Lavery, the confessor to the Pioneers. 'Vincent,' the priest had told him in the darkness of the sacrament, 'if I were a young man I'd be on the boat beside you.'

Great fellows they were, the Pioneers. Great times he'd had in that huge room above the drapers', not a bit less enjoyable because of lack of spirits, never mind what the detractors said. The Pioneer Total Abstinence Society, a group with high ideals, considered that liquor was the ruination of the sap and flower of Irish manhood. Why did the Irish take to drink? It was an interesting question to Vincent, one he'd put his mind to often. Without profit. His daughter, too, he'd never wanted to admit that Magdalene had that problem. Now he feels he must. He must begin to tell the truth about the midnight phone calls to her mother. Years ago they started. Cam was still a child. Magdalene would phone and berate Ellen, saying she had never loved her, neither of them had. He knew she said it, though she never spoke to him in those states, and Ellen and he were silent when she hung up the phone. It was her mother she abused. She wasn't right; it wasn't that he hadn't loved her, it was that he didn't know what to do with her. A pretty girl who couldn't hold a thing two minutes in her head. Wanting to dress up, going in for playing parts. Nothing to do with me, he'd said, looking at his daughter, unable to get his mind fastened on the kind of person that she was. Unstable. Insubstantial. Odd that she'd made money. She could put her mind to that.

It was a terrible thing for a mother to drink. He'd seen Cam coming to them in the mornings, saying nothing about what her mother had done. Coming to Ellen to be given breakfast. Ellen and Vincent had admired her. They'd felt real admiration for the child. They didn't have to say anything to each other about their feelings for Cam; each watched how the other behaved. She was the only girl child Ellen ever liked, and you saw why: Cam's heart was loyal and she didn't ask for help. She wanted to be around you but there was no needing things from you. You'd take your hat off to a kid like that Dan, too, the two of them, looking after each other. Brother and sister never closer. It had surprised him that his children hadn't liked each other. Though it shouldn't have: he and his brother hadn't liked each other. He'd left home to escape his brother's hate.

And he'd been right to, right to go to Cork, a green boy, fifteen years of age, apprenticing himself first to the ironworkers Smith and Pearsons, Ltd. He'd taken up the offer that Mr. Leary, who ran the mill in Dromnia, had let him know about. He had a great friend in Cork City, he'd told Vincent, who had a great place for a boy with a fine mechanical sense, like himself.

As a young child he'd found his way over to the mill. He'd been drawn to it. He passed it on the way to school, when he took the walk he liked, beside the river. The sound of the mill wheel fascinated him, and, timid as he was, he had approached it. The machinery had made him dreamy. He remembered now the first time it had happened, how he'd lost himself – in the intricacies of the machine. The gears, the axle: he mooned over them as poets mooned over the mountains or the sea. He would fix his eye, and then be lost. No Vincent, no more body, no mind trying to get around the coiling and incomprehensible ways people acted, what they thought, their hates, despairs, their cruelties.

Mr. Flannery, the manager, who worked in the mill office, was a Protestant. Vincent had taken his fancy. A stern, fastidious bachelor, with pencils showing from the pocket of his old tweed jacket, he had a reputation among the men who worked at the mill for being gruff but fair. The men respected him. Vincent had decided as a child that that was his desire: to be admired for his justice, for his knowledge, by men who worked under him. Only he knew he didn't want to sit behind the desk; he'd want to be there with the other men. With the machinery.

He'd left school at thirteen to work at the mill, because he knew it was the life for him, the life he liked, men working, simplified by their endeavors, pleasant to each other, rarely speaking, but the silence functional, not ominous like the long silences between him and his brother which hung in the air between them like rows of hooks. The men would say to each other, 'Would you pass me that?' or 'Could you hold that for me?' or sometimes no need even to say it, for you knew, you were caught up in it, what it was you were to do, what help of yours was needed. When something went wrong with the machinery, you felt like a circle of fathers standing still above the sleeping or the ailing child. Machines brought up in him a painful tenderness. He felt, always, that they were trying. He could help them in their failures. Their failures were not their fault.

Jack Lafferty, the mill attendant, had been kind to him as well. Vincent had often thought Jack Lafferty must have considered him an odd one. Eight years, nine years old, and standing at the wheel like it was heaven, or like it was water in the desert, or the most gorgeous woman in the world. He'd talk to Jack about the workings of it. One day Jack let him watch when the stone stopped dead in its turning and he had to prize the floorboards up to check the gears and find the problem. Come with me, then, he had said, and Vincent followed, stepping carefully and watching, watching, for at his first look he knew he understood the thing and longed to get his hands on it.

He liked how the time went. It was the end of the day before you knew it. He'd not minded being indoors in the finest weather, even, which surprised him: he'd loved his walks out by the river and the caring for the animals. But he had left that, once and for all, and left off schooling when he was just thirteen years old. He was happy he had found his place.

The father had been glad of it. A trade, he said, a fine thing, meaning what he wouldn't say: Remember that the land is going to the older brother. None of this is yours. The mother had regretted it, taken to heart the lamentations of the teacher, who'd said Vincent should go on with schooling, for he had the gift. The mother had loved the book of poems he'd won for his mathematics, loved to have him read out to her the songs of Thomas Moore, like they were poems. In the book it said that Moore had been a friend of Byron, the great English poet. He'd have been a Protestant, though, Moore, which made it less remarkable that he'd been friends with a rich Englishman. Terrible among the Irish, Catholics hating Protestants, and the hate back. Even now there was bloodshed because of it. He'd never taken a position back at home. 'Keep out of it,' his mother had warned him as he'd left for Cork. 'Keep out of politics. You'll only soil your hands. One band of villains armed against the other. There's no hope in it.'

He'd loved his mother and hadn't wanted to cause her worry, so he had kept out. She'd been glad that he'd joined the Pioneers instead. He was sorry now that he hadn't been in the Irish Question. By Easter 1916, he was in America, but it had been fermenting all the time in Cork. The parties, so confusing and so numerous you couldn't keep track. The papers full of it. Confusing. He'd been confused by the First World War and hadn't taken a position. It was before he met Ellen. She'd taken a position. She'd been against it. He knew that if they'd been in Cork together Ellen would have read the papers, holding them close to her nose as if she could find the truth by reading closer. She'd have been able to make her way. She'd have been in the thick of it, and him too. That was the great thing about Ellen, she'd bring you out into the world. She was a great one for seeing the big picture. 'We're citizens of the world, Vincent,' she'd say. 'We can't forget it.' It was one of the first things he remembered her saying to him. So young and fresh and high-colored, her features sharp, her dark hair shining, in her twenties, but she looked much younger to him. He didn't know her real age, that she was older than he was, till they were married. 'And if you'd known, what would you've done?' she said, teasing him, playing with his hair. 'You'd have stayed away from the old crone. Just as well for you it never came up.' He let her tease him but it was as well, it was a blessing. If he'd known that she was older, he'd never have approached her. He'd have thought she was above him. He'd always thought that, but he thought that in her youth he'd give her some protection that she needed. If he'd known that she was older, he'd have felt that he had nothing, not a thing that he could give her that she didn't have herself.

He felt if they had met in Cork they'd have been involved in the Great Struggle. She denied it. She had no interest in the Irish Question. The Irish were bog trotters, she said. They mucked up whatever it was that they touched. Let the English take them all in hand and make a decent country of them. What could you expect of them, a rosary in one hand, a pistol in the other, a flask of poteen in the pocket just in case their other remedies should fail them. There was no tenderness in her for her own country. None.

But she was wrong about herself. She'd have seen the injustice of the English and been stirred. Injustice moved her, and her hatred of it made her great. She'd given up too much of that part of herself for the family, and it was wrong for her, he knows it now, but at the time, what could you do? What could you do when the times were against you, against who you really were?

For his own mother, family was everything. He'd been happy with his mother. People didn't seem to have fond memories of their parents anymore. His memories of her were fond.

He knew himself her favorite. Perhaps because of the long space between him and the younger girls. For six years she had not conceived. Mysterious. And then she'd conceived four more times. In those years he was her companion, always with her as she did the woman's work. She'd trusted him to gather eggs and help her with the milking. Together they planted the kitchen garden, and in another plot they'd both felt a bit ashamed of in front of the father and the older brother, they grew flowers. Flowers they'd been told they had no business growing. Sweet peas. Hollyhocks. Ellen had grown those flowers too. Nowadays people didn't go in for them so much. They liked these modern flowers with their new sharp colors. Modern plants were what the sisters wanted. 'Vincent,' they'd pleaded, 'we want petunias and geraniums. Coleus.' In their blue station wagon they'd brought home what were called 'bedding plants.' It wasn't how he liked to do things, or the kind of flowers he liked. But to please them he'd planted them out. They'd flourished. And how glad the sisters had been, how grateful. It had made him courtly, manly, their women's praise, old as he was and even though they themselves were nuns.

It had hurt his mother when he went to Cork. But it had been a good thing. It had been for his advancement. Had he been wrong doing things for his advancement? Had the priest been right, that Father Sullivan, whose voice he still could hear? Had this been his sin, materialism? He was interested, it was true, in the material. Not money. Objects. It was important to him that a thing should be well made. He might, for all that, have stayed on at the mill in Dromnia. But he had left because he could not bear to live beside his brother, having to take in all that hate.

His mother had the countrywoman's belief in the root evil of all cities. Be careful what you eat, they'll steal your money, don't speak to a woman, the milk is full of coal dust, take your tea black, look for a picture of the Sacred Heart before you choose your lodgings. What to her was danger had been what stretched out encouraging and beautiful before his eyes. He'd walked each inch of Cork, the first of his cities. The names came back to him, vivid, exciting names. Patrick Street, the Grand Parade, Anglesea Street, Cool Street, the Vicar's Lands. He'd loved the harborside, the busyness and action of the ships, the goods unloading and the shouting of the workers on the dock. The warehouses for storing butter, tea, silk, parts of carriages, or furniture. Medicines. Soap. All those things manufactured in dark factories, their brick or stone fronts as inviting to him as a home. His first real job after his apprenticeship was in the brick-front headquarters of Capwell Carriage Works, assistant to the smith there, Owen Dawson. A hard man, unhelpful, not wanting to teach the knowledge that he had. He'd moved from there after consulting Mr. Leary back at the mill in Dromnia, who'd recommended Owen Dawson and whom he didn't want to disappoint. 'Weigh the pros and cons, Vincent, of any decision you make. Weigh them honestly.' Sound advice it had been, and he'd followed it always, had lived by it. Not Ellen. She'd make a decision in an instant, she could feel it on her skin, the right thing, she'd say, and then she'd do it and she'd not look back. But had she always been right? She'd got the proportions wrong. She'd framed it badly. Her ideas were right: hold fast; keep faith, be what you stand for. But she hadn't done it. What she'd done was to keep people out. She'd mocked him in the end; she'd stopped being who she had been. But he knew that even now she was expecting him to keep his promise: Don't let me be taken away, don't let me die among strangers. He had convinced the others that he wanted to go home.

So now he'll go home. He dreads going back, he's been happy at Maryhurst. But he can't say that. At eighty-eight you owed it to people to be the man you always had been, so that they could believe in things and go on.

Weigh all the pros and cons. Give equal weight to each. He'd left the firm of Capwell. Owen Dawson had no will to teach him. The men in the place drank on the sly and muttered constantly against the foreman, who was a time-server and a fool. Vincent realized that only two things kept him there. The first was the twice-weekly visits of Mr. Capwell himself, resplendent in his morning clothes, his spats, his white carnation. The second was the wording of the advertisement in the Cork *Examiner* which made him proud of his association with the firm: 'Capwell Carriage Works,' it read,

> Having had a long varied and practical experience in all classes of work, and being thoroughly conversant with the requirements of the Trade, the public are assured of having their orders Executed in a prompt and satisfactory manner, strict attention being paid to repairs of every description at strictly moderate charges. Trial respectfully submitted.

He'd felt it was an honor to be part of such an organization. He was linked up with serious words again, like the words from the pulpit, 'conversant' and 'satisfactory' now, instead of 'eternal damnation' or 'apostasy' or 'sins against the Holy Ghost.' As time went on, however, he began to know his worth. Then he began to read with care the other advertisements in the Cork *Examiner*. One day, the first of May it was, the year 1911, he saw two advertisements by the same firm. The perfection of the wording, fitting as it did his talents, his need for employment, and his preference that the employment should be in a firm of grandeur and of style – these came together in the two ads in the paper the same day. The first was an ad to attract potential customers. 'Twelve Prize Medals Awarded,' read the headline. 'McArdle & Sons, Carriage Builders, Warren Place, Cork.' Then there was white space, and the eye dropped down.

> Invite an Inspection of their Carriages, comprising all that is most Modern, Elegant, and Up to Date. They have also a very extensive variety of cars and carriages at their showrooms.
>
> McArdle & Sons employs the largest staff of workmen in the South of Ireland, and personally supervises each branch of the Business to give the greatest possible attention to the Materials, and special care being paid, using only what is highly Seasoned, they are thereby enabled to guarantee all their work the expertise

of which is attested by the large number of Prize Medals they have received.

Prize medals, and the greatest possible attention to materials. He could remember now how he had held the newspaper away from him, then put it down. And then he saw below that advertisement, in another column, the same firm, McArdle & Sons, had advertised a place.

Smith's Helper wanted at McArdle & Sons, Carriage Builders, Warren Place, Cork. Must be a sober man. No other need apply.

A sober man, no other need apply. He could remember how he'd folded up the newspaper, completely, perfectly, as he did every day, to be added to the pile beneath his bed in Mrs. Tierney's house, for there was great stuff in the newspapers in those days, stuff you'd felt you'd re-read at your leisure, poetry and essays, Swift and Dante, he'd read about in the newspaper, and the great Cardinal Wiseman, and all sorts of information about nature. Things he still remembered, like a piece about the fierce cats of Cat Island, near the Cape of Good Hope, animals so ferocious they could be tamed by no man. You didn't get stuff from newspapers like that nowadays, it was a disappointment. He'd loved learning all sorts of things about the world. When Cam and Dan were young, he'd subscribed to *National Geographic*: the built-up yellow piles of them made him feel prosperous and safe. He still kept his subscription up.

He thinks of Mrs. Tierney's filthy house. Poor soul, a widow, he supposed she'd tried, but it was still a dreadful place, in the courtyard with the other houses, dismal, and the shouting of the angry mothers, all their patience gone from being poor, the dirty washing-up water, the drunks at night, berating or apologizing. He'd been miserable there, but felt too sorry for Mrs. Tierney to move. Perhaps if he'd had better lodgings, he'd not have left for New York.

That day, in Mrs. Tierney's house, he unfolded the newspaper and forced his eye to move slowly once again down the advertising columns, to be certain that his eye would read correctly what he feared he'd only dreamed. But no, he hadn't dreamed it. The same words called up to him. He put his cap on, made his way through the dark courtyard to Warren Place, to look for himself at the building that housed McArdle & Sons. Nothing special on the outside, red brick, a bit of undistinguished ivy climbing up, high windows, desolate at that hour, blue and empty with the workers gone. He'd wanted some sort of message from the stones themselves, but no message had been forthcoming. The edifice did not proclaim itself superior to Capwell Carriage Works, as he had hoped it would. He weighed both sides: he had a sure place at Capwell, they knew his worth and he their weakness. But he would never rise there, as he'd hoped he would. He'd slept on it, and in the morning he walked back to McArdle's and presented himself to the manager, a Mr. James O'Rourke.

It bucks him up to think of James O'Rourke. He'd been a father to him, more than his own dad, not that he hadn't loved his father, but the dad had not looked after him. James O'Rourke smoothed over everything with McArdle's for him. Later James O'Rourke had told him, 'I knew from the first you were the lad for us. You had a feeling for things. I could see that. And of course your being a Pioneer did you no harm.'

Not only James O'Rourke was at McArdle's. Vincent had had the good fortune to meet Martin Ferris there, the greatest good fortune except of course the gift of meeting Ellen. It was terrific times, working beside Martin. Born partners they were. They started the saying then, and said it always to each other, until Martin's death, was it five years now? Six. 'Partners we are and partners we shall be.' They'd said it all those years.

Both of them lived to be old. As young men they had not imagined that. A war could cut them down, an accident. They had been ready for those things that had not happened.

Martin was adventurous, quick in his mind, like Ellen. And impatient like her. But he was capable of studied concentration when a problem gripped him. Great talks they'd had, sitting on the quayside, smoking cigarettes. Everything under the sun came up in those discussions. Women, God, the bosses, the economy. Martin was a socialist. He'd lost his faith, although he said he respected Vincent for keeping his. (It was strange, in middle life he became quite religious.) Because of Vincent he joined the Pioneers, but quit soon after. The boys were not his type, and he said he couldn't stand the presence of the priest. 'I get the creeps around the blackbirds, Vince,' he said. Little by little, Vincent stopped going to the Pioneers himself.

Cork, too, bored Martin. If Vincent suggested that they save up for stall seats at the theatre, Martin would bring up the theatre in New York, and say his brother'd written about hearing Caruso at the opera. Always Martin's talk was about New York, so when he blurted out that he was saving for his passage and wouldn't Vincent consider going with him, together they'd be sure to get ahead, Vincent was not surprised. He'd heard about the flat Martin's brother had, the unions that the Church could not put down, the opportunities for education. America was a place you could stretch your legs and take some giant steps, not like this godforsaken country, where your every movement was hobbled both by priests and by poverty. They'd walk along the river Lee and Martin would talk about New York as if he'd been there, and soon Vincent wondered what it was he'd seen in Cork. He thought that everything he liked in Cork would be a hundred, no, a million times superior in New York. He'd miss his family, but he could help his parents and his sisters so they'd not grow up dependent on the older brother's whim, the girls could marry as they wished, for love or pleasure.

He consulted Mr. Flannery back home, and James O'Rourke and Father Lavery. Their advice was all the same: America was a place for a boy with go; he'd keep himself back in this country. The time was now.

He thinks about the day he told his mother.

'I knew it, I knew it,' she said, rocking like a child desperate for a sense of movement. 'I knew it when you left for Cork, I knew it was only the first of it and it would end at this.'

The father quieted her, ashamed at her woman's outburst. She responded to the father's hand around her wrist.

He learned something from that about the life his parents had together, the life they'd had before the children came. He thought of them together, planting out their first field in the spring before the brother's birth. 'I'll have that one day,' he said to himself then. 'One day I will marry.'

He'd waited till only a week before his passage before telling them. He thought it would allow his mother less time to grieve. But she felt tricked by his waiting, began to suspect he'd had it in his mind to go for years. It was between them as they embraced, as they clasped hands, measured their hands together, their game continued from his childhood, laughing now that his hand was so much bigger. He allowed her to arrange walks for them that he knew led her to say to herself, 'This he'll not forget.' And smooth it down in her mind, one task done, a piece of linen mended, or a blanket put down in the chest for winter. And on the day before his leaving, he made no attempt to stop her tears when she said finally the thing he dreaded, 'After you leave, I'll not see you again.' He knew how she needed the spilling tears; he'd not deprive her.

Though it made it hard for him. He wanted to be thinking of New York, the great streets and the buildings, the discussion groups he and Martin would join, the job prospects ahead of him. Thinking of those things would help him before his journey; feeling his mother's weeping body thrust against his own would never help. She was pregnant; he'd been shocked when she'd told him. Shocked to have to think of her as a woman still young. 'You may never see this one I'm carrying,' she said. 'You could die never knowing the face of your own brother.' She was sure it would be a boy.

'I'll be back in five years,' he said, knowing that he lied. The countryside was strewn with absences, the promise that he'd made his mother had been made a hundred times in this same valley, and had not once been kept. He let her do all the things she needed to do, take him to all the places, but he allowed his own mind to wander. As he walked with her on a bridge over a small creek, holding her sobbing body, he concentrated on the age of the old stones, the stress of the bridge, its span. In his mind he was calculating problems in arithmetic. How much weight could the bridge bear, how many crossed it every day, and would there be, one day, a point where there would be too many, causing the edifice to just collapse.

After telling his parents, he'd gone back to Cork to collect his things and then came home again three days before the journey. It was a foolish thing, impractical, to go home so he could leave from home, having to make the journey passing right by Mrs. Tierney's, but he'd wanted it. They all had, even the older brother.

He remembers now what it was called, the whole town gathering before one of the young people went off: 'the American wake' they called it. Never before had so many people gathered in his house. He didn't like it. It was a bad thing, the family's cavorting and their loudness. It stole the time. He'd wanted to sit, holding his mother's hand. He'd wanted to talk quietly to his sisters. But all the children in the room were vexed with tiredness and Margaret and Julia fell into their beds unhappy and perplexed, unwilling to take off their day clothes that far into the night. He'd wished his mother or his father would stay up with him. He feared sleep.

But they all slept a few hours.

It was the father who came in to wake him, dressed as Vincent had rarely seen him. He stood in the silver light and Vincent's heart flew up: today would be the last day he would see his father. He was wearing a new waistcoat with a gray-and-black front and a white back. 'Time now,' he said, not looking at his son and pointing to the kitchen as if Vincent were a guest and needed guidance. In a stupor, the mother dished out stirabout and splashed the milk into it for him, as if he were a child. The older brother came in from the milking, glum, respectful, asking what time was the boat, though they all knew it, they had talked of nothing else. Margaret and Julia played at his feet, happy in their excitement. They'd lived so little of their lives with Vincent in the house that his leaving didn't mean much to them. The older brother slung the trunk into the sidecar, nodded, said 'Good luck so,' and turned away.

Then they were off. They made two stops, one to the parish priest, one to Marin Cowley, who was blind and couldn't come to the do the night before. The mother asked couldn't they make another stop: she wanted him to have one of the postcards people took with a packet attached and the words printed on it: 'A packet of real shamrock seed.' The picture on the postcard showed a bridge in a circle. The circle was made by a quantity of shamrocks in a horseshoe shape and then 'Forget not the land of your birth' in letters that joined the horseshoe into a circle. He put the postcard in his pocket but it worried him. He remembered the notice in the post office warning that if the shamrock had roots it was 'capable of generation in America.' Customs would heave it off the dock. This was the kind of thing he feared, the home custom that could keep you back, the stern rules he had never heard of, the men in

213

uniforms, like princes, raising up their white gloved hands and saying 'No.'

He rode out of the town with his mother and father. The little girls stayed back with the neighbors, the brother claimed he couldn't leave the animals that long. They'd met up with Martin, just as they'd planned, at the railway station. He'd been a great help, with his high spirits, encouraging them all to see the sights. The big hotels, 'Too rich for our blood now, but give us six months, folks, and it'll be a week there, room with bath for all.'

Martin took the father up the hill in Queenstown and pointed out to him the look of the rooftops. 'The Pack of Cards,' they called those houses up along the hill. The roofs were alike as cards, and spaced that evenly. 'Isn't it great to think of that,' the father said, 'that kind of name for a thing.' Vincent had stayed down by the water with his mother; it was not a climb, he felt, someone in her condition should be asked to make.

'Will we not make a visit, then?' the mother asked, her eyes on the Cathedral. He feared Martin would refuse and cause his mother anguish worrying that Vincent, in the company of an apostate, would lose his faith. But as usual, Martin rose to the occasion. When Vincent thanked him for it later, he said that it was nothing, he was interested in architecture, it was the building he was concentrating on and not the superstitions that the building housed. 'They were irrelevant to me,' he'd said, leaning out over the boat rail when they talked about it. Vincent had been impressed with his friend's using the word 'irrelevant,' and the breadth of his mind allowing him to think about a church as just another building without fear of blasphemy or being struck down.

But Vincent had done the same thing that day in the Cathedral, thought about the building, and his heart scalded him for seventy-five years each time he thought that in his last hour with his mother his thoughts had not been with her, but on the engineering problems that the Cathedral, still under construction, had presented to his eye. The building was completely surrounded by scaffolding. And as he walked with his mother, he saw her body was made heavy by her grief at the leaving of one child and the burden of another growing in her. But he didn't dwell on it. He thought of the line the columns made, the way each column carried a certain weight of roof. He could not pull his mind away from

214

the idea that the work the scaffolding did on the outside – the iron crossbars, angles, cubes, harsh, ugly to the eye – was being done on the inside by these impressive columns, each topped with a lady's head that looked Italian, more to him like opera singers than like saints. So, when he said to his mother, 'Let's take a turn outside,' it was not her he thought of but the way the scaffolding supported the tall steeple. And that was in his mind as they embraced at the dockside, and as his father hugged him and said, 'Earn well, so you'll soon come back to us,' he was thinking about the limestone quarries where the stones of the cathedral had come from. When his mother put the bit of hen's dirt in his pocket for good luck, and he laughed at her, as she had wanted him to, for her superstitions, his eye, over her shoulder, was on the steeple. He kept looking at it, not at her face, crumpled up with weeping; his last sight of home was not his mother's handkerchief waving at him but the half-constructed towers of Saint Colman's, which he still thought more impressive than Saint Patrick's on Fifth Avenue.

His mother was right; he'd not seen her again, nor the child she was carrying – a boy, as she'd predicted, who'd died only a year ago, whom he wrote to every year at Christmas. And every year, on his birthday, his youngest brother had received a birthday check. The amount, Vincent could take a pride in saying, had kept up with the rise of the cost of living.

Martin had made the voyage a great time, chatting everybody up, the girls, the sailors, learning everybody's plans, and playing cards into the night. They'd walked around the deck and talked about their lives, how they were just beginning, how the past was past and everything in the world was theirs. They only had to take it.

Now, in his room in Maryhurst, he wonders if he'd been wrong to come. He might have settled down in Cork. He'd liked it then, for its compactness, it suited him to live in a city you could walk around in just an hour. He might have risen far in McArdle's. By now he might have owned the factory. Ridiculous. The factory'd gone under when the automobile caught on. What was it now: a gas station, Cam and Dan told him, they'd looked it up for him on their trip over. For all he knew the building had been blown up by the Black and Tans. When you went over the past, you didn't imagine the objects changing. The houses in your mind remained the same, the street, the furniture. But while you had gone on with your life, the objects had gone on with theirs, had crumbled, withered, changed beyond all recognition, disappeared.

Of course boys like him and Martin would come to America: they'd been brought up on the dream of it. Chicago, Butte, Philadelphia were more real to them than the Wicklow Mountains or the Giant's Causeway or the Galway Bay. America was an invented country and yet one where people they had known had gone and prospered, not returning, sending money home. And exhortations: Pack up, come with us. Their voices rang across the ocean like the voices of the damned crying for clemency, or like the siren crying: Follow; like the Angel with the flaming sword or like the angel breaking, with a touch, the prisoner's chain. Of course he and Martin would come over to America. It could only have been that way. When he'd gone back that once he saw he had been right to leave. But he could still feel the pain of it. The songs could make him feel it. Yet he liked to listen to the songs.

When he first came to New York he'd go to the theatre, to hear the women singing those songs. He'd think about them now; he'd let himself. 'The Woods of Kylwyne.' Fanny Brayton sang it; he remembers her now. In the Tara Hall in downtown New York she sang between the dance numbers:

My heart is heavy in my breast, my eyes are full of tears
My memory is wandering back to long departed years
To those bright days long, long ago
When nought I dreamed of sordid care, or worldly woe
But roved a day, light heart boy, the woods of Kilaloe.

It was great, the way some of the songs could make you see things you thought you'd forgotten. Like the second verse of that same song:

There in the springtime of my life and springtime of the year
I'd watch the snow-drop start from earth, the first young buds appear
The sparkling stream o'er pebbles flow
The modest violet and the golden primrose below
Within the deep and mossy dells, beloved Kylwyne.

216

He loved to see a fine woman singing a song like that. You never saw it now. And people used to sing around pianos. Families did. He'd always hoped to have that. Ellen wasn't musical.

He remembered hearing the music of the pianos and the voices summers when he lived in Jersey, in that first house, Mrs. Kerrigan's.

Hoboken. Weehawken. The names he thought romantic because they seemed to be Indian. (He'd looked it up once in the library. They were.) Home after work, still dirty, for the only wash-up was a filthy zinc bucket full of dirty water. It shamed him to come home so dirty. Mrs. Kerrigan was kind; she said nothing when he took so much time at the sink. He thought of the spring evenings, the summer twilights that stretched out like silk, the soft air urging, and the yearning on his skin. He'd walk the streets, past houses that he learned were owned by one man for his family alone. In each house was a child or children learning the piano. They did not play their instruments well and yet the music pleased him. He heard them playing scales that flowed like grain passing from hand to hand. And on the river you could hear the sounds of voices. Mandolins. Perhaps the songs of lovers. In the parks, for free (the country was a miracle), bands played for hours. Great songs, German music, waltzes he didn't know the names of. There was nothing like it in the whole of Ireland. Young girls passed, their arms linked, their light sleeves touching. He would have liked to put his lips to those sleeves, to take off the hats, carefully unbutton the bodices, and with reverence reveal the white flesh of those girls who walked like angels to the music. But he spoke to none of them: he didn't have the right. All day he did work that an animal should properly have done. He dug the subways. He lived in heat and filth. But when he saw those houses with their trees, and heard the music, the piano music coming from them, he believed he would do better. He would have a house with trees around it that the snow would lie on in the winter, that in summer would keep the house shaded and cool so that when his daughter practiced the piano she would never feel the heat.

Theresa had been musical. He'd loved that in her, it was why she'd been his favorite. He felt that of the three of them she was the only one he knew. He heard her singing to herself as she played with her dolls, as she dug in the garden, and he asked her when she turned seven (the age of reason) would she like piano lessons.

He had not asked Ellen first. He knew that if he did, Ellen would convince him of the folly of it. It was a terrible aspect of her, the jeering side of her, her hardness at what she called his foolishness. 'Your damn ideas,' she'd call them. 'They'll put us in the poor-house.' She liked to think she was the practical one, the one who knew the world. But most of the ideas she thought were right had come to nothing. She never knew that about herself; he was glad of that.

'Your damn ideas,' she'd said when he told her about the piano lessons. 'Perhaps she'll play the piano for us all when we're on the street. We'll be in need then of some entertainment.'

But he held out against her. One day he told her to make a place in the living room, there would be a piano in the house next day, some friends of his were bringing it around. He'd kept an ear out at the station for news of a piano, and had heard, finally, of an aunt of somebody, her only son a priest, who'd died out in Bay Ridge. The family was selling up her things. 'Would there be a piano? I've been keen for my girl to start with lessons,' he'd said to the fellow and was told that he could name a price. They'd both been pleased. That fellow knew another who'd transport it if you gave him a day's notice and a drink or two on either end. Vincent had been uneasy about that; they kept no drink in the house except for holidays. But he bought a bottle. It was right to do. His girl would be able to play piano and make use of her God-given gift. It was America, where you used your gifts.

Ellen wouldn't stop her dreadfulness about the business until he faced her with the rage he knew she feared. And she was right to fear it; when it came upon him he knew himself to be fearsome. No, that was the thing: he didn't know himself. A thousand times he had confessed it to a thousand priests. His temper. Again and again it had led him to the mortal sin of anger. It surprised people too, who thought him easygoing. It surprised him in himself. He'd seen himself raise up his fist, as if it were another person's, and bring it down on something. He'd never struck a person in his anger, thank God. But no, that wasn't right. He'd struck his son. The shame of it still. To strike a boy. And John dead now, a boy in his plane, landing in trees, they told him. For a moment he could see it among the leaves, and it seemed beautiful, the plane, light, resting in the trees, the branches holding the resting boy, his eyes closed, not in death. Like Jesus said to the sisters about their brother Lazarus: He is not dead but sleeping. He always thought that one day John would simply wake up, open his eyes, and clamber down unaged, out of the plane, back into the house, where they would still be waiting.

He'd struck his son, his son would not come back, his son was dead. He could see the War. He saw it gray-faced, crushing. War was the raised fist (his fist) that loved itself as it came down.

At the time of Ellen's bad behavior about the piano he had put his fist through glass. 'This is my home. If I say we'll be having a piano, we'll be having it.' He'd frightened Ellen. She could see his bloody hand, the hole in the center of the windowpane. She took a look at his bloody hand, and then went silent. And said nothing again, not a word, about Theresa and the music.

What a thing to fight about so bitterly, a child and her piano music, a fight so bitter that nearly sixty years later he can still remember it. It had brought out the hateful side of Ellen, the trampler, the destroyer. They'd fought too, he remembered now, about a gramophone and about John McCormack. She'd made fun of the Irish songs that gave him pleasure. 'Kathleen Mavourneen.' 'Molly Bawn.' The greenhorn cod, she called it and made faces, pretending to mouth the words, as he sang the songs. He broke the records, smashing them on the floor when she mocked him. She'd not done it again, but he'd never had the heart to replace the records, they'd never again had John McCormack in the house. Great the things now they could do with music. John was telling him. Compact discs, they were called. You'd never believe the fellows weren't in the room with you.

It was terrible to think of fights. Why had they fought? 'You're not in charge of the world, Ellen,' he'd shouted at her once. 'You're not the head of the Holy Roman Empire.' He'd raised his voice, he'd shouted, he'd wanted to hurt the woman that he'd shared a bed with, watched in childbirth, in the nursing of children. But there was that part of Ellen that could hate things so. Music and dressing up for church. Things you couldn't understand a person hating. Certain types of flowers. Some she liked, the ones they grew themselves: sweet peas, hollyhocks, hydrangeas, dark blue or white. The pinkish ones she hated. She hated petunias. 'Look at their prissy faces; I'd never have one around me if it was the last living thing on earth.' Hothouse roses could put her in a rage. She hated certain foods. The word *hors d'oeuvres* could drive her mad.

She said she hated things that weren't of use. But that wasn't really true. There were some useless things she loved: the figurines of Presidents, cordial glasses she would fill with sherry every New Year's Day. A golden thimble she'd brought with her from home. Display was what she hated. You kept things to yourself. You kept them hidden. You took them out in privacy, you hugged them to your body. You did not show off. You kept your feelings to yourself. Anger only was allowed.

She had not loved Magdalene, and Theresa, and would not pretend to. John she had loved. And later, the surprising love for her grandchildren: Cam and Dan. She loved them because she respected them. Theresa she had feared, and she had been right to. Vincent knew the hardness of his daughter's heart. Theresa didn't love, though she said she loved God now. He hoped it brought her comfort. Everybody needed that.

Theresa you could not touch.

She'd been so musical. Fine-looking too. Her mother's skin and eyes that looked right through you. Not like Ellen, though; Ellen was fiery. You wouldn't say there was anything warm about Theresa; no, warmth was not a quality of hers. He'd liked her best of all the children. Her containment. She could keep things to herself. He believed now she kept these things because she grudged them.

It had pleased him to see a girl of his at a piano: her straight back and her clear high voice. Sometimes after supper he would ask her to play for him. He'd hear the angry banging in the kitchen: Ellen furious that Theresa had got out of drying dishes, knowing it was her job. It was Ellen's time to read, while the girls did the dishes; Theresa playing the piano cheated her of that. She knew better than to cross Vincent directly, though; she'd seen how much the music meant to him, and that she wouldn't win.

He loved the sad words of the songs Theresa sang for him and the music that went deep. It brought back everything, the greens of the woods around the river, the river itself, his leaving his mother forever. Once Theresa agreed to learn for his sake a song called 'The Old Bog Road.' There was a part in it about a mother dying that he lets himself cry over now, though he hadn't let himself when he was younger, a father of a family, a husband, he didn't feel right letting himself go then. But now he's alone in a room that will allow him anything. So he can cry thinking of the words. My mother died last spring. When Ireland's fields were green. Then something, something, and something about snow-drops and primroses piled up beside her bed. He'd lost it now. He's an old man. Many things were lost.

It was a dreadful thing, Theresa and her mother. Ellen in the kitchen banging pots and muttering 'Lazy good-for-nothing.' He could hear her angry words and see Theresa playing on as if she hadn't heard. Then getting up when she had finished, closing the piano, turning to her father with a smile that he knew to be terrible: she had vanquished her mother and she hadn't turned a hair. He pitied Ellen then, but still he loved his daughter, loved the cool-ness and the sureness of her. He hoped that she would marry a good man. She had, Ray Dooley was a good man, you'd always say that of him. But she hadn't loved him. He knew his daughter couldn't give a man that thing that Ellen had given him.

Perhaps he, as a father, had been at fault. Perhaps he'd frightened her about men and the way they could be to a girl. He knew he ruined the music for her. She began having friends over. They would stand at the piano and sing. He saw the way the boys looked at Theresa. And the songs she sang he thought were trouble. The sad songs she sang for him, the songs he'd heard standing outside the houses with the great lawns and the trees, the songs the bands played in the parks when the girls walked together with linked arms, the songs he'd bought her the sheet music for: she never played that kind of song for the young men. The songs she played for them were hard, and dangerous. Some words didn't make sense. One he had hated: 'Ja-da, Ja-da, Ja-da Ja-da jig jig jig.' And he didn't like the idea of a young girl singing 'Body and Soul.' He'd get cross with the young men staying late and filling up the ashtrays. One night he lost his temper. The young men did not come back. To punish him, Theresa gave up the piano. How they loved giving out punishment, his wife, his daughter. Masters at it. He could see their joy.

As a young man, he'd not known the side of women that could punish. His mother hadn't been like that. His sisters and the girls he dreamed about, their pale long dresses sweeping the damp grass: where was the punishment in them? Hardness, he'd thought, came from the world of men, the world he worked in. The men were terrible in the subways. His first job had nearly killed him with

221

the hardness of the labor and the sense he had that if this was life he should die and get it over with.

Terrible days at first, he couldn't get used to working underground. The heat, the stink. Exhaustion in the bones and worse: filth you could never get away from. The zinc bucket with its two inches of greasy water. Hateful. Who'd wash up in that? And the beast's work that required no mind: digging, nothing to understand, no complicated thing you held and turned around and got the knack of. Nights you were too tired to get the good out of the country. Only Martin was never tired and Martin's enthusiasm bucked him up. He dug the I R T. He said it to himself each time he rode it. I dug this out. Not his usual pride. His usual pride was: This I understood.

But he didn't have to do the unskilled work for long. Perhaps he'd never have had to if he hadn't followed Martin's lead taking the first job going, a job Martin's cousin put them on to and helped them get. If he'd waited and considered all his possibilities he might have lived a while on the money he'd brought and saved himself for work commensurate with his skills. But Martin Ferris was not your man for waiting. 'Jump in' was his motto. He was like Ellen in that. Though Vincent only did this work for two months he'd never forget it, and understood from it that men could be made to labor like animals. He saw what it did to them, and yet it didn't take their lives. Which he had never understood: it would have taken his if he had stayed. But he saw the ad in the newspaper and answered it.

He wanted work that would use what he knew. And so he left Martin, and took a job at Acme Tool and Die, a dark stone room in a warehouse in Long Island City. His boss was German, a grunting, silent man. Words he used only to find fault. The two of them were alone in the stone room without a window. Nine years of it: every morning he was sick to death with the idea of that room.

But because he hated the room and the German it wasn't so impossible to leave the job when he agreed to get the mother.

He'll let the image of the mother, the horror, come into this room where nothing dark can be absorbed. He'll think about it now. Usually, he makes the image go away. But now he understands that it may be the most important thing about him: that time, what happened to them all.

He came home one day, to find Ellen in the dark. She'd pulled down the shades; the children were off with her friend Delia; she lay under the covers trembling.

She'd always told him that her parents both were dead. But now, refusing to look at him, refusing to let him look at her, she tells him everything about the mother. Then she tells him about Anna Foley, who cares for the mother; Anna Foley has written; she herself is dying; Ellen must get the mother now or there'll be nothing for it, the father will have to be in charge.

She rocks from side to side beneath the covers. He'd like to hold her but he can no longer hold himself. Who is this woman in his wife's body, his wife who feared nothing, her beauty gone, the light no longer in her eyes, her white skin coarse and ill-looking?

She begins to beg him. She, who prided herself on having to ask for nothing. Her eyes are wild, like the mad women at the dockside offering everything for anything a man will give.

'Why did you never tell me?' he asks her; far away from her, standing across the room.

She doesn't answer him. She tells him only she's afraid to go back home. She, who was afraid of nothing. She says her father will have her arrested. She tells him that if the mother stays in the town, the father will kill her.

She rocks herself, crying, and to stop her he'll do anything. He can't have this for her, this self she's become. But he will close himself up from her. When he sees her face he will grow cold.

But he will do the thing for her. He would never not do it.

He makes the plans for the journey: He is young. His body and his life hum with health. He says to his good friend Martin, high up, it seems to Vincent, in the subways: 'Do you think there'd be a place for me in a month's time, a month or so, I'd say?'

'Any time, Vince. A man like you. I have friends in Signals. They'd give their eye teeth for a fellow with your knowledge.'

He doesn't tell his friend Martin the full tale of it. He says: 'There's trouble in the family. I have to be taking a trip home. Ellen has to stay here with the baby.'

'Vince. With your brains, you've only to walk up to the foreman and say, "Take me on tomorrow." You'd be taken on.'

'And if it didn't happen right away, Martin, could you give me a leg up?'

Martin is a bachelor. Doing no one knew what with his wages. Still in the boarding house and still no entertainments, despite all his talk at home about the opera, the lectures, the night classes for the workingman.

'Vince. I would, of course.'

He goes off with Martin's promise. He tells Frank Bremer, the hard German in the stone room where he has worked, that he won't be coming back. He takes his wages from the silent, furious man. And he allows his wife to pack his bag. He doesn't write his family to say he's coming home, to his own country. Theirs. He doesn't see them, so as not to show them Ellen's shame. For her keeps it in the dark, away from sight.

On the boat he remembers the promise of the first trip over and the hopes. He looks back at his life in America. Good luck. Jobs, a wife. Children. But it is built on nothing. He's been made a fool of. It was all for nothing. She'd used him. The woman he had loved had never loved him. She'd have married any man she thought that she could fool.

All right, then. He'd close his heart. He'd go on living. It was what you did.

Even with all these things on his mind, out at sea his pleasure in his body rises up, breaks through. The sorrow, the betrayal, all he had thought impermeable can give way for moments to his pleasure in the sea air in his lungs, his lungs filling and emptying, marvelous things, a great machine, the body. He is stirred by the prospect of open ocean. He wants to take one of the pretty girls and tell her his predicament, talk love to her, squeeze her warm fingers, tell her how he's in need of pity, and then take her, right in the open air, in all her clothing, take her in hunger, anger. And to spite his wife.

Even though she's deadened all that was the center of her, her real self, still, the thought of her body, ardent for him, stirs him as he stands and looks out at the water or walks up and down the deck. Ellen. The dark bright thing that is her wanting of him, growing and then satisfied but never over, both of them wanting each other.

'Ellen,' he says to her, looking out at the black water, 'knowing me so, how could you have done this thing?'

224

He vows that he will close himself forever from her. He'll not be near her again.

He's back in Queenstown. His mother is dead now. He thinks of the last time he was here with her, his mind not on her, but on the scaffolding, still in place ten years later. The father is nothing in his mind. The brother's hardness still keeping him away. He'd have gone back to see the sisters, Julia, Margaret, the cheerful one he hardly knew. And the boy child he had never seen. He'd go back for the place itself. The river and the bridge. The mill and Mr. Flannery. He'd be glad to tell Des Flannery about his progress in America. But no, he won't go. He'll remember the brother's hate and Ellen's shame. No one's affair but hers.

And his.

On the train to Cork City, he is once again the young free man he'd been there, full of projects. But he doesn't linger on in Cork. He goes right to Limerick, from there to Gort, and then by farmer's cart to Tulla. The familiar look of all the vegetation presses him hard.

She'd told him not to go and see the father.

'Tell him nothing,' she said, pulling at his hands. 'Speak to Anna Foley only.'

She told him to take the mother away by night.

He knows he can't do it in that way. Although to honor Ellen he will see the mother first.

The morning breaks while he is in the cart. The stars, covered with mist, seem smaller to him than they had been in America. He tries to calculate the time. In New York, he'd be closing up the house, walking from room to room, turning off lights, smoothing pillows. He cares more for the furniture than Ellen does. She said it was simply that he got away from it all day. By six o'clock, she said, the furniture became her enemy. He sees her with her hair braided for sleep, but she herself is not ready for sleep, fiercely reading by the inadequate light, the rosy glow of the lamp with its soft pink lampshade. Her vanity: she does not like the hard light on her undressed skin. For this she sacrifices her eyes' health. And because of this, he imagines, she has to wear spectacles. He'd found it funny that he had a wife in spectacles. He knows she likes herself in them. She needs them only for her reading, and, wearing them, she is stamped by them, known as a person who reads. He never told her how she charmed him in this way, her spectacles, her nightgown, and her braid. She doesn't like to think he watches her. Reading, she likes to think she is alone.

He doesn't want to think of her now with this tenderness.

But how can he not think of her so? Here on the roads she'd walked on as a child, how could he not allow her to become part of it all?

He will not. He tries. She will not be kept out.

The child on the white road.

He knows at once which is the house. Hidden behind a copse of dreadful trees, cruel firs, dead-looking grasses with their clutching roots. The farmer in him sees the land impossible for cultivation. The firs let through a puff of smoke and a glimpse of the house's stone. No care here for this house, but it is Ireland, there's no care for many of the houses.

The dead heart of the house makes itself visible as he walks up the road. Why would you enter? says the air around the house. This is a place of punishment.

He knows he must break through this curtain of dead air, must enter the place. And with no weapon but his healthy body. For a moment he fears that he cannot. All his youth, health, joy in life, belief in the benevolence of fortune urge him back. And what, in opposition to all this, would press him on? He fears the face of the now ruined mother. And the face of Ellen, mocking him: 'I needed a young man and you were willing, though I had to make you think I loved you. So that you would do this thing.'

But as he stands where she'd stood he knows her terror, the defeat she feared each morning stepping out of that house. Her courage and, each evening, her terror once again. About to enter that house, he feels that he is standing on one side of his life and that when he sees the mother's face he will cross over to the other side. But he knows he can do it. He is overcome with tenderness for his wife, Ellen, for all that she has been. Her history rises up before him, the child, girl, woman, the first blood, childbirth. Looking up, seeing the mist that rises from the brown grass and the smoke between the trees, he hears the sound of Ellen's laugh, her voice discussing an idea, sees her eyes that shine, in pleasure and in anger, and he knows despite everything she has loved life, she has loved him.

He knocks at the door. Who will answer. What will he see?

A voice behind the door asks who he is. He gives his name and the door opens.

He is not afraid. He knows this.

He is no longer afraid.

A woman like the women he has always known looks out at him.

'You've come,' she says.

He takes off his hat. The house is dark, the trees purposely left to block the light. And in the darkest corner sits the mother, silent, looking as if she were made of stone.

'I'm Miss Foley,' Anna Foley says.

She offers him a stool so he can sit beside the mother.

'I'm Vincent,' he says to the mother, 'I'm Ellen's Vincent.'

The mother is looking into darkness. No part of her stirs.

He takes photographs out of his pocket. Ellen. The two children. He puts them in her hands.

She doesn't look.

They sit.

'It's useless,' Anna Foley says. 'She's past all that.'

'Perhaps you'd like to see the pictures.'

'Well, I would of course,' she says, smiling for the first time. 'Though she's sent a lot.'

She looks at the three photographs. Theresa at her baptism and Magdalene hanging on to her mother. Stand up straight, he tells Magdalene in the picture. Even in the photographs she is unhappy. He speaks to the child in the picture. It will get you nowhere, you can see it's what your mother doesn't like.

'You've done well by her,' Miss Foley says.

He nods, to thank her.

'Mrs. won't be a trouble to you. She's as still as anything. And clean too, you can see that. She would never soil herself.'

His young man's modesty is outraged at these words. He wants to say: You shouldn't say these things to me.

★

227

He weeps that night in the commercial traveler's room in the hotel in Gort. For Ellen, for the picture of the young clear-eyed mother on the dresser in New York, and for the ruination of a mother that took all the joy from Ellen's girlhood, hollowed it out, and put in horror, terror, courage, black remorse, the tearing, scalding shame. He understands everything. He knows why she lied to him. It was the business of her life to keep the mother from the world.

Inside the house he sees the moist stone walls, he feels the stone floor's coldness through his boots, he knows it is a house built to shut out warmth and lightness. The old woman sits in darkness by the window, or is walked by Anna Foley to the table or the privy. She's grown enormous, like a statue, ancient, gray, the white clear skin of the young mother darkened now, with patches beneath the eyes, around the mouth. And like a man she has the makings of a beard, a mustache.

He wants to kneel before the mother, so like a statue. Pray to her.

He can smell the death on Anna Foley's skin. She holds her side when she walks over to the table with the teapot.

'Can I help you, Miss Foley?'

'Thank you, no, you've done enough.'

Suppose she grows unmanageable on shipboard? He prays to the benevolent God he thinks of as an honorable landlord, a good boss. 'I have done this thing. My duty. Now You must help.'

He walks, terrified at the thought of going to the town to see the father.

'The man could kill me,' he thinks, 'he would not be wrong to try.'

How could he not fear?

A man feared mortally by Ellen. She, who was fearless. A man who shut up one wife in a house designed for darkness, and who took another wife. 'Common law,' he believed, was the word for it. Common to whom? And whose law? He tries to understand there is an underside to things he has no knowledge of. Of course he knows about it, as he knows of drunkenness, but he'd lived his life to keep himself back from it. No one he knew had practiced vice.

But Ellen's father, a practitioner of vice, could be capable of having lived as he had lived, of any act. It was like what they said: after the first mortal sin the rest was easy. One letting go and the boulders rolled, side over side, and never stopping until death and the sinful body racked by endless torture but the worst torture the soul's knowing it was kept forever from the face of God.

But in this life the vicious father clothed still in his living flesh could raise his hand, bring down the fist, the hammer, present the loaded gun, the knife.

He knows that it is possible that he will have to fight the father to the death.

He is given a lift once more in the cart. Into the town this time, to Tulla. No different from a hundred Irish towns. He is lucky to be there on market day: there'll be more people on the streets. More witnesses in case the father tries to kill him.

All the years in America had made him forget the treeless Irish towns. They'd a lesson to learn from the Americans, though of course they never would. He thought of the great trees even on Main Street, Flushing, trees even near the Elevated. Planted, perhaps by Protestants. But Thank God for them.

And there were trees in front of their own house, his and Ellen's. The maple, so full in spring and lush in summer. In the fall a burning bush, a torch, a flame above their heads. The chestnut in the back in summer offering up its flowers, white and ceremonial, like candelabras, or like chalices.

Only in the treeless streets of Tulla does he understand he has become a man of property. And that there's no reason to doubt things, or to be regretful. He'd been right to leave. The too-wide streets, the endless stone and mortar, the dark faces of the poor children, and the resignation of the women waiting for nothing to happen while the men make deals, bad deals for somebody, and then celebrate in the pub, giving their money to the likes of Thomas Costelloe, his Ellen's father. T. Costelloe, publican. He thinks of Jesus: publicans and sinners. Well, the man was both a sinner and a publican. His father-in-law.

In what law?

He'd never understood the love some people had of pubs. And Costelloe's was one of the worst type. In the dark air, the smoke, the smell of beer makes him unable to believe in his own breath. Men spit on the stone floor, then drag the sawdust over their own spits with heavy boots, as if to cover up.

He asks for the proprietor. Some farmer points to a man sitting morosely at the table. 'Thomas Costelloe,' the farmer says.

He thinks the farmer must have misled him, or that he himself misheard. He knows the kind of man the father is. Large, Ellen had spoken of his size; handsome, she had said that too, with stiff black hair that grew up like a brush. That was what she had told him. He asks another farmer to show him Thomas Costelloe, the owner of the pub. The farmer points to the same man.

Vincent had never thought himself quick-minded, but this rupture of his imagination makes him ill. He wants to lie down somewhere.

Right there before him sits the father, neither large nor handsome, neither fearsome nor eaten up by vice. Light-boned, narrow, with the stooped shoulders of a man grown middle-aged in business, largely bald, with tufts of grayish hair and tawny eyebrows that seemed as if they ought not to belong to him. A gray mustache covers the too-dark lips of the drinker and the Irish smoker's yellow broken teeth. High cheekbones, the fine beloved cheekbones of his Ellen, give the face a harsh air but the dark eyes (Ellen's) with their dirty-looking whites make him look sickish, as if his digestion has not for some time been good. As if he once had been a judging man, but has given it up, as he has given most things up, and settled into disappointment.

How can this be the father? He sees nothing to fear about the man. He even feels a bit apologetic for his youth, his looks, his life with the man's daughter in the fortunate country they were thousands of miles away from, so obviously the superior of this. He feels understanding saturate him, the slow stain of it spread unevenly through his conscious mind. He sees the pity of his Ellen's life, the loss involved in it, the admirable woman she became. And he is saturated too with tenderness for her and pride in what she is. He knows her then as the girl who thinks this wretched fellow, doubled over by regret, is *someone*, is a force that could even imagine lifting up a hand to stop her in her will.

The man knows who he is. Still, he feels the need to say: 'I'm Vincent MacNamara. Ellen's Vincent.'

Just to say their names. To hear their names in this room.

The man nods, indicates they should go across the street to another of his establishments, the Feed and Grain. He allows Vincent to lead the way, like a condemned man, knowing that the verdict has been reached and is out of his hands.

The Feed and Grain is high and light and open. Thomas Costelloe lifts up the counter and they walk to a back room where all the books are kept. The records. The two men sit across from each other on high black stools.

'Ellen feels it's time now that her mother should be with us. Miss Foley, her caretaker, has notified us that she herself appears to be in failing health.'

He hears himself talking like a newspaper. He doesn't know where he has got the words.

He sees the father's shoulders fold into themselves. The chest, hollow itself, contracts. Then the man shakes himself like a dog ridding itself of dirty water. And Vincent sees Ellen's gesture when she is determined to get on: the head, lifted, he knows, in false confidence. And he prepares himself to argue with this man.

But no, once more he has misjudged.

'Ellen would know,' he says. 'I'd have to be giving you something to cover my wife's expenses. You didn't get here on a magic carpet.'

Vincent does not know what to say. What would Ellen want?

He says, 'It's not required, sir. We're comfortable in America.'

'It's Ellen's due. It's all hers after I've gone. Not that she'd take it. But you're to tell her that it's coming to her. Now that she has children, she might see things in a different light.'

Moved to pity for the man who he believes deserves none, he presents the children's photographs. The father covers the images as if they hurt his eyes.

'And there's no need getting Declan O'Fallon to drive you up the Gort road in the cart. I've men enough to help you out with that. And with the other transport. One of them will see you get to Queenstown safe. That far at least.'

He allows the father to spend money on arrangements, a motor-car. (In one week he has forgotten that American streets are full

231

of cars, but in the whole town of Tulla only Thomas Costelloe owns one. He hired someone else to drive him.)

Vincent allows the father, the transgressor, to spend money. He picks up the suitcase full of underclothing that has been bought new. (By whom? Costelloe's other wife? Vincent has had no glimpse of her, and is grateful for it.) Anna Foley packs the underclothing with a tight-lipped, disapproving face. 'That's the first I've seen of linens for her that've not been sent over from America.'

He thinks of Ellen secretly packing up underclothing for the mother, who has turned herself into a man.

He will not tell Ellen about the money he allowed the father to pay out. But in the iron bed in the hotel in Gort, under the gray bedspread, greasy, smelling of cooked cabbage, he feels he has been delivered. He can have a first-class compartment: he can close a door. Keep her from sight, from company. He need not have the dread of the stone-eyed gibbering woman on a ship's deck crowded with voyagers. He need no longer fear the public beds, facilities. But still he fears what he will have to see of her. Anna Foley assures him that she can see to herself, will dress herself with some encouragement. How much encouragement and of what kind he doesn't know.

They make the journey home.

He is American now, a citizen, there is no fear that they will fail to let him in. No reason for the old terror, of making a mistake and then being sent home a fool, a laughingstock, a failure. The memory still comes to him, of the journey over, the sea air and Martin chatting up the girls, Martin, too, sneaking above deck to first class for just a glimpse, then down before they catch him. And their lives ahead of them. He remembers that he thought perhaps he'd join the merchant marine. A great life, looking at the sea all day, all you could learn about it: winds, tides, the movement of the stars, the working of the engine. He'd longed then to know it.

It is years later, he is older, much that he had hoped for has taken place. He is better off than he dreamed; he has more than he would then have known to ask for. But on this trip his skeleton is rigid with anxiety. The mother, whom he cannot now afford to regard as human, could do anything. Anything, and he could never stop her. The idea itself is mad, his taking her. Sometimes she speaks: 'Who are you? Where are we going?' He says, 'I'm Ellen's husband. We are going to America.' She stops listening, or else does not believe him. Perhaps she believes that he is carrying her off to her death, a death she would not raise a hand against. Dying would be so easy for her. He can see that. Natural.

He never leaves her. Only when she sleeps he walks ten, fifteen minutes at a time around the deck. First class, his dream, but he cannot enjoy it. Thomas Costelloe has given him a fortune so that he can pay the stewards. And more money so that all her meals can be brought to the cabin. Ellen's father had thought of that. The stewards call Vincent 'sir.'

On rough days she is sick. He holds the basin for her, washes her vomit down the sink, puts out a change of clothes, then disappears. When he comes back she has done it, dressed herself. He could go on his knees to her in gratitude.

At home Ellen has grown afraid of him. He does not tell her: I was moved to tears for the childhood that was stolen from you. He does not say: I took a fortune from your father. It would not have been possible to bring the mother to you without his help. He does not tell her, till years later, that the father planned to leave everything to her. When he does tell her, she turns from him, as if even his knowing taints him.

She was happy with the mother in New York. Those were the years that she was quiet in herself, and settled in. She paid attention to the house. She gave up reading. John was born then, the one of the three she liked. An easy baby. For two years, three, while the mother lived with them, life went on inside the house the way it must, he thought, for sailors in a submarine. They were lulled as if they slept and rose each morning to the murmur of the water. Outside was nothing they could live in, nothing to do with them.

It was terrible for the girls, though, Theresa and Magdalene. The mother frightened them. Ellen saw that and it made her turn from them once more. It was another thing for which they never could forgive her.

He saw his wife become a thing he'd never thought she'd be: devoted. The impatient girl he'd loved to watch in argument, her hair falling down, pinning it up as if it was ridiculous to bother, he'd seen this same person holding the old lady's hands grown swollen and fattish from her idleness, the square nails as tough as any man's. He saw her make the special foods for her mother and stay by her while she sat, looking at something else, never looking at her daughter, never giving back the daughter's glance of love.

He'd liked their life that way for a while, but then it seemed wrong to him, the way Ellen wanted to keep back the world. She'd not been born to live like that. And in the winter evenings when he'd come in, he'd feel her cheek hot from the house, he'd hear the sound of children bickering, Magdalene always the wounded and always at fault. And in bed at night, rather than reading with her glasses that he loved, she'd turn the light out, turn to him not, he felt, from ardor but because otherwise she was so bored. Her body slackened in those years. Still it was lovely to him. Always the body of the woman he had loved.

And does he love her now?

Sixty-six years of life together and he can't say.

He knows only that he doesn't want to go home.

He likes his life here.

He likes his simple life.

Sister Roberta knocks and comes into his room. In tears. She holds in one hand a tight bunch of marigolds and in another a black plastic bag full of tomatoes and yellow squash. She's not a pretty girl; tears don't help her. It isn't fair, if you were pretty tears never hurt your looks, if you were not they always did.

And by what name can he call her? Strange to comfort a weeping girl and call her Sister. She always says, 'Call me Roberta. Bobbi.'

He can't. She is who she is. A nun, and not like other people. Consecrated. She made promises. That she would never marry.

She thinks her father doesn't love her.

He knows better than to say that parents always love their children. He doesn't say, 'No, Sister, I'm sure your father loves you. I'm sure you must be wrong.' He knows that she may not be.

'Vincent,' she says. 'I feel like I'm losing my best friend.'

She sits down heavily, right on the floor in front of him, and like a child rests her head on his knee.

He wants her to get up. If Cam finds her like this, she'll be savage to her. At the same time, he relishes his ability to comfort this poor girl, not usually unhappy, but unhappy now that he is leaving.

'Now, now,' he says, patting her head. 'Now, now.'

He knows almost everything about her life. More than he knows about any woman in his family. But none of the women in his family was born with Roberta's simple nature, kind, patient with the difficult people, urging, cajoling, encouraging the ones who want to sit and wait for death. Acting as if she herself doesn't believe in it, death, or in its strength, its pull for the old and tired. As if she cannot understand this sentence: *I have had enough of this life.*

As if it is the last sentence she could ever understand.

She believes, she tells him, in eternal life. But it can wait, she says, the here and now is where I live.

The here and now?

He wants to tell her there is no such thing.

Since he was a child, the idea of the present seemed to him a terrible thing, a shapeless thing. You would grab at it and it would flee from you. As a child, desolate in the simple fact of his aloneness, he could terrify himself by asking, often standing on the thin border between wakefulness and sleep: 'When is now, when is it becoming the not now, the past? Already it is swallowed up as I try to give it substance. And I too am swallowed up. I am nothing. Nowhere I stand is firm.'

He didn't think of calling for his mother. What comfort could she give him? Already possibly not existing herself, possibly a figment as he was, unplaced. Even as a grown man, when his flesh chilled as the water went down the bathtub drain, as he followed the sound of it and watched its vortex, he couldn't comprehend his wet cold flesh with certainty. His own wet flesh horrible to him, he wanted and didn't want to go to Ellen.

What would he have said?

Have you ever thought it is quite possible that all this may not be?

There is no place on earth?

No present, therefore nothing, and therefore no place.

She would have mocked him. Made a story of him.

She would have been right to.

He wondered now why he had never known how she had failed him.

Until now.

But he can't even imagine another way, a person you could go to, saying anything, expecting to be understood. It's the difference between him and Sister Roberta: he knows she can imagine such a thing. It's why she's here.

He strokes her dull curls (she had got herself, proudly, a permanent); he's glad to comfort her, she's free of mockery. In its place is belief.

He wonders how a person comes to have a simple nature.

She believes her father doesn't love her. But he must have loved her at one time.

Or else, he wants to tell her, you would not have this: a simple nature. At some time in your life you must have felt safe. You still do. Even now, when you're sad. You always expect that there will be some person near to dry your tears. Some person whom your tears will interest. Or you have made that person up. Or perhaps it's God. And have you made Him up? But this is why she has a simple nature. She can always imagine someone to dry her tears.

He thinks: My mother had a simple nature. I had one. But for me it had nothing to do with tears. Because I was a man. It was because I could forget myself in the world around me. When I thought, *There is no place on earth*, I would go to a place like the mill. I would say, *Things work. I understand them. Therefore there must be a place.*

He wants to tell Sister Roberta about Ellen's father and mother and to say: Nothing happened to you like that.

He thinks of Ellen's mother.

Five years she lived with them. The years of Ellen's false simplicity. Her slackness. Then the mother died. Sitting up, she died, and, dead, her face showed no change of expression. Ellen buried her in peace. Then she became herself again.

She read the newspapers. He'd come home, not to the warm flaccid cheek, but to the heated one, inflamed by her proof of public injustice. She'd wave a newspaper at him before he had his coat off. 'Read this, read this. The common criminals.'

The house piled up with newspapers. Yellow clippings proliferated like spoor. The false years of her caring for the house were over. You would think he would have minded. He did not. He felt he'd got his wife again, and wanted her again. Her fine-cut nostrils flaring as she called out, 'Herods, thieves.'

Only when he became a union man did he begin to understand the world.

'Come back, come back,' he urges the far past. He knows his mind is undependable. But now he wants it to work. He wants to say, I am old now but I see the lit-up past. He is sitting in a chair covered with olive-green plastic. A chair he doesn't like. He is stroking the hair of a girl, a nun, who is kneeling at his feet, her head on his knee, weeping because he is going home. To the house he has lived in over sixty years, so that the woman who has been his wife for sixty-six can die beside him.

But he doesn't want all that. He wants the lit-up past. And it comes back. The darkness of the subways and his fear, skill, comradeship, loneliness in the work, horror of darkness. The first days come back to him. His greenness when he has to ask for help.

'The diagrams, the "prints" we call them, are up on the walls. You teach yourself here, before you go out,' Bill Walsh said.

He'd no experience with anything electrical; Martin's cousin said a smart fellow could pick it up.

He is in anguish now, because he needs a certain book and he cannot tell Sister Roberta that he wants her to get up so he can find it. That he wants to stop comforting now so he can lay his hands on something, on a sixty-year-old book whose title would make her think that he had lost his mind. He knows he brought it with him; no, he hadn't, but Cam had. She was good at finding the things he wanted, bringing them, not saying it was foolishness. A good girl. She stood up in court for people. You had to do that. People needed that.

She'd brought the world in to them; she'd gone out to it, both she and Dan. Ellen had sent them out. She'd not go herself but she would send her grandchildren as messengers. Each piece of news, fact, accolade, accomplishment was in part her treasure. Like a miser's, her face lit up with all the gold they brought her from the world.

He hadn't brought that book with him at first. That was the

terrible time, when he could think of nothing he desired except his death.

His memory goes back now, not to the lit-up time but to the dark room where he has fallen; no, not fallen, Ellen has knocked him down. His leg is broken. He has broken every window in the front of his own house.

Theresa comes.

Then Cam comes to the hospital.

In their hating they try to cut him up. He is *mine. Mine.*

They say, 'I think that I had better . . .' or 'It seems obvious to me.'

The ambulance boys strap him to a flat plank. Like a corpse. As they do this, he wishes: If only this were my death.

And in the hospital he can think only that she always meant to hurt him and show him the mockery, the trickery, of all their life. That promises mean nothing. That he'd been a fool to believe in a promise. She had known it all along but covered it to hide her strength.

And then one day Cam said: 'Granddaddy, I've found such a good place for you. On the Island. You can feel the ocean in the air.'

Be polite, you mustn't hurt. . . . He had thanked her. He could see her tears.

'What shall I bring you? Any books?'

'No, nothing, no. They'll have the television.'

Life had come back to him here at Maryhurst. After some time he realized he didn't want to die.

Has he enjoyed his life? Parts of it have been enjoyable.

You could look back at your own life and see it broken into parts, divided like a field cut up for different crops. But when you were living any part of your life, that was the whole of it. You didn't say, Eventually there will be another part of life from which this will be separated. Even the breaks, the new starts, terminations, crossings over. You didn't let go of the part of your life you were living. Nothing became the past while you were living it.

Things bled from one part of your life into the new part so that it seemed a piece, and when the terrible times came that was the trouble. You believed it never would break up. The past became the past only when it could no longer wound you. And then you lost some kind of interest in it. It became less real to you. You could no longer recognize it as your life. Only some thread reminded you that you were always the same person. Birth to death, you were the same.

He'd always thought that. Now he thinks he may be wrong.

He may not be the same man who was brought here eight months ago intent on working on his death.

He keeps trying to look back on how it happened, if he's a different man from the man who'd come here eight months ago. He feels his understanding darken with his failure to make sense even of his own life.

Perhaps if he tries to go over the events.

First this happened, and then this. Then this.

But what he never can call back, never has been able to, is whatever it is between the pieces of the past. *Between the then this and then that.* The separation. The connection. How can things be separated but connected?

Had Ellen understood all that?

He pities her, in her silent fog.

He pities the girlhood they had stolen.

But he doesn't want to live with her again. He doesn't want to be in the house with her.

He'd thought he had a simple nature. But now all these things make him see that he has not.

The poor child, kneeling to receive his comfort and yet consecrated all the time the bride of Christ, he'd thought she had a simple nature. But perhaps no one did.

Sister Roberta had helped when he arrived. At first her happiness had been a grievance to him. Too much life when he was wanting to prepare for death. As if she'd walked into the room of a headache patient singing cheerful songs, when every loud note on the brain pulp was agony.

But her belief had saved him, her belief in life. That it was worth it.

He thought even now that she believed because she knew no better. Still, he could say that she had saved him.

Didn't Jesus say that to a blind man or a leper, somebody like that, 'Go thy way, thy faith has saved thee'?

He sees now that people, he did not exclude himself, appeared to need the idea of faith. It couldn't be a lie.

This is the lie: life is worth the living. This is the lie you needed. What was truth?

Pilate had asked that. Vincent had been told from the pulpit that he asked this because his pride had made him blind. Jesus right there before him and he had to ask. But Vincent understood Pilate. He praised him for the courage of the question. Most people didn't want to know.

He'd always thought he had been one who did want to know. But now he knows that there is only one thing he wants: life. He wants now to go on living. He is hungry for it. Every aspect of it interests him. He could use another hundred years.

He wants to enjoy his life.

No one he knew had ever lived like that. It was a thing the young had thought up, not his children or their generation, but the generation after that. Camille and Dan.

Did this interest in enjoying life actually make them enjoy it? How did you tell? How did you ever tell with people? So much for us, he thinks, was what we had to do. And yet we thought about the world.

Suppose he turned to Ellen and asked her. Suppose that she could understand, even though he knows this won't be the case ever again. Everybody tells him that. But suppose there are moments when the fog lifts and she can understand. Suppose he turned to her and said: 'Have you been happy?' He'd never done it. Never once in all their lives. He doesn't know what she'd say.

If she's the woman that she always was, she'd tell him he was nothing but a fool. Her scorn for him would make her lively once again. She throve on it and treasured it. Without it he imagines she could never feel her heart pumping its blood, the volumes of it he's read about, to her limbs, her lungs, her brain. Scorn made her feel real to herself, contempt assured her she drew breath.

High-colored. Beautiful. She'd sweep her hair up from its tender place of exile, its escape, there at the part of her neck he loved best, the nape, the hollow where the two muscles formed a cleft. She'd turn to him, made lively by her scorn, and say:

'I've always feared I'd inadvertently connected myself to a crackbrain but mostly you were clever and kept it hidden until times like this, when it's all up. There's no more hiding it. You're cracked. Happy. And who'd be happy in a world like this?'

She'd turn political. She'd say they wanted to keep you busy with soft thoughts like that – are you happy – so you'd turn your eyes away from their thieving tricks.

And yet, knowing all this, now that it was too late, he longs to ask her: 'Were you happy? Did you much enjoy your life?'

Although if he were asked he'd say: I didn't think about it. What I did seemed at the time the only thing to do.

But is she the woman that she was? Sister Loretta, who had a master's degree for studying old people, says it's impossible to think of her that way. But suppose she is. Then why did she do that to him? Knock him down like that. But if she isn't, who is she, then?

He feels his brain harden around the problem. He's heard that the brains of old people, which aren't fed by the quantities of blood that rush up when the brain is young, grow hard. He knows that he should understand. But he can't.

Now Sister Roberta's unhappiness begins to weary him. I am an old man now, he wants to say to her. I get tired.

But the truth is not that he's tired. It's that he's curious. He wants to be looking at his old book.

But he'll sit still for her. He'll do that much.

He doesn't think they're wrong to be concerned about their happiness. Perhaps if he and Ellen had done more of it, more for the children, thought about their happiness, it would have done some good.

It never seemed to him his children had been happy. It didn't seem that they'd enjoyed their lives. The two living ones, Theresa, Magdalene. The hard, resentful mouths of women in their sixties who haven't got what they once wanted. The presence of Theresa makes him wince. The furious stiff hair. The tight lips, lightly colored in. The nails that longed to tear, polished bright pink. As if, so colored, they could appear kind. And Magdalene, deformed now with her missing breasts. Her drinking. All those late-night calls. 'Neither of you ever loved me.'

She was partly right. He wished that he could tell her that, 'We tried but we didn't love you enough. We did what we could at the time.'

Too late now, the damage done, and he can see his daughter eating up her own child's life. Only he thinks now Cam is happy. He doesn't know why. For many years she held herself with the posture familiar to him in so many women: *I will do what must be done*. Now he sees something in her movements, in the way she walks, that reminds him of something Ellen had when she was younger. As if moving weren't just a duty. He doesn't know what to call it.

He hopes that Cam has happiness, now that he believes in it.

He keeps his body still.

He'd love just a look at the book before they pack it up, pack all his things for the trip home in Cam's new car. A Jeep. A Land Rover. He admires the car, the name. He'll like that, driving home in a new car. He'll keep his mind on that.

'Oh, God, Vincent, you must think I'm an awful baby.'

Sister Roberta gets up on her heavy legs. Wipes her wide face.

'We'll meet again,' he says, and memories of songs come to him. He is glad of the memories, they allow him to show this girl, for all she is a nun, some gallantry.

She kisses him on the top of the head and suddenly runs away.

He lets the room be quiet for a second, makes himself be still, not to forget too quickly what seemed to be her grief.

Could she have felt real grief, and then got up and gone away like that so fast?

Slowly he gets up from his chair. But that's all right, he knows about it, they can no longer surprise him, these small failures of his body. He goes into his wardrobe with its built-in mirror and four drawers where he keeps the books he doesn't want out on the shelf.

He runs his fingers up and down the leather cover.

You'd never see that kind of cover now.

He opens to the first page.

Rules and Regulations
for the
Government
of the
Operating Officers
and
Employees
of the
Engineering Department
Interborough
Rapid Transit Company
Manhattan and Subway Divisions
To Take Effect July 1st 1924

This book is the property of the Interborough Rapid Transit
Company, Engineering Department, and the Employee holding
it will not receive his final pay until it has been properly returned
to the company.

One of the few instructions in his life he hadn't heeded: one of the
few laws he had not obeyed. He'd drawn his final pay and had not
given back the book.

The rules themselves (he thought) were really like Commandments. He thought of Moses with his beard holding the tablets
and the people waiting. Grateful. Knowing now what was the
right thing to do.

He'd liked having those exact rules in his work. They made
things seem nailed down. Specifications – 'specs' they called them,
the same nickname as for eyeglasses. But they were like Commandments he was happy to obey. No, more than that, or less. Not
happy. It let him know who he was.

He turns now to the section of the fragile book entitled 'General
Signal Rules.' It is page 107. Small pictures of the signals indicating
section breaks. They bring his youth back to him. Representations.
Stop and Stay. Proceed. He is a young man once again who loves
his work. He is a young man who came over and in terror took
the first job that he heard of. Digging, although he'd been a skilled
machinist. But he'd never thought of waiting, he'd preferred to
get a job alongside Martin Ferris. The year was 1913. Men were
needed to construct a great tunnel, to join up Brooklyn and

Manhattan. The Whitehall Street–Montague Street Tunnel it was called.

Terrible work he hated. He did not want to be that young man now. Not now, on this last day in the place where he has been happy, he doesn't want to be the young man doing filthy work he hates and is ashamed of. Or working all day beside the German. He wants to have his good work life, the first job in America that was his pleasure and his pride: signal repairman. Though he was not that at first, of course, he was assistant, starting at the bottom like you had to then.

He turns the pages of the book to the 'Rules Governing Signal Repair.'

Repairmen shall make frequent detail inspection of all apparatus under their charge and must make renewals of defective parts before a failure may occur.

They shall take up lost motion and see that no studs, pins, or holes are allowed to become worn more than $1/_{32}$ of an inch in any direction.

They shall see that cotter pins are in place and that they are in good condition and properly spaced.

They shall see that signal blades are securely fastened and kept bright and that all lenses and roundels are kept clean.

They shall keep the bearings of all moving parts free from grit. Care must be taken to use just the right amount of oil and not flood the parts with oil. Old oil must be removed and the parts wiped before re-oiling.

They shall inspect switches in operation every day, and shall see that the locking bars are not worn more than $8/_{36}$ of an inch in any direction. Plungers on facing-point locks shall clear the locking bar one inch when withdrawn and shall have a throw of eight inches.

They shall not permit any foreign wires or any attachment foreign to the apparatus to be placed on signal apparatus.

They shall keep all exposed contacts clean and in perfect adjustment.

They must not break series of relays.

If waste paper collects about switch or signal apparatus, they shall report it immediately to the supervisor.

He did all this, and all the words are objects to him. They bob up now, they swim up in his mind, he has no need to send for them. 'Lens,' 'roundel,' 'cotter pin,' 'plunger,' things called 'frogs' and 'dogs.' Maintenance. Repair. Keeping up. Holding back. All the things that life took away, ground down. He loved the thought of this.

He worked his first section of the track as assistant to Charlie Weaver, then with Dan Clark, the boy who assisted him. He won't think of Dan Clark now. Not now. Later.

Now he'll think about his area of track. The Broadway Line, the IRT, of course. He never would be anything but IRT. The oldest line, the most outstanding. His area was between 103rd Street and 125th. Each day inspecting, oiling, keeping free of oil, of grit, replacing, and reporting. And you had to have your wits about you every minute. Every minute there was something that was your responsibility that might, while you had been away, have taken it in its head (the things had minds and natures, he was sure of it; some wanted to please you, some took pleasure only in your defeat) to grind itself down, smash, or turn useless.

Those signal fellows were some bunch. Thought themselves the elite of the whole system, and perhaps they were. Terrific skill. Quick-minded. They had to be, and they knew it, and would hold it over you, but that was all right, you felt they had a right to it. You'd hear stories about near misses, terrible catastrophes. Great tragedies averted by a fellow's wits and speed. You didn't hear their names, of course. Catastrophes averted never made the papers, but the men knew among themselves. It gave them pride, they liked the danger, the signal fellows, the aloneness, in the towers or the tunnels. By themselves in darkness, everything depending on their wits. If they didn't like that sort of thing they didn't last in Signals; they moved on.

They drank a terrible amount, they were known for it. They

called themselves the cowboys of the system. And their talk was terrible. The names they called each other: Ragass, cheeseballs. They were famous for their drinking and their talk. They said he had lead up his ass when they thought he couldn't hear them. They were like soldiers among themselves, like desperadoes. You'd see fellows missing fingers all the time.

They loved the life.

He'd loved it too until the thing happened with Danny Clark. Now he must think of it; he owes Dan Clark that much.

Danny Clark was his assistant. An assistant kept an eye out: that was his whole job. The trains came rushing by, they weren't going to stop for you so you could do your job. That was the point of it: you did your job and you didn't stop the trains from going. That was what it was all about. So the assistant kept an eye out for the trains and secondarily on the equipment.

You could say that Dan Clark hadn't done his job. But you would never say that. Dannyboy, a good boy, a joking boy. His jokes were the death of him. Now Vincent must live that again, must not dishonor the young boy who'd been cut down in his prime by a joke. He must not dishonor the boy by his refusal to relive his death.

Vincent arranges his mind. First I will remember the year. The year is 1925. And the month: August. It is steaming hot, the tracks are hot as hell and black, the worst time of the year to work, the summer months. They are repairing signals on the local tracks. Vincent is removing a cracked lens. Dan has the replacement in his hands.

Dan was a Dublin boy, a city boy. Vincent had thought perhaps that was the problem: city life could breed unsteadiness. Too much excitement for a young person.

He remembers a song that Danny sang.

I left me ould mother wid one little brother
And came to this country when scarcely a boy
And though I am Irish and lived on the parish
I'm first cousin German to Patrick Molloy
I came in short breeches that often lacked stitches

Had nails in me shoes fit for horses to wear
My mother'd not know me, but if you would show me
I'd quick know me mother and Dublin of yore.

He even remembers the name of the song: 'Teddy McGlynn from the Town of Dublin.'

Danny had liked bragging about the things he did with girls, though Vincent never did believe him. He was such a boy, Danny, with his arms too long for him, his legs as skinny as a stork's, his popping Adam's apple. Girls would not be taken by his looks. Vincent was silent when the boy said dirty things about what he did with girls, hoping to indicate he didn't like that sort of thing talked about. Though he didn't want to hurt Danny's feelings. He suspected Danny talked that way because he thought it made him look manly, and in fact most of the other fellows working Signals would have liked the talk and joined him in it. But Vincent had never gone in for that himself as a young man, and now, Ellen having been to him what she was, he could never. He was fond of Dan, although he lost his patience when he saw Dan's mind wander. He could have bitten his tongue off for what he said to him once: 'We'll both pay with our heads for your daydreaming. Is that what you're after? The two of us in coffins? Is that your plan?'

He shouldn't have been so impatient with him. He could have taught him better if he'd had more patience.

What was Dan Clark thinking at the moment of his death?

They were repairing lanterns on the local track. Dan held the lens. He was still holding it after he was dead. He was singing some song, Vincent remembers that. It could have been the one about Teddy McGlynn or something different. Vincent tries to remember the song's name as if remembering will make things turn out different. He gives up.

Danny Clark is holding the lens, singing. And what happens next? Does he lean back? Or lose his footing? Why hasn't he been looking for the train? It was his job to keep his eye out for the train, not just the local, the express as well, he knew that, he'd been told. Vincent asks God, whom he no longer is sure listens: Why would a boy be cut down?

He is weeping for a boy sixty years dead. He weeps as much for this as for his own son, dead in the trees of France.

Vincent remembers: he is taking off the old lens. All his mind is fixed on loosening the screws that have grown tight as the devil. Then, in one second, he sees the boy fall back. He sees the train that can't stop. No time between when it is not happening and when it has happened. It is over in a second. It never began.

The train stops, too late, at the next station. It switches to a local track. Too late. 110th Street. Vincent is alone with the smashed body of the boy who never knew he died. The smashed glass of the lens lies all around him, sickeningly colorful, like scattered candy on the track. Vincent knows you do not move the body. He stands still. He waits, stands watch until the proper people, the authorities arrive. They all suggest that he go home.

Obedient, he goes back to his locker, changes clothes, washes at the small filthy sink, and goes home. He never in his life felt so alone as that day on the train, the Flushing Line, thinking: Not one of these around me knows about it.

He can't remember telling Ellen about Danny Clark. Perhaps he never did. Or perhaps he told her later and didn't make much of it. He knows two things: that he did not describe it to her, and that she gave him no comfort. What did that mean about the things he could not have told her? Did it mean that there was nothing between them? Only living beside each other for a long time in a house? Perhaps it meant he could have lived with any woman. Or was it Ellen's scornfulness that kept him from telling things to her, that made him keep things to himself? Did it mean she'd never loved him? Or that he had not loved her? How did you live beside a person and not say things?

Because you didn't much believe in the good of it. Because there were certain things you did believe about life, things you learned when you were young that you didn't forget. To others, words, tears, lamentations, crying out, refusals shouted, accusations flung upon the ground could represent relief – 'It was a weight off my heart to tell him,' 'I felt a stone lifted from me' – Vincent had always felt it was better to leave the stone in place. You didn't shift the weight, because the movement could bring danger and the weight had goodness to it in that it pressed things down.

Though he and Ellen had never said things to each other they felt the same way about life. It wasn't that they hadn't loved each other; it wasn't that they were nothing to each other. It was that they believed the same things about life. You took the things that you were given. You did not cry out.

There was the one time that she did and he had tried to stop her. He'd been wrong then, he'd seen it immediately. She had lost her son. She was right to cry out, to take the pins from her hair and try to rip the hair of her head out, thrash like the wounded creature that she was. He should have let her. After that, she'd closed down something to him and had kept it closed. He'd not stopped her in anger or in shame. He'd just felt the danger for her, in opening herself up like that.

He'd done nothing to expose his grief. My son. My promise. The promise he'd never kept. He had never been a father to his son. He'd been no better to his son than his father had been to him. Worse. He'd never felt any closeness to John. He'd always wanted to keep him at arm's length. Something about his son was irritating to him. He felt things came too easily for John. He pleased his mother doing nothing. And, later on, the business with the girl. Ellen had been right about her. He wondered what had ever happened to her. Once he'd seen John empty a full ashtray from his car right onto the pavement of the church parking lot. The time he'd hit him it was for coming home drunk. He'd hit him for having worried his mother. Ellen had paced up and down the house that night like a starved animal. She'd been reading something. She'd put it down; pretended to go into the kitchen for a glass of water. But she'd been looking out the back window for John. When Vincent went into the bathroom, she went out to the sidewalk to look up the street. Finally John came back home, singing under the front-porch light. A nonsensical song, Vincent remembers. 'Mairzy Doats.' The nonsense of it made him hit his son in the face.

Only after he was dead did Vincent realize that John had been a good boy. It was only that he was lighthearted, and none of the rest of them was. That was why Vincent had never understood him, he hadn't let life press him down to a shape Vincent could recognize.

But when John died, Vincent felt it was he who should have died. He'd never known his son. His son had died a stranger to him, never having lived his life. At night he'd wake up in the dangerous moments before first light and think, 'No sense to go on living now.' It had seemed easy to him, letting himself go into death. Now that his son was dead. His son that he had never known. His son whom he had struck for singing underneath the front-porch light.

Vincent puts down his book. He can't read any more about the signals. After Dan Clark he left the Signals. Left his pals that were good to him, including Martin, who had felt let down. But he could never take pleasure in the job again. The fellows in the signals, who were used to things like this, had a way of talking about it he couldn't be a part of. They said, 'A boy dying like that, in one way, it's a blessing. A song on his lips, weren't you after saying that, Vincent? That's the last he knew of life, a song on his lips. He never knew what hit him; he never felt a thing.'

How did they know? He'd never say that to the mother. Mrs. Clark. He felt she blamed him: You were older, you should have been looking out. She never said that but he felt she thought it. He knows that he went to the funeral but he can't recall a thing about it. He remembers Ellen went. That means he must have told her. But what? She must not have asked him much about it. That was good of her. She loved knowing things usually, wanted to know everything about the world, wanted to know about it without going out into it. She feared direct living of a life. It was the life she lived as a girl beside those parents that had done it to her. She grew up thinking that if you went out to the world, if you rubbed up against people, they might know your shame. One word could do it, cause the edifice to collapse, the edifice you'd built so carefully to keep the shame hidden. A look, an indication: everything could go to smash. Better to stay inside the edifice you'd built. Keeping watch; keeping people out.

It wasn't that she wasn't interested in the world. She always wanted to be one who took things in, but from a safe seat in the house she never loved but hated leaving. The only things that made her break out were political. When she was all het up on politics, you couldn't keep her home.

She was most alive in those days when the union was beginning to be formed. He'd bring the newspapers to her. A lot of people were giving out a lot of different newspapers at the shop gates. He brought her home the *Daily Worker*.

They were good times for him too. After the death of Dan Clark he applied for what he had been trained to all along, machinist's work, at the Kent Avenue Power Plant. He remembers talking about those days recently. When was it? He remembers. It was when Sheilah was doing that thing for the night-school class, when she was supposed to be getting him to talk into her tape recorder and then she'd write it up. They gave her a mark for it, too. 'Oral history' they called it. He thought that was amazing. Then she got a raise at her job for taking that course. He had a hard time following the line of that. But it sounded good for her and so of course he said he'd go along. He'd tell her what he could remember, but he said he didn't know what good it would do her, an old man telling his life story. 'Not your life story, Granddaddy. It's oral history. Just tell the truth. Tell me about your job,' she'd said, 'just wait one second, let me test this thing.' She pressed the buttons on the machine; then she was glad she did. One time she'd forgotten to check and a whole tape was lost. A black family she counseled. Of course she couldn't ask again. 'All right, Granddaddy, talk about your job.'

'It was a good job. I was proud to be associated with the IRT.'

'Why were you proud?'

He tried to answer what she wanted. He felt sorry for her. She was always the child with the worst luck of any of them. If there was a rusty nail, a piece of broken glass, she'd step on it; a patch of poison ivy, she'd go through it. When she woke from her naps her eyes were always crusty and her mother blamed her for it. It hurt him to hear Theresa talk to her. And then leaving the convent like that, under a cloud, marrying a priest, you'd have to say that there was shame in it. Thou art a priest for ever. They said the ones that left never got over it. Although they seemed all right, the two of them. So maybe that was wrong too. Maybe some of them did get over it. And the little boy seemed nice. She was a good mother to him, warm, although her mother hadn't been. And she was proud of him, her Diarmid. But she had what every woman in the family had. That set mouth. Angry. Judging. He saw her hating Cam. Who did Cam hate? Sometimes he could understand why Cam would hate her mother. But that couldn't be right. She did everything for her mother. She was at her beck and call.

So he told Sheilah that the IRT was the best line, the oldest, and the shops were by far the most advanced of any in the system. Which meant the world.

251

'Tell me whatever you want, Granddaddy. Tell me about the shops. Whatever you can remember.'

He remembered quite a lot. The big shop of 147th Street and Lenox Avenue.

'It was quite a place,' he told his granddaughter, who listened to him, holding a machine, so she could get a pay raise.

'What do you mean, Granddaddy, when you say "quite a place"? I mean, do you mean that you liked it? That you liked working there?'

He wanted to tell her: You're asking the wrong questions. Questions like that are not the kind I like to answer. He wanted to describe how the place looked. As he had done for Ellen.

'It was a huge place, that old shop. Of course they took the whole thing down, they had to. Two blocks it took up. That's why some people will tell you it was on One-forty-eighth when to be exact you should say One-forty-seventh Street. Everything was there: Inspection, Maintenance, Repair. We replaced parts there. Everything you needed for the system we made there. It was a huge place, all sorts of departments, blacksmiths working, tinsmiths, carpenters, even weavers to weave and reweave the caning for the seats. You can remember that, I think, you're old enough, the caning on the seats. There were a thousand of us working at a time there, and a night shift – not as large, of course. Two hundred fellows. It was made of concrete, the shop itself, "reinforced concrete" they call it. There were those huge doors at the bays, we called them "bays," the bays held different things, different equipment. You could hear the racket all the time those doors made going up and down. The doors were steel, you know.'

This wasn't what she wanted to hear. She wanted to hear about his feelings. 'Did you like working there? What did it feel like to work there?'

'It felt great. You felt proud to be a part of it. A small cog in a big wheel. You did your best.'

He couldn't tell her of the love, the peace that fell upon him when he walked into the shop, buzzing with each man doing things that he was good at and machines you felt it was an honor to be working with. He'd walk in every morning. The wave of the place would lift him up, its fast smooth movement a delight to him. 'Here, Vincent,' one of the engineers would say, handing him plans. 'Could you make this up for me?'

252

He'd take the blueprint. And his mind would sink down, into the lake of this new problem. There was nothing in the world but this thing that needed to be made, constructed. And you could do it. You gave yourself up to it and in the end presented it, what it was that you'd done. Or they'd say to you, 'Vincent, we want fifty-three fittings pronto, hole $^{73}/_8$,' and you'd have to make them. You thought at first you couldn't; then you realized you could. You gave them what they asked for. You ground the wheels to make them perfectly round. They had to be perfect or they were useless. And you couldn't make mistakes. It didn't matter what was going on around you: noise, heat, bad language or bad temper; 'We need this thing, goddamn it, I said we need it now.' Sometimes you looked up at the windows in the ceiling and the light came down. You thought: Ideas come to me like this, the thick light straight through the glass, coming down in a line. He couldn't explain it all to Sheilah. 'I felt I was swimming in one of those seas where the water keeps you up. I felt I was part of an important enterprise. My mind was always taken up.'

Instead of all this, he said into the machine: 'It was a great bunch of fellows I was working with. You felt they'd share and share alike.'

'And what was the ethnic component of the workers?'

'What did you mean by that, dear? The different nationalities?'

'Yes.'

'Well, we were mixed. A lot of fellows from overseas, not just the Irish. German fellows. Poles. A lot of them well educated, you'd get your more skilled fellows in the shop. You could learn a lot.'

He had learned a lot about the world there. High ideals they had, some of those Europeans. World peace. No national boundaries. One world: the international republic of workers.

It was there he'd first heard talk about the union. 'The union talk got started in the shops and barns; well, it was natural, because in the other jobs the men were isolated, alone, maybe a pair of them, but they weren't together to talk among themselves out on the tracks.' He told Sheilah that but she didn't seem interested. She wanted to know about his feelings.

'It felt great being there,' he said. 'Every day you felt great.' She turned her machine off. He knew he'd disappointed her. He didn't know what it was she wanted, but it was something he couldn't give.

He is sitting in a green plastic chair that is pretending it is leather. Leatherette. His youth fills up his veins. The old blood, tired, hopeless, vanishes. He breathes again the air of his youthful hope.

He'd been in on something, he could say that. He'd seen something historical. The making of the Transport Workers' Union. He'd been part of that. When he'd signed on with the IRT he'd joined the Company Union, the Brotherhood; he'd known no better. Martin too, for all he was a great one for the TWU later on. They'd had no choice but to join the company union. He'd thought at first it was great stuff the Brotherhood could do for you. The libraries at all the major terminals, the recreational facilities with pool tables and lunchrooms. Hot showers. Just for them. For the workingman. 145th and Lenox, 180th Street, Van Cortlandt Park had one too. At the time he thought it was a great thing for the men, their lives were hard, living in boarding houses, some of them were filthy, and the terrible long hours and the danger. Though they boasted about these things, you'd see it took its toll. So many of them at the bars the minute they got their paychecks. He'd seen a few others lose their mind. One walking the track, they all were terrified, him shouting he was all right, the train couldn't hurt him, he was Jesus Christ, his body had been glorified. So many of them marrying so late, they said they didn't have the money, but you felt it wasn't that, they didn't have a taste for married life, they held back from it like so many did at home.

He had only loved one woman in his life, and minutes after he had met her knew that he loved her. He saw the things she had, the treasures she would bring: Courage, a quick mind. She could make decisions, see things. He wanted a life beside her. She was a tree on a high ground that beckoned. Irresistible. There was no kind of life apart from that. Nothing he'd want to live.

So, when he brought Ellen to meet his best friend and Martin warned him, 'Don't be rushing into anything that you'd regret. You haven't got it too bad now. The job's good and your time's your own,' Vincent felt a door come down between him and his friend. Though he said nothing, or 'There's a lot in what you say.' But in his mind: 'My life is with her now.'

And was it still?

He doesn't want to go back to the house where they had lived, where children had been born and sheltered, and the mother sheltered, or hidden, and the news of the son's death received, and the children of children, history, ideas they'd had about the world. How could he not want to go back to that place?

Because she isn't the person she had been.

And if she isn't, there's no sense being with her.

He doesn't want to live again under the tyranny of that nurse who filled the house with noise and theft. The theft he saw and couldn't stop. When he'd said, 'A silver brooch of my wife's seems to have been misplaced,' she'd answered him in her false accent, pretending she was from the South (he knew she wasn't really). 'Darlin', you gave away so much of that old jewelry to the girls, Theresa took a lot of it, remember. You get things mixed up in that old head o' yours.' But he knew that brooch hadn't been given away, it was one he'd given Ellen when they were courting, he wouldn't have let Theresa have it. He told Cam and even Cam couldn't stop her. The nurse, Mary Davenport, stood in her white uniform, in her white shoes, her stiff hair like a weapon. She said to Cam, 'If I'm not trusted, I'll just have to leave.'

That terrible time. He knew Mrs. Davenport had falsified her time sheets, she had not bought groceries that week and claimed she had, and Cam demanded strict accounting. Cam stood in front of the cabinets asking, 'Exactly which of these purchases was made this week,' in a lawyer's voice, the voice that could stand up to everyone, talk to judges and make some people go to jail and some be given money and protection by the court, Cam that knew Latin like a priest, his Cam. The woman shook her finger under Cam's nose like Cam was a bad child, shook and shook her finger so it was in Cam's face. 'I will not be doubted and I will not be abused. I'll quit this instant. And you'll see. She won't live a day after I quit, it'll be on your heads. Go on, now. Just come in with me, we'll tell her to her face. We'll tell her that I'm leaving and it's you that's sending me away.'

Cam called her bluff. They went into the room where Ellen was strapped into her bed. The nurse went up to her and said, 'Your granddaughter here is trying to get rid of me. She wants to separate you and me, it's what she wants to do.' She leaned over Ellen, putting her big face into Ellen's face, the face that was a skull.

And Ellen, Ellen who feared nothing, Ellen who stood up to everything, lay back, her hand a claw, her arm bone, grabbed the hand of the nurse, and began to whimper, then to cry, opening her mouth, showing everyone her gums.

The nurse turned to poor Cam, with a look of triumph on her thievish face. Cam backed down. 'Let's keep stricter accounts from now on, if possible,' she said.

The nurse said, 'Well, it's not my problem.'

As if that meant anything. As if any of them knew what that meant.

He won't think about it now. He has only an hour left to be in this room he has enjoyed, where he has learned again that he is interested in living life. He wants to remember hopeful times when he was happy, young.

The year is 1933. The shop is full of talk of a new union. The Brotherhood does nothing for them, gives them a sop – the libraries, the recreation halls – but they are slaves, they work like slaves, they are humiliated and in danger and uncared for. He recalls a speaker standing on a platform at the shop gate so the men would hear as they left work, 'Even the slaves in early civilization had a few hours for recreation, but for transit workers it is work, sleep, and a few hurried meals. We are unable to go to our bosses and talk to them like men, looking them in the eye, man to man, not with eyes to the ground like a dog.'

He listened to the speeches and the conversations of the men who seemed to him full of ideas, great ideas for the world. He took the papers that were handed out at the shop gate. He brought them home to Ellen.

The children were older now, even John was independent, the mother was dead, Ellen had gone back to reading. Every day she was more hungry for the talk he'd listened to about the union, for the plans and the ideas.

'Then what was said?' she'd ask him, leaning forward like a girl. 'And what was said to that?'

One day a fellow at the shop, a machinist like himself, asked him would he sign up with the new union. Hundreds of other fellows had signed up. Vincent said he would sleep on it. What he meant but didn't say was he would talk it over with his wife.

'Of course you will, why wouldn't you, you're not a coward

and you never have been. All your life you've never done an act of cowardice and never will.'

He said, 'We're in the middle of a black Depression, I could lose my job for this, in a minute, they'd love it, there's thousands of guys wanting a good steady job like mine. You just must realize I'm putting my job at risk.'

'Of course I realize it. What was there ever of value in this life that couldn't be put at risk? Our whole life was a risk, think what you risk every day of your life living beside someone of my bad temper.'

'We've done all right.'

He wants to kneel down before her where she sits, bury his head in her apron, she is the mother he has left, the mother of his children, comfort to him and support. And at the same time he wants to stand up beside her, he can feel her grow erect because of this, their taking up a larger life. He wants to take her hand, to walk to some high place with her. At the same time he wants to plant kisses on her body, kisses of praise, of consolation for the sadness of her childhood that was stolen from her, kisses for her bravery, her love of life. But she would never agree to it in the morning; he doesn't ask her, it would shame the both of them, his asking.

She says, 'Come help me feed these foolish creatures.'

It is June, a Sunday. She puts grain into the pocket of her apron and a bit into his hand. Joyfully she opens the screen door, the springing sound is hopeful to both of them. She calls the chickens to her. She's had chickens since the mother came; and they'd been handy, particularly with the Depression, and the garden she began first for her mother throve and was her pride.

They scatter the grain; the birds feed on it and he takes the children off to church. It is a Sunday. She'd never go, she hated everything to do with it, the priests, she said, and their black hearts. You take the children if you like, but expect no help from me. I'll not listen to their catechism; I'll not hear their prayers.

The girls to spite her have grown pious. They kneel with their heads on their folded hands.

He prays for the success of the new union and vows to Saint Joseph, the patron of workers, that his membership in the new union will not stand in the way of his faith. Some priests were dead against it, since the Communists were giving strong support.

257

'Where are the priests to give support?' Ellen said, when he'd spoken to her about his worries. 'The Communists are out for us, rain or shine. The priests are in their churches, worrying their beads like old women. Taking tea in the houses of the rich.'

He felt she'd be a Communist, like her friend Bella, only she knew he'd be upset.

He signed up for the union in June of 1934. All of that year there were weekly meetings of the union held at the shop gates. And soon after he joined, there was an outdoor rally in the Bronx, a thousand people showing up, and stirring speakers telling them their day had come. The speakers had had rotten eggs thrown at them from passing cars, rocks, broken glass. They were undaunted. All that summer he and Ellen went to rallies in the open air, in neighborhoods where the Irish were strong, Hell's Kitchen and Bay Ridge, which had a lot of fellows from the BMT. Bella would come along, the three of them like a big family. Bella approved of him at last and when he wouldn't sign with the CP when she asked him, she'd laugh and say, 'You will one day.' Ellen said she would but didn't like giving her name to anybody. Bella never challenged her; 'All right,' she said, 'Ellen, I know you're with us. A comrade through and through.' Ellen had smiled with pleasure. He knew she wouldn't join unless he joined.

Bella came to them Friday nights. The three of them went to meetings and rallies every Friday night. After their meal of fish.

That fall, or maybe it was '35, an organizer at the shop asked if the MacNamaras would be willing to have their house serve as a meeting place for a small group to discuss plans and work out strategies. He said the leadership encouraged small meetings, five fellows or so, that way in case there was a spy among them only three or four of them would lose their jobs. 'You talk it over with the wife,' the fellow said. Vincent couldn't think of his name now. 'Sometimes the wives get scared.'

'Not mine,' said Vincent, 'she's a great supporter of the cause.'

The man laughed, not kindly. 'Talk it over with her first.'

She was thrilled. 'What's the use of a house like this if it can't be used for something important. It's an honor and our privilege to open it up.'

As if it was a thing she'd always done, opening up her house. As if she hadn't kept the house closed, furiously, to strangers.

Nearly everybody was a stranger to her.

They'd moved to Queens Village in 1922. And though she talked to people in the shops, was friendly, bantered with the neighbors, she invited no one in the door. If someone came, a woman, offering her some gift, or food, asking her advice on schooling for the children, which they often did, or asking her advice about their gardens, she'd talk to them on the porch or at the door or in the back yard. She was genial; they left glad they had spoken to her. But she never let them through the door.

He didn't have to ask her why, knowing it was a habit from the time she felt the mother must be kept from sight. But this habit of hers didn't make it easy for the children to have friends. He felt that it was to spite her that Theresa had used her music and her looks to bring people around. She never seemed to like the people.

So when, in 1935, Ellen agreed to use the house as a meeting place for the five fellows from the shop who needed a place to talk about their plans, their ideas, fears, procedures, he was doubly grateful, knowing it didn't come easy to her. But she seemed happy with them there. They'd all sit at the kitchen table. She'd stand at the sink, holding back at first, then entering into the talk. They saw her brains and appreciated her. Except for Martin, who'd become one of the group, though the others were from the shop and he was still in Signals. 'My advice, Vince, for your own good, is keep the wife from butting in.' He was thinking of asking Martin not to come after that crack, but the others valued him. They thought he could be useful in recruiting signalmen. He wasn't, though. They were a strange lot, signalmen, and snobbish too. They didn't want to mix with the unskilled workers. Funny, because the machinists, who really were the skilled ones, were happy to mix with everyone. When Martin reported his failure in recruitment Ellen lost her temper and said he must not be trying. Vincent saw his friend go white around the lips. He knew that they'd never liked each other. She'd been right in seeing through some things in Martin, the drinking, the big talk. And he was still mad IRA; she said she didn't believe in causes that were strictly national. Though probably that was Bella talking through her.

They'd fought about it once, Ellen and Martin.

'Have you forgotten it's your nation,' Martin said. 'And what John Bull's done to it.'

'Ah, the bull's got into the cow, is that it? I say, burn the place down. Good riddance to it. The Irish have a talent for two things and two things only, getting drunk and stepping on their own two feet.'

After that, there'd been nothing but hardness between the two of them. Martin told Vincent he thought it shameful that a mother would not kneel beside her children in church. Seeing the hardness between Martin and her mother, Theresa curried Martin's favor. He bought her an expensive prayerbook for her Confirmation. As her Confirmation name she took Martine.

Martin stopped coming to the group, warning Vincent that the leader of the group, John Hogan, was a Communist. Of course Vincent had known it all along. After Martin stopped coming, Theresa took up her disapproving air when the fellows came by.

'Godless Communism,' she'd say with her sharp, beautiful lips. 'At Fátima, the Blessed Mother begged us to fight to the death against it. To pledge ourselves to the conversion of Red Russia. To give our lives to return it to her arms.'

'Russia was not a Catholic country,' said Bella, who was there, hearing it all. 'If you'd tell the Orthodox priests the Pope was on their side they'd turn Red faster than you could say "Ash Wednesday."'

And Ellen laughed, joyous in her ally's victory against her daughter.

Every Friday night when the groups met, Theresa, looking her best, dressed up to kill, made a great show of passing by the men – of course they stared at her, she was a stunning girl – people thought Magdalene was better-looking, but he'd take Theresa anytime – saying in a loud voice that she was on her way to church.

'On Friday night?' Ellen would say, unable to keep silent.

'Devotions,' Theresa would say, tilting her stylish hat.

And Magdalene, made sick by the turmoil, the anxiety of having strangers in the house, by the anger of her mother and her sister, took to her bed. John, young, indifferent, listened to the radio in the front room.

What were the things they talked about? He can't seem to remember now. Something about a new kind of squeegee the company wanted to force on the men so they could work more quickly and more of them be laid off. Some workers in the Jerome Barn refusing to do whitewashing. A 10-percent pay cut. The demolition of the Sixth Avenue El. All this is vague to him. What he remembers is his pride in Ellen, in himself and in his fellow workers, their courage, the ideas they had, the important things they talked about, the sense that they could change things in their lives. That they would see things change.

And they had. But before the great strike it had been finished for him. He had had a heart attack and had to leave his job. No more commuting for him, the doctor said, and no more of this union excitement. 'Not unless you're interested in seeing your good wife a widow and your children orphans. If you're interested in that, go on doing what you're doing. The good lady will look lovely, I can see, in black.'

The doctor said this in front of Ellen, who looked back at him in terror. He was surprised. It had not occurred to him that his death would mean so much.

When it happens he is at work in the shop. Sitting at his bench, looking at plans the engineer has given. He feels a tightness in his chest. Fire. The surprise of pain. And the conviction: Now I see.

No one is there around him. He doesn't want to call out. His helper will be by in time. In a strange calm he calculates the chances of his death. He concentrates on going towards something. A shape. A dark circle. But desirable. Not undesirable, the end of everything. Whenever this time has come back to him, he recollects that at that moment there was only the circle, dark, but shining in the distance. Shimmering. Disintegrating at the edges as if it has been touched by some corrosive thing. Yet beckoning. And he is anxious to approach it. It takes up his attention, the circle that can be disintegrating. He has no sense of regret for what was left behind or of a yearning for a life to come. Only of the shining, dark, disintegrating circle in the distance drawing his life from him. Drawing him to itself. It is more interesting to him, more arresting than his pain.

The helper comes and he is taken to a hospital. Saint Clare's – he tells them he prefers a Catholic hospital. The fellows in the shop see him off as if he were leaving for a cruise. All the time he knows he will not be back.

Ellen comes in to be beside him, not forgetting to make a bad face behind the nuns' backs to make him laugh. She doesn't bring the children with her for a while. She says she doesn't want to disturb him but he knows she wants him to herself. She is taken up by the idea that he was almost snatched from her by death; and that he will not die now, but will be with her. The girls know they are being kept away, and it grows into one more thing for which they never will forgive her. He can see this as it happens, from his bed he sees it. He knows they store up her offenses. Even now, women in their sixties, they take them out, examine them like jewels, precious for having endured. Shining, intact. Their grievances against their mother.

In bed for three months, he reads all about the strike. A triumph for the workers. The Kent Avenue Power Plant in Queens. The BMT too, a surprise that it should happen on the BMT, the organizers hadn't done nearly as much as they had with the IRT. The union men took up their stand in front of a panel of circuitbreaker switches. If they pulled the switches, the lines that they controlled could be put out of service in the twinkling of an eye. People could be killed, hundreds of people injured. A brave plan, an audacious plan. It worked. No one was hurt. Not one hair on a worker's head was harmed, or on a passenger's. Thousands of men braved it to support the sit-downers, risking their lives, their jobs. And then, triumphant, the union was recognized. All the dreams, plans, words that had taken shape around hundreds of kitchen tables just like theirs had been realized. They had their strength.

But he was not a part of it. And though the fellows came to visit in his three months' convalescence, and told him enthusiastically what he'd missed, that he was one of them, he knew he wasn't one of them and wouldn't be again. He followed the doctors' orders. He quit the Transit Authority.

His body had prevented him from taking part in the one event in history he could have said he'd helped lay groundwork for.

He remembers now, they came to tell him all about it in the hospital. He'd been feeling all right, coherent, but when they begin to talk to him he feels himself move away, as if he were sick with a fever. He is lying in a state that seems between wakefulness and sleeping although it has nothing to do with sleep. His bafflement makes him feel that he is standing off, far from them, watching. He can see what they are telling him about, but it doesn't touch him. He hears the roar of the men's voices, he knows all about the building. The power plant. Power. It is an idea and the exact opposite of an idea. The impulse is obedient, you have only to flick a switch. Darkness, the cessation of movement or its opposite – light, movement – occurs. A hum like the hum of the race itself emanates from the center of the plant. The wires that are everywhere are dangerous, death-dealing. Men stand, shifting from foot to foot, ready perhaps to die. All of it becomes only an idea to him, and his friends, who had spoken in the same way at his kitchen table of the world ruled by the workers, tell him what went on. But they believe they are describing a real occurrence. To him it is abstract. His pain in having been kept back from it makes him believe that it has not been real. He allows himself luxurious infirmity. He drifts into an invalid's thin sleep. The power plant hovers above the ground like a palace in the *Arabian Nights*. At any moment it can cease to be. He does not want to come out of this. He is alone; the building moves above him, light and insubstantial, signifying nothing. Causing nothing to begin to be.

He took a job in Queens so that he wouldn't have to commute. It was a good job, Patent Scaffolding. The problems he worked with interested him. How to set up an outside structure that modeled itself on the eventual inside. Holding the workers as they made the thing becoming itself. Scaffolding was all function. There was nothing beautiful about it, that was not the point of it, to look beautiful. But you couldn't make mistakes. Men's lives depended on you. He admired engineers. He wished Dan had become one. But ideas were what the boy liked. He'd seemed to have no love for things.

Vincent had thought himself a shallow person because only palpable things won his greatest love. He was never sure whether he'd loved the body of his wife, or the idea of her. Would he go on loving her dead? He'd wondered about that. Now he would never know. Her body goes on, but he no longer loves her.

For more than twenty years he took the plans the engineers came up with, making models of the scaffolding that they designed. Good work, he liked it. But the pride he'd had when he worked for the subways, like you were a part of something great, that had been lost. Some days he felt a child could do his work. And sometimes just to ride the subways hurt him.

Ellen understood that. When he got sick the company offered her a job in one of the change booths. She refused, knowing it would be painful for him: her a part of it, him not. Her able to join the new union and him not. He knew at the time that she'd have liked to join the union, would have taken the job for that alone, but she said nothing to him. He was grateful. She was not like other women. She'd known that about him. Perhaps another woman wouldn't have.

Bella got her a job with her at the millinery. Ellen had lost her skills for fine sewing, but the work was too simple for her, it tired her, and the commute tired her. But she was happy seeing Bella, having lunch together made everything up to her. She never made a new friend. And never told him she'd joined the Milliners' Union. His eyes fill, remembering the time she was taken to the hospital with gallbladder, and he'd gone into her wallet to find the card that told her blood type and found the union card. She'd never said a word about the union, and never gone to the meetings, though Bella was active and he knew it would have pleased her, given her something to take her mind off John's death. John's death changed everything. She'd closed a door down and shut it for good. She never forgave him for stopping her grief. Or was it that she blamed him for helping her bring to the world one who would be lost? Or was it that she knew he'd never been a father to his son?

The War ended. She stopped working so she could be home with Dan. They became parents again, slower, more patient, better to Dan and Cam, he thought, than they'd been to their own. She kept on at the Democratic Club, but after Roosevelt's death her political attachments never were as strong.

With John's death they became old people waiting for their greater age. Not fifty yet, they softened to the expectation of their death. After Roosevelt's death she turned her passion to the children of her children. Into Dan and Cam, seeing them gifted, she poured her fearful love of the outside world. They would go out to it. She'd make them ready as she had not made ready her own. She'd shelter the gifts and the gifted children.

She took no interest in Theresa's children. He'd tried to make it up to Sheilah and to John. But he found their pain exhausting: he was too old for children in such pain. He'd liked Marilyn. He'd liked the ease of her, the way she took pleasure in things. It hurt him that she'd been foolish in her life. Sex was her downfall, he could see. Still, she was lovely. He'd been proud when she came to visit here at Maryhurst. The whole place had brightened up. It disturbed him to see that his friends had liked her being there better than Cam. That wasn't fair, although he understood it. Marilyn had only to walk into a room. That was her gift.

But if they'd been in trouble, it was Cam they'd have gone to. He knew that.

After his work ended he did not know how to say what his life was. His life had been his work.

On that tape Sheilah expressed surprise. 'If you came here, Granddaddy, as a skilled machinist, why did it take so many years to get a job commensurate with your skills? Was it your Irish heritage that held you back? Statistics show the Irish don't achieve as they could be expected to. As a nationality, they don't live up to their potential.'

'I did what I felt I had to. They were hard times. You didn't have so much choice.'

He took the job digging because he could get it right away. He took the job with the German because he was fed up and he'd seen the ad. He took the job in Signals because Martin worked in Signals, and after the time he'd taken off to get the mother, he couldn't afford to wait around.

But he had asked himself, and after sixty years he didn't know the answer, if Danny Clark hadn't died, would he have stayed in Signals all his life? Or would he have pushed ahead to get the job that he was trained for? The job that he deserved.

Someone is knocking at the door. It's Sister Otile.

'Well, Vincent,' she says. 'Ready to go?'

And to his shame, before a woman, he begins to cry. He walks to the wardrobe so she won't see him, pretending there's something he needs to get. He says, 'Be there in just one minute, Sister.' She says nothing.

She says, 'You know, I could say something to Cam.'

She and Cam are friends. This is the reason he is here. Cam met Sister Otile, whom she calls simply Otile because they worked together for some women who were beaten up by their husbands. The two of them, to spend their time on that. Generous of them. Wonderful, the both of them.

He says, 'The family's expecting me. Cam's worked her fingers to the bone setting things up so that I can go home.'

'Vincent, you're an old man. You've got certain rights. The right to live the way you want.'

'But what about my wife's rights?'

'In my professional opinion, Ellen would be just as well off here as home. I'd put her into a room just down the hall. What's she got going for her there? Some crackpot who steals the silver? We're not big on silver here. It doesn't turn our heads. No class.'

'She's happy with that Mary Davenport.'

'She'll be happy here. She wants to be with you. Being with you is what makes her happy.'

'You don't know her,' he says, and then, fearing that he sounds rude, adds, 'She'll be together with me when I go home.'

Sister Otile is not sympathetic. 'Vincent, you know what I think. You like it here. We like to have you. For one thing, you save us money. If you leave, we'll probably have to put Roberta back into therapy. Think of it this way: if you stay you'll be saving the community thousands of dollars. To say nothing of my own life. No one but you likes to hear my John McCormack records.'

Vincent smiles.

'In my opinion, your happiness should come first. Not some sixty-five-year-old promise that has no meaning anymore.'

Vincent nods.

'You know I could talk to Cam. Cam will do anything you want.'

He looks up at her. 'I told everyone I was going.'

'*Un*tell them, Vincent. Let Cam deal with the family. She's a lawyer. People pay her to do this kind of thing.'

He shakes his head. Refusing.

'Vincent, I always said it. You're a stubborn mick.'

★

He isn't listening; she is still talking but he isn't listening.

He is thinking about his house.

When he retired in 1961 from the job at Patent Scaffolding, his life took on the rhythm of a woman's. Seasons, meals, the house itself became important.

He would go back to the house.

In honor of the years when the house had been the center of his life. Their lives.

Years watching the apple tree turn pink, then yellow-green, then somber green in the high summer, in the autumn seeing the heavy fruit streaked yellow and red. The darker, later red. They'd gather it, he and Ellen, even when the grandchildren were gone. In summer there were mulberries. She was clever with the windfall fruit. She loved the ease of the collection and the growth free from her care.

Slow years and always in each other's company. An hour or two apart from each other, him in the basement, her cooking, the two of them eating their big meal in the afternoon and after it the sweet sleeps in the rooms now at opposite sides of the hall, far from each other. Their serious reading: tearing articles from the newspapers. Colored people beaten, kept from schools, John Kennedy, Vietnam, where Johnny went but Ellen refused to see him off. 'Suppose he dies there,' Vincent had said. 'He'll die, then, from his own stupidity,' she said. She turned her back on a boy she'd been at least kind to.

But he did come back. Johnny came back.

Great children they all are and they're waiting now. Waiting for him.

History, the son's death, the dead Presidents, the pictures of the weddings, graduations.

The windows he had broken. Fixed now. Johnny'd fixed them, Cam had said. Without his asking; he had been ashamed to ask.

The house that had been their life.

Why had she let so few people in the house?

That was why he liked it here. People came in and out, you

talked to them, lent them a magazine, offered them a sweet. They gave you things.

Why in all the years were there so few people in the house?

So few outside the family.

Martin, Delia, Bella.

Theresa's friends, whom nobody had wanted.

The union people, only for a while.

He had loved his wife. Now she's waiting for him. She waits for him to keep his promise.

He thinks: I always wanted someplace where people could just come in. Someplace to sit down, be themselves, and feel that they were happy.

V

1

Two blocks, or less than fourteen hundred feet, less than five hundred yards, separate the home of Vincent and Ellen Mac-Namara from the house where Cam lives with her husband and her mother. Cam decides to drive.

If she didn't drive her car between the houses, if she walked the distance in her normal way, it would be proof that she didn't believe her mother would return with her to Vincent and Ellen's house, where Magdalene has promised that she will appear in honor of her father's homecoming. Where he will take his place again beside his wife so they will die together in the house, which everyone believes is what the two of them want.

It's the last thing Vincent wants. He is happy where he is; he doesn't want to leave Maryhurst and his friends the sisters and his cronies, who pretend to envy him his homecoming but really don't. He doesn't want to leave the simple garden with its easily grown vegetables, perennial spring flowers, and the others that are guaranteed to give no trouble: zinnias, marigolds. He doesn't want to leave the card games, songs around the white-painted piano, magazines, stashes of food brought to rooms between and after mealtimes among friends, advice easily given, taken or ignored, long days broken by TV sports events or press conferences given by the President, the governor, evening Mass (voluntary, sometimes even some of the nuns can't make it), and the short sleeps of old age, unfrightening among the furniture where no past life has set its mark.

His family believe that he has spent his time longing for this day of his return.

Cam pretends to believe that she will any minute make the two-block journey with her mother strapped into the seatbelt on the passenger's side, smoothing down the trousers of one of her ten identical pastel trouser suits.

John is outside in his grandparents' back yard. Away from his mother, out of her sight, he thinks again that maybe he will sign up for a nursing course.

Sheilah is in the kitchen, still working on preparations for lunch. She is thinking: Of all of them, only I have a life worthy of unequivocal respect.

Dan is thinking of his grandfather. He is thinking that the old man is coming back to a dying animal to die himself. He is thinking of his daughters, wondering if it's good for them to see this. He thinks it may be good; at any rate, he wants them to see it. Whatever it is, it will happen less and less frequently in the world. They may not see it again, two lives, two bodies, together until death.

Theresa thinks she bears the word of God within her and quite soon she will lay hands on her mother and her mother will be healed.

Marilyn thinks: If I brought my children back here, if I learned to live without a man, if I started again, but here, where I was known, where I was at least not unknown, it might be better.

All of them, except for Cam and Dan and Marilyn, believe that they are lucky to have Mary Davenport to look after Vincent now, that she will take the extra burden in her competent and forceful stride.

Not one of these things is completely true. Some have elements of truth in them; some are wholly false.

Ellen believes nothing. She lies in her bed sleeping, crying out, cursing, crying, falling back to sleep.

Cam drives the two blocks hoping that her mother will be getting ready. As she drives, she prepares her annoyance. Her mother will not yet have chosen which of her pastel trouser suits she will wear. She will be walking around her bedroom, still half undressed. Cam stiffens herself in case her mother isn't wearing her prosthesis, forcing Cam to see her empty chest. She vows she won't look; her mother should spare her that, but if she won't Cam knows enough to spare herself.

She walks into the house, already prepared to be angry. She turns on the light in the front hall. It's still afternoon but this house always seems to need more light. She and her mother argue every day:

'Turn the lights off, Cam. Why make the lighting company more millions than they have?'

'I pay the bills, Mother.'

'If you love to waste, then waste. I thought you were the one that was big on this energy crisis.'

Above the light switch is a photograph. It is a picture taken in the twenties of a mother standing in a garden with her little girl. The child is small, two or three years old. The mother bends above her in an arc of intimate instruction, leaning and about to pick a blossom from a flowering tree.

The light falls, straight and plain, on the figure of the child. The child is obviously dressed for the picture. Or perhaps she is always dressed like this. The dress is bell-shaped, stiff and frilled, made up of rows of tender lace. There are hundreds of small buttons, tiny as milk teeth, opalescent or covered in some version of the cloth that made the dress. The mother's hair is collected into bunches at her ears; it must be morning, perhaps this is how she does her hair for sleep. She's wearing a peignoir trimmed at the neck and sleeves with velvet, or it may be fur, some trim it's impossible to name for certain in the dark hallway where the photograph is hung. And Cam would never move the picture to a better light. She hates the picture. She would be happy if it fell and smashed. She has no idea where her mother got it; it seems always to have been around. If it fell and smashed, she would be pleased to see the shards around the floor. She wouldn't see to it that it was re-framed. For a while her mother would keep asking her when she was going to get it re-framed, and she would say 'Soon,' pretending she'd just forgotten. But she wouldn't have forgotten; she would have refused. Her mother would almost stop asking; three times a year, perhaps, she'd bring it up. She would put the picture in a conspicuous place, and Cam would put the photograph back in the closet, where it would lean against the dark back wall. She would know that she could keep the thing a ruin, that it was in her power, and she would.

But the photograph won't fall. It will stay where it is, kept there by the mother as the representative of what she would like to have been and believes she was. It will be kept there by the daughter as a proof of her mother's ability to deceive herself. Neither of them need say anything to the other. They never speak about the picture. They both know everything about it.

Each day, Cam wants to tear the picture from the wall, shake, literally shake it underneath her mother's nose, and say, 'I know what you think. You think we were like that. We were never like that. There was no tree like that. You wanted nothing to do with gardens. You hated gardens, because your mother was good at them. Nothing grew beside our house. One thing: a lilac bush you had no right to, that flowered every April, the envy of the neighborhood. It was just like you to have a tree like that.'

Each day, Magdalene sees the picture and thinks: This is exactly how it was. We were like that. I remember, we were lovely. I remember every morning we were just like that. I never understood: we could have been like that forever.

Cam flicks on every light between the front door and her mother's room. One in the dining room, two in the upstairs hall. She even turns the light on in the bathroom, though she has no thought of going in.

'Ready, Mother?' she calls out.

Of course, Magdalene has known for several seconds that it is her daughter walking through the house. She knew it but allowed herself to hope that it was someone else. Bob, Kevin, one of her friends. A burglar. Someone resolved to do her definite and final harm. A harm that people will feel sorry for.

She imagines the killer's face. He has no face; he's wearing a black mask. He ties her to her chair; he gags her. She knows she could die at any minute. But he doesn't kill her. He hits her on the head with his gun. She blacks out. When she wakes up, her room is empty, ransacked. She touches her hair and feels patches of sticky drying blood. She's helpless until Cam comes home. Cam sees her and starts crying. She unties her, bathes her, dresses her in nightclothes, puts her to bed. The police come. They interview her in her bed. She can't remember anything, she says. They understand. They tell her she was very brave.

'Mother, it's me.'

She hears the accusation in her daughter's voice. She hasn't done a thing and already Cam is angry with her. It takes all her strength away from her just to hear that voice. Cam never believes in her, never has. She never thought that Magdalene would make it to her parents'. Magdalene thinks now that she could have done it if only somebody had been there beside her, having faith in her, encouraging her when she felt bad. But nobody encourages her.

Nobody believes in her. Nobody knows how hard it is for her to do the simplest things. Things that are simple for other people aren't for her. She has her dizzy spells. Her trouble breathing. Nobody understands all that, because she doesn't tell them. That's why they won't understand why she can't make it to her parents'. Because she keeps things to herself. That's why nobody understands. That's why she's all alone.

She sees Cam in the doorway. She can't stand to look at her, she looks so angry.

'You're not dressed,' Cam says.

Magdalene shrugs. She stands up and walks over to her vanity table. She sits down, looks in the mirror, and puts on an earring. She's wearing her bathrobe; she put it on over her clothes because she didn't want to soil them when she put on her makeup. She takes the earring off. She looks at her daughter's angry face in the mirror. In the mirror, Cam looks back at her.

Neither of them knows who will speak first. Which one will say the words. The accusation. The excuse. They look at each other in the mirror. Cam shifts her weight from foot to foot. Magdalene sits still. Neither of them says anything. And then the time comes and they understand that Cam will say it:

'So you're not going after all.'

Underneath her bathrobe, Magdalene is dressed. At any moment she could change her mind. It isn't over yet, the possibility that she could change her mind.

'I thought I would, Cam. I honestly thought I was going. You see how far I got. Though it wasn't easy, even to get this far. Just to get dressed made me so out of breath. And dizzy. Spots in front of my eyes everywhere. I had to keep stopping for drinks of water. Only little sips. I was just terrified of throwing up.'

The words Cam won't say are blooming in her throat like knives. *Faithless. Inconstant. User. Parasite. You can't do anything. Not even for your father. Or for me.*

She doesn't say these things to her mother, who is crying. She swallows the blooming knives and says instead, 'Maybe you'd better just lie down.'

Magdalene toddles over to her bed, unsteady, as if she were drunk. She isn't drunk, although she has been drinking; when she's drunk her gait is steady. Drunkenness focuses her mind. One step follows another. Her desires shine before her and solidify. Drunk, she reaches out. Each thing she touches is the object of her dreams.

Now she lies down on the bed. She points to her feet, indicating that Cam should remove her shoes. Cam does, with such revulsion she can hardly breathe. She lifts the lavender cloth pumps off the veined puffy feet, the feet with twisted toes, crippled from the cruel shoes of fashion, the toenails painted pale, their yellow hidden under polish the shade of evening shells. Magdalene's eyes are closed, she covers them with her right hand. She can't bear to see her daughter but she calls it migraine. Blindly she hands over the lavender pearl paste earrings.

'In the zipper bag,' she says.

'You told me once, Mother. About the zipper bag. I heard you fine the first time.'

Magdalene becomes contrite. She becomes a child. She says, 'I know you did. I'm sorry, Cam, I know you did.'

Cam puts the earrings in the zipper bag. She puts the wooden trees into the high-heeled shoes. She doesn't understand this care, this choosing, and this maintenance of clothes that go nowhere, clothes that Magdalene wears for minutes, then takes off. These costumes of deception, self-deception. These hours of selection, preparation, garments put on, judged, adored. And then what happens? This is where Cam's mind always darkens, where the shutter closes and the images go black. What happens then? What could possibly happen? What goes on between the admiration there before the mirror, the last loving pat, and the final decision: I cannot.

Mother, she thinks, seeing Magdalene, one arm over her eyes, one up above her head, as if she lay on a beach, waiting for something wonderful. And then, *Not my mother.*

How can you have become this to us both? You are everything I never want to be.

Does Cam say, when the sweat breaks on her upper lip, when the salt taste of her revulsion rises up in her dry throat, when all this comes upon her every time that she has contact with her mother's flesh, does she say: *Yes, of course I understand. I must despise this which was once my home.*

Does she say: *Mother. Of course now there is horror, you betray me by the softening and drying out of that firm flesh I loved. You show me what I will become, each falling vein reminds me of my ruin. I will become you.*

She says nothing to her mother. She would never say such things. Even if she knew them, she would never say.

2

People who know them both say how remarkable it is that two people, a mother and a daughter, could be so unlike.

Cam responds to this observation, casually. 'I often wonder myself,' she says. 'How can I have been brought up by someone and be so different. The truth is I wasn't. Brought up by her. I was brought up by my grandparents.'

The daughter denies the mother. Not for her the fashionable romance dragged up, patched together, by her friends and fellow feminists. Mother and daughter reunited after years of misunderstanding and discord, discovering each other in the nick of time. *Mother. Darling. We are the same. Only the wicked system made us push away.*

She listens to her friends saying how they'd been taught to downplay the mother's value. Dangerous, of course, the adored object of babyhood tending the house and solitary in her indoor life. Of course you felt the father was exciting, out in the world, bringing home the bacon, news, contagion of the world. Of course the father was the hero and the mother the poor second best.

We understand it all now. And, thank God, in time.

When her friends speak like this she doesn't even pretend interest. When they talk about their mothers she feels like a Bolshevik listening to White Russians talk about the old life. She listens to them in another city, where they all now live. But it is a city of strangers, it is not her home. The lost past, this idyll that they mourn she had no part of.

Sometimes she lies about her mother's glamour. Or she believes she's lying, but in concealing her mother's present, she is telling a kind of truth, the truth of Magdalene the young widow staring the public pity for her state right down, out in the car each morning in her suit, perfumed, her smart foot light on the gas pedal of the Buick she bought herself.

Songs. Show tunes. The permissive and luxurious night outings of the single mother and her only child.

The child as escort. Boon companion. Ornament and prize. Out. Out on the mother's arm.

There are some things they've always loved. Musical comedies, movies with dancing. Across the brackish water of their years of failure they can meet and join hands over the songs and dances of the beautiful and tender movie stars, their only real relatives. They are sisters watching in the dark. Humble sisters to near gods. They watch, sing, join in, and forget. They forget Magdalene's hacked breasts, and her drunken accusations, her self-publications and displays, Cam's silent reproaches, her turning away. Even now they can sit in the dark eating the treats of movie darkness: bonbons, malted-milk balls, caramels. Even now, on the mother's bed, an island, they can sit in front of the huge television Magdalene bought. Sixty-five inches. Fifty channels. All remote control. They watch *Top Hat, Babes in Arms, Three Coins in the Fountain, Gilda, Daddy Long Legs, Born To Dance*. And they are happy as they were always happy, watching, singing, each illumined and protected by the glowing pictures of impermeable lives.

But when these images are needed – the luxuries, the faces, the bodies that flicker and then disappear, the luscious melodies, words that are lozenges of joy – when they are needed do they come to hand? Now, covering her mother with a cotton blanket, the same shade of purple as her trouser suit, trying to cover her mother and yet not have a moment's contact with her flesh, the flesh that makes her sweat break out, now do the words of songs, even the name of *one*, *one* sentence they have dreamed of from the movies, come to their lips?

Not one.

At the door Cam shouts over her shoulder, 'I'll be back, I don't know what time.'

She goes down to her room.

She raises the receiver of the phone. She calls Ira. She will ask

him if they can live together. Anywhere. Her house, the empty
house, or his apartment. Or somewhere else. She has money.
Other people do these things, she'll tell him, other people do them,
we could too.

She wants to say to Ira: I can't give my mother one more second
of my life. I won't draw or fail to draw another breath on her
account. My husband and my mother can live without me. They
may do better. It's only my self-love that keeps me here. I am
in love with my own image, the honorable one, honoring the
promises.

Yet I do not honor them.

I honor you.

I am a faithless wife.

I do not love my mother.

As she dials the number she is thinking of the faithless wives of
movies. How quickly they turn into murderers. And the ungrateful
daughters, dancing while their famished mothers labor through
the night.

As the phone pips – the modern signal, stripped of romance and
powerful intent – she waits to hear her lover's voice. 'You always
answer the phone like you're expecting the sheriff,' she tells him.
Even before he answers, she knows she can't say what she'd just
thought of saying. It's impossible, she thinks, we'll never live
together.

She knows she couldn't say to Vincent, 'Granddaddy, I'm
moving in with my lover now.' It would be a ridiculous sentence,
she thinks, the product of the modern age. Antibiotics and a
loosening of sexual mores. He would never understand.

She thinks of Vincent's face, grown dark with disappointment
when she tells him. She can never tell him. For her to have a life
with Ira, both her grandfather and her mother would have to die.
How easy it is, she thinks, to wish the death of another person.
Is considering it wishing it? No. She doesn't want Vincent dead.
She doesn't want him absent from the world. She does not want
him lonely among the rootless dead. She wants him in the world
with her. But she would almost rather see him dead than hurt
him.

When she hears Ira's voice, the sound of it makes her blame
him. Blame him for what? For the sentence she has formulated in

her brain, the wish for two people's deaths, which, without him, would never have been able to exist.

'Where the hell were you?' she says.

He answers: 'In the shower, sweetheart.'

She thinks he wouldn't call her sweetheart if he knew what was in her heart. She would like to cry. She would like him to come and take her away. She would like him to meet her grandfather. None of these things is possible.

She tells him that her mother won't go to her parents' house. Won't be there to meet her father. As she promised.

'Well,' he says, 'you have to understand.'

'Nothing,' she says, 'there's nothing that I have to understand. You're the one that has to understand. My mother, as always, got exactly what she wanted. My mother always gets exactly what she wants.'

'All right,' he says.

'All right what?'

'Can you come here now? For a little while? Before you get your grandfather.'

She knows that they are in the house now. Waiting for her. Waiting for her and her mother.

'They're all waiting for me,' she says.

'Just tell them. Tell them that she's not coming. That she's sick. Then come here and be with me.'

The gift of a simple sentence. *Just come here and be with me.* His simple sentence allows her to say one as simple.

'I want to be with you,' she says.

It is Saturday. It's all right to go to Ira's apartment; her in-laws, the Ulichnis, have gone to Pennsylvania. She'll go right now, for just an hour. She'll call her grandparents' house, tell them the news by phone. Tell a lie on the telephone. She'll say: My mother needs another hour to get ready. She just needs a little bit more time.

Sometimes, when she knows she will be with him in a little while, the last minutes before she sees him are unbearable. She can't wait to see him, she feels that she literally cannot wait. Every one of her cells seems lit up. Pinpoints of expectation dot her skin. Her bones empty themselves of solid matter. Her neck, like an expectant bird's, stretches out.

She thinks of how lucky she is. How fortunate, she thinks, to have a body, to be young, healthy, capable of pleasure, no, not only pleasure, this bodily joy. She grabs her purse. She flies out of the door like one of the carefree teenagers she worshipped in the movies. Her hair swings out behind her. She runs to her car.

But then she sees her husband driving up the driveway, pulling his car in beside hers, holding his hands like a visor above his eyes as if she were something that hurt his vision. All the quickness in her body seizes up, as if she had been riding on an elevator which suddenly stopped in the basement, landing in the darkness, failing to open up its doors. She smiles, the flinching smile she always gives him. She thinks it must be terrible for him always to be greeted as she greets him. Tenderly, she sees his yellow short-sleeved shirt, his striped tie, his brown pants and black fake-leather belt, his gray suede oxfords with a line of black making a horseshoe shape around the toe and arch. I'm sorry, I'm sorry, she wants to say every time she sees him. Why don't you leave me, she wants to say. You're a good man, you could be happy. You could have a life without me, why do you let me cut off your life?

They never touch. It must be ten years since she's kissed him. She puts her hand on the top of the car door, where the window would be if it were closed rather than open, where his arm would be if he hadn't moved it inside the car when he saw her approach.

'Hi,' she says. 'You're home early.'

'I took a personal day,' he says. 'I thought you might need me around.'

'That was nice,' she says, 'thank you.'

'Your mother all right?'

She snorts. 'She never meant to go. She's up in bed. I guess she'll stay there.'

'Want me to stick around?' he says. 'In case she needs anything.'

'No,' she says. 'Whatever you want. You want to come over to Linden Street after he's home? I don't know that I'd recommend it. With that crew.'

'No,' he says, 'you know I'm not one for parties.'

'Some party,' she laughs. 'Fun at the house of Atreus.'

She realizes he doesn't get the reference; it's another thing she's done to him, after everything else, one more thing.

'Thanks a lot for being so thoughtful,' she says.

He shrugs. 'Things were slow anyway. Down at work.'

'Anyway, it was really nice.'

'Never mind,' he says. 'It doesn't matter.'

In the car, driving to Ira, she begins to cry. What could she do for Bob to make things better? She never wanted to hurt him, but she understands that marrying her, meeting her even, was the worst thing that could have happened in his life. She knows it's too late for him; she wishes he wouldn't go on being good to her and her mother. Doing things around the house. She wishes he'd run amok, set a fire in the basement, burn them both up in their beds. It's what we deserve, she says to herself. Both of us. No, not her. It wasn't her. No one did anything but me.

She stops at a pay phone. She forgot to call them at her grand-parents'. Marilyn answers. Thank God. Marilyn. Later she'll tell Marilyn the truth.

For now a lie, useful, simple, handy as a bottle opener, will serve. For the hundredth time, she's appalled by what she'll do to be with Ira. Lies, betrayals, jealousies, all the things she satirized or vilified in other women. Sometimes she wants to stop every-thing with Ira, because what she feels for him has made her a person she would otherwise never have been. She is *subject* to her feelings. She is, more often than ever in her life, a person doing things she can't approve. A person she can't recognize as still herself.

Once she got a glimpse of herself in a bathroom mirror. She was shocked at the sight.

They were together in a hotel for the weekend. They had slept too late to get room service. He went out to get a paper, coffee, some sweet cake. She was alone in a room he had just left.

She washed her face. She looked into the mirror above the sink. Her own face surprised her pleasantly. It looked so happy. His shaving things were on the shelf before her. On the ledge was a little wavelet of his shaving soap, delicious as whipped cream. She scooped it with her second finger as if she were stealing frosting from a cake. Then she rubbed the cream between her breasts. It disappeared; she was pleased at this absorption. Her eye fell on his shaving kit: black, oblong, nearly empty. Its brass-colored zipper cut a gash through pimply Leatherette. She forcefully disliked the object; it beamed out enmity when she looked at it; she didn't know why. And then she understood. She looked at a label, green and white, an airline sticker with his name and old address in his ex-wife's handwriting. The handwriting she hated, the boarding-school girl's slant printing: proof of a privilege the woman, she knew, had done nothing with. His ex-wife was a failure, Cam had thought with brimming happiness. To think of her made Cam's lip curl. How could he? Why her? And if her, why me? The label present in the room with her struck her as an assault. Polite, well bred, it staked the other woman's claim. Cam felt herself seized by inspiration: she felt it in the roots of her hair. Stiff figures, illumined, whispered in her ear. Told her that if she could rip the label off in one magic, ritual stroke, leaving no trace, no corner, no shadow of residual glue, that she would have effaced the other woman's claim. She and Ira would be happy for the rest of their long, happy, and prosperous lives.

She didn't allow herself to catch her own eye in the mirror. Approaching the bag as if she were about to crack a safe, she hesitated, studied the angles, then proceeded. There was only one chance for victory.

She succeeded. Her heart was filled with joy. She ripped the label up and threw it in the toilet. Her heart guiltily pounding, she flushed the evidence. Bathing her burning cheeks, she saw her eyes in the mirror. The lurid eyes of bloody triumph.

She was horrified. She thought: My God, look at what I've turned into. A primitive, living by signs and portents, turned on by the obliteration of another woman, whose only crime was to take her place before me in a bed. Everything I hate I am.

She thought she'd tell Ira: he'd make it into a joke and it would lose its force.

She never told him. She was too afraid.

She sees Ira is glad she didn't ring the bell, that she used the key he has had made for her. She sees he's spent the minutes since they talked laying out food. He likes to feed her. Nothing nourishing. Starches and salty foods, Boursin, halvah, peanut M & M's, Pepperidge Farm Goldfish, Entenmann's Sour Cream Cake. It always surprises her, the decorative small dishes in which he presents these foods. An odd set of possessions, she thinks, for a man who doesn't own a colander.

They eat the food they both know is quite bad for them. He tells her a story from the office. He asks about her cousin Marilyn. Her fate: the pliant, pretty, sympathetic girl, top in her class in nurse's training, the disastrous marriages, the helpful teenage children, handsome as herself, all this has won his heart.

He knows he mustn't say anything to Cam about her mother.

He picks up her hand. They recognize themselves again as lovers. They lie together on the bed. There's not much time. When they are finished they hold each other, stroke each other's backs with languid fingers. As if they had all the time in the world.

And then, behind her eyes, Cam sees her mother's face. She is thinking of herself as a child, this kind of torpid summer day. She is thinking of herself in her serious and heavy single braid, sitting alone in the small room behind the curtain of her mother's shop. Her mother is grateful for her quietness, proud of it; she shows it off to other women, customers and employees, as if it were a talent whose cultivation she had fostered and paid money to develop.

He knows she's thinking about her mother. He can recognize it now, the wall that drops between them, the door that shuts. He can never ask her about her mother; whatever she tells him he has to pretend to agree with, even if he thinks she's wrong. He made two mistakes with her; he won't make them again. Once he tried to defend her mother's dependence on her, saying it was hard for Magdalene, she was afraid. Cam gave him a cold look. 'That's right, the slaveholders were afraid too, weren't they? Frightened to death behind those fucking white columns, weren't they? Chattering their teeth against their julep cups.'

'All right,' he says. 'I'm sorry, I didn't understand.'

'You'll never understand,' she said bitterly. 'No one will.'

He felt himself shut out, as she had shut him out another time – but that time he didn't know why. They were talking about their favorite topic – the differences between the Irish and the Jews. 'Of course we thought the Irish were a bunch of crazy drunks,' he said. 'God, I remember a song my grandfather used to sing. "Shikker Is a Goy."'

He sang in Yiddish, then translated for her. The drunk is a goy, he sang, thinking she was amused, the goy is a drunk. The goy is a miserable drunk because he's a goy.

The look she gave him froze his heart. 'Very funny,' she said. 'Know any coon songs, any wop songs, any chink songs? Maybe you could sing for the KKK picnic. You'd be a great hit.'

Only a year later, one night when she told him about the

mother's nighttime calls, to her grandmother, her aunt, told him about her running up and down the stairs with her hands over her ears saying, 'Hang up, mother, hang up, it's late, they're tired, please hang up,' did he understand what he'd done. He held her and he let her cry, fearing that later she'd be angry that he'd seen her that way. But she hadn't. Only one other time she told him something about her past that made her cry. About her hysterectomy. About how her mother didn't visit her in the hospital, about how her grandmother smuggled in food, how her grandfather cried one night in the chair across from her when he thought she was asleep. He often wants to comfort her; he wants to tell her he's the person who can comfort her. But he knows he can't say it. That's why he likes to give her all this food; he wants to make her happy.

He wonders if she knows how much he'd like to live with her. He can't press her, he understands she'd see it as a burden, his desire, which is not unequivocal, not constant: he admits it to himself.

Many nights in his bed, mornings alone eating a solitary break-fast, he yearns for her with a racking pain. But many days – his days of sixteen-hour work – he is relieved that he can put her from his mind and that she isn't waiting – for his conversation, pleasantness, for the vacation he will never take with her (his holidays are for his children, who are both away at college). He's grateful that he needn't think of her out shopping for the prettifying and domesticating object that will become, in time, the source of reproach. Grateful that with her he needn't engage in conversations over re-doing the bathroom, over swatches of material, glassware, china. He is terrified of the imperialistic life of women in a house. She doesn't live like that. She talks to him about the world; they're interested in it. Her hunger is to change the world, not the house. He remembers his anguished attempts to satisfy those domestic hungers in his wives: the time he bought a child's paintbrush and spent a week painting antique molding a quarter-inch at a time. He recalls agonized trips to paintshops, wallpaper books that blurred before his eyes. 'Anything you like, darling, is fine.' To which they'd answer, 'Admit it, you don't give a shit. Admit you just don't give a shit.' The women's tears, his guilt: Why do I fail to be a normal man inhabiting a house? Sometimes he's glad that Cam has her own house and leaves him in his, which he need never think about, where he can come only to bathe and sleep.

Cam begins to get up. 'Don't,' he says, stroking her back. 'We have a little more time.'

She gives herself up to what she really wants. She puts her head on his shoulder. This wanting to be beside him, which has become a physical need with her, like the need for food or sleep, frightens her sometimes. But now she isn't frightened. She lays her head on his shoulder. She thinks: 'I don't even remember who I was before him. Someone different, someone strange to me now, someone not knowing what I know.' She thinks, 'If we weren't together, something in me, what can I call it, something, would be shot dead.'

3

Imagining her grandparents at her age, adjusting a tube attached to her grandmother's nose, and dreamy in her competence, Marilyn thinks: It's probably too late for me to have an ordinary life.

She thinks about the body of her grandmother. Light now, the bones nearly visible, the sparse hair having long ago given up its springiness, its luster, and its weight, this body that has long ago dissociated itself from the spiritual is itself a dying animal, and seems now to Marilyn to stand for something rather than to have its own existence.

She remembers once opening her grandparents' kitchen door. Vincent was kneeling on the floor in front of Ellen, who was in a chair. He was holding her bare foot in his hand. He was cutting her toenails. On the kitchen floor there was a blue enamel basin filled with soapy water. She must have soaked her feet in that, taken her foot out of the basin only moments before.

He was holding her foot in his hand. He was drying it with a white towel. In a leather case on the chair where she was sitting were ivory-handled scissors and a series of small knives.

Marilyn stood in the doorway and watched them. Silent. Frightened. Not knowing why she should leave yet feeling she was witnessing something she should not. She was frozen in the locked stare of the transgressor, hypnotized by what she must not see. She knew that she was looking on her first intimate act.

Ellen's back was towards her, Vincent was kneeling, concentrating on Ellen's foot; he didn't know Marilyn was in the room.

She saw by Ellen's back that she was suddenly alert. Silently, Ellen tapped Vincent. Vincent got up from his knees. She put her stockings on. He dried the little knives and scissors on the towel.

Ellen said, through furious clenched teeth, 'What were you doing coming in like that?'

'It's all right for her,' Vincent said.

But Marilyn knew it wasn't all right. She was ashamed of herself. And ashamed for them, doing this in the daylight. She thought her grandmother would stop liking her. She only liked her a little, but even that could stop. In liking Dan and Cam, it was as if Ellen had used up a pile of coins, unable to be replaced. She wasn't nice to Sheilah, but all right with John. She always liked boys better. Marilyn saw this and accepted it as she accepted what she knew about her own mother. She knew her mother disliked all her children, but as the oldest, because her mother was less tired when she was more needy, she believed she had suffered least. Their father loved them, and their grandfather. But that wasn't enough. They all knew it was second best. Ellen had liked her a little; she was terrified of losing that.

Ellen grew genuinely fond of Marilyn only when she brought her bastard baby home. She liked Marilyn as a hippie, with her sandals, peasant blouses, and unshaven legs, her baby slung in front of her or carried on her back. Had Ellen liked her then to spite Theresa? She said: 'It's a good thing, you've gone looking for adventure.' She liked having a descendant with dark skin; she'd powdered Jeremiah's brown behind as if it were a new fruit she had heard of but had never come across. She'd liked all of Marilyn's husbands, all three of them. She admired them for their imaginative failures. She defended them against Theresa's acid comments and Ray's abashed, shamefaced apologies and Vincent's worry they would do Marilyn harm. She liked them as voluptuous and healthy animals, for all Marilyn's husbands had been quite good-looking; handy too, around the house.

★

Why was he holding her bare foot? Why was he on his knees before her in the kitchen? Why was he cutting her toenails? What did it mean about the two of them? She thinks of her grandparents' physical life. The various components of it, food, dirt, animals, children, childbirth, menstrual blood, fluids of sickness, sex. It isn't difficult to think of Vincent and Ellen as lovers. Easier for Marilyn to think of them as lovers than her parents, with her mother's horror of disorder. Soil. Theresa had told them to eat nothing at their grandmother's. She isn't clean, Theresa had said.

All the delicious foods, the warm sweet puddings, heavy breads, carrots spilling their moisture into meat and taking in that juice, all those succulent foods were made dangerous by the mother's word. Theresa would come into her mother's kitchen, take the dishes from the cupboards, and wash them before she put them on the table. Did she do this to enrage her mother? No, though that was part of it. Theresa believed in contamination. She would bring her children up in modern life, safe from her mother's filth.

Marilyn smooths one of her grandmother's braids, in homage to her grandfather's devotion to her. He was, he is devoted to you, she thinks. How did you make him be like that? And why haven't I?

She wonders if any woman could now. Devotion. She wonders what the word could mean. A wholeness of attention. Fixed regard. The body's posture: bending towards. Here I stand, bending towards you. There is nothing you cannot ask.

She thinks of her grandfather's body. Sexual even now. Women responded to him, knowing his sympathy for them. The women at the home with him. The poor nun that Cam made fun of.

All of us, even Sheilah, we all felt favored in his sight. But we were wrong. Only his wife was favored.

He wasn't a good father, she thought. The children of lovers are orphans. Someone had said that to her once. His devotion was to the body, the idea, the past and changing present of the physical existence of his wife. This had robbed his children of a childhood. Each one of them was starved. She didn't know about Dan's father. But about the daughters she knew. Magdalene, Theresa: the daughters had been starved. You saw the hungry look around the eyes, the mouth.

Vincent had liked Theresa. But as a child, she must have seen his gaze fixed on his wife. Which the harsh child Theresa never had forgiven. Never would forgive. Theresa could never share regard.

Marilyn thinks of her mother's harshness, of her frightened father, flattened out. How could a daughter of Theresa's inspire devotion?

She wonders if Cam has. With this lover, Ira Silverman. She'd never thought it would happen to Cam, she'd thought it was what made her different from Cam: she had a sexual life, Cam had chastity. She had abundance, Cam was spare. Cam was honorable, she was physical. Cam's honorableness had desexed her, as Marilyn's physicalness had made her weak. Ashamed, Marilyn thinks: I've loved Cam all my life, but I was glad that I had something she didn't. Now it doesn't split apart, the world that they divided up. The crack, neat, down the center, so the crystal breaks apart in perfect halves, no longer stays straight. It's ragged. Marilyn is without a man; she runs the Clínica de Salud, she's a force in the community – its physical as well as its political life. And Cam is happy with a lover. Cam is like Ellen now: the beloved of a man.

But no, Marilyn thinks, she doesn't have what Ellen had. Neither of us does. She has something, but not the whole. She can't sit with her mate out in the garden and call out his name, saying: 'Bring me the sweater from the back of that chair. Is the light on in the kitchen?' She can't come to holidays, throwing off her coat, brushing the snow from his collar, scolding, 'He'll catch his death one day. He never wears a hat.'

She can't have any of that, the wages of legitimate and sanctioned coupling. Her sterling cousin now is an adulteress. *Adulteress*, a word that shines, metallic, luminescent, charged.

But Marilyn is happy for her. She thinks of poor Bob Ulichni. And of Magdalene. The weights dragging her cousin down. Cam deserves some kind of simple happiness.

Marilyn thinks that it has always been she, after desire took its course, who bent her body in the posture of attention to the man. She has bent, curved, hollowed out her body to make a shape accommodating to the men, the errors, of her life.

She knows she will again.

Marilyn uncurls her grandmother's hand and lays it flat on the nylon sheet. She thinks that no one in this world could get what Ellen got. For a moment she is angry at her grandmother. Jealous of her. But she thinks of her grandmother's pleasure, her belated

289

pleasure, in her, Marilyn's, life, of her grandmother's surprising support, of her affection for these grandsons-in-law, and these children of different fathers. She holds her grandmother's hand. She thinks of her children in the new house she has bought them. Not a nice house, she knows that, but they're happy there. Without a man. All of them like it better that way. A weight has been lifted off them, the presence of the angry husband. The punishing father.

Her children. She wants to tell her grandmother something about the children. Ellen moves her head. Opens her eyes, seems to understand that she is seeing something. As if understanding, for the moment, were within her grasp.

Marilyn wants to say how good they are, the three of them, her children. Good children, Gran, she wants to say. Are they happy? Who asks that now? Who could tell?

She says to her grandmother, bending towards her ear: 'You had a life. That's what I want for them. That's all I want. That they have a life.'

She goes to the back steps to have a cigarette. Her brother, John, is there already, smoking. Of the whole family, only the two of them still smoke. The kinship pleases her, it is something that they share, although she's seen, in working in the hospital, terrible deaths from lung cancer. She should know better; she should stop; she should urge John to stop; there is nothing on earth good in doing what they are doing. Yet she's glad they're doing it.

She leans her head on his shoulder and he flinches at the touch.

She wants to say: How has all this happened to you? You used to have so much.

'Don't jump, it's only me,' she says.

He laughs or grunts. His teeth are terrible.

She wants to say: I remember your white teeth, those square teeth, they were bluish white.

'She all right?' he says.

'Resting.'

'It's good, your being here. I don't trust that other one. What the hell did she do to the old lady to get her hooks into her that way?'

She sees his anguish at the presence of Mary Davenport, who offended Vincent. Of her taking up the family space. Or else he never would have said 'the old lady.'

'You see it sometimes,' she says. 'Ellen confuses her with someone from her childhood. She doesn't see who she really is.'

And you, she thinks, what do you see? And how do you live?

'I'd like you to come out again sometime,' she says. 'Stay longer, though. Stay in the new house. The kids would love to see you.'

He came once. She never knew why. Something she couldn't give him.

He drove all the way across the country and then stayed one day. She wants to say: What happened, that time you came? What did you want that time?

She doesn't say it. She sits silent, smoking.

He says, 'Yeah, well, I've got this new job now. Tough getting time off when you're starting.'

He was married that time he came to California. Better off.

What happened to that marriage? No one knows. *That* marriage, thinks Marilyn. We use the word *that* in front of the word *marriage* as they never would. Our parents. Our grandparents. As if marriages were replaceable. As if they were interchangeable. You got another, and you went on with your life. Which was the case. So you were right to say 'that' marriage, implying another one.

It was easy for them all, the family, to act as if it hadn't happened, that marriage. But not for Marilyn. She'd liked the wife. *The* wife. How can I call her that? Jo, her name was. Josephine? Marilyn never knew.

She remembered the cards in his suitcase. Had he wanted her to see them? She'd sat on the single bed, her twelve-year-old Vincent's bed, as John unpacked. She'd shoved the suitcase over, lying on the bed, resting her head on her propped arm like a happy teenager. She was always glad to see him. For a little while he didn't seem like a ruin. She saw the cards on top of the neatly folded shirts. Hand-drawn messages on index cards. 'Don't miss us too much. We miss you.' And the other, 'Daddy. John. We love you with all our heart.'

Jo's children called him Daddy. Marilyn was happy at that. She thought he must have a life.

She thinks of Jo's looks now. Poor Jo. She had the kind of hair that meant a man would treat her badly. Murdered hair. Dyed, dyed, and dyed again, each time a desperate color.

Marilyn walks now with her brother up and down her grandparents' back yard. He was supposed to care for it in the time Vincent has been away. She sees that he hasn't done a good job and wonders if the sprouting weeds will be a source of agitation for her grandfather when he comes home. Vincent is almost ninety years old. Has he decided in the last part of his life that he will give in to the tendency of the world to destroy order? Or has his refusal to give in to this kept his back straight and his fingers competent? She'd like to stop walking now, stoop down, and pull up weeds. But she's afraid that it will hurt her brother, so she doesn't.

She thinks about a barbecue they had for her, John and his wife, Jo, on the patio of their apartment in Virginia. It had the heavy desolation of apartment complexes built on the cheap to suggest contained, professional existences: childless lawyers who will live here for the period of their establishment until they have grown ready for the larger house, with its responsibility of sloping lawn. The truth is far from this. The truth, she'd learned from being there, the truth that hung above the flat, inadequately insulated roofs so that the air brings the tenants no refreshment, even on the clearest days, is that these are the homes of single or re-married mothers who are waitresses or clerks at the cable-TV office or the Office of the Warden of the County Jail. Or of divorced men, refusing to hang up even one picture or to buy one dish towel. Rowdy groups of boys in their early twenties, menswear salesmen, television salesmen in department stores in closed-off malls. A year, two years after their completion, these places – called Dutch Garden, Tudor Village, Tara – all decay. The bad building, the cut corners, rise up like the family insanity that can no longer be concealed. The Styrofoam tiles fall from the kitchen ceiling; the tin lighting fixtures bend; the beige linoleum cracks and buckles underfoot. The fake brick of the patio becomes undone in the first winter. Fights break out in the parking lot. Men take off in their angry cars, leaving no forwarding address. The women and the children, torpid from abandonment, sit around the greenish swimming pool.

The day that Marilyn was there, at John and Jo's apartment, John cooked hot dogs on a hibachi. Jo opened the sliding doors and brought out mustard, paper plates, and mayonnaise. She was wearing cut-off jeans and a red-checkered halter. Her hair was caught up in a clip. The shorts cut cruelly at her thighs. Her stomach hung over the too-tight waist; her midriff rippled and her breasts looked choked by the built-in brassiere of the check halter.

John looked up at her. 'You look like hell,' he said, and turned away, back to his cooking, and to light a cigarette.

Three years later, in her grandparents' garden, Marilyn decides to pull a weed. She should have told her brother not to speak to his wife, to anyone like that. Not to his wife, who was so good to him, who loved him. She should have warned Jo he would leave her, that it wouldn't be her fault, that there was nothing she could do or had done. It would happen. One night he wouldn't come home from work. One morning he would drive away and that would be the end of it. She should have said something, not just stood up as she did, asking if she could do anything to help, saying how much she loved a barbecue, how lucky they were to have this nice patio. She should have stood up then and said: 'This is hopeless. This is terrible. Do something.'

John sees her pulling up the weed.

'You think I'm as fucked up as everyone else. You think I can't even pull up their fucking weeds right.'

'Don't get paranoid,' she lies, 'I pulled a weed.'

'It's not like you're such a hot shit about it. Your property always looked like a piece of shit. Every house you ever lived in looked like a piece of shit.'

'You should see this one, Johnny. This one is the worst.'

She will not let him hurt her. No: he has hurt her. She has not made her surroundings beautiful. *Will not*, her husbands have told her. *Cannot*, she has always said.

She won't let her brother see that he has touched her shame. Or afterwards remorse will make him shameful. Shame causes him to suffer and strike out. The ripples of his shame will cause a tremor to go through the family house. Who knows what object the tremor will cause to shatter or break.

Go on, she tells herself. *Go on to something else*. But what? Like a roulette wheel, her mind spins blindly. Can she bring something to rest, a topic, an idea that won't cause him anger or remorse? Her brother, like a burn victim, must be approached with care. Only a few intact spots can be touched.

Animals, she thinks, he likes animals. She remembers that he has a dog.

'How's your dog?'

'Good.'

She sees there isn't much conversation possible on the subject of animals. Not with him.

'He does OK while you're at work?'

'Jesus, Marilyn, what the fuck do you think? What do you want him to do? Go out and get a job himself? He hangs out in my room. Mom doesn't want him in the living room. She doesn't want him shedding on the broadloom.'

Broadloom. Her mother's word. The fierce saving for it: pennies stolen from the family pleasure. And the pride, the interdictions: Don't walk on it with your shoes on. No food on the broadloom. Forbidding her father to smoke in the room with it. The yearned for, unapproached God. And her brother is still there.

She has nothing more to say to him. She wants to help, but she will never be of help. There is no helping him. She knows that. He knows it. When she tries, it only makes it worse.

'I'm going to go back in to Gran now.'

John shrugs.

He wants to say, 'Don't go because of me,' but he knows it wouldn't come out right, she'd think he was just being a shit. Sarcastic, trying to sound smart. He wishes he could make her understand that he knows he made her go, but he didn't want to. Now he understands why he didn't pull up the weeds. Now he knows that he was right. His mother should have done it. Got down on her goddamn knees and pulled the weeds out of the ground if she cared so much about her parents. But not her. Couldn't get her out of the church to do anything that anybody cared about. Now he remembers why he didn't pull the weeds. It wasn't his job. It was his mother's.

He wishes he could make her do it. He'd like to push her down to her knees, shove her nose into the dirt, make her get her hands dirty. Say, 'You could do one goddamn thing for your family. Why should I have to do everything?' He knows there's no way he could make her. The two of them could stand in the same spot until the end of the world and he could never make her.

But it's her job. He's not going to do it now.

He sees his grandfather's face. His grandfather will be disappointed in him. He feels furious. What right does the old man have to be disappointed? Then he remembers Vincent's asking him and his saying yes, he'd do it. 'Yes, Granddad,' he said, 'you don't have to worry, I'll handle it.'

But he hadn't handled it. And now his grandfather will be disappointed. Of all the looks he makes people have on their faces, this is the one John can't stand most. He wants to run away again so he won't have to see that look on his grandfather's face.

He kneels down on the stones. Maybe if he works very hard he'll be able to do it. He knows he can; he'll just work really hard. He pulls up weeds, some with white flowers, some with oblong pointed leaves. Twelve of them are on the ground, uprooted, taken care of. Then he hears his mother's voice. He sees her standing on the grass above him.

'Better late than never,' his mother says.

What does Theresa think as she stands looking at her kneeling son?

Is she sorry for his failures, that he can't make a life?

Is she ashamed and worried that perhaps she has had some part in it? Does she believe the science, gossip, journalism of the age that points its finger at the mother? At the first sign of rebellion, bad grades, drug abuse, sexual deviation, financial disgrace, the mother is examined under the cruel public light of her children's history and has no chance of ever being judged free of fault. Has she felt stupefied by this glaring, public light?

Is she anxious for his future? For his life after her death?

Is she proud, touched by his kindness to her parents? It is he, after all, who planted the garden. Without him, only the perennials, and not these zinnias, nasturtiums, marigolds, would have appeared.

Is she tempted to bend down, to touch his head in memory of his childhood hair?

None of these things. She is thinking: One night he will kill us in our beds.

Ray Dooley is looking at his wife and son. He thinks: I always failed him. I didn't protect him from her. I never gave him what he needed. How else could he be?

John hears his mother's voice. He understands he has to try to hurt her. It's the only way to stop her. She has to be stopped. No one can stop her. But he has to try. This will please him. This is the only thing that he can think of that would please him in this life.

'I can't think why you left it so long,' she says.

'Nope. I guess you can't.'

Ray wants to step between them. Walk away from her, he wants to tell his son, she'll always win.

'I hope your grandfather doesn't find out about your latest stunt. This fiasco at the new job. I hope it can be kept from him for a day or two.'

He bares his bad teeth at her.

'Well, I guess he won't find out if you keep your fucking mouth shut. Which, let's face it, is probably out of the fucking question.'

'Lovely language,' she says, turning away from him. 'I just thank God your grandmother can't hear you. I thank God your grandfather's not around.'

'Why don't you go fuck yourself?' he says.

She turns away from him, walks in the house. Something in her is satisfied. She feels she has shed light on something in the world, properly exposed it. It has described itself in its true colors. Something has been cleansed: stripped bare. She is happy now; at peace. What she has done has made a kind of truth. She can rest now. Everything is open. Nothing is covered up.

Ray Dooley wants to say: 'Why did you let her?'

Marilyn wants to take her brother's head, cradle it in her arms, and let him cry. But he wouldn't cry. He is wounded; he is poisonous; he would bite and claw and try to wound her; they would both be covered soon by fresh, deliberately drawn blood.

Everyone walks into the house. Except for John. He stays out in the garden, on his knees.

He pulls ten more weeds. He counts them: ten. He throws the last one on the ground. Then he stands up.

He gathers up the weeds and throws them in a fury down into a basket in the dark garage. He walks out of the yard. He won't wait for his grandfather. He'll go somewhere, he doesn't know where yet, but he won't come back.

He gets into his car and drives, to give offense, too fast up the short street. He slams his brakes on at the stop sign.

★

They shape themselves around his loud departure. It is the fissure around which they walk, carefully measuring each step. They group themselves around the dangerous rupture of the adolescent male. He will come back and act against them. Nearly forty, he is still the boy they fear, the male with strong limbs, quick reflexes, the fist that can at any moment raise itself against them, bring itself down, cause a death.

Marilyn is ashamed. *If I hadn't picked the weed*, she thinks. *I started everything.*

Ray Dooley thinks, *They see how I have failed to be a father to my son.*

Sheilah thinks, *Now they know, they see how I have always been much better than my brother.*

Dan, ashamed of his own fear, thinks, *I have never known what to do.*

Theresa thinks, *Now they see how I have suffered. Now they know.*

And in the silence, shaped around the cleft, the guttural, inhuman noise of Ellen's cry boils up. Speech without communication, words unmoored from meaning, thrown out, an offense. *I will remind you how frail your grasp is upon what you determine to be human. At any moment you can be the animal I am.*

None of them knows who should go to Ellen.

Marilyn, who has the training?

Theresa, the closest to her in blood?

Dan, the most beloved?

Sheilah and her father know that it cannot be them. They move to the outside of the oblong borders of the room.

The other three hesitate. None of them wants to make the point.

If Cam were here, she would move quickly. And this would make Theresa move. Marilyn and Dan would be relieved of the responsibility to act. They feel this at the same moment: the absence of the forceful presence. Dan fears that in another moment Theresa will feel what they have felt and realize that, to spite Cam, she must go in. He walks towards his grandmother's room, hesitates a final moment in case one of the others has been seized by need or impulse, then walks in.

★

He wonders what it signifies. This sound. Ellen's moaning. Pain? They've been told it's not. The doctor has assured them all that she feels no pain. But why should they believe him?

The doctor said: 'You have to understand what pain really is. A message of the nervous system, a collection of impulses signaling some malfunction. This is not what she's experiencing.'

'What, then?' Dan asked.

He says, 'Well, for example, if the fan blew against her arm and caused some of the surface hairs to move, she would experience disproportionate sensation.'

He doesn't understand.

'Too much sensation,' the doctor says slowly. 'Something a normal person wouldn't register might cause her to cry out like that. But you wouldn't call that pain. For example, you wouldn't medicate someone for a thing like that.'

'What would you do?'

'Try to ignore it. It doesn't mean that much. It sounds terrible, but just don't take it seriously. It's just scrambled messages. Just what I said: a disproportionate response.'

'But why not keep her medicated?' Dan had said. 'Obviously, she's experiencing some kind of distress. Why not block or mask that?'

'We'll save the medication for when she really needs it.'

'How will you know? At what point will you call this pain?'

The doctor gives him a wounded, or exasperated look. *How could you doubt my competence? With my training, my knowledge? What do you hold against it? Your sentiments? Your instincts?*

The doctor says, 'I'm afraid you'll have to trust me.'

But Dan does not.

If this utterance is not meant to communicate her pain, what is it meant, then, to communicate? Her outrage? Perhaps that. Her outrage that she cannot choose, discriminate among, keep out, the pushing and remorseless random beats, all the impressions that refuse to sort themselves out, as the rules of sanity demand, into the essential and inessential.

Of course she's outraged. Her outrage is visible. Visible in the clenched lips and toothless gums ground like a prophet's teeth, in the wet phlegmy consonants of the incomprehensible words, syllables (only you know that they're curses). In the fists, hardened into weapons, in the thrashing head on the bird neck, what can you read but outrage? But the eyes are calm, as if the mind, cut off from its expression of itself, has seen a serene vision. Not a happy one, but one that brought quiet or the knowledge that to fight is futile: why not rest?

The dead eyes and the utterance of death.

Why should she go through it? What was so wrong with death that it should be kept back? And why this thrashing animal, avid still for its animal life?

Dan has no need of God to explain death. His father, brilliant in his flaming death, the god in the machine grown incandescent, deaths he had known, even unreasonable ones, have not made his spirit rebel like this sight that he sees before him. Even the deaths of children, the terrible violent deaths of victims murdered in their innocent sleep, have not made his heart cry out like this. Those deaths, even the worst of them, had not rendered the dead in-human. What has happened to his grandmother? He fears that she no longer has a soul.

He wonders how, being the man he is, he can have used this word. Living as I live. Doing what I have done. What do I mean by this word? Using it, I know that it has meaning. But what meaning is in this word?

And what would be the thing it represents? Some object or some faculty whose function is to understand the impulses: sights, sounds, tastes, odors, pressures, letting up of pressures, harmony, discord, at least that. To comprehend and to assign a meaning. To take in some impulses and refuse others. To be able to say: I will use this, this other is of no use to me.

And would this faculty go on then to eternal life? His grand-mother had not expected it. She fought with the priests. 'I'll not be prayed at by a Coughlinite. I'll not be in the same room with a fat-faced idiot who thinks Franklin Roosevelt is Satan walking on the earth. What has their God done for them but cause them to cower, sneer, claw at every stranger, every new idea?'

She wouldn't go so far as to say there was no God. Only that she wanted nothing to do with Him. Dan guessed that for Vincent's sake she'd never say there was no God. She'd keep that safe for him, knowing her force, knowing that if she spoke all that she suspected with the power of her arguments, her tongue quicker and cleverer than his, he might be forced to give it up. This God that she could see had brought him comfort. She didn't want him to have to give that up.

What differences had it made in their lives? Of the two, he was the more at peace, she the more seeing. She had force; the steadiness was his. If you wanted the truth of something, you would go to her. If you needed comfort, though, you'd stand just near him. The closeness of his body meant the world was safe.

But it wasn't a safe world. She would tell you that. Yet she relied on her husband to give her safety. And sometimes in her haste she'd fail to see him. Sometimes in rooms you'd see her little flick of panic if she couldn't get him, in an instant, in her line of sight. The sight that now saw nothing.

Or what did it see? The face of God approaching, reassuring as her husband's? No, she'd have fought that. Faith, she'd said to Dan once, is throwing good money after bad. Faith for Vincent was one more steady, honorable investment, like the workman's pension fund, an allocation from a dutiful and careful life.

Now, watching Ellen sleep and grateful for her momentary peace, he thinks: What is my faith? Faith of our fathers. Probably a hoax but one the world did not seem better off without.

He doesn't want to be a person who dislikes the modern world. He knows what went before it was no better. The sorrows of the past were terrible. Yet people yearned to copy the past, as if it were the thing that could make them whole. Around him at every turn, it seemed, shopping malls were being built to look like Williamsburg or Boonesboro. He could hardly go into the house of a friend of Sharon's without seeing a dreadful reproduction – a plywood veneer only, held together by glue and two-penny nails. Come see our dry sink, they would say. In the middle there would be an arrangement of silk flowers which the wife herself had made. Touched by their blunderings and wounded by the bad design of the objects among which they lived, he spent whole evenings in houses struck dumb by the furniture. He kept wanting to say to these people, friends, relatives of Sharon's, *How are you trying to live? It wasn't like that. What do you believe you have bought with your furniture? The past was terrible. It wasn't what you think.*

In college, when he studied primitive societies, he'd not been optimistic enough to go on with the work. Yet he loved in them what he had loved about his grandparents: the sense of keeping the thread you were born holding between your fingers. Of not letting go.

Even now she won't let go.

Even today he will come back to her.

But who will Vincent be coming back to?

And who will he, Dan MacNamara, waiting for his death, look around the room to see?

Not Sharon. No.

His daughters? Nearly strangers to him. He had tried to make them not feel tied to him, to keep the passion of his yearning for them secret from them. He was always leaving, or they were leaving, the point was not to make the leaving agonizing. So you kept back the scalded feelings and the longings. You did not cause them to think that in your old age they must make a home for you. You let them be free. At least that. Yes. That most of all.

What did his two daughters have faith in? Staci tells him that in her high school, affluent, suburban, all the kids steal from each other.

He doesn't ask: Do you steal? He assumes the disgust with which she speaks of the events means she doesn't. Yet he would never ask.

And if she doesn't, why doesn't she?

Better not to ask.

Darci believes in everything. Poetry, drama, art, the stirrings of the soul. Above all, in the great urban centers of the world. Paris, London, New York, Rome. Her tears spill over for a beggar, her fist comes down on the table at the treatment of the Nicaraguans, she loves her new best friend, Rebecca. She loves Camille. She says she loves him. 'Daddy, I adore you,' she says at least once a day.

When she says this, what does she mean? He is afraid to believe that she means simply what she says.

Staci believes in keeping herself safe. He wonders if it was he who did that to her. Would she have always been that way?

No, it was his fault. He made her unable to believe in life.

It was not believing in anything that made her eyes blank. Her blankness hurts him and makes him feel ashamed. Nothing interests her. As a young child she had been petulant, withdrawn, easily bored, and easily provoked to hot, uncleansing, and unsatisfying tears. This tendency, perhaps it was a decision, to find nothing in the world desirable, transformed itself in adolescence to a gift. She became the model teenager. She understood in every situation what was wanted, who was wanted: she became that person or that quality. Infinitely variable or infinitely on her guard, she had the sensitivity to change of children brought up starving, or nocturnal animals unnaturally introduced to light. Dan felt she could become a criminal; sometimes, seeing that nothing within her was durable or passionate or fixed, he saw in her eyes the same look he'd found in the eyes of criminals he had defended, whose clear guilt he knew. He feared for her, and each success reported from two thousand miles away made him fear more. She was selected for new, special computer classes; she won yet another trophy for high jump; she made cheerleading squad. 'That's great, honey,' he'd say, and his heart would freeze, the hollow in his throat would fill with air. He would see that by his leaving he had taken from the cradle that first ordinary gift of youth, belief, and cut its throat.

There was nothing in Staci's behavior you could fasten on as worthy of correction or of blame. She'd seen Sharon's weakness, and understood that it was in her interest to please her, particularly since Darci would do nothing to please her. And she worked to please her, though each time she succeeded Dan saw the contempt behind her eyes. Dreadful, he thinks, dreadful. My daughter's eyes are dreadful to me. And I have planted the dread.

4

Marilyn comes to the door to tell him it is Magdalene on the telephone. She wants to speak to him. She cannot for the life of her imagine what's become of Cam.

I simulate, he thinks, more than the plywood furniture, more than the plastic shillelaghs and the papier-mâché turf. I simulate the idea of the good, caring man. He knows that Magdalene thinks she can trust him. He can comfort her. In her mind, her daughter, who has left her house two hours ago, is on the highway, splattered dead. He knows he has to simulate concern.

Yet in the process of his simulation he begins to feel concern for Magdalene. He hears the game, flirtatious voice.

'How's my best boyfriend?'

'Over the hill, Mag. I'm too old for you.'

The satisfied laugh. Cigarettes and whiskey. *You, a man, remember what I was.*

'Listen, my fine bucko, where would that daughter of mine have gone to? She left hours ago. I thought she'd be there.'

'Maybe she went to the office. Maybe she's left from there to get Granddaddy.'

'No, she said she'd come back. She said she'd come back to check if I'm feeling better. I'm hoping against hope, Dan, you know that, to have the strength to be there when my father comes home. You know how hard I'm trying, don't you, Dan?'

'Of course, dear, everybody knows.'

'Cam seemed so annoyed with me. But I just wasn't up to it. So I thought after a little rest I'd try again. She said she'd come to see if I'm feeling better. If she'd just give me a hand. But she probably won't, she was so aggravated with me.'

Dan realizes the nature of his faith. He believes in human frailty. He sees the wholeness of all life, the intricate connecting tissue. It is this, this terrible endeavor, this impossible endeavor. Simply to live a life. Magdalene, trying to live her life, presses on Cam, who turns then to her lover, leaving her mother terrified. Cam is happy in a man's arms, but she must leave the arms to go to her mother, who will fail her. To the grandfather, whose body fails. To bring him to his wife, the avid animal who refuses to fall into her death. He sees his aunts, uncles, his cousins, children, Sharon, and his clients, battered, battering, divorcing and divorced, enclosed in a thin porous globe. He would like to embrace them all. He would like to say: You must believe this. I understand you all.

Standing in the hall of his grandparents' house, holding the old black telephone, he is in love with humankind. He looks at all the ornaments, the figurines. His grandmother collected them. He remembers all the ones that Vincent broke, flinging them through the windows to get help that awful night. He mourns the lost figurines. But there is Franklin Roosevelt, intact. An eagle of the Bicentennial. A scroll shape of the Constitution. Among these significant social-historical remembrances there are other puzzling objects. A beaded-glass Florentine slipper with a dark-blue cuff of plainer glass. Maroon vases with borders of gold depicting scenes of eighteenth-century pastoral fantasy: the lords and ladies hatted and bewigged. What had they been thinking of, his grandparents, treasuring these? What dreams, divorced from everything they lived by? Simply to be lighthearted. Simply to be concerned with having a good time.

He sees the dark piano with its clutch of photographs. Only Theresa had played the piano. Poor Theresa. Now he can feel pity even for her. For you could see what she had been. She had her mother's angry quickness but without Ellen's vision of a better world. Surer than Ellen, but not brought up with nature, she had none of Ellen's physical softness, her tenderness for the male. Theresa could have become something. She could have run a corporation, sent men to their deaths. Would she have been happy? Better than now. Armed to the teeth with God. Her children were impossible for her. Unfortunate Sheilah, ruined John, and Marilyn, who had a sex life Theresa could not forgive.

He sees his own heart suddenly watching himself watching others. He dislikes himself. The porous surround that held the whole of humankind, his love, dissolves, and all of it is hateful to him now. Watching himself watching, he disbelieves his own benevolence. He sees himself incapable of one authentic act. Everything he does seems to him simulated. Purporting to love humankind, he sees now that he was loving only the vision of himself loving.

He turns his mind back to Magdalene on the phone.

'Maybe Cam just went shopping,' he says. 'Maybe she'll be back soon.'

But he's lost interest and Magdalene knows it. She is hurt by her quick fall from grace. He cannot rouse himself to praise her or to joke in some way that would do her homage. He thinks: She's worse off now than before she called.

'I don't know if I'll have the strength to make it, Dan. The heat is brutal, they say. And the humidity. That's what gets me, Dan. Not so much the heat as the humidity.'

'All of us, Magdalene, it gets us all.'

'What do you think, Dan? Do you think I can make it?'

'You know I'd love to see you, Magdalene. You're always a sight for sore eyes.'

He hears her giggle. She believes him.

'Dan, you're too much.'

Dissembling, simulating, he has made her, for another moment, whole.

'I've got to go, Mag. Here comes Darci. Running like a banshee, for a change.'

'Great to be young, Dan. She's a great girl you have there.'

He listens to Magdalene, who hasn't spoken, he reckons, a sensible word in thirty years, as if she were the possessor of a deep, abiding truth. 'She's a great girl you have there.'

He thinks, Yes, yes that's the truth. Nothing I've done has crushed the life from her. He sees her running up the stairs, her comical red hair, his as a child, though it was never allowed to be wild as hers is. Weighted down, slicked, threatened, cut, you'd never have known it for the same hair that springs out of Darci's head, exuberant and vivid, stubborn, full of life. And the large limbs they got from Vincent, long, thick legs and arms. The heavy torso. And the round breasts. He can see his daughter has become voluptuous. Do men see her as that? He hopes and does not hope so. He would like her to be desired. But what father wants to think of his daughter as the object of men's lust? Never mind, now. He'll put the thought from his mind.

She leaps onto the front porch. The screen door, challenged by her forceful entry, squeaks reluctantly and bangs. He sees Theresa register her disapproval. He would defend his daughter to the death. But how can he defend her from Theresa and her kind? The tight-lipped, fine-boned, sharp-eyed calculators and recorders of *faux pas*, excesses, errors of good judgment. Their accusations always are just. If Theresa should say, 'My goodness, Darci, there's a sick woman in this house. You should come in more quietly. That door won't stand rough treatment, it's as old as I am,' if she should say that, no one would be able to accuse her of injustice. And if he should say to her, 'You and your kind are murderers. Your cold breath puts out life. You've done it to your children. You will not to mine,' he would appear fanatical. Absurd.

He won't say it. Theresa, after all, has said nothing. She has only pursed her lips over her porcelain teeth. He sees it in the tight mouth. The instinct to crush the beating heart, snap the fluttering wing, muffle the tender gesture. In her silence it is there.

He will defend his big child with his body.

He leaves the hall and runs, as heavily as Darci has, to meet his daughter. He half-lifts her off the ground in his joy of embracing her. In her buoyant flesh he feels her faith. What she believes in she is right to pour her soul into. Like the dying animal, her grandmother, she hungers, she is avid, simply for life.

'Can I see Gran?' she whispers to her father.

He takes her hand and leads her to the room.

She tells herself to look at her great-grandmother, keep her eyes open, not to look away. She tells herself she has to, it will help her to know something about life. She has to be open to the whole world, afraid of nothing. That's what she has to do if she wants to be a great actress. Great actresses know about life, they aren't afraid of it, so they can play everything: queens, wanted women, war nurses, Greek heroines, Shakespeare. Everything. That's what she wants. So she has to look at her great-grandmother; she has to make herself not be afraid: she can't allow herself to look away.

She takes Ellen's hand. It's light, a death hand, a bone, paper, a hand full of its dying. When the hand grips, she grips back. I'll learn something from this, she says to herself, it's important. And these words I can't understand, they have something to teach me. I can't be afraid to learn what it is. I can't afford to be someone on whom something is wasted.

Ellen raises her head. She bares her gums and clenches them together. She says something, no one can understand it, but Darci knows it is a curse, and she's afraid of it: she doesn't want to be cursed, it's too strong for her, it's too strong to do her any good. And then it happens to her, that thing that happens to her often now: in the middle of an experience, she turns from being the person that she wants to be – interested in everything, learning from everything, afraid of nothing – and becomes the child she was. She wants her father to take her away. She wants to burrow in her father's large, safe body. She wants to turn away from her grandmother, with her clenched gums and her cursing nobody can understand, and run to her father's arms, saying, as if she were the child she doesn't want to be, 'Save me. Save me from this.' But she knows that she must not.

306

Dan sees that Darci wants to leave but cannot find the way to break the grip, the grip of death on life. He thinks she is afraid that, if she lets go Ellen's hand, Ellen will fall into her death. Yet more than anything he sees she does not want that hook hooking her into death. He sees all this. And he will make it stop. He can; it is in his power to do this.

She is a big girl, but he is much bigger. He can stand behind her so that she knows there are some things she need not do. He is her father. He can say, 'Let's go now,' and allow her to be free to go.

He does say this. And she looks up at him, the child's pure gratitude, saying nothing, but she lets him take her hand, lead her away.

He will take her away, through the room of people. Theresa, whose looks he will not allow to touch her. Marilyn, who will be kind. Ray, who can alter the course of nothing. Sheilah, whose instinct is to ruin happiness. He will take his daughter to a cool place selling sweets. They will sit across from each other talking seriously. They will let sweet liquid slip down their sad throats. He is her father. He can make this happen.

He walks into the living room with his arm around Darci's shoulder. Staci is sitting on the couch, reading the *TV Guide*.

'Want to come to Howard Johnson's with us, Stace?' he asks.

'Unh, unh,' she says. 'But you can drop me off at the running store. They said they might have a job for me. Part time.'

'Sweetie, you have your lifeguard job. You don't need another job,' Dan says.

'I just hate vegging out,' Staci says. 'So if you can just drop me off there. You don't need to wait. I'll walk back.'

'Sure,' Dan says. In the car, the three of them are silent. When Staci gets out, Darci begins singing. 'Mairzy doats and doazy doats, and little-lambs-ee-divey.'

'A kidd-le-ee-divey too, wouldn't you?' he joins in.

They hold hands walking into Howard Johnson's. After they order, she takes his hands and looks into his eyes.

'Daddy, does it make you very sad?'

He wants to tell her everything. Simply to have her understand his life. Yet he does not want to be the yearning boy, the child who watches every woman in the supermarket and from details –

the movement of the skirt, the click of the closing pocketbook – tries to invent the solid mother. To replace the vaporous unbodied image from the photographs he hides, the ones he knows he's not supposed to have. If Darci believes that he is suffering, he fears that it will stop her flight. Instead of telling her his sorrow, he tells her how his grandmother rang the doorbells of strangers for FDR, refused to talk to neighbors who wouldn't join her in denouncing Joe McCarthy, all the colorful boycotts and feuds which led to nothing but made Ellen feel she lived a vital life. He tells Darci about her great-grandmother's fierce reading, and her friendships with Bella, with Delia, and about her fear of meeting the teachers on Open School night, but how she then charmed them, she and Great-Granddad. He does not tell her of his shame that on those nights he was not represented by young, confident parents, joking with the teachers, saying, 'Don't forget to give him what for if he opens his mouth in the wrong place.' Instead his grandmother, reverently stroking the textbooks, caused him to choke back tears of mortification. He doesn't tell this to Darci. He tells her only stories of courage, pride, and tenderness, so she won't be discouraged about life.

'Daddy, did you talk to Cam?'
   'She talked to me.'
   'And will you do it? Will you talk to Mommy?'
   'Sweetheart, your mother will be terribly upset. It's your last year with her. She'll want you home for that.'
   'Believe me, Daddy, she'll be mostly glad to have me gone. Daddy, I belong here. Not there. I belong with you. You know that. Just stand up to Mommy. You know I'm right. We'll all be happier. She just has to stop pretending she likes having me around. With me gone, they'll be happy as clams. Up at six in their jogging suits cleaning the bathroom tiles with toothbrushes and bleach. Come on, Dad, you know I belong with you. We deserve to have one year together. Just admit it, you adore my company. And I adore yours. Cam'll talk to Mommy if you don't want to. If you're afraid.'
   'I'm not afraid, Darci. But I don't want your mother to be hurt.'
   Darci snorts. 'Believe me, Daddy, she'll get over it. Daddy, just admit it's a perfectly brilliant plan, that I was perfectly brilliant to

have thought of it and that I'm your favorite person in the entire world.'

He raises his hand, as if he were a witness in the box.

'The truth, the whole truth, and nothing but the truth,' he says.

'Does that mean you'll talk to her? Soon? Right now? There's a phone back there. Go on, while you're psyched.'

He takes her face in his hands. 'I promise I'll do it, my love. But not in Howard Johnson's. Not in front of all those thirty-seven flavors.'

'Tonight, then.'

'Yes. After we get Great-Granddaddy settled in. I'll call tonight.'

She jumps up and crawls into his side of the booth. She covers his face with cool sweet kisses.

'If you'd only understand that you are the most perfect person in the history of the world, Dan MacNamara, if you'd only listen when I tell you, you'd be a hell of a lot better off. And the other lucky thing: you have the perfect daughter for you. Right? Admit it. Nobody makes you happier than me.'

The extravagant words frighten both of them. The truth of the words (they know them to be true) brings them great pleasure. But little help. There are all those others. Mother. Daughter. Sister. Lover. All those who should have equal claim. And the slight shame of it – they are happiest with each other – excites them. It shines like a glimpse of lightning in the dense air of ordinary life.

He thinks: I could leave Sharon. Let her have the house. Rent a small apartment in Manhattan. Live there with my daughter. Walk on the streets with her. She loves life. Like Cam, like Ellen, she has the gift to find life interesting. To be avid for it. I have not had this. But with her perhaps I could.

But then the other faces, hurt, justly angry in their accusations – Sharon, Staci – bulk and thicken in his mind. Of course he never could. He and Darci must live as if she'd never said that sentence. But something will change. She will be near him this last year, before her life apart from him. The rest of her hopeful life. He'll make Val see the rightness of it. She's always been a woman who believed in justice. She'll see that this is right. And Darci can live with Cam, her favorite. How will Darci's presence make that heavy, dark house change? The vivid presence of a girl. Can it cut through the heavy atmosphere? The weighing depression, offense, shame? The lie of all their lives that they are better off like that, together.

Something new will happen.

At least that.

Leaving Howard Johnson's, on their way back to Vincent and Ellen's, Darci is thinking: I am happy, I am perfectly happy. She knows she can't touch her father's sadness for long, but for moments, she knows, she can. She is the favorite. She is her father's favorite person in the world. Knowing this, she thinks she can do anything. She thinks to herself: As an old woman, I'll remember this, that I walked beside my father, I was seventeen, and I knew nothing was too much for me to do.

5

Sheilah is trying to decide whether or not she'll fight with her mother.

Often a kind of hunger comes on her, an itch, a compulsion to unravel the tight weave of her mother's presentation to the world. She thinks she is the only one who understands her mother, who really knows what her mother is made of, as if she had made her herself, as if her mother were a construction Sheilah has assembled. But it isn't that, she isn't the creator, the assembler. Her interest does not lie there, in building up. Her attention, her ambition focus on demolishing her mother. Her mother is the house she would bring down. Her life has been a hammer with which she taps, looking for the stone that, touched, will crack, and cause the edifice to fall. Sometimes she has touched the weak stone: her mother's vanity. Resisting, watchful, she has seen her mother grow exasperated with her failure to have molded a daughter who could in any way do her credit in the world. On occasions when she knew her mother wanted a demonstration of family rigor, family smartness, Sheilah would malinger, dawdle, hang behind.

Then she could see – once, twice in her childhood – that underneath the stone façade that everyone thought was the complete woman there was not only the arsenal they feared but, below that, one level down, pile after pile of mousy dust, where even rot would be impossible, where nothing bred. Spiritual vanity was the last shield for what Sheilah alone understood was at the bottom of the structure that was known in the world as her mother. Despair. The sin against the Holy Ghost. The sin that denied life.

Vanity of spirit. She'd been counseled on it in the convent; she had not been able to root it from herself. She hadn't tried. It was too valuable, and what it covered unimaginable. She understands her mother's vanity of spirit. She knows that this is the vulnerable spot. Slowly, for she has all the time she needs, all the time in the world, she raises her precise, her specialized, her expert tool.

'Gran's not much better. Did you notice a difference in the time you were alone with her? I mean, were there changes in that time?'

She sees her mother freezing over, and recognizes what she sees: the dangerous black ice of troubled pride.

'Not for the moment, Sheilah. Not much change that I could see. What were you fussing over in the kitchen? Aren't we going to have lunch?'

Theresa sees her daughter and her mother trying to entrap her. Weak, the both of them; she always was the strongest. Her daughter cried and fell and constantly caught colds. Her mother lived in filth. She bred filth, disorder. Her underwear slopped over the backs of chairs on tops of piles of newspapers she'd never read. You had to wash every dish that came out of her cupboard before you'd dare to use it. She wouldn't use hot enough water on her dishes: you couldn't talk to her. She chose the filth she lived in, as Sheilah chose her drooping shoulders, the curve of her spine, her lank, dull hair. Theresa looks down at her nails. Pink, shining, perfect. She has learned from the Scriptures what she always knew: weakness, illness of the body, is not the body's, it is weakness, illness of the spirit. Theresa suspects her mother knows her to be powerful, but resists, in order to refuse to give her credit. And she knows that Sheilah sees her failure, and wants more than anything to expose to the world that she can't heal her mother by her laying on of hands.

'What were you doing in the kitchen all that time?' Theresa says to Sheilah. 'I thought I'd go mad with the sound of that electric knife. God knows what it did to your grandmother. What were you doing with it?'

'I was cutting up some cheese, Mother. I was cutting Muenster cheese.'

'Muenster cheese? With an electric knife.'

Theresa starts to laugh. She puts her hand over her capped teeth to hide her laughter. Then she stops trying to hide. She sits down on the kitchen table and rocks back and forth, holding her sides. She says: 'People are supposed to be right-brained or left-brained. You hear that all the time. I wonder what you are, Sheilah? Something we haven't heard of yet.'

Sheilah sees her mother: confident, victorious, rocking with laughter, sitting in what was Ellen's chair. She understands the ridiculousness of her every act. She knows her mother knows this about her, and she's right. Her mother has always been right. She'd wanted to make a nice luncheon spread for Dan. There are so few people in the world she likes, or who she feels like her. She worked a long time to cut the slices of cheese so she could spread them in a pleasing shape. A fan, almost a flower, a tomato at the center, the cold cuts radiating out. But Dan forgot that he'd said he would stay for lunch. Darci came and he forgot that he told Sheilah he'd love her to fix lunch for him. His daughter came, that noisy, clumsy, horrible girl, and he was taken up by the pleasure of her existence. No one had ever looked happier than he did with his daughter. They forgot everyone. He forgot her.

She stands, watching her mother laughing at her, remembering the moment in her life she had thought would be great.

But it wasn't great. She thought she'd planned it right, keeping quiet, not allowing people to observe her being pious. She had not been pious. No one had asked, but if they'd asked the watchful child with her white columns of legs, the mortification of dark hair on her white forearms, if they'd asked her: 'Do you think there's a God?' she might have said 'Who?' Losing interest. Her interest was in the moment, the announcement dropped like the first news of war in a rapt, crowded theatre: 'I have a vocation; I'm going to be a nun.'

What she hadn't understood was that for the announcement to have been of interest, to have shocked, the one making the announcement would have to have earned the interest of the audience by something in her prior life. She had been so long the person people preferred not to regard, her stare had been so well understood as fault-finding and contemptuous that people had grown relieved not to attend to her. So that when, in the last months of her senior year in high school, she announced to everyone that it had become clear to her that she had a vocation, no one was particularly interested. It was no different than if she had told them she was going off to business school or to study dental hygiene. She was leaving the family, she was leaving the world, and no one mustered up the interest to express amazement, reverence, or even horror or alarm. Her grandfather seemed moderately pleased. He said it was a hard life, but a lovely one, and had its own rewards. Her father asked had she thought of the sacrifices. Blushing, he mentioned a normal life. Children, he said, a family. Then he took away even that comfort by saying, 'But I guess none of that meant very much to you.' And he too turned away his eyes.

Sister Hilda, who had been her confidante, had told her that a nature such as hers, demanding, with a tendency to finding fault, might find communal life a special challenge. Convents are not peopled with saints, she had told Sheilah, only sinners trying to be. Some have a long way to go, she had said, laughing the laugh that nuns did when they gave information to the outside world which revealed, in fact, nothing, but seemed to be opening a window to a secret life. Sheilah felt that Sister Hilda had lost interest in the middle of a sentence: she saw her eyes wander behind her glasses to some girls making noise in the corridor. And Sheilah realized that Sister Hilda would have preferred a vocation in any of fifty other girls.

She couldn't remember if her mother had said anything directly to her. She couldn't call back her mother's face the night of the announcement. She remembered the date. July 11, 1965. But not her mother's face. Had she, even at that great moment, feared the white, empty center in her mother's glance, when it fell on her, the vacancy that said: For me your existence is nothing. You are no one. Your life has never been worthy of my regard. She remembers her father looking frightened, her grandmother saying 'Nonsense,' her grandfather trying to create a distraction so that she wouldn't hear what Ellen said, trying to steer them all away from expressing their wrong feelings: Marilyn's embarrassment,

313

John's scorn. When she calls back her mother's face she sees only the outline of a face. What she remembers is another time, soon after the announcement, her mother's voice, answering her father. Her father is saying he's worried. 'It's a hard life,' he says, 'they give up so much.' Her mother's voice, bored at even this much attention to the subject, says: 'Cut your losses.' And her father, her weak father, says nothing. Not 'How dare you say such a thing. How dare you speak that way of my beloved child.' He says nothing. 'Cut your losses,' she says. Turning back to her reading: giving the subject no more time.

And in the end even the drama Sheilah'd believed would electrify the family never took hold of their imagination. It withered before it rooted or became quite real. They allowed it to wither, mercifully, because it so quickly turned into comedy, the worst, most common sort of farce. There was the circle of events: her novitiate, profession, her teaching history in the high school, her education in civil disobedience, her political activism. Closing with the snap of the photographers' cameras as she stood at the motel door with Steve.

So why shouldn't she be cruel now? Why shouldn't she get back at Dan for sitting on the couch so happily with Darci, not thinking of her, not remembering that he let her down. She sees the other daughter is with them. Staci. She recognizes the malignant vengefulness of the less favored child. She sees in the avidly law-abiding girl her own taste for punishment. Futile, she would like to tell her: it is the thirst that never can be quenched. She sees Dan looking at Staci as her father looks at her. Saying with his look: Forgive me, I cannot give you the one place of honor. There is no room for you at the center. I would give you the real thing if I could. Don't think it's your fault.

Who else's? The trick, the precious trick of the beloved object. To do nothing and earn everything. To try for nothing, and by not trying, to win.

She wants to say to Staci: For people like us, outside this circle of favor, forced as we are to punish, to draw blood, how could there even be forgiveness?

Sheilah sees Staci has inherited the luck of her mother's severe good looks. Valerie. Remarried now. So she will have this. Staci will have the power to make men suffer. Starting with her father. She is frightened by the furious child, leaving childhood. Staci forces her to stand back.

6

Staci won't look at Sheilah. She knows she can make something come onto her face that makes people afraid to come near her. Her eyes fall on her aunt Theresa. She doesn't know if she can make her afraid, but she knows it's important. She has to keep her back. She looks into Theresa's eyes and sees her own eyes, those eyes that make people want to look away from them, as if they were a spot of heat people couldn't bear to fix on. But what people see isn't heat, Staci knows, but coldness, coldness that makes them scared. Most of the time no one can stand up to her. Maybe her aunt Theresa can. But she won't let her. Not today.

She won't let Theresa force her to go in to look at Ellen. Her great-grandmother makes her angry. It's important to Staci to be in control. Most of the time she is. No one can take her by surprise; no one can make her do anything she doesn't want to do. If other people do things they don't want to do, she knows it's their fault. She thinks there is a cover you can put around yourself, surround yourself with if you're careful, if you're smart. She knows that there are things around, everywhere, wanting to break in, to steal, poison, contaminate, take over. But if you keep the cover tight around you, if you look around you at all times, you can keep things back. Her great-grandmother has lost the cover; she has given it up. Anything can go into her or come out of her. Staci hates that; she hates her great-grandmother for making her think about it.

Staci knows she can make herself not think about it. She can think about her life, the way she wants her life, the way she's made it and will keep it, if she doesn't see Ellen's eyes again. She can think about the high jump: the hurdle she knows she can clear, again and again, if she wants to enough. She always wants to. She can think about the sound of her computer: even, safe. She wishes her great-grandmother would die so that she wouldn't have to see her anymore.

But she can't make that happen. She'll try instead the other thing: she'll keep her aunt Theresa back. She'll make her know that there is nothing she can do to her: nothing in Staci is within her reach.

'Has anybody heard from Cam?' Theresa asks.

'She might have gone to work,' Marilyn says. 'Or shopping.'

'At a time like this?' Theresa says.

'I'll try the office,' Dan says. 'She had her briefcase with her. Maybe something came up.'

When Dan leaves the room, Theresa comes up behind Staci. She puts her hand on Staci's shoulder.

'I'm sure you want to see your great-gran, don't you, Staci. While she's peaceful and asleep?'

A sheet of metal is shaken out between them. The sound is alarming, thunder, the flapping of metal wings.

Staci knows that Theresa can only come up to her like that, say things to her, touch her, because her father left the room. He always leaves her. He can't think about her long enough to remember there are some things he could stop if he would just stay near her. When he comes back, she'll make him believe that not for one moment of her life has she wanted him to be close. But it will be too late. Because the thing he could have stopped will have happened already. While he wasn't there.

She has to prove to Theresa that she can't be touched, that it doesn't matter, she can do anything or nothing, it's all the same. She shrugs her shoulders in a way she knows will infuriate Theresa. She shrugs her shoulders so Theresa will think she could do this or that, or anything, be anywhere, doing what any-body wants, any person in the whole world, something Theresa would think was horrible, disgusting, and it wouldn't matter, Staci could do it. She won't look at Theresa so Theresa will know Staci doesn't think she's worth looking at, saying yes to, or no.

She walks into her great-grandmother's room. She sees her great-grandmother sleeping. The cover around her life loosens a little; seeing her great-grandmother, she knows that she is still a child. In silence she implores the sleeping woman: Stay asleep.

316

Don't look at me with those eyes that have already seen the things I guess at but don't have to name if you don't say them, those eyes that see nothing, everything. You don't need the sight of me. And I need *not* to see you. I need you not to look at me.

She squints so that before her eyes is not a woman, but the idea of what she can bear Ellen to be. She makes the shape of Ellen circular and unalive. Unchangeable and closed. Undecipherable. She makes Ellen round and indistinct. She makes of Ellen nothing she has to recognize and therefore fear.

But she's still frightened. Ellen may move; Staci can't help that; she can't prevent that movement, and in the movement Ellen may grow distinct. Distinct, she will become the thing that Staci fears. She begs her great-grandmother: 'Don't open your eyes. Remember, I am still a child. You are dying but are still adult. You have power over me, duties towards me. It's your duty to not become the thing I fear.'

She counts the seconds: twenty, twenty-seven, thirty-one. To make Theresa understand that all this is nothing to her, she has to approach the bed. But not touch her. She won't do that.

She hears Theresa come behind her. She can hear her breath. Theresa is nervous; she doesn't know if what she wants will come about. Theresa wants Ellen to look up, curse, see Staci, make Staci see her. Staci is praying to the sleeping woman: *Don't.*

Theresa puts her hand on Staci's shoulders, the shoulders Staci shrugged to make her furious. Lightly, she squeezes Staci's shoulders, as if she wanted to encourage Staci to relax. But Staci won't relax; she knows she doesn't dare to.

'See how peaceful she is,' Theresa says. 'Why don't you bend down and kiss her. On the cheek. You'll remember it all your life.'

Underneath the hands that mean her harm Staci can't stop her shoulders stiffening. There's no choice now. She is walking into it, she has no choice. At any moment it could happen: the terrible eyes. She prays to her great-grandmother: *Don't.*

She forces herself to put her lips on the damp forehead underneath the hairline. She puts her lips to her great-grandmother's skull.

It is over. She can walk away now. Ellen is still asleep. Her eyes never opened.

Now that she's safe and there is room for it, Staci's anger rises up. Where is her father? How can she hurt him now?

She wants to say: 'I shouldn't have had to do these things alone. You've always made me.' But she can't say it. That would leave him something to say. She wants to leave him nothing.

She walks to her sister, who is looking through a *Reader's Digest*. 'Where's Daddy?'

'On the telephone,' says Darci, knowing from her sister's voice that she plans to hurt her and not wanting to meet the eyes that will enjoy the hurt.

Staci sets her lips. She sits beside her sister.

'Who's he talking to?'

'I don't know. He's trying to find Cam. It might be Magdalene.'

On the telephone, she thinks, talking to someone, helping someone, when I was the one who needed him, only he didn't notice.

In the hall, fearing for his daughter, Dan listens while Magdalene begins to cry.

'Where is she, Dan? What could have happened to her? Do you think she's been in an accident? She's not at the office, I've tried there. What could have happened to her, Dan?'

He'd like to turn his back on the whole lot of them. He tries to think of a place where he could be happy. He thinks of a modern house, open, looking out on a bay or among trees. He thinks it would be nice if Darci could come often, feeling free to leave whenever she wants. He sees each object in the house: tools on the wall, a white dish, cup, and bowl. Blue or green cloth napkins. Books about migratory birds. He wonders if it would be possible to live a life where he didn't feel an obligation all the time to lie. A life that wasn't a semblance of another thing. He wonders if he could ever live without feeling it was his job to comfort or shore up with lies. He wishes he could say to people: I *can't* help you. There is nothing I can do for you.

He feels angry with Cam. Off with her lover while she should be here. Forgetting everything to be in bed with some man who doesn't love her, doesn't appreciate her, is grateful because she makes so few demands, doesn't ask to be the name on his next set of alimony checks. Dan doesn't want to have a picture of it. Cam's white arms and legs that he has known since childhood, her large buttocks pressed down, comic Ira, white and fat, sweating above her.

When she should be here.

'Maybe she went on a walk, Magdalene. Was she upset when she last saw you? Maybe she went on one of her walks so she'd be calm to pick up Granddaddy. I'm sure that's what she did.'

'How would I know if she's upset, the way she treats me? You should have seen how she was to me. I was desperate. I threw up every bit of lunch I had, not that I have a big lunch, ever, but every shred went into the toilet. Then I was so weak, I saw these things in front of my eyes, circles, one inside the other, what do you call them. Concentric. Luckily I lay down just in time. I got to my bed just in the nick of time. A minute later, I'd have been sprawled out, right on the rug. God knows. I could have hit my head. I just thank God I lay down when I did. God takes care of me, you know that, Dan. We're all in God's hands, from the minute we're born to the second we die. Young or old, the tiniest baby to the oldest person in the world. That's where we sit, right in the hands of God. Of course my daughter doesn't believe it. She thinks we do everything ourselves. Especially *her*self. Upset? When isn't she upset with me? I can't do one blessed thing right for her. You'd think I had that spell on purpose, when I almost passed out on the floor, the way she acted.'

'I think she was really hoping you'd get over here in time for Granddaddy's homecoming,' Dan says.

'How could I, in that condition? You'd think with her brains she'd see that. I couldn't put one foot in front of the other, no less sit up in this heat. The whole afternoon. What I thought, what I was about to tell her, was that if I had a little time to rest, to pull myself together, she could come and get me later. But then she ran out of the house so fast. God only knows where she went, and believe me, I'm not asking. And where is she now? I'm ready to be picked up. I'm ready for it now, and where is she?'

'I'll come and get you, Magdalene.'

Magdalene is silent for a moment. Dan can hear her take a breath.

'Oh, Danny, I'll tell you, it's too late. She's done it to me now. I just can't do it, knowing what she thinks of me. You know how nervous I get when Cam starts criticizing. Everything I do she jumps on. I don't have to tell you that. You know how she can be. You know, Dan, I'll tell you this because I know you'll understand. I wouldn't tell another living soul. Do you know what the tragedy of my life is? The tragedy of my life is she's my worst enemy. My own daughter is my worst enemy.'

'Oh, Magdalene, you don't mean that,' Dan says.

'The way she looks at me, Dan, of course I make mistakes. I'm afraid to make the first move, she jumps on any little thing. Do you know what it's like to feel you can't do anything right for a person, Dan? You'd think my sickness was my fault and not my curse. No, Danny, you're as sweet as ever to me, but I couldn't make it now. Not in the mood she's in. I'd be humiliated the whole time. Just let me stay here, out of the way. That's the way she wants it. You see what she's done to her poor husband. The two of us, we might as well be in prison, and her with the key.'

Dan thinks of Cam. Go off with him, he wants to say, go off with this man if he makes you happy. Leave the lot of us. Go off and don't tell anybody where you went.

'Just lie down, Magdalene, and take a rest. Tell Cam if she comes home to call here just so everybody knows when to expect Granddaddy home.'

He walks into the living room to see Staci. He sees that she has suffered and that she wants to hurt him. He sees her intelligent, effective will to hurt. She won't look at him: not yet. She'll make him hunger for the look that she won't give until she knows that it can hurt him.

'You O K, sweetheart?' he says.

She shrugs. 'I'm a little upset.'

His heart quickens: She's opened the door. Perhaps now he can comfort her. He can be of some help to her in her life. He puts his hand on the top of her head.

'What is it, sweetie?'

'Sharon,' she says. 'I think she's hurt that you won't let her come here. It makes her feel just terrible, like you think she's a leper, not good enough to be with your family at a time like this.'

Theresa does not look up. She is pleased at this justice. The adulterer is shamed. The threatening child does damage. All in their places, in the nature of the truth. Theresa hears her mother cry out. 'I'll go to her,' she says, rising, full of the power she has always known is hers, rising from the brown corduroy chair.

She walks into her mother's room and sits down in the chair beside her. She takes her mother's hand. She prays to the spirit. But before she calls the spirit in to heal, she says to her mother, silently, what she has always wanted her to hear.

'Mother,' she says, 'there were some times when I was happy. Not because of you. You never made me happy; nothing about you was for my good.

'You were distracted. You felt you lost the world for us. For me. It was our fault. Later, when you didn't mind being in the house, it wasn't for us you didn't mind. It was your mother. I watched your mother; she became an animal, a man. Even now I fear her fate. You tended us but thought only of her. The stone mother you served, the mother without language, secret, kept apart.

'I saw my father's eye move from me whenever you came into the room. He could make you not distracted: I could not. I saw him feel your pull and move towards it. Towards you, away from me. There was nothing I could have from him that he couldn't at any time take back and give to you. You taught me I could count on nothing. The pull between the two of you was like the current that made electricity. I knew if I got too near it it could throw me out of my life, and it was nothing I could help.

'So I decided to want nothing. I would hide everything I had. Open fondness for an object of love brought out my hate.

'I decided, Mother, to punish the crime of revealing desire, joy. I decided to bring down my fist. I decided I would hold my knife against the stretched, vulnerable throat. I would shed blood, loving justice. Only then would I be at peace. I want to tell people what you always told me: you are nothing, there is nothing that is yours.'

She leans over the bed, and kisses her mother on the forehead, on the eyes, the ears. She asks the spirit to come there, where she has kissed, to cleanse, to bring light to the darkness. She presses her mother's hand. She prays: Come, Holy Spirit, come.

Ellen opens her eyes. She begins shouting, cursing from the throat. Communicating nothing. Useless language, living only in the throat. Only horror. But the eyes do not mirror the horror. They mirror nothing. Only her refusal to cease to be.

She curses everything. Everything falls under her malediction for the crime of continuing to be. She curses, not to change the state of anything, or even to punish, but to name.

Theresa tells herself she will not fear the eyes that are no longer human. She will say to the unclean spirit in those eyes: Rise up. Her mother will live out her days a model patient in the serenity appropriate to the approach of death. Theresa lays on her hands.

The mother rises up. She will not allow herself to be approached. Theresa tries to keep her down, to hold her by the arms, the torso, the shoulder. Ellen screams louder. The words can be made out. *Help. Help.* Theresa will not pray aloud, but silently. With all her strength, she urges the approach of the strong spirit.

The mother will not give up resisting. Her body is nearly all bone; it serves her still; it allows her to resist. She will not soften herself in compliance. Theresa stiffens her fingers, grips the shoulders, which are bone, pushes down. She knows her mother is putting all her strength into the effort to be against her. The mother strains and pushes. Theresa holds her down; she won't allow this thing, this rising up. In her mind, the words of the spirit drown her mother's words. *Help. Help.*

But no one else can hear the spirit. Someone comes in, thinking they can help Ellen as she, Theresa, obviously cannot. Someone is behind her. It's over. She's failed. She knows this. She must let go. She must loosen her grip. She must pretend that she has not laid hands on her mother.

'It's all right, Mom,' says Marilyn. 'Don't be upset. She seems to have become agitated for some reason. No one knows why she does. It just happens. Don't be upset.'

She must appear now to have wanted nothing, to feel nothing, to be free to leave. She looks at Marilyn and thinks, *My daughter.* And she is enveloped in contempt.

She will not heal her mother. Her mother will resist her to the death. She prays for her deliverance from the sin of pride, but really she is praying for another chance at punishment so she can be again at peace.

Her husband sees her. He recognizes in her eyes the fresh desire to humiliate. And he thinks: Long ago, when I first recognized this look, I should have taken the children from her. In the middle of the night, we should have gone, lived in our car, driving by night across the country to a new place, where we would have had new names and she would not have found us.

He hears the back door close quietly. Theresa has gone to sit on the back porch. Then Marilyn comes from Ellen's room. Ellen is quiet. Marilyn has given her an injection to bring on this quiet. Will it bring her death? Ray Dooley sees that his daughter Marilyn is frightened that her mother will go into Ellen's room again and disturb Ellen once more. He wants to say to his daughter, I can't lift my hand to help you. I never could.

7

Cam's eye falls on her watch. One minute, she thinks, just let me have one more minute with him. She makes her body flat against him. They are face to face. His sex is hard against her. He could enter once more and he starts to. 'No,' she says. She refuses him. Things have to begin being over. He doesn't listen. She gives up wanting to refuse.

There is a shelf, painted black wood, above his bed. Before they make love, he pushes the stacks of books to one side and brings glasses of cold water there and little dishes of salty foods. Today there are cashew nuts and Japanese crackers in the shapes of other foods. Vegetables, fish, peas green as jewels. He gives her water, he holds her head to drink as if she were an invalid. He hands her the small pieces of food, piece by piece. So that, when the dishes are empty, she has already left him. He does this for her, lets her leave him first. It's his house, she has all that life she must go back to. He can stay in the place where she was present after she leaves him. So to let her leave him while she is still there is, he feels, the least that he can do.

He hears her in the shower, her impatient dressing, her cruel brushing of her hair.

He hears her on the phone:

'All right, Mother, if you're that weak, lie down. Just make yourself some soup. I have to go now. I'm late. I had to do some things for work . . . No, I'm not at the office. Have some cheese, then, if you're too hot for soup. You can have one of those new frozen dinners I got you for supper. Ask Bob to help you with the microwave. Maybe you could eat with him.'

And then another call. 'Theresa, this is Cam. No, I'm not really late, not at all, no. They're not expecting me out there till four. I'm sorry you were inconvenienced. I'm about to leave. We'll be back at six, six-thirty at the latest. He's been all packed for days. He's chomping at the bit. I don't know where you got the idea of two o'clock, Theresa. I'm sure I never said it. Just tell Dan I'm about to leave, will you. Or is he there? No? Well, tell him I called. Thanks a lot.'

Ira suggested that she bring Dan with her to get their grandfather. For Dan's sake and for hers. He knows Dan doesn't like him. He understands the brotherly mistrust, the rudeness, the clipped address considered right for the defiler, the avoiding glances, the cynical, fractured half-sentences of a man who has no talent for withdrawal or half-truth. Cam said she'd ask Dan, but it was only to appease Ira. He saw that; he understood that she wanted the job to herself. She wanted her mission. He hears the relief in his beloved's voice when she hears that Dan is out – she couldn't have asked him anyway, there was no way he could have come.

She bangs the phone, clicks shut her pocketbook, her motions furious. She furiously jangles her keys.

'Poison,' she says, 'the two of them, their voices make me feel like I've been poisoned.'

She kisses him on the mouth but he knows she has left him. Long ago, when he gave her the final bit of food.

8

Before she gets her grandfather, she decides to visit the house left to her by her old teacher Edith Blake. Her house. Her property. For two years, since Edith's death, she's left it empty, a scandal to the neighbors, an untenanted house. It is as if she is reproaching them with Edith's death. Her *deadness*. As if she were blaming them.

She pays a boy, one of the neighbors' sons, to cut the grass in summertime, to shovel the snow in winter. If a windowpane is broken, she sees to it that it is fixed immediately. She has had a sump pump installed in the basement; she has had a painter repaint the blistered trim. All these attentions make the neighbors more uneasy. They can't console themselves with the idea of a forgetful landlord, far away. They watch her visiting the house. They see her going in the door. They don't know what she does inside.

Inside, the waste of living space, the uselessness of what was made, above all to be useful, the shelter that shelters nothing, only the air that it surrounds, the excess of emptiness, the wrongness of it, is voluptuous to Cam. She bathes herself in emptiness as if it were the sea. Eternal. Dependable *Mare nostrum*, she remembers. Our sea. Our air. *Mine*.

She wants to know this house, not as an enclosure for human need, but in itself. Not as a place for furniture and food. No sinks, couch, counter, furniture, picture, bathtub, bed. She wants to see the joists, the cornices, the woodwork unobstructed by softening objects, the curtainless windows, the carpetless stairs, the kitchen without table, pot, or knife, the blank, blind walls. She wanders from room to room. She is in love with the angles of the door frames, with the hinges, with the sloping floor, the staircase that ends abruptly near the window looking out to the lush garden with its day lilies, its junipers, its holly – male and female – its hydrangeas – pink and blue.

Proprietorship soothes her. She looks up at the ceiling. There is a stain there, in the shape of a fat bird. She feels hopeful, breathing in the unclear air.

She thinks of Ira. Does she want to live here, in this house, with him? Women and men in houses. She's grown to dislike the idea.

It's the source of all the problems, she thinks, sharing living quarters. She's begun to think that any man who lived in a house with his mother shouldn't live in one with a woman till they're both almost dead. The stories he's told her about his mother make her feel she's right, that it's the reason they remain happy together: they don't share a house.

He told her about playing ball in the streets. It was the most important thing in life, he said, those games. Life and death. He was chosen first, he told her, not because he had talent, but because he was quick and he could pay attention. Nothing got in his way. All the windows, he told her, were always open on the street. He'd be in the middle of a play, something crucial to the game. He'd hear his mother's voice, calling him to come in, to do something that minute for her, it couldn't wait, take some soup up the block to his grandmother, go down to the drugstore, help her lift something, close something. When he heard his mother's voice, he said, he felt like he was drowning. He felt she didn't want him to live.

He told her about eating his mother's food. He didn't like to eat. He didn't like desserts. Every day his mother made four desserts to coax him. He'd open the refrigerator when he came home from school and see four desserts. She threw away the ones he didn't eat the night before, or gave them to his father. Every day he swore he wouldn't touch one, even if it tempted him. He said he kept his vow.

'Didn't you ever like life at home?' she asked him, jealous in some way of the attentive mother. 'Didn't your mother ever do anything right?'

He said he liked it when he was sick, a little sick, a little feverish, when he could really have gone to school, his mother knew it, but she decided to be indulgent. He liked sitting on a chair when she put fresh sheets on his bed. The cool sheets when you got back in them were like heaven. She'd come in after a while and play cards on the bed. He'd liked that, he remembered.

Cam looks around her empty house. She wishes she could forget the stories about Ira and his mother. She wishes she didn't have to think about mothers and sons, men living in houses. She wishes she believed a man could live in a house with a woman and not feel he's being drowned or starved.

★

326

She walks upstairs into the room that she would make the bedroom. She imagines waking beside him in the morning and thinks
perhaps it's worth anything for that. To wake beside him every
morning. To be able to believe in that.

She walks back downstairs. She doesn't know what's worth
what. The air, thick with the dust that travels down a ray of light
as if it were a portent, an alphabet, seems to her an element that
she must learn. Learn properly to be herself.

When she is herself, she'll live here. She doesn't know with whom.

But not with her mother. Her mother has never seen this house.
And she promises: I will never bring my mother here. Then she
modifies: My mother can come sometimes if she likes, but only
as a visitor, a guest. My mother will never live in this house.

9

She is driving on the highway, driving east, thinking of her
mother.

She's begun to worry about her. She keeps thinking about her,
lying with her arm over her face, her feet puffy when she took her
shoes off. Her ankles might have been swollen too; Cam doesn't
remember exactly, but she thinks they might have been. Magdalene never exercises and only eats processed food. Sixty percent of
her calories at least come to her in the form of liquor. At her last
checkup, the doctor said her blood pressure was high, that she
should watch her sodium. But all the things Magdalene puts into
the microwave are sky-high in salt. Cam's tried to tell her to
eat fresh foods; she bought her unsalted sunflower seeds and
whole-wheat crackers. Magdalene just left them in the cabinet.
Cam knows that in the summer old people who have a tendency
to high blood pressure are more prone to strokes. Her mother said
she saw spots in front of her eyes. It could be nothing; her mother
is always inventing symptoms, or exaggerating them, but Cam
remembers hearing somewhere that people see spots in front of
their eyes before they have strokes.

She pulls into a 7-Eleven and dials Maggi's. Tiffany, who works at the desk, gets Kevin for her.

'I know it's Saturday, I know it's busy, but pretend you're glad to talk to me.'

'I'm pretending,' Kevin says.

'She decided not to go,' Cam says.

'You know what I love about you, Camille? You know what my favorite quality in you is? Your ability to be surprised. Like you believed, you actually believed for one minute that your mother might go out of the house. I know you: you thought it actually might happen.'

'All right, so I'm an asshole. I'm well known for it.'

'Luckily, you have other gifts. You just come from Ira?'

'How did you know?'

'I can always tell it in your voice. For about five minutes you sound like you're not headed across the Donner Pass.'

'So if I'm so terrible how come you hang around with me?'

'You're a good customer. I live for the day when you come in, every six months, for a trim.'

'Will you go over there?'

'My last appointment's five o'clock. I'll go then.'

'I'm on my way to get Vincent. Otile thinks I should leave him there. What do you think?'

'I think it doesn't matter what I think. I think you all hear some whistle outside ordinary human register, like dogs, that other people don't hear.'

'Tell me, Kevin, I need to know what you think.'

'I think Mrs. Sullivan should definitely go for the cellophane. It'll bring out her hidden highlights. I'm about to tell her that now.'

'Otile is such a goddamn nun, you know? I feel like I'm going to the principal's.'

'Call me when he's settled in. I'll go eat something with your mother, but we're going out after that. So call me late.'

'Where are you going? Someplace nice?'

'Of course. If it's good I'll take you next week.'

'Promise?'

'Promise. Mrs. Sullivan's beginning to fidget in her chair. You know what that can mean.'

'Call me tonight. Wish me luck.'

'Just bring Otile a holy picture. That'll calm her down.'

She gets back into the car. The traffic is beginning to be heavy.

She wishes she didn't have to be at odds with Otile, who is one of her best friends, whose opinion she respects.

She admires Otile's love of movement, a longing to strip down her life and the life around her, as if all the years in coifs and wing sleeves had made her wild for action and change. She and Otile share a sense that they're responsible for other lives, weaker lives, and they take their place in the world with the knowledge of this, ornamenting them like epaulets. Oddly, Cam chose Otile as one of her few confidantes about Ira. After she had, she was partly sorry; she wondered if she'd wanted some sort of clerical sanction for adultery: the sacred personage who'd bless her in her sin and tell her to go on. She told Otile at least partly because Otile was so practical. She had a strange idea that Otile could come up with a plan that would make everybody happy: She'd be with Ira. Her mother, Bob, her grandparents would somehow prosper by the move. Everyone would be grateful for this new breath of fresh life.

Otile encouraged her to move in with Ira, which made Cam feel she understood nothing. 'I like his jokes,' Otile said. 'You need someone to make you laugh. You can be a real pain in the ass sometimes. All of them will get along fine with you five miles away. Bob won't notice that you're gone, your mother will be crazy, but she's crazy anyway. And she'll bury all of us, as well we know. Your grandmother wouldn't know at this point if you were living in Timbuktu.'

'My grandfather would know,' Cam said.

'Your grandfather is a surprising man.'

'Yes,' she'd said, 'but he hasn't stopped being himself. He'd be heartbroken if I left Bob and moved in with a man who'd been divorced twice.'

'You could marry Ira. Go for three.'

'Thanks, Otile. I love it when you're worldly.'

'You know what your problem is, Camille. You're just like all the goddamn Irish. You like the idea of a thing better than the thing itself. You like standing for something better than being something.'

'Well, what about you, *Sister*?' Cam said unpleasantly. 'You don't go out in the world just as yourself.'

Otile lit a cigarette. She smoked like a teenager: symbolically. Often she didn't finish her cigarettes. She smoked badly, as she used profanity badly. She hadn't grown into it, she'd forced it when she was too old for apprenticeship: the fit was always rough.

'I use what I stand for to my advantage,' Otile said, looking at Cam with hard eyes. 'It allows me to do what I want. *You* use something, an idea, to allow you to do something you *don't* want to do. There's a word for that, you know: "fucked up."'

Cam had listened. She always listened to Otile. But in the end, she felt Otile's advice was useless. There was too much she didn't know about. Their conversations about Ira had been colored, after a while, by Cam's sympathy for Otile's untouched life. She'd told Cam she'd been in love once, and knew herself beloved, but she hadn't so much as held the hand of her beloved, who'd been married. Otile knew nothing about the unreliability of sexual love, or its deceptive powers. Suppose Cam moved out of her house, dismantled the structure of several lives, and in a year found herself out of love? Or found that Ira was? It happened all the time: Cam had handled hundreds of divorces; it was the most commonplace story in the world. Seeing what Otile had done to Maryhurst, Cam knew that she understood nothing about preservation.

She couldn't listen to Otile's advice. Otile had told her that Vincent really didn't want to go home, that he'd be happier at Maryhurst, but he didn't want to let the family down. Especially not Ellen.

'Let him off the hook, Cam,' Otile had said. 'Tell him he should stay here. Make something up. Let him enjoy his life for once. God knows he's earned it. He's finally got a life he can enjoy. He's a very sociable man and, because of your grandmother, he's never been able to live that way. Let him live his last days in pleasure.'

Cam felt herself harden against Otile when she'd said that a week ago. She wanted to tell Otile that she'd never got over her early training: like all nuns, she felt exempt from boundaries, she felt it was her privilege to intrude. Cam spoke to her in the voice she'd learned to use with subordinates who'd overstepped the mark.

'I think I know my grandparents better than you, Otile. They've lived their lives together. They belong together, these are their last days.'

She turned away from Otile, sorry that she had let her know about her lover.

She drives up the gravel entrance to Maryhurst and parks the car in a lot a hundred yards from the house. She wants Ira. Her longing for him makes her lean her arms on the car roof and lay her head on her own arms to get a moment's rest. She has no idea what she should do. So many of them: Bob, her mother, her grandparents, Dan and Darci. Ira, of course. Ira especially. All those lives would be re-shaped by her decision. And she has no idea what's right.

She walks towards the house. She tries to imagine where the heart-shaped flower beds had been. Lovingly, as if she were saying the names of the family dead, she says the names of the varieties she's been told once formed the flower beds: pinks, lilies of the valley, peonies, moss roses. She touches the pocked shoulder of the statue of the girl whose plumed hat has been eaten into by the weather.

Vincent is waiting in the corridor with all his bags. Sister Roberta, wearing her Sister Power sweatshirt, is sitting on the orange Leatherette couch beside him, crying softly.

Cam gives Vincent a kiss on the cheek. She is always shocked at how young, how lively, his skin feels. Her grandmother has withered; he has stayed intact.

She knows he wants the leaving to be over quickly. She rings the buzzer outside Otile's door.

Otile says, 'You know you're making a mistake.' She is brusque in her goodbyes. Brusquely, she hands Cam the gray envelope with Vincent's records.

'I'll call you, Otile,' Cam says, kissing her disapproving cheek.

'Do that,' she says, not looking at Cam. She walks over to Vincent.

'So, Vincent, you're leaving us,' she says. 'Keep one thing in your mind, though, will you do that? There's always a place for you here. Anytime. Just call up O. T. Ryan. I'll come for you in my helicopter.'

'Thank you, Sister,' he says, not looking up, 'but I'm glad to say you've seen the back of me at last.'

10

He is sitting in the car and looking out the window. He is thinking: 'It is August, the sky is light still until eight o'clock. But soon it will grow dark much earlier. In no time at all the sun will disappear by five: the air will be that vivid shade of blue I am too old for. Children will be throwing balls, one to another, shouting at each other. Then they'll realize they can no longer see very well. They'll begin to miss the balls and blame each other. They'll walk together toward their houses. "Good night," they'll shout, "good night," but the words will take on distance. They will close their doors. They will become invisible. In seconds, the sky will turn completely dark.'

The thought of the coming winter makes him rub his hands together with anxiety. He thinks of all that could go wrong. Storm windows; burst pipes. The thought of the house's needs and weaknesses exhausts him. He was glad to be a few months without this sort of worry. He doesn't trust anyone else to do a proper job. And now he doesn't even trust himself. He is rubbing his hands together, afraid of the twenty-four wooden storm windows that somehow must be put up. He can't remember now who did it for him the year before last. He knows he mustn't ask Cam. Not now.

He thinks of his friends at Maryhurst. He thinks of Ellen and her curses months ago, the night of his fall. They say she's failed; she can't walk now. They say she's heavily sedated and she might not know him. They say he must be prepared.

He's going back to keep his promise.

He doesn't want to go back.

Cam watches her grandfather looking out the window. She wonders what he's thinking, if he's unhappy, expectant, but she would never ask. His profile is beautiful in the car's unclear light. Strong, princely. She'd like to say: 'You look like a handsome prince, returning to his kingdom.' But he wouldn't know how to respond to something like that. She holds his hand, undeformed by age; the high blue veins are signs to her of his masculinity, not hints that he is aged or infirm. She'd like to pull the car over to the side of the road, put her head on his shoulder, and say: 'Tell me what to do.' She'd like to tell him about Ira, ask his permission to move in with him, to marry him, to leave her husband and her mother in the house without her. He tears his gaze from the outside and smiles at her, squeezing her hand.

'You're the finest in the land,' he says to her.

'And the music is something grand,' she teases back.

'It's good of you to come and get me.'

'Granddaddy, as if I'd even let anybody else.'

They both laugh. He pats her hand, and takes his hand away. She can see he'd be happier if she had both her hands on the steering wheel.

'So, everybody's waiting for you with bells on,' she says.

She realizes that there's almost nothing she can say about anybody in the house that wouldn't upset him. She's afraid that if she starts talking about Marilyn, the news of Marilyn's divorce will slip out of her mouth. Theresa, John, Sheilah, and Ray are out of the question as a topic. She doesn't like to think about Staci, ever; when Staci's face comes into her mind, she tries to make it disappear.

'Did your grandmother seem peaceful?' he asks.

'Yes, fine, she's having a good day,' Cam says. She has no idea what that means, what would distinguish a good day from a bad for Ellen. Sleep, terror, rage: she knows her grandmother's life is lived only in these three states. She doesn't want him to be worrying about Ellen on the ride home. She tries to think of something to distract him.

'I think Darci's going to be with us next year. I think she'll go on living with me till she goes to college.'

'Well, that's nice,' Vincent says.

Cam realizes she's confused him; he's trying to figure out why a child would not be living with her mother in her customary home. Or at least with her father, who has a home as well.

'You know, Granddaddy, she wants to be an actress. She's been doing very well in her classes in the city and if she lives with me she can be near to them. It's a great opportunity for her.'

'Well, that's fine, dear. It'll be good company for you.'

'And Dan will be glad to see more of her.'

'Yes, of course, that's something too, isn't it.'

'She's such a delightful kid, Granddaddy, really. She enjoys her life so much: she's living it to the hilt. I think every day is an adventure for her. It's great to watch.'

He tries to remember being young, what it was like to think of each day as an adventure. But he can't do it now. He'd like to just look out the window, to think of simple things, the growth along the roadside, when the trees will lose their leaves, to try to push away from him the idea of Ellen knocking him down, cursing at him, walking down the road like that, just in her nightgown, with the car horns honking, and his breaking all the windows to get help.

Cam pulls the car in front of the house. She comes around to help him out. He notices the blue hydrangeas, purple at the center, and wonders when this happened, this turning color. He wonders why the color changed. Is it that they are fairly near the sea and the salt air, as he's read, turns the flowers? Or is it some new poison in the air, some chemical, so that what looks interesting is only the first sign of blight? This is the kind of question he can't answer anymore; he no longer even knows where to look for the answer. He didn't think this way at Maryhurst, among his friends, among the mothers and their children, with the quiz shows and the President's news conferences, with the white piano and the shiny furniture that never needed care. He remembers that he didn't think this way, the way he was just thinking. He can't remember now what he did think about there, but he knows it was different. He can't think which is a better way to think.

He looks at the sharp marigolds. Their leaves, he thinks, are like the leaves of carrots. And their flowers are carrot-colored. He wonders if there's a relation, if there even could be, between the two species. He hears the creak of the last porch step. It brings him back to himself.

And he knows he is right to be there, that there never was a choice.

★

He walks through the living room, waving his hand at people, like a politician. He waves at his children, his grandchildren, his great-grandchildren. He has no time for them now.

He is on his way to his wife.

She hears his step in the room and opens up her eyes.

He believes that she can see him, but he's not quite sure.

A NOTE ON THE AUTHOR

Mary Gordon is the author of three earlier novels, *Final Payments*, *The Company of Women* and *Men and Angels*, and a collection of short stories, *Temporary Shelter*.